ARMAN'S FREEDOM

DAVID PARKS

Arman's Freedom

Copyright © 2022 by David Parks

All rights reserved. No part of this book may be reproduced or used in any manner without written permission of the copyright owner except for the use of quotations in a book review.

ISBN 979-8-88758-002-9 Paperback

ISBN 979-8-88758-003-6 Ebook

Scripture quotations marked CSB have been taken from the Christian Standard Bible®, Copyright © 2017 by Holman Bible Publishers. Used by permission. Christian Standard Bible® and CSB® are federally registered trademarks of Holman Bible Publishers.

Published by Soncoast Publishing

P.O. Box 1503

Hartselle, AL 35640

www.soncoastpublishing.com

*Corrie, Anna, Auston, and Julie, this book is dedicated to you.
May Jesus be your fire on the darkest of nights.*

CONTENTS

INTRODUCTION

This book was born out of a dream and a fourteen-year-old girl embarking on a novel.

The Dream: This began with a conversation I had with a young Iranian many years ago about what had happened to him over the weekend. It was a dream that ultimately convicted him of sin and also included enough about Jesus to make him want to come to me to once again hear the gospel. At this point, I needed no particularly insightful words. Just good news of grace to someone anxious to jump into the forgiving arms of Jesus. I had many other conversations with Iranians who desperately longed for freedom from their oppressive government and were busily executing their plans to find long-term visas to other countries. I eventually learned to ask the question, "What is freedom?" as a way to have conversations about the gospel. The central character of the book is very (emphasize "VERY") loosely based on the young man who had the dream and the theme of freedom comes from the multitude of conversations I had with Iranians, whose longing I learned to feel as my own.

The Fourteen-year-old: My oldest daughter, Corrie, has always been both a reader and a writer. Even as young as six years old, she made little booklets for her younger siblings with stick figure drawings on 8x11 sheets of paper, stapled in the middle. *The Gummy Goat* was a family favorite. Later she would be inspired by *The Chronicles of Narnia, Harry Potter,* and especially *The Wingfeather Saga* to the point where she wanted to try her hand at writing a full length novel. She called it *The Evergreen* and I loved it. I didn't know a lot of high school freshmen writing novels and she didn't either, so it was kind of a solo project. She wanted feedback and I was happy to give it, but I was only going to critique it so much. After all, I'm her father and I mainly just wanted her to enjoy it and keep writing. So I eventually had the idea that it could be fun if I tried my hand at it as well, mainly as a way to share the experience. I've been a teacher, missionary, minister, tennis pro, and perhaps a few other things, but I'd never written a novel. I was fairly sure, however, that she'd gotten the storytelling from me and so I thought, "Why not give it a shot?" I've been genuinely surprised how many vacation days I've been more than willing to give up just to sit in a coffee shop and indulge my creative side. I've also discovered that sometimes you can learn a lot about yourself through your children. One more thing about her and then I'll move on. There is one random corner of the book - a short scene, a couple of pages in length - that she wrote years ago. It's a good thing the older Corrie hasn't asked me to take it out because it's staying. By the way, I'm writing this on her twentieth birthday. Happy birthday, Corrie.

Speaking of my children, I hope you like the cover. If not, I would keep that to yourself since my middle daughter, Anna, drew it. I'm amazed by her talent and if there was any way possible that I could insert a 5x8 portrait of her visualization of the opening lines in *The Color Green* by Rich Mullins, you would be unfolding it at this moment. Shoutout to my wife, Jenn, for coming up with the basic idea for the book cover. What an incredible honor and joy to be your husband! My two youngest are also a treasure to me. Auston is my tennis buddy. Julie is the smart, sweet, and laid back one you can't help but love. I'm so proud to be called "father" to all four of my children. From the very beginning of this work, it was my great hope that they would want to read it and be encouraged by it as well. This should explain the dragon.

As I considered what I would write about, it was natural for me to think back to our experiences overseas and interactions with Iranians. I also saw an opportunity to illustrate how and why the gospel has translated across cultures.

I love teaching missions, and I want others to love it as well. Not just *know* it. *Love* it. As I've heard Andrew Peterson say multiple times, "If you want someone to know the truth, tell them. If you want someone to love the truth, tell them a story." As you read this book, I hope you learn to love Arman. I hope you learn to love the Iranian people as well as I attempt to tell their recent history in a Forrest Gump style of historical fiction. Most of all, I hope you experience a greater appreciation for how Jesus has saved us from our guilt, shame, and fear and has lavished his followers with the unfathomable honor of being children of the Most High.

As I mention that phrase - "historical fiction" - I feel like I need to let you know what I'm doing with facts versus fiction. There's a major event in the book that happens in the "present" of 2010 at the Petronas Towers in Kuala Lumpur. This is fiction. Descriptions of other places and events, such as local restaurants and a Hindu festival called Thaipusam are based on reality. I lived in Malaysia for over five years and it's an absolute pleasure to describe to you the sights, sounds, smells, and tastes of a place and people I love. The back story, which occurs in Iran, references many events and dates from the Iranian Revolution in 1979 to major protests in 2009. All of these, to the absolute best of my knowledge, are actual historical events. Even the one about the man on the moon. The story and the individual characters, however, are complete fiction. I'd like to thank Martine Fairbanks of Soncoast Publishing for giving this book a chance. I assumed I was going to self-publish when Bryan Gill (author of *Devils in Alabama*) suggested I pitch the book to them. Because of the overlap of what I teach with the story of Arman's

Freedom, I called it "missiological fiction" and Martine fell for… liked it. She also helped me make this a much better book than it would have been. Martine has been great to work with and I'm truly grateful for her investment.

WOUND CARE

Arman took pride in his ability to calculate shortcuts and usually claimed victory even when his original ideas took just as long as normal routes, but this time he knew he was wrong. He'd only been in Malaysia for a week and was already weary of the inconvenience of walking around the grounds of the Bandar Raja secondary school, inconveniently lying between his university and his condo. Thick red gates circumnavigated the precious green space like flaming swords, warding off the uninvited, but he'd been wondering if it was possible to cut across the field. He glanced down both sides of the road to see if anyone was looking, then defiantly crept through the gated entrance and walked swiftly to the side that would be the straightest path home. At least, as swiftly as his tight jeans and flip flops would allow. Failing to see an exit where he had hoped, he began following the edges of the fence for a way out, only to find an impenetrable row of steel rails covered in chipped red paint. Eventually he wandered out of the open field into a grove of palms and rain trees, reminding him of his hometown in Iran.

The wide bowl-shaped rain trees, so beautiful in daytime, were less welcome at night as they placed a blanket between Arman and the city lights. Walking through his new home in the evening normally felt like the entire urban landscape was illuminated by the same source, as if the moon itself penetrated the atmosphere, peeling back the dark to reveal the hustle and bustle of Kuala Lumpur night life. The sudden blackness, therefore, had a disquieting effect. His instinct told him to go back, but his inquisitive nature got the better of him, so he continued looking for an exit in the foreboding shadows. The only sounds came from his flip flops and the faint noise of traffic.

The silhouettes of the rain trees were mesmerizing. With long horizontal branches shooting out in every direction, dipping downward as low as four feet off the ground before swooping upward, they would have normally served as an engraved invitation to hop on and climb up. They did, in fact, draw his attention just enough so that he left the security of the fence and wandered into the middle of the grove, but there just wasn't enough visibility for him to feel comfortable with anything but admiring them from the ground. As he walked underneath one of the trees, he reached out his left hand to caress a limb. What he felt instead made his hands tremble and his muscles stiffen into bones.

At first he thought he was feeling the edges of a strange type of bark, but his fingers pressed into the surface too much for it to be wood. Suddenly, the "limb" moved sideways and threw Arman into a crashing panic, causing him to lurch in the opposite direction until he tripped over a thick root. He heard a shrieking hiss and caught a glimpse of two large fangs, the only visible parts of the creature as they glistened in the meager light available from nearby street lamps. They swiped through the open space above him, making him grateful he fell. He pounced to his feet more quickly than he thought possible and darted through the trees. His only visible means of defense were his flip flops flying haphazardly through the air. The wound on his face flared intensely, but it was his chest that made it almost impossible to run.

In the midst of a wild sprint, he listened for anything running or slithering from behind. He was fairly confident what he had seen was a large snake and, since he had run about fifty yards and was getting close to the edge of the trees, he assumed the lack of noise in his wake was a good sign. As he looked back, there was just enough light to see the ground in the grove, convincing him the immediate threat had passed. He stopped to catch his breath and began to settle down. Arman ran his fingers through his wavy black hair and thick beard, only now realizing he was barefoot. Then he began to laugh at himself and think through how he'd tell the story to his cousin, who was also his roommate, as he continued out of the school grounds. Just as he was walking past the last tree in the grove he heard the same shriek directly above.

More than one giant shrieking reptile?!

He caught a glimpse of a large triangular head and a sharp dark tail as he fled toward the gate where he entered. Again listening for any noise behind him, this time he was determined he wouldn't slow down until he was a long way from the snake-infested school. Street lights provided a measure of assurance as he darted past the short palms lining the side of the road, but he'd been scared so badly that he didn't stop running until he was fully three blocks away. He continued his panicked sprint until he lacked the strength and breath to move another step. He put his hands to his knees, struggling for air, and looked several blocks down the street behind him. Not a reptile in sight. He slowed down but continued to walk away from the school even though that meant he was going in the opposite direction of his condo.

Winding through the unfamiliar neighborhood, he happened upon the neighborhood night market, a beloved aspect of Malaysian night life he'd heard about but had yet to experience. In fact, he'd spent very little time outside at night since his plane landed a week before. Food stalls lined the left side of the road for about a hundred feet. The sight of nasi goreng (fried rice), naan, fried cantonese noodles, and nasi lemak ("fat rice") had a calming effect even though he hadn't tried much of the local food. A stall full of open coconuts, still filled with milk, was an unexplainable comfort to the young man whose hands were still quivering from fleeing a mysterious serpent. Feeling safe in the crowd, he decided to look around for a while to take his mind off of his terrifying experience and the pain in his chest.

He walked through rows and rows of semi-cubicles bulging with gifts designed for gullible tourists. Each section featured aggressive salespeople promising him better treatment than they normally would give others. "For you, special price," was the constant refrain as he walked past watches, toys, and endless "local" wood-carved gifts made in other Asian countries.

"Arman!" The loud voice to his right with the clear Iranian accent was Farzin, his cousin. He was next to a durian stand motioning for Arman to join him. Known as the "king of fruits" in Southeast Asia, durian is both the most popular and most hated food in the region. Approximately the size of a large pineapple, it is light green and covered in spikes. The inside is white with large seeds covered by a milky substance referred to as the "meat." The smell is so putrid that most hotels and buses have "no durian" signs posted at their entrances. Even those who love it say, "Tastes like Heaven. Smells like Hell." When foreigners visit Malaysia, it's only a matter of time before they are given the "durian dare."

As Arman walked closer, he noticed a mischievous grin on Farzin's face. "You've been here for a week, Arman. It's time to try it!" Farzin had been in Kuala Lumpur for over four years and was now working on a master's degree. Since Arman arrived he had happily taken on the role of host and was ready to lead Arman through the necessary rite of passage.

The young Chinese man selling durian happily joined Farzin's chiding. "We need to see if you really belong in Malaysia. You taste it for two days, but you like it lah!"

As he continued to goad Arman in whatever way he thought would help him make a sale, Farzin began to see the look on Arman's face and grew concerned. He also noticed both that Arman was barefoot and the red scar protruding from his ankle.

"Are you okay?"

"I'm fine. It's just the smell of durian," said Arman, hoping to both deflect attention from his disheveled state and prevent being pressured into eating the creamy rotten onions in his hands. The spikes on the durian suddenly looked like the teeth of a python. He knew it was illogical to think one of the snakes could be nearby, but he stole a glance down the road behind him anyway.

If any of them were following me, I'd hear them before they were close. He questioned his own sanity even as he considered this probability.

"You know I'm coming for you!" Three voices screamed in synchronicity inside Arman's head. One of them was sharp, clanging, and ear-splitting, like the central steel beam of a skyscraper being shredded in two. Another was deep, rhythmic, sonorous, and almost attractive. Like a bard singing an ancient poem, sad and semi-detached. The third voice was feminine, harsh, and panic-stricken. The voices clashed horribly, but they spoke simultaneously. The world around Arman became blurry and unstable. He clutched his head with both hands and looked down at the ground, desperately trying to balance himself. The durian man didn't take the hint and continued to badger him to try a bite.

"Real men eat durian!" He had a rough voice and a laugh like a chain-smoking hyena.

After about ten quiet seconds passed, Arman successfully convinced himself he really hadn't heard anything. It was just his imagination. As the night market slowly came back into focus, he gathered himself and felt he would be able to act normally. He decided he would tell Farzin about the snakes and the pain in his chest, if for no other reason than to just change the subject and avoid the rancid taste in his mouth that he knew he would regret tomorrow. And the next day.

Then the familiar shrill.

He looked into the space behind and above Farzin and the salesman and saw it. Stiff and too shocked to move except for his lips, he only managed a silent scream. What he saw was clearly impossible. The "snake" had three heads merging with a thick and long black body. The end of its tail formed a sharp, arrow-like shape that looked as if it were made of metal.

And wings.

How can it have wings?! This was the only thought Arman's terrified mind could form.

The salesman, who was only laughing harder now, cackled, "Just a fruit, man! Don't be so scared lah."

The terrifying creature descended from behind Arman's companions, smashing into a row of mangosteen and jackfruit stands. The salesman squealed in a high-pitched voice which Arman thought was almost as impossible as a three-headed snake with wings. Men, women, and children raced through the street in horror, the more unfortunate of them trampled underneath the chaos. Arman and Farzin were quickly behind them, weaving their way through the chaos like crazed motorbikes dodging cars in Kuala Lumpur traffic.

The monster thrashed its tail back and forth, scattering coconuts and hurling the entire stall of durians toward the fleeing crowd. Approximately fifty spike-covered stink bombs shot like missiles in every direction, one of them impaling Farzin in the back of the head. Arman slowed down to help his unconscious cousin. He was shocked to see the durian was actually stuck to him, but before he could consider what to do, he looked up to see the dragon rocketing in his direction. The voices came back to him, this time thundering like a thousand waterfalls as the monster opened its mouths to speak.

"You know your sin! Now... it's time for retribution!"

Arman looked up to meet the stare his tormenter, his final mistake. The six-eyed gaze of Dahag immobilized him like Medusa. Just when he thought his body would be crushed with a three-pronged attack from its mouths, the creature raised up and brandished its silver claws in his direction, but this was just another distraction. He raised himself slightly higher, this time whipping his long tail underneath his legs toward Arman. The last thing he saw was the steely tip of Dahag's tail plunging into the center of his chest, multiplying his pain and sinking him to his knees.

～

Arman woke up screaming and soaked in bloody sweat. He clutched his chest with both hands as Farzin jumped out of bed to turn on the lights.

"What happened?!" asked Farzin, though he had a good guess.

"Just a bad dream." Arman covertly moved his arms downward, though he really didn't need to. He was wearing a dark t-shirt as usual, effectively hiding the wound.

Farzin continued to look at him with both genuine concern and a bit of amusement. "It must have been horrible."

"It was a snake."

Arman laid back down and rolled on his side, facing the wall. Although he'd forced a smile, it was clear he didn't want to talk about it any further. Farzin turned the lights back off and went back to sleep.

About fifteen minutes later he heard the unique whistling sound that always accompanied Farzin's deeper stages of sleep, so he crept out of his bed and into the bathroom. The humidity smothered him more than usual. As always, he hated leaving the relatively cool bedroom, fan blasting on high, to walk directly into the tropical heat. He splashed cold water on his face and felt the immediate sting of Dahag under his beard. Lifting up his shirt cautiously, he made sure he didn't do anything to further irritate his chest wound. He peeled off the large bandage with the same care, revealing blood and pus dripping from a newly formed crack in the ten-month-old second-degree burn. *Will this never heal?*

He would occasionally go weeks without any significant pain and conclude that things were improving, only to have another incident. Most of the five-inch scar looked okay, but blisters continued to form and reform, occasionally bursting at inappropriate times. He gently washed his chest wound with water, careful not to crack open another blister. As usual, it was a painful and tedious process. As usual, he made sure no one could hear him wince in pain.

After spending the time and effort to apply a fresh bandage, he was covered in even more sweat, of course, so he decided to take a shower. A careful shower, where you don't stand directly in the water and, instead, cup your hands together to make sure you only wet the parts of your body that you want cleaned. The ankle burn on his left foot, though not anywhere near as serious, was yet another annoying reminder of his foolishness. The first drops of water would always feel like the pin-prick of a needle as he would hold his breath and count to ten, waiting for his body to adjust. As irritating as this was, he actually preferred it to wearing a bandage. It required less work, cost less money, and perhaps the suffering would atone in some small way for his sins.

Arman's mind wandered back to his dream. He finally remembered the durian and laughed under his breath. *Death by durian. How appropriate. I'd rather have my head bitten off by a dragon.*

He rehearsed how he would describe this part of the dream to Farzin. It would be an edited version, not the entire story. And definitely not the *back* story. Even though his cousin was aware of the problems that began earlier in the year while Arman was still in Iran, there were many details he didn't know. The unedited story would have to include the fact that this was simply the latest twist on a recurring nightmare. It would also reveal memories too personal and too shameful for Arman to discuss with anyone. Even his favorite cousin.

The Ahmadinejad years aroused a great deal of embarrassment among many Iranians, especially those in the city. His presidency evoked the culmination of feelings birthed in the early years of the Islamic revolution. Initial excitement turned to hesitation. Hesitation turned to distrust. Distrust to fear. Fear to anger. And anger to hopelessness.

Some Iranians blamed the coming of Islam itself and embarked on a re-identification with their ancient Persian roots. Their *pre-Islamic* roots, to be specific. Like most Iranians, Arman had already taken great pride in their collective memory of King Cyrus the Great and the famous Persian empire of old. More recently, however, he'd embarked on a discovery of Zoroastrianism and the henotheistic god Ahura Mazda.

One of his more incidental discoveries of Zoroastrianism occurred while attending a cultural festival during Nowruz, the Iranian New Year. An older gentleman in olive green traditional dress solemnly and confidently took a nearby stage to perform a Naqqal, the dying art of Iranian storytelling. Arman was initially skeptical, having never seen this, but was quickly enthralled by the brilliance of the man's skills. With arms waving, dramatic acoustic instrumentals in the background, and an impeccable memory, the man wove the ancient myth of Kirsasp to flawless prose. Verse by terrifying verse, he told of a three-headed monster bent on murdering all of humanity. The cunning and demonic dragon named Dahag, currently in chains, was prophesied to burst its bonds at the end of the world, wiping out a third of all human beings on the earth. The Naqqal ended with his countenance lifting and the instrumentalists strumming in triumphant rhythms as he sang of the hero, Kirsasp, coming back to life to once and for all slay the six-eyed embodiment of evil.

The performance thrilled Arman and was soon emblazoned into his memory. He didn't believe the story was true in a literal way, but it connected both with his desire to see justice done and his longing to bond with his ancestors. He retold the story to himself for months to come.

Unfortunately, his love of this story produced in him a love of dragon myths in general. Most of these were not a problem. He didn't read a lot of English novels, but he managed to work through the Eragon series, which was his favorite. Mostly, he watched movies. Any and all movies that featured dragons: Dungeons and Dragons, Dragon Hunters, Dragon Heart… he loved them all. It was all just good fun until he read about an ancient dragon myth connected to Islam. In this story, the dragon is an emissary of Allah sent to punish, or "sting," men and women for their sins. This dragon was fierce, merciless, inescapable, and close enough to his view of the reality of God to be genuinely horrifying.

After Arman's arrest and overnight imprisonment, the Islamic dragon merged with Dahag and began tormenting him in his dreams. The nightmare was never the same. One night the memory of his indiscretions and culpability before the Almighty would lead to Dahag piercing him straight through the chest. In a variant of the dream, Arman was sometimes quicker and more deceptive in the encounter, allowing him to outrun the beast. The chase always seemed to inflame the wound on his ankle, however, and no matter how far away he was, the voice was always present. Accusing. Convicting. Tormenting.

On other nights, a memory of the disgrace Arman had caused to descend on his family, combined with the estranged relationship with his father, led his scaly tormenter to electrify the small wound on his face, sending shock waves through his veins. Mercifully, these dreams didn't return every night. It was approximately every other week. They didn't always end with him screaming and bleeding, either. Nevertheless, each night as he laid down, the fear of Dahag was on the forefront of his mind. The merciless three-headed dragon of guilt, shame, and fear seemed ever-present, always watching, always ready to pounce.

2

SELAMAT DATANG

"Where are we going, Farzin?"

"I don't know yet. All I know is that it's time for you to get out of the condo and away from the school cafeteria."

"I was just fine. I promise." Actually, Arman was bored out of his mind and grateful that Farzin had finally made some free time for him. He'd arrived in December of 2009 to have time to get adjusted for a January start at Bandar Raja University and was feeling quite lonely.

"After you discover the magic of Kuala Lumpur nights, you'll thank me."

The soft lighting on the streets of Bandar Raja neighborhood are just enough to reveal the roads, sidewalks, nearby link houses, and endless palm trees and banana leaves. Even at 10:30 p.m., it seemed the night was just getting started. A Chinese couple in shorts and t-shirts passed by walking their Chihuahua. An older Indian gentleman accompanied by a woman in a sari casually made their way back home. Malay boys kicked a soccer ball back and forth on the way to City Center, a relatively small mall compared to the seven and ten story behemoths just a few kilometers away.

Looking up to the northeast he could see the ever-present

Petronas Towers. They beamed from the center of KL like twin diamonds. A north star among a sea of endless city lights, they have a reassuring presence that remind sleepy citizens both where and who they are. They seemed to cry out to the modern globalized world, built on the common language of science and a thousand trades, "We are here. And we are contenders!"

"Wait. Were those tables and chairs in the parking lot earlier today?" Arman was pointing toward an open air restaurant at the end of the nearby shop lot.

"No, they weren't. That's part of the magic, Arman! Every night the nasi kandars break out chairs, tables, string lights, and…" Farzin paused for dramatic effect. "The projector screens!"

"Are they always showing soccer?" Arman tried unsuccessfully to avoid acting excited.

"Yes, cousin." Farzin spread his arms wide, palms facing the nearest large screen. "Yes, they are!"

Approaching the mall, they noticed even more open-air restaurants and other sights that would become common for him in the coming months — the western options of Starbucks, The Coffee Bean, McDonald's, Baskin Robbins, and KFC. It was quite an appropriate picture for the city and the country in general. The local and the global looking at each other out of the corner of their eyes. McDonald's and mamak. Mosques and megamalls. Shop owners in Chinatown selling the same mass-produced trinkets found in every local marketplace in Southeast Asia. The freedom promised by endless material and entertainment choices within the confines of overt control from an Islamic government.

The juxtaposition of it all reminded him of "Jihad vs. McWorld," an old article in The Atlantic. Tribalism and globalism side by side, pulling each other together and pushing each other apart at the same time.

"Want to go to Ali-Baba's?" The wide array of restaurants was enough to make Arman hungry, if not adventurous.

"Wait. Have you had any of the local food yet?"

"I've had it for lunch the past three days in the cafeteria. I think that's enough to last me for a while."

Farzin smiled, shook his head, and assumed his role as the elder of the two. "We're within a quick walking distance of Thai, Chinese, Malay, and Indian food and all you can think about is eating more kabobs?!"

"Are you saying you like smelly fish?" countered Arman.

"You can't eat at Ali-Baba's for every meal off of the school campus, Arman. Besides, cafeteria food is bad wherever you are. Did you ever love the 'Persian food' at your high school?"

For a brief second, Arman's face contorted and his eyes narrowed. "I wouldn't feed that to my worst enemy."

"Okay then. It's the same here. This time I'm just going to choose for you. Tonight you're going to discover nasi kandar."

Nasi kandar literally means "rice stall" in Bahasa Malaysia, the official language of the country. Found in almost every corner of the nation, these restaurants include a strong mix of Chinese, Malay, and Indian cuisine.

Arman sat down and immediately a young dark-skinned Indian man approached to ask for their drink orders. "Two teh tariks, please," responded Farzin while looking at Arman with a confident smile. The young waiter bobbed his head in acknowledgement and walked away.

"I'm surprised to see so much Arabic writing on the walls," observed Arman.

"That's because all of these restaurants are owned and run not just by Indians, but Muslim Indians. They're often called "mamak" in Malaysian slang, which is why the restaurants are often just called 'mamak' instead of nasi kandar. Some of them think that the word 'mamak' is racist, so I just say 'nasi kandar.'"

Arman looked around and noticed people from the three main ethnic groups, along with some who appeared to be internationals, were present. A surprising mix of ages were there as well. Children in pajamas past 11 p.m. were walking around their parents' tables stuffing tosai into their mouths. When their food came, Arman looked down at a large round dish apparently made of tin with one large section for bread and three small sections for sauces. It was roti canai, a basic Indian flatbread, served with mint, dal, and chicken curry.

Before tearing a piece of bread to dip into the sauces, Farzin formed a wicked grin and, in a breathy voice completely unknown to Arman, said, "You've gotta ask yourself one question: 'Do I feel lucky?' Well, do ya, punk?!"

Arman stared blankly for about five seconds before Farzin finally gave up hope he would recognize the line.

"It's Dirty Harry!" This obviously didn't help Arman, so he added, "You know, Clint Eastwood?!"

"Ooohhh… okay," replied Arman, offering a halfhearted laugh of recognition. This seemed to appease Farzin. Arman was lying, of course. He never understood Farzin's obsession with American action movies and had learned long ago that he would either pretend to know the movie or have to listen to his incredulous reactions followed by long explanations of movie history Arman cared nothing about. The path of least resistance was his preferred option.

"Alright, Arman. Time to see if you can ever like anything other than kabobs and ghormeh sabzi."

He dipped the bread into the various sauces. First the curry, which was spicy, but not too spicy. Dal was the safer option, though still quite savory. It was the green mint sauce, however, that took him completely by surprise. Each new flavor exploded from the bread into Arman's mouth until his skepticism had been thoroughly annihilated. Farzin could clearly see he was being vindicated.

Arman's smile of satisfaction faded and he began staring through his food, rotai canai dangling from his left hand.

"What's wrong?" said Farzin. "I thought you were liking it."

"No, it's not the food."

"Well, what is it?"

It always seemed precarious to try to talk about deeper thoughts with his older cousin, but Arman took a risk.

"The Christmas party you invited me to sounds great, but…"

"But what?"

"Let me ask you something." He looked Farzin in the eye. Farzin wasn't sure if he was grinning or frustrated.

"When you meet people from the West, do you ever feel like you need to say, *Hi, my name's Farzin. And I'm not a terrorist?*"

Their first response was to laugh. Farzin almost lost some of his teh tarik before he calmed down. Then he got quiet, swirling his roti canai through the chicken curry.

"The quick answer is yes. But you can't let that bother you, Arman. Most of them know it's only a minority of us that are extremists."

"You're right, of course. But do you think my thick beard makes it worse?" Arman again looked down as he talked.

"If that's a concern," said Farzin, "then why don't you shave it? It's not like all Iranian students here have beards like ours." Arman decided to overlook Farzin's comparison of their beards. His cousin was clearly seeing what he wanted to see in the mirror.

"Honestly, it's not a big deal." Arman wanted to play it off and move on with the evening. "I was just curious if you sometimes felt the same way."

The truth was that he'd shave off his thick beard in a second if he could. His ultimate dream was to move to the western world and become a journalist. He wanted to expose the bullies of the world, including his own government, and have a respectable career at the same time. And there weren't a lot of western journalists with thick black beards.

The real reason he kept the beard was to hide the scar that happened in the extremely embarrassing incident with the fire last year. He simply wasn't ready to talk about it with Farzin. Or anybody else for that matter. So he effectively changed the topic of conversation and continued to have a good time.

For Arman, it had been a long time since he enjoyed a meal. It conjured brief memories of sitting around a dinner table with his father, mother, and sister in their home in Tehran. His sister trying not to laugh at one of Arman's jokes, his mother gingerly carrying in his favorite kabab koobideh and fresh shirazi salad, and his father gazing at him with a look of approval as he teased his sister.

Whatever hope or joy these images brought to him, they evoked intense pain many times over. It wasn't boarding a plane that brought these joyful family gatherings to an end, however. It had been many months since he experienced this happy scene and he knew without a doubt that he would never again have an enjoyable evening with all of his family, for multiple reasons.

Arman quickly pushed these thoughts out of his mind. If things were going to be different here, it wouldn't happen while incessantly feeding himself with negativity. He desperately needed a new start and, for the first time since he arrived, he felt a glimmer of hope. He knew, however, that it wouldn't just happen. He must discipline his mind. He must fight for it. As his favorite Iranian poet, Rumi, wrote nearly eight centuries before:

Until the juice ferments a while in the cask, it isn't wine

If you wish your heart to be bright, you must do a little work

Arman finished devouring what would be only the first of several dishes that evening without saying a word. He then sheepishly looked up to Farzin and grinned.

"Okay, so my opinion about Malaysian food might have changed a little."

"Selamat datang, Arman."

"What does that mean?"

"It means, 'Welcome to Malaysia.'"

Arman walked home by himself, stomach full and a heart that was beginning to feel like he could live in this place. It was approximately a month before his world would collapse.

3

ROJAK CHRISTMAS

As Arman wiped his palms on the waist of his blue jeans, he recounted his fears about the evening. First there were issues that were common to anyone in their youth. He knew almost everyone there would be older than him. He was an eighteen-year-old journalism major who had yet to take a single class and was was about to hang out with a group introduced to him by twenty-two-year-old Farzin, who was working on a masters in electrical engineering. This, of course, seemed small compared to the extreme self- consciousness he felt over his facial scar and his beard.

I wish I could go home right now, shave off my beard, and burn the hair on the balcony.

When Arman used his fingers to peer through his bushy facial hair, he saw a discoloration that made it look scaly, inspiring him to privately refer to it as Dahag. The reality was that his heavy beard covered the reddish mark almost completely and most people never noticed it.

But there was something else causing a significant amount of apprehension as well. He'd been told that most of the party was going to be just hanging out, but it was made clear that there would be a time where they talked about the birth of Jesus. Arman had little difficulty trusting the group that had invited him to the Christmas party. The nagging thought he couldn't get out of his mind, however, was about his own countrymen.

Will there be other Iranians there besides Farzin? Will they think I'm wanting to convert and tell the religious police in Iran?

His mind turned toward an old childhood friend who had turned into a radical. The suffering he caused Arman was as profound as it was personal. Arman dreamed in vain of one day getting revenge and somehow getting away with it. The first part seemed easy enough. The latter was impossible. Fortunately, this particular enemy was now a world away.

In a dark turn on the same topic, a guilty thought escaped. *And just how much do I trust Farzin?*

This sounded like a ridiculous question considering that Farzin was his cousin, but such were the depths of distrust among Iranians when it came to matters of sharing unsanctioned religious thoughts. Deep down, he did trust him. He pushed the question out of his mind and continued his journey.

Either way, he was determined not to live his life in fear anymore. Not here, anyway. This night held the promise of new friends and the excitement of taking part in in a global celebration he had only seen on satellite television. Beneath it all, however, were two deeper motivations that served as twin engines forcing his feet in the direction of the Marbury's house for their church's Christmas party. First, he was genuinely curious about what these people believed about Jesus. Second, the very act of walking down Jalan Bandar Raja toward this gathering felt like… rebellion. Sweet. Delicious. Rebellion.

So Arman walked through the open gate, placed his shoes and socks with the large gathering of sandals and flip flops on the shoe rack outside the door, and proceeded to do exactly what he had spent a vast amount of time and energy desperately trying to prevent his sister from doing.

Arman walked through the door and into a sensory explosion. Colored Christmas lights hung around the entire perimeter of the ceiling, and crisscrossed through the middle as well, casting a red hue throughout the living room. It was immediately about thirty degrees colder as well, not the usual feel of any condo or house he'd visited in Malaysia, even when they had air con units. *Is this central air conditioning? I don't know what I'm smelling, but please, please let it be halal!* Approximately a million lights blinked to the beat of some very loud and happy Christmas music as they reflected off of gold and silver ball ornaments.

"Hey y'all!" said a tall and happy woman coming out of the kitchen. Arman guessed it was English, but wasn't entirely sure. A tall woman in her sixties wearing a fuzzy red and white sweater ran over to the latest guests and enveloped one of them in a hug like a venus flytrap. The victim looked to be American, approximately in his thirties. From Arman's vantage point, he seemed to be entirely cocooned inside her embrace with the exception of a few locks of light brown hair, helplessly waving in a stream of air coming out of a nearby vent. He was absolutely paralyzed with the thought that he could be next. Just a few weeks ago, even shaking hands with the opposite sex was a new and uncomfortable experience. Now he was whispering a silent prayer for it.

As the hostess was winding down her assault on the other guy, she turned sideways and aimed a beaming smile at Arman. While the American's body was still mostly shrouded by a picture of Santa's backside on her sweater, Arman decided to act preemptively. He straightened out his arm, leaning forward with his rear end sticking out unnaturally behind him, effectively putting as much distance between himself and his hand as humanly possible.

"My name's Barbara and this is your new friend, Matt Fuller!" She dismissed his hand with a casual flick. "Honey, if you're gonna hang out with us, you're gonna give me a hug!" As she threw herself around Arman, his arms remained stiff and immobilized while his eyes shifted to the other guests in a silent plea for mercy. After an embrace that seemed to last at least as long as his plane flight to Kuala Lumpur, Barbara mercifully let go of him and enthusiastically led the way toward the rest of their party. As he stumbled along behind her, Arman's hair and even his eyebrows were somehow disheveled.

The next person to greet Arman was Tom Marbury, Barbara's husband. He was approximately the same height as Barbara, had thick gray hair, bronzed skin, and eyes that were both intelligent and playful. He smiled under his thick mustache and greeted, "You must be Arman. Farzin's told us all about you!" He had a clear Southern accent, but not as thick as his wife's. He gave Arman a firm handshake and added, "Merry Christmas!"

"Are you Farzin's cousin?" Matt asked.

"Will that be a good thing or a bad thing?" Arman smiled, hoping his joke would land. Matt hesitated, pondering the question as he stared through a collection of snow globes on an end table.

"Well, I'll just say that I come from a land where people are supposed to be innocent until proven guilty." Matt offered only a slight smile, just enough for Arman to be sure he could laugh. "I've been looking forward to meeting you, Arman! Come over and sit with us." Matt led him over to a collection of folding chairs and introduced him to Yusuf, a thirty-four-year-old pastor from East Malaysia. After greeting a few newcomers, Tom joined them as well.

As they were getting to know each other over plastic plates full of spicy chicken curry, sweet potato casserole, and an assortment of colored and sugary desserts, Yusuf pointed to the colorful group of people in the room. Chinese Malaysian, mainland Chinese (the phrase they use to describe the Chinese people who still live in China), a couple of Malay students, Indian Malaysians, and several international students. "Do you see that, Arman? Now that is rojak!" Yusuf laughed at Matt's use of Bahasa even though it was correct. Matt looked at Arman, speaking in an amused voice. "I became convinced long ago that it's against the law for Malaysians to refrain from laughing when they hear a white man speaking Bahasa."

"Rojak's a fruit dish," laughed Yusuf. "Yeah, but it literally means 'mixed.' We have quite a mix of people here tonight."

Presently Wilson, a Chinese Malaysian with thick straight brown hair worn just above his eyes, picked up his guitar and started casually picking a tune next to the Christmas tree while Jessica, also Chinese Malaysian, prepared her microphone. The students rearranged chairs and couches to face toward them as Yusuf handed out sheets of paper with song lyrics.

As they began singing "Joy to the World," Arman assessed the quality of the guitar playing to be adequate, but nothing special. He drew the same conclusion for Jessica who had a pleasant voice that was mostly on key but often off beat. He was a bit startled, however, with the enthusiasm of the singing from the students singing along. They didn't conduct congregational singing at his mosque in Iran, so this was completely different. It was uncomfortable for sure, but that didn't mean he disliked it. On the contrary, in the end it was the chorus of voices that would stay with him the most as he looked back on this night.

It was a good thing he had the words in his hands. Trying to catch the words and meaning of phrases sung in English so quickly would have been difficult otherwise. Even so, he found himself continuing to read particular verses multiple times while they were already on another song. He was particularly drawn to this one:

> *Long lay the world in sin and error pining*
> *'Til He appeared and the soul felt its worth*
> *A thrill of hope, the weary world rejoices*
> *For yonder breaks a new and glorious morn.*

It was satisfying to know most of the English words on the sheet of Christmas songs.

He did, however, get stuck on "pining." He felt like he understood what it might mean from the context of the sentence, but he didn't know for sure. He already knew from the Quran that Jesus was born of a virgin, so a song about his appearance connected with Arman. *"A world with sin and error, yet there is hope, rejoicing, a glorious morning, and our soul has worth."*

After five Christmas carols, Yusuf stood up in front of the group with a warm sincere smile and proceeded to tell the story of the birth of Jesus. Arman recognized him as a humble, soft-spoken man who obviously believed what he said and honestly cared about people. By this time, however, Arman retained very little mental energy for careful listening in English. In the end, he wouldn't remember much of Yusuf's carefully prepared message.

Yusuf concluded speaking with a prayer that didn't include a rug or anyone bowing on their knees toward Mecca. As everyone began moving about, Arman took that as his cue that the formal worship time had ended. Yusuf closed his Bible and walked toward Arman.

"Thank you for coming tonight, Arman. It means a lot to me."

"Thanks for inviting me," replied Arman, who reached for Yusuf's hand. "Everyone has been very kind." He started to say something, but stopped short just as the words formed on his lips. Finally, he garnered his courage and shared some burning thoughts.

"I just want to make sure that you and Matt as well as the others know that we're not all terrorists. Those people don't represent us. In Iran, our poets are very famous. They've helped most of us understand that all religions lead to God if you follow that path sincerely." Yusuf smiled, but offered no reply. "So I want to say that I respect what you believe," Arman continued, "and I pray that God blesses you for showing acceptance to me." Arman started to walk away, but then remembered a question he wanted to ask.

"Yusuf, what does 'pining' mean?"

"It means 'longing.'"

Arman turned his head slightly sideways. "That's my name. That's what 'Arman' means."

Yusuf grinned, but spoke in an unmistakably sincere voice. "Well, Arman. What are you longing for?"

Arman laughed it off. "Seconds," he answered, impressed with himself for remembering the double meaning of the English word, and promptly making his way towards the serving table for more chicken curry and another teh tarik. Despite outward appearances, he took the question seriously.

Easy answer for that one… Freedom.

Only now did Arman begin questioning why Farzin still wasn't there. Regardless of the reason for his absence, this meant Arman was the only Iranian present. He wasn't sure if this was a good thing or a bad thing. Just then he heard Barbara's familiar multi- syllabic greeting to a latecomer and looked up to see tufts of blonde hair poking out from under the Santa sweater. He assumed it was another western visitor until he heard the voice.

"It is such a pleasure to be your guest."

The insincerity of it was the first thing that stood out. The high-pitched and generally annoying intonations were the next. Combined with the Persian accent, Arman had no need to wait for further confirmation this was Habib, his personal tormentor who wasn't supposed to be anywhere near Kuala Lumpur. And if this was, in fact, Habib - the young man dedicated to the radical religious leadership of Iran - then he didn't exactly show up to celebrate Christmas.

Without the slightest hesitation, Arman flew up the stairs and into the sitting room on the next floor. He stood close enough to be able to hear what was going on downstairs, but far enough away to where he couldn't be seen.

He'll tell the secret police I've become a Christian. An infidel. They could send me to jail when I go home… If I go home.

The moisture on his hands left finger-shaped imprints on his jeans. He looked around him to see what he would do if Habib came upstairs. There was one large bedroom to the right, which he assumed was Tom and Barbara's. It was a large room with a king-sized bed, multiple mirrors, a TV, and a long sliding glass door to the balcony. There were two rooms on the left, both of which were closed. Arman thought that must be the rooms of Jessica and the other students who lived here.

As soon as he heard the first footfalls on the stairs, his choice was forced. He quickly but quietly opened a door to a student's room and hurried to find a place to hide. He wasn't surprised by the dark, but he was, however, unnerved by the movement next to him. Just enough light came in from the window for him to see two pack-n-play beds, each with a baby sleeping inside. The child nearest to him rocked his head back and forth on his pillow.

Please don't cry. Please don't cry.

He wanted to pray to Allah, but he wasn't entirely sure whose side the Almighty would take.

Barbara's voice echoed just outside the door. "Habib, I'd let you use our bathroom, but it's a complete mess. Let me see what the girls' bathroom looks like." She opened the door and reached for the light, but halted all movement when she saw the portable cribs. And Arman. The light came through the door and exposed his upper torso and face as he unsuccessfully tried to hide behind an end table. He had his index finger to his lips and a plea of desperation in his eyes. Barbara quickly backed out of the room and closed the door.

Without the slightest hiccup, and in a voice that bordered on a giggle, she said, "Oh, dang! I forgot the Fuller twins were sleeping in there." She laughed as naturally as she did when Arman talked to her downstairs. "Sweetheart, I'm afraid you're just going to have to be brave enough to face the wreckage of my make-up and curlers."

"Oh, it's perfectly okay, Ms. Barbara." Arman could picture Habib's plastic smile and the way he would bend slightly and look down when he tried to impress elders with his great respect. Just the sound of him made Arman's chest wound flare and his ankle burn. "My mother and my sisters are exactly the same way," laughed Habib.

A few minutes later he heard Habib exit and realized that Barbara was waiting for him in the sitting room.

Is she guarding me?

"Thank you, Ms. Barbara. It actually wasn't as bad as my home." He laughed in that loud and squeaky voice that Arman hated with his entire being.

"Well, that's a relief, I guess," she replied.

"Ms. Barbara, are there other Iranians here? I don't want to sound like I don't feel welcome, but I'd feel more comfortable if I could just sit with one or two people from my home country."

He's been sent to Malaysia to find Iranians to turn in! Arman's instincts were confirmed.

"Oh, I'm sure there's one or two from Iran downstairs. There's so many people, it's hard for this Southern lady to keep up! I just get so confused with all the different countries. I'll tell you what. Why don't you just sit next to me and I'll just keep you under my arm and love on you for a little bit!"

In Arman's mind, the picture on Habib's face went from a fake smile to genuine horror. He breathed a deep sigh and ran his hands through his beard, trying not to disturb the babies with his strange mixture of stress and laughter.

After the immediate danger had passed, Arman found his way under a single bed and remained motionless for fifteen minutes.

Should I go through Tom and Barbara's bedroom, exit the sliding glass door, and climb down?

He didn't like this plan since it would mean climbing down in the front of the house and he was guessing that Habib wouldn't last long while under Barbara's wing. Every idea he considered seemed futile, but staying too long would make others suspicious about what he's doing. He didn't want to have to explain himself to everyone, so he crept out of the room and tip-toed to the top of the stairs. He found an angle where he could peek into the living room while being almost entirely guarded by the rails. After he was satisfied there was no sign of Habib, he cautiously descended into the living room.

"Arman!" Tom waved him over. He was with Yusuf, Matt, and Barbara on the comfortable leather couches that Arman had hoped earlier that he'd get to try out. The only empty seat, however, was next to Barbara, who had her arm over the head of the couch. She winked at him. A mischievous grin revealed the wrinkles around her eyes, even with the generous make-up.

"For some reason, Habib didn't seem entirely comfortable being the object of my affection." The others laughed as Arman stood still in wonder. He never expected them to understand what was happening. Barbara removed her arm and leaned toward the other side of the couch. "For you, I'll be on better behavior, I promise." When Arman had entered the house, he was confident that Barbara was culturally clueless. Now she was a genius.

Arman sank into the plush leather and tried to think of something else besides Habib. After a few deep breaths, he surveyed the end table on his right and admired the manger scene, an antique barn covered by a fine layer of moss, replete with shepherds and wise men, glowing in the light of a red and green Tiffany lamp. He recognized Elvis's voice as *Blue Christmas* blared in the background. Picking up a snow globe the size of a soccer ball, he watched as the slightest movement showered tiny white motes across a pine tree forest. He still hadn't met Christine, Matt's wife, but he was enjoying watching the scene on the other side of the living room, as she was on the floor with their oldest two daughters, 4 and 7 years old, spinning around in circles to the amusement of the students. Elise, the oldest, had blonde hair and blue eyes and reminded Arman of a Barbie doll. Grace had flaming red hair and looked like nothing he had ever seen. He watched in wonder as her confident walk swung her ponytail back and forth.

"How about some apple cider?" Tom's smile somehow matched the picture of the Grinch on his sweater.

"Thanks," said Arman, unsure of whether or not to ask who the green creature was.

Regardless, he was feeling more at ease around these new friends. Whatever discomfort he initially felt with Barbara faded as it was clear she was completely comfortable with him. "You need to know," Barbara teased, "I have a real weakness for men with heavy beards." She winked again and, looking toward her husband, added, "Not scraggly little mustaches clinging to a man's lip like a tumbleweed." Arman blushed under the facial hair and curled his fingers on his knees. Tom pretended not to hear and, while elevating his voice, continued his conversation with Yusuf, who was to his right. "Did I ever tell you about the first time I met my wife? She took one look at my muscles and my Burt Reynolds mustache, and I spent the rest of the night trying to pry her off me!"

"You wish, honey!" she countered. "I actually spent the rest of the night holding my finger up" - she held her index finger up sideways in an attempt to block her sight of Tom's upper lip - "trying to imagine what you'd look like without that stupid thing!" They cackled loudly and at the same time. "You know I love you, Tommy," she sang with a broad smile and approximately fifteen syllables.

Arman was amazed to find out that both Matt and Tom worked in the Petronas Towers. Tom worked for Shell Oil and his window overlooked Kuala Lumpur traffic from the seventieth floor. Matt was a journalist for Reuters and worked on the thirtieth floor. "You're a journalist? That's what I want to do!" said an excited Arman. He peppered Matt with questions and dreamed of the life he's always wanted.

Arman had just begun to thoroughly enjoy himself until he began to think about Farzin.

Why is he still not here?

The easy explanation is that Farzin is once again distracted by his new girlfriend, Banu. They'd met a week ago and Arman had barely seen him since.

Why have I still not met his new girlfriend? I don't expect to be asked to go on dates with them, but how is it possible that I've seen him so little over this week and haven't seen her at all? She's met him outside our condo four times and he just rushes out to meet her instead of introducing us.

"Is Farzin coming tonight?" asked Yusuf, as if he was reading Arman's thoughts. "I thought so, but I think he's with his girlfriend."

"I didn't know he had a girlfriend." Matt smiled at the thought. "I hope she enjoys action movies."

Tom laughed and added, "If he does show up, it won't matter that she's here. He'll still be quoting Schwarzenegger and Stallone."

There was a knock at the door and as Matt looked out the window, he saw it was Farzin.

"How long do you think it will take, Tom?"

"About five seconds," he said flatly.

They walked in and Arman lost his breath. His hands were suddenly clammy even in the artificially cool air. The overhead light near the door seemed to be shining directly on Banu and only Banu. His gaping mouth was as dry as the gingerbread cookies. The expression he wore didn't look like puppy love. No, this was something more grave. Like he had seen an angel. Or maybe even a ghost. It was as if Banu's very presence was a complete impossibility, both beautiful and horrifying at the same time.

Tom glanced at Barbara to see if Arman's stunned reaction was really that obvious. Barbara was clearly giggling. In fact, everyone had noticed, except for Matt and Farzin, who was delivering a well-rehearsed Sylvester Stallone line.

"They drew first blood, not me!" His guffawing would've echoed off of the walls if it hadn't been for the music in the background. Matt unrolled his eyes to observe an awkwardness in the room that even Elvis couldn't fix. All conversation had stopped, even among the college students, and everyone was trying to think of something to say to ease the tension.

Unbelievably, Arman was still staring. Farzin turned and saw that Banu's smile had long faded, her nervous eyes pleading for him to do something. Finally, Arman snapped out of it. He rose from the couch and sprinted upstairs. He appeared to be crying.

After Banu's unnerving entrance and Arman's abrupt exit, everyone moved on and proper introductions were made. Barbara and the girls liked Banu's green blouse, which she had purchased just for the occasion, and they gushed about her shiny jet black hair. It was pulled back into a tight bun with just the right amount emerging from the center. She had light skin - made even lighter with the make-up - bright red lipstick, and long golden earrings. Although everyone was friendly enough, at an appropriate time she squeezed Farzin's hand and attempted to pull him gently toward an adjacent sitting area down the hallway which was currently unoccupied. He didn't get the hint, of course, so she physically dragged him to privacy.

"Why is your cousin staring at me, Farzin?! Is he some kind of a creep and you didn't tell me? Is that why you didn't want to introduce us?"

"I never said I didn't want to introduce you!"

"Well you sure came up with a lot of reasons why it wasn't convenient for me to come in!"

"Look, there's nothing weird going on. I have no idea why he did that!" Farzin pleaded.

Their conversation got heated enough that Arman was already sitting on the chair across from them before they even noticed he was there. He gently cleared his throat and stared at the floor, searching for words.

"Banu, I'm sorry for acting like that." Farzin raised his eyebrows in an expression of satisfaction. Justice was being done. He wanted peace to be made quickly and turned toward Banu to encourage a forgiving response. Instead, he was jolted with surprise as Arman continued.

"Why didn't you tell me, Farzin?!" he asked incredulously.

Stunned with the accusation, Farzin responded with equal force. "What are you talking about?!" His voice was strong and confident, but his eyes were uncertain.

"Are you serious?" replied a perplexed Arman. He was searching Farzin's face for honesty.

"Yes I'm serious! I don't know what you're talking about!" Again, his eyes equivocated as he strained to look forward.

Banu, who was as confused as she was upset, glared at Arman and blurted, "Tell me what's going on right now or I'm leaving!" Arman's eyes filled with frustration and as he realized he was upsetting her but, at the same time, revealed stark wonder at the sound of her voice. He looked at Farzin, then back at her and gathered himself. A soft, flickering candlelight was visible through the tears welling up in his eyes. Finally, he exhaled, "You look like Mahnaz."

He buried his face in his hands as his body shook in sorrow. Banu was even more confused now, but as she looked to Farzin to confirm Arman's impropriety, she saw compassion instead.

He looked at Banu as if to say something, then paused and swallowed hard. "Mahnaz is his sister," he finally explained as he slowly reached over and put his hand on Arman's shoulder. Banu felt a certain amount of empathy because of the intense emotion, but she knew there had to be more information.

Finally, since Farzin couldn't think of any way out without filling in the blanks, he added, "She died last year. During the protests."

As the cloud of mystery lifted, Arman slowly reached into his pocket and pulled out his handphone. It was a flip phone with a three-inch screen and a sliding keyboard underneath. He reached toward Banu, who took the phone and, for a few seconds, truly believed she was looking into a mirror. Her mouth dropped. The lipstick, the large brown eyes, thick eyeliner, light skin… she could see it wasn't her now, but it was as close to an identical twin as she thought possible. Her face softened and she suddenly felt a strong and inexplicable affinity for Arman. Just moments ago all she saw was a creepy bearded guy who couldn't stop staring at her. Now she saw a young man who loved his sister. She wanted to hug him but didn't want to inappropriately interject herself into the holy moment. Banu wiped a tear and whispered a prayer to Allah as they sat in long silence.

Arman left the party with Farzin and Banu. It was a quiet walk back to Bandar Raja, all of them having much to ponder. Arman still had to practice restraint to refrain from staring at Banu even though he had already attained a certain level of acceptance of the situation.

Over the course of the next few weeks, however, the three sons and daughters of Cyrus became inseparable. While Farzin and Banu grew closer to each other romantically, Arman and Banu developed a familial bond that seemed to strengthen each day.

Sometimes Arman would marvel at the way her laugh, a spontaneous grin, or a kind word would remind him of Mahnaz. A subtle furrowing of the brow would rekindle a joyful memory of his sister in the low-lit dining room of their home in Iran. He would feel her warmth and remember how close they were. It would remind him of the heartbreak of losing her and his anger toward those responsible. It produced sparks of hope that one day he could be with her followed by the stark reality that this was impossible. All of these thoughts could materialize in less than a second, leaving him trying to hold onto all of them while simultaneously continuing a conversation in the real world. In the end, it wasn't the pain that triumphed. It was the joy.

Banu had experienced enough in Iran during the past few years to elicit more than sufficient compassion for Arman's loss. She felt both a bond and a sense that fate drew them together. Consequently, not only did Arman gain Banu, but his relationship with Farzin was restored as well. Previously, Farzin had been unconsciously hiding Banu from Arman, staying out late with a girl whom his cousin had never met.

But now everything had changed. They were family.

Arman walked home feeling like he was one step closer to finding a home in this world. In the very near future, however, this kind of hopeful thinking would feel like a bitter and distant memory.

4

TOURIST DAY

Yusuf, Arman, and Banu stared upward along with the rest of the tourists on the walking trail of the Kuala Lumpur City Centre (KLCC), a large entertainment district comprised of the Petronas Towers, a large mall at its base, an aquarium, and an impressive outdoor recreation area, where they were standing in front of a massive banyan tree. A collection of tree trunks, formed by "aerial roots" growing downward from its branches, sprawled across an area about twenty feet wide. The tree provided a much needed relief from the oppressive heat and humidity, as well as a sense of age and mystery, regardless of the fact that it was the new and shiny things of the world that drew the people to this place. Staring through the branches, they could see the Petronas Towers leaning over them, occasional reflections of sunlight forcing their gaze downward.

"What are you doing, Farzin?" Banu asked. He was standing behind one of the tree trunks as if trying to hide, but a full half of the black leather jacket he was carrying was visible. Undeterred, he remained motionless, just in case. Banu shook her head and continued her conversation with the others. Arman assumed she was too excited about their much anticipated tourist day and their eventual visit to the crosswalk connecting the massive twin buildings to let Farzin get under her skin.

"This tree always reminds me of the fishing village where I grew up," said Yusuf.

"You lived in a fishing village?" Arman's curiosity was piqued.

"Until I was ten years old my parents and four siblings lived in a small town in Sabah, East Malaysia. It's about twenty miles from Sandakan. If we weren't in school, we'd fish in the morning and swing off the banyan trees into the Sulu Sea in the afternoon."

Farzin broke his silence to jump out from behind the tree trunk and grab Banu. He screamed as he briefly shook her. "Boom!" Then he proceeded to laugh, as if his mission had been accomplished. "Admit it. You jumped!"

"You literally shook me, idiot!" Banu was only mildly irritated. Arman had seen worse.

"So when did you move to Kuala Lumpur?" Arman hadn't turned his attention from Yusuf, who was becoming more interesting by the minute. *How is he not sweating in this humidity?*

"I moved to KL to go to seminary and prepare for the ministry. I thought I was going to move back, but I guess the city called me. I like it here, but I take every opportunity I can to get to the mountains or a lake. And now you know why I brought you to the banyan trees first."

Banu smiled in wonder, her dark shiny hair glistening in a sliver of light reaching through the leaves. Her white tank top and pink shorts reminded Arman of his sister.

"It feels like there's something spiritual about them," said Banu. "Maybe that sounds weird, but the way the trunks are arranged are beautiful and haunting. They look like…" She hesitated, searching for the perfect metaphor.

"Like giant skeleton legs?" said Farzin, who was studying Banu to see if she would finally crack a smile.

"No, not like that at all." Not even an eyeroll.

"That's all I can see now." Arman admitted. "Can we go to the mall?"

"Yes!" cried Farzin. It was the little things that excited him the most. And today he was giddy with anticipation. They got their tickets to the crosswalk at 7 a.m. and still had hours left to just roam around the KLCC until their 1:10 p.m. appointment.

As they approached Suria KLCC, the six story mall at the base of the Petronas Towers, Arman pointed at the jackets carried by both Banu and Farzin.

"Why are you carrying those things with you when it's so hot outside?"

"Because," Banu replied, "it's always freezing inside the mall!"

"Okay, but did you really need them to be that thick?"

As they walked through the glass double doors into the mall, the shock of cold air hit Arman first. As he pretended not to care, Farzin and Banu slowly unfolded their jackets, sliding their arms into the sleeves while looking at Arman with raised eyebrows.

"Whatever." Arman looked to Yusuf for instructions on where to go. After all, he was their host today.

Banu and Farzin held hands behind Yusuf and Arman on the way to a popular computer and technology store, lost in each other and the wonders of the Chinese New Year's decorations still hovering throughout the cavernous center of the mall in late January. Red paper lanterns and dragons floated alongside them, as if pointing the way to the glory down the hall. Massive red letters spelling "Gong Xi Fa Cai!" floated through the space behind the dragons.

"Where did you get that shirt?" Yusuf asked Arman. It was a basic white t-shirt with a design of two simple shapes. One looked almost like a tombstone and another had the appearance of a staff, with "coexist" written in religious symbols in the middle of the latter.

"Actually, I designed it and had it printed here a couple of weeks ago."

"Well, it's interesting," replied Yusuf. "What does it mean?"

"The larger shape is a tablet and the other shape is a staff. It's a reference to Moses and the Shepherd, a poem by Rumi, one of our most famous ancient poets. I put 'coexist' in the staff because I think the meaning of the ancient poem and the modern symbol are similar. All religions are the same."

"So what about you?" asked Yusuf. "Are you religious?"

Arman looked back to make sure Farzin and Banu weren't listening. "If I'm honest… not really."

"Have you studied the major world religions?"

"Of course," replied Arman, who became suddenly quiet. The reality is that he hadn't studied the Eastern religions much at all. He just had a strong distaste for the religious extremism in his homeland and was determined to be a dignified and tolerant person.

A vast array of metal and flashing screens revealed they'd reached their destination. Skyscraper IT lit the remainder of the hallway in front of them as they suddenly had the task of deciding what to do first.

It was 11:15 a.m. and this would be the last taste of normality Arman would experience for a long time.

Banu chose to peruse the long cases full of handphones. The iPhone 3GS and the Samsung Eternity were the shiniest of the offerings, but there were a generous amount of used basic Nokia handphones as well. The guys, however, made a beeline to the gaming area. In no time at all Farzin and Yusuf held the game controllers for the PlayStation I, competing on *Dragon Age: Origins*. Arman, who had suddenly become uninterested in the PS3, reflexively placed his hand over the scar on his chest and aimlessly browsed a section of old used video games.

This left Arman alone for the moment. Alone, that is, until an overly aggressive salesman began trying to sell him on every single gadget in the store. He was Chinese Malaysian, slightly taller than average, muscular build with a tight-fitting shirt, and flashed a smile wide and bright enough to make nearby screens look dull.

"Want to try the new Batman on the Wii?" asked the young man standing approximately one foot away.

Arman stepped back as slowly as possible in an attempt to avoid being rude but also to avoid being so close he could see his entire body reflecting in the young man's teeth. "No, thank you."

"Then you should try Prototype on Nintendo DS." The young man, whose name tag read "Adrian Wong," was obviously not easily deterred. His smile only grew shinier and more powerful.

"Look," said Arman, "I'm not going to be able to buy anything except perhaps a used video game, so it really doesn't make sense for me to test new gaming systems. Adrian's smile actually diminished a bit and morphed into a knowing grin. He put his right hand on Arman's left shoulder as if they were old friends and changed his tone to one of acquiescence.

"Okay lah. I see that you've made up your mind here. You're not as easy as your friends," he said with an infectious laugh. He looked at the others, who were about twenty feet away and unable to hear the conversation over the noise of dragon fighting, and spoke in a lower voice.

"I know this may sound weird or too good to be true, but if you agree to try out a new system I just received, I'll pay you fifty ringgit."

"What!?" replied an incredulous Arman.

"I know. It's weird. But a client developing this system wants feedback from gamers and he's willing to pay well for it. Every time I get someone to play for at least ten minutes and give me brief feedback, I get fifty ringgit as well."

"Then why are you only asking me?"

"I would ask the others," said Adrian, "but…" He cast a furtive look toward the man behind the display case next to the cash register. "I can't let the store owner know."

This didn't make much sense to Arman and he started to just walk away when Adrian grabbed his hand and inserted fifty ringgit.

"Just ten minutes."

"Okay, whatever."

Adrian walked him to the back of the store and pointed toward a door that seemed to lead nowhere. "The door leads to a long narrow closet with shelves on either side. When you get to the end, you'll see a red plastic bag on the floor under the shelves to the left.

It will have a device that looks like an iPhone and a large black mask. Just press the on button for each of them and you'll figure it out quickly. The game's called "Free Flyer." You'll love it! See you in about ten minutes." Adrian flashed an assuring smile and a wink as he moved Arman toward the entrance. Seeing that the store owner couldn't possibly view him from where he was standing, Arman slipped inside.

The shelves and the entire closet in general were in complete disarray, games and other IT products shoved onto the counters with no particular rhyme or reason. Poles that had once helped shelves stand erect were strewn across the ground next to leaning storage bins. Arman stepped over poles, tangled extension cords, and old yellow computer monitors to reach the end of the closet. He easily spotted the red bag, pulled out the handheld device and the mask, and, just as Adrian said, found it very easy to turn on. He slowly pulled the mask over his eyes and ears and entered a stunning new world that immediately surpassed all his expectations. It was 11:21 a.m.

5

COLLAPSE

"Don't call an ambulance lah!" pleaded Adrian. "He'll be fine."

Farzin was clearly irritated and his famous temper was about to make a grand entrance. "He's *my* cousin and I don't care what you think!" The veins in his neck revealed he was now acting on instinct.

Arman was regaining consciousness just as things got heated between them. Still disoriented, Arman looked around to try to figure out how he got here. He remembered walking into the closet, but how he found himself on the floor remained a mystery. As he placed his right hand on the back of his aching head, which felt like was still swelling, he saw his foot still tangled in a few cords and began to put a few things together.

Adrian obviously didn't want his boss to find out what he's been doing behind his back and, in the process, revealed that he cared little for Arman's welfare. As Farzin turned around to call the paramedics, Adrian reached from behind, grabbed his handphone, and brazenly stared straight at Farzin, daring him to do something.

Farzin didn't hesitate. He grabbed the muscular salesman by both shoulders, shoved him against the wall in a rage, and screamed two inches from his face, "Don't push it! Don't push it or I'll give you a war you wouldn't believe!" He pulled him toward himself and shoved him against the wall again. He threw him backward a few more times, then paused to see what his adversary would do. Adrian's face grew ashen. He involuntarily dropped the phone, which landed on the side of his foot and slid toward Banu. Farzin glanced at her to see if she would grab it, but she was frozen.

As Arman sat up, now wide awake, he looked at the others. Banu appeared frightened. Mouth gaping, eyebrows raised in astonishment. Yusuf, who just entered the closet, was difficult to read, but it looked like he was about to step in if things got more heated. Neither of them wanted to do anything to provoke the young man who was easily taller and stronger than Farzin.

In the midst of the drama, no one had realized the significance of Arman sitting up. Not even Arman. Farzin was the first to snap out of it.

"Arman!" He threw Adrian to the side and bent down to hug his younger cousin. Yusuf and Banu joined in with a mix of "Thank God!" and "Praise be to Allah!" Adrian saw a chance to cut his losses and made a move toward the door. As he did, Arman smiled. He knew what this meant for Farzin.

The food court in Suria KLCC became the backdrop for the celebration of Farzin's triumph. Restaurants from virtually every part of the world were represented in the large open space, with specialty drink offerings nearby. They sat next to an enormous window, revealing a water fountain the size of an Olympic pool below. It was 12:30p.m. and the crowd was beginning to peak.

"You know that was a line from First Blood, right?!"

"You said that already." Arman replied.

"And who's the actor that plays Rambo?! Huh?"

"Arnold Schwarzenegger."

"You can't be serious, Arman!"

"I'm not. You've said 'Sylvester Stallone' ten times already."

"Stand up, Arman! Let's act it out again!"

"If you shove me against the wall one more time!"

"Have mercy on this poor young man," laughed Yusuf. His usually tranquil demeanor had vanished. While Arman had finally become irritated, he was hopelessly lost in laughter. He'd never seen someone so obviously drunk on testosterone as Farzin was at the moment.

"You realize you didn't actually punch him, right?" Banu feigned disappointment and looked out the window at the fountain. Farzin's mouth flew open for a split second, then he caught himself.

"I'm not falling for it, Banu. You know you can't get enough of this." Farzin raised his arm and kissed his bicep.

Arman stole a few glances at Banu to gauge her response. Despite the obligatory comments to prevent Farzin from getting a big head, it was clear by the way she was smiling at him that she was both proud of her boyfriend. As Arman considered the scene unfolding before him, he couldn't help but grin. Farzin re-enacting his heroics, the ridiculous movie line, the beautiful girl looking at him with admiration… It may be a bit shallow, but he knew without a doubt that, for his cousin, it was a daydream come true.

As for Arman, he wasn't irritated that they had all but forgotten his injury. Quite the contrary, he was relieved the attention had been taken off of himself. His head throbbed more than he wanted them to know and his memory of what happened inside the closet was slowly coming back into focus, increasing his embarrassment in ways he would never want to explain to them.

While the others were mentally occupied elsewhere, Arman became aware that something was off, beyond just the pain. It wasn't terrible and certainly didn't warrant alerting his friends. He just felt… cloudy. As he would turn toward the window or look up to talk to someone, it seemed to take him a second longer for everything to come into focus and respond appropriately. The accident obviously had more of an effect on him than he wanted to admit. Drawing attention to how he felt, however, would also draw attention to what he was doing in the closet in the first place. Since he didn't want a lot of questions, it was an easy call to just keep moving on with the day and pretend nothing had happened.

~

It was finally 1:10 p.m. and they were about to step onto the elevator to the crosswalk, or the "SkyBridge," as it's called. As Arman stared down at his ticket, he glanced at Farzin and Banu, both now wearing the black leather jackets they'd been carrying around all day.

The hostess, a young Malay woman wearing a short and elegant black dress, led them out of the elevator and onto the SkyBridge. After a few words about the Petronas Towers and the sites that can be seen from their new height, she dismissed them to view the city at their leisure.

The two-story bridge, connecting the twin towers on both ends, was stabilized by two pair of large steel pillars spreading from underneath the center of the crosswalk toward the buildings in an inverted V-shape. Silver beams, visible through the ceiling, rested horizontally on top of the large open windows all the way down the crosswalk. It was a spacious opening and there was plenty of room for everyone to look out of either side of the bridge.

Arman had developed an intuition for when Farzin and Banu wanted to be alone and this seemed to be the case as the viewing began, so he joined Yusuf as he wandered over the green beauty of the KLCC park below. Palms, ancient banyan trees, walking trails, a wading pool for kids, water fountains, a sprawling playground, and a mammoth steel whale jutting out of the water offered much for conversation. Then, of course, there was the endless sea of skyscrapers, high-rise condos, and traffic congestion uniquely visible from the bridge. It was hard for Arman not to feel superior to the tiny matchbox cars stuck in traffic while he roamed free on top of the world.

Happy tourists from all walks of life asked strangers to take their picture, with many variations of desired backgrounds, facial expressions, and cheesy poses. A few of the girls next to him stared at their phones, quickly posting trophy photos to their new Facebook and WeChat accounts. Some leaned over the rail to get closer to the glass window while others were content to avoid the rail altogether.

A new group exiting the elevator included seven young men and women, approximately college-aged, whom Arman instantly recognized as Iranian. He didn't know any of them, but it was clear that Farzin and Banu did. The young Persians immediately walked up to them and exchanged several embraces. Arman, who was watching them out of the corner of his eye, noticed the other Iranians, like Banu and Farzin, were also wearing black leather jackets. *Did I miss a text? And why would they want to wear anything like that in the tropics? Sure, it can get cold in the mall, but…*

Something began to bother him. Was it jealousy that these people he didn't even know were spending time with Farzin and Banu when he was clearly given hints to leave them alone? Was he feeling left out of the loop regarding the fashion choice for the day? Or was it their collective countenance? Arman turned away from them and stared aimlessly out the window opposite his cousin and Banu, his misgivings increasing by the second.

He suddenly felt someone reach into his back pocket, not surreptitiously, but with enough force to knock him forward. He spun around to see Farzin winding his arm up as if to throw his stolen wallet down the walkway. His first reaction was both a slight relief combined with irritation, assuming it was just a lame joke. He didn't believe he was actually going to throw it. As Arman waited for the inevitable line from an action movie, Farzin slung it with all of his might from one end of the crosswalk into an opening in Tower 1, completely off the bridge, then walked in the opposite direction toward his new companions. Stunned and confused, Arman glanced at the crowd of people where his wallet landed and quickly decided he would retrieve his wallet first and demand answers later. Normally he would have cursed at him for something like this, but he was too unnerved to know how to react.

He sped across the bridge as fast as the crowd, strollers, and children would allow. *Where is it!?* He scoured the floor where his wallet had landed, but a new stream of visitors exited the elevator at the worst moment possible. As they cleared the immediate area and entered the bridge, he saw nothing on the floor.

"Is this yours?" The voice came from his right. He looked up to find a young bearded man in a green t-shirt holding his wallet in one hand and his identification card in the other.

Arman grabbed his belongings from the young man's hands, offered an abrupt "thanks," and immediately turned back toward Farzin. All of the tourists had cleared the center of the walkway and were contentedly peering downward through the glass, allowing Arman a clear view of Farzin, Banu, and their friends on the other side of the bridge. His eyes met Farzin's and his body immediately went numb, legs wobbling as he fell helplessly to his knees. Farzin's expression was somber and apologetic, but Arman knew it wasn't about the wallet. Then his face hardened and his eyes turned to stone as he looked away. Banu was maniacal, fists clenched and eyes alight with a demonic fire.

"Noooooooo!" Arman's wound seemed to burst into flames as he wailed a tortured scream. The chatter of the SkyBridge visitors was quickly supplanted by panicked silence as everyone swung their heads toward Arman, anxiously awaiting and fearing his next move.

Behind the tourists, visible only to Arman, nine young Persians flew open their jackets and reached toward their waists.

"Allah-O-Akbar!"

6

THE MAN ON THE MOON

"Allah-O-Akbar!"

Hundreds of young men and women flooded the streets around Tehran University as the incredible news spread by word of mouth. Zia Tehrani, a 21-year-old college student, darted out of her dorm room and sprinted toward the joyous crowd.

"What happened?!" Her shouts to the dancing revelers fell well below the decibels of their wild chants. Suddenly she felt someone grab her from behind and promptly twirl her through the air like a rag doll.

"Did you see it?!" Her older brother, Ali, set her down roughly, breathlessly awaiting her response. His long and wide smile revealed the gap in his upper teeth as he gazed in expectation at his younger sister. His eyes were stupefied with bewilderment, like a young man in love. Zia's sleeveless red dress revealed tone muscles, but Ali was tall and strong enough to toss her around with ease and playfulness.

"No, I didn't. I don't even know what you're talking about!"

"How can you not know?!"

"Just tell me, you idiot!"

Ali laughed as Zia displayed her usual spunk and defiance. He

45

didn't mind keeping her in suspense, even if it meant that she was actually becoming angry.

"They saw him on the moon!" he finally explained. "Saw who?!"

"Ruhollah Khomeini!"

Zia paused in wonder at the moment, still not completely understanding. She glanced toward the heavens, but the moon had already dipped behind the Alborz Mountains. "What do you mean, 'Saw him on the moon?'"

"Thousands of people all across the country saw a clear image of his face on the moon! It's a sign! Allah sent a sign!"

Zia smiled, again studying the crowd around her. "Allah-O-Akbar!" still bounced off the walls of her beloved university.

"Did you see it?" She was now only half-smiling, eyebrows narrowed, forehead creased with doubt. Ali rolled his eyes and slumped forward.

"Really?! So many people all over Iran see evidence that Allah is granting us our freedom from this tyrannical ruler and you won't believe?!"

"I didn't say I didn't believe." Her voice was unusually weak.

"Then why are you spoiling this for me?!"

It was ironic that Ali, the science and engineering graduate, had no problems with believing the fantastical story even as his sister, the history major, seemed skeptical. Yet it was completely consistent with their personalities. Ali, the tempestuous leader with a strong sense of justice. Zia, while possessing a romantic heart and passion for literature and poetry, was usually led by rationale in the real world of everyday events. This wouldn't be the first time, however, that Ali jumped in with both feet, pulling Zia along in his wake. "Look around you," he continued. "Don't you see this is our chance?! The time is now and Allah is with us!"

It was Summer 1978 and Tehran was simmering with revolution. The push toward an Islamic republic was just beginning to surface, but the discontent started much earlier and over entirely different issues. The king, Mohammad Reza Shah, had devolved from a leader who modernized the country to a corrupt despot who made deals with western powers, mostly the U.S., which benefited the ruling class but left the majority of Iranians in the cold. All speech critical of the Shah was silenced through the state-run media and dissenters were imprisoned and tortured. The SAVAK, secret police established by the Shah with the help from the CIA, were as universally despised as they were feared. The bulk of the earliest intellectuals who banded together to protest these abuses didn't necessarily want to overthrow the constitutional monarchy. They just wanted more constitution and less monarchy.

As the winds of the protests subtly shifted in favor of the religious clerics - especially toward Khomeini - and the people learned of the great freedoms that a truly Islamic government would guarantee, Zia found herself just as swept up in the unfolding historical drama as her impulsive brother.

She forced a change of countenance and embraced Ali. "You're right, big brother. This is our chance." In that moment, Zia made a conscious decision to disregard whether or not the reports of Khomeini's face on the moon were true or not. "What did it matter?"she told herself. The only thing that was important to her, and untold thousands of others enveloped in that magic moment, was the momentum gained toward finally overthrowing a corrupt and violent monarchy. Surely both Allah and King Cyrus smiled on these hopeful people dancing around her, their thirsty mouths open wide in expectation of the monsoons of freedom lying just around the corner.

In the coming days, the historian inside occasionally raised concerns about where all of this was headed, anxious about the lack of a clear plan for a future government among the anti-government leaders. She quieted her fears, however, by repeating the lie that had sabotaged the ideals of millions before her and would haunt the Middle East for decades to come. The Trojan horse of a thousand revolutions.

Nothing could be worse than this.

7

SURVIVAL

The explosion thrust Arman backward and slammed him into the elevator. Only half conscious, he looked toward the bridge desperately hoping none of this was real. Clouds of smoke still poured from Tower 2. A cold chorus of screams from men, women, and children whom he couldn't see sent a terrifying chill through his limbs. The last glimpse of Farzin and Banu replayed in his mind as he lay immobilized just off of the bridge on Tower 1. Intense grief and hopelessness left him too numb to care even about his own survival.

"I can't move!" wailed a panicked female voice to his left. "Get her! Please get her!" A young Malay woman in a bright red hijab grabbed Arman's shirt and attempted to shove him toward the bridge. In the midst of shocked and wounded tourists running to his side of the bridge, Arman noticed two things at the same moment. First, he realized the end of the crosswalk connecting with Tower 2 was completely unhinged and it was only a matter of time until it would crash to the ground. It wasn't falling directly downward, however. The V-shaped cross beams below holding steady, it instead was rolling to his left, both southeast and downward. The bridge leaned slightly and people were beginning to slide to their right as

49

they fled to safety. The second thing he saw was the baby stroller slowly rolling away from him.

Arman reacted instinctively, leaping to his feet, holding his ground as fleeing tourists ran into him, and rushed toward the stroller. He grabbed it with his left hand and had just begun to run backward when the bridge violently lurched downward and to his left. He fell on top of the side window, which gravity had now selected as the floor. The combination of a steeper angle and slippery glass made it impossible to move back up to Tower 1. With one hand on the stroller and the other trying to balance himself, he slid backward and fell further away from the frantic mother. Glancing down, he caught a quick glimpse of the baby boy. All he could see was dark curly hair and a tiny grey t-shirt.

He grabbed the rail with one hand and maintained his grip on the stroller with the other. All he could do was hope that the child was strapped in well. Finally, he realized that he could use the hinges where the rail was attached to the window as footholds to push himself upward while pushing the stroller with his hands. Inch by terrifying inch he made his way back toward Tower 1. Just as he thought he'd made it, his foot slipped off of the hinge. It happened so quickly and unexpectedly that his noble desire to save a child collapsed under the weight of his instinct for self-preservation. He let go of the stroller, clinging to the rail with both hands. As quickly as he realized the horror of his actions, he looked up to see the falling stroller jerk to a stop. Glancing to his right, he saw a dark hand reach down, clutching the stroller and pulling it up to safety. Arman was embarrassed by his failure to hang on, but incredibly relieved the child was okay.

An ear-splitting noise above him revealed that the connection of the SkyBridge to Tower 1 was rupturing. As the top half wrenched away from its anchor, Arman could only grasp the rail in hopes of survival. The bridge was now at a forty-five degree angle as he looked down at the handful of others still clinging to life. Halfway down the crosswalk he saw a face he recognized.

"Yusuf!" Arman cried helplessly to his new friend. A friend whom he trusted. A friend who trusted Arman. And Farzin and

Banu. He held onto the same rail currently preserving Arman's life. Arman could see empty space beneath Yusuf as the bridge was so far forward and downward that the other end no longer revealed the side of Tower 2. As he looked deeper and more intently at Yusuf, he saw the last thing he expected. Peace. Yes, Yusuf was still climbing, but there was an inexplicable calm about him.

It was clear to both of them that there was no time for Arman to help even if he could. Yusuf looked upward toward Arman. "Tell me again. What is it you're longing for?"

The connection to the bridge again ruptured above him, this time almost completely. Arman was close to Tower 1, but was now out of strength to climb. He felt a strong hand grab him by the wrist. "Push with your feet! Hurry!" The guy who had handed Arman his wallet had returned to save his life. He put both feet around the rail and, without a solid foothold, pushed up with all his might. The young man in the green shirt pulled him off the bridge and continued to drag him until they were both at least twelve feet away from the edge of the abyss. They looked backward just in time to see the last beams connecting the bridge rupture in two as the entire structure drifted out of sight. Yusuf was gone.

8

———

THOU DOTH PROTEST TOO MUCH

"Wake up, Zia! Everybody's going back to the streets."

The air in Zia's dorm room was thick with perfume. Dilruba had become impatient with her in recent weeks. Sure, Zia had joined in the protests like almost everyone else, but she seemed a bit lacking in fervor as far as her roommate was concerned. After shaking Zia awake, Dilruba continued to add a third layer of make-up to complement her golden hair, carefully rolled into a glorious beehive.

Zia rolled over and sat up slowly. Staring at the floor, she rubbed her eyes and scratched her head while studying the patterns formed by the lines on the large tiles below. They had a hypnotic effect in her drowsy state. At first they seemed to form a spiral, spinning faster and faster until she saw almost nothing but a dizzying blur. She blinked and it appeared like a maze, her eyes consciously trying to follow it to the end, but always leading back where she'd started.

"This is almost ten days in a row," Zia complained. "Are we ever going to start classes again?"

"Is that all you care about?! Your studies and your career? Would you be content to succeed as a teacher even if your students are occasionally taken off to be tortured at Evin Prison?"

Zia was awake now, but not yet angry. They'd been through this several times already and she knew where it would lead. Zia stressing the need for order amidst chaos so they could be prepared for a victorious future. Dilruba scoffing at anything short of full-scale rebellion. The real reasons for Zia's lack of enthusiasm remained hidden, even to herself.

She decided to employ the weapon of silence this time, allowing her eyes to linger on the floor a minute longer and then casually lying back down as if nothing had been said. For her roommate, who was even more feisty than herself, this was the equivalent of Zia taking the gloves off. She responded in kind.

Dilruba put her lipstick down on her desk with unusual force, brushed her hands all the way down her green blouse until it reached the edge of her mini skirt, making sure to remove any unsightly wrinkles that would detract attention from her youthful curves. It was an annoying ritual she performed every time they were getting ready to go anywhere that included boys. This time, however, the ceremony appeared to be performed as a threat, Dilruba now directly facing her. The claws were out.

"I'm beginning to think you're SAVAKI," she said coolly. The vicious swipe connected with flesh, drawing first blood.

She shot up from under the covers. "How dare you!" responded an indignant Zia, now standing face to face with the tigress before her. "You know what they did to my brother! To my family!" Her shiny brown hair swung wildly in her face as she seemed to be watching herself from above, not fully in control of her words. "Has anyone in your family been detained?! Tortured?! Of course not!" It was a clear reference to Dilruba's uncle, a lower-ranking member of the discredited Senate. She preferred to pretend he didn't exist.

Dilruba slowly returned to the mirror, backing down but not sheepishly. She watched out of the corner of her eye as Zia began to put on her clothes. She considered it a win, suppressing her smirk as she continued to scheme toward her ultimate objective for the day.

Zia continued to brood over the accusation as she was getting ready, silently replaying the crimes of the SAVAK, the Shah's despised secret police. They lurked throughout all corners of society like invisible tentacles, incessantly retrieving recriminating information on dissenters and feeding it into the king's giant beak. Ali experienced their stranglehold when, shortly after graduation and landing a job as second in command of a bridge construction project in a small town near Tehran, he criticized the Shah in front of the work crew. While complaining about the budget allotment for gasoline and oil, he carelessly quipped, "Why don't we just pay it directly to the United States and their minions in Sa'dabad Palace?" He regretted it even as the words were warm on his lips. He never found out who the informant was, but it must have been someone well-connected. Ali was pulled from his bed in their parents' house in the middle of the night, taken to Evin Prison, and both tortured and interrogated for three days. Four prison guards bound his hands, punched him in the face until his left eye was completely closed, and urinated on him while he helplessly writhed in pain. Before he was released, they made it clear he should shut up unless he wanted them to come after his sister and parents next time. He returned to work, face disfigured and dark blue, to be promptly handed a termination letter. In the following weeks of job searching, he discovered he'd been blackballed from the entire industry. Currently he worked behind the counter of a movie theatre and still lived with his parents, a bleak future looming.

By the time Zia had thrown on some make-up and her latest sleeveless shirt, the tension had died down. She knew better than to take her blonde friend too seriously.

"I talked to Kamran yesterday," said Dilruba. "He's supposed to be in front of Kharazmi Boys School this morning."

Zia knew what was coming next as she stared blankly at her incorrigible roommate.

"He'll have a friend."

It was November 1978 and the revolutionary protests had reached their pinnacle. The bombing of Rex Cinema in Abadan in southern Iran, which had been effectively blamed on the SAVAK although many signs pointed toward religious clerics, killed over four hundred people in August. September 4, the last day of Ramadan (or "Eid-al-Fitr"), became a rallying point for dissenters. The fervent protests which followed lasted for several days. Hundreds of thousands of citizens marched the streets, many clashing with soldiers desperately trying to maintain control. September 7, the soldiers lost their composure, firing into a crowd of protesters at Jaleh Square. Dozens were killed, prompting a massive backlash. They called it "Black Friday" and responded with ever-increasing numbers on the streets throughout the nation.

Ayatollah Khomeini cemented his leadership of the movement with his clear condemnation of the shootings, pointing the finger directly at the Shah. He demanded a government that was both democratic and Islamic, earning him prompt exile to France, where he gained the attention of the Western media and actually improved communication with the leaders of their movement despite the distance. A wide range of Iranian society was still represented within the masses on the streets, but the center of gravity among the leadership had clearly shifted toward the religious clerics, Khomeini firmly in charge of their ranks.

There were lots of smiles and giggling as Zia and Dilruba approached Kharazmi Boy's School. There was a girl's school across the street and virtually all of the high school students had flooded the boulevards and nearby courtyards for weeks. The mix of secondary and university students electrified the atmosphere, adding both fuel and fun to the demonstrations. The protests were mostly sincere, but these young people hadn't experienced as many opportunities to get to know the opposite sex in their entire lives as they had in the last month. As one would expect, this added a different element to the daily gatherings. The guys were mostly well-groomed, even the hippies for the most part, and the girls dotted the crowd in glowingly colorful array. There were more tight dresses and blue jeans than chadors and hijabs, which were probably more comfortable in the brisk Fall weather, but both styles were well represented. The distant snow-capped Alborz mountain range appeared as cinematographic light reflectors for the unfolding screenplay below.

Zia's face stood out in the midst of the laughing youth. Not because she was pretty, but because of her vacant brown eyes. She had no intention of enjoying herself or helping Dilruba with Kamran, her latest male target. She anticipated that after they found the boys, Dilruba would introduce her to Kamran's friend in an attempt to separate into couples, gaining Kamran's full attention. She would thwart her roommate's scheming by refusing to leave her side and insist that their entire focus be placed on the actual protesting part of the protest. She would shout more diligently and poetically than Dilruba as well, gaining an upper hand in their next dispute.

The guys approached from behind, catching Zia off guard as she turned to meet them. She never really noticed Kamran. His friend, Jalal Javadi, was tall, clean-shaven, and had long wavy brown hair. He had intelligent brown eyes framed with round wire-rim glasses and a soft, clear, and light complexion. He wore brown pants widely flared at the bottom, a white shirt with thin collars, and a brown leisure coat. He briefly offered a polite and kind smile that communicated friendliness without being too eager. Zia replied in kind, smoothing her hair over her right ear and briefly studying the asphalt.

She was vaguely conscious that Dilruba had been talking, but the first words she actually discerned were, "Is it okay if we move ahead by ourselves for a few minutes and look for Kamran's brother?" She was holding Kamran's arm firmly and already moving away before she received an answer. Zia feigned objection, happily acquiescing despite her convincing deadpan performance.

Zia and Jalal continued their march (or was it a waltz?) toward Tehran University alongside their fellow dissenters. After an awkward introduction, conversation came easily and they began to get to know each other. They were the same age, both studying at Tehran University, and had many common tastes and perspectives on life. He talked briefly about his studies in journalism, but he was much more content to ask Zia about herself. Topics included King Cyrus, the Pahlavi dynasty (which included the current regime and much critique), and her favorite poets.

"Who's your favorite poet?" inquired a grinning Jalal. "I can't choose a favorite," she insisted.

"I'm sorry, but you have to." Jalal playfully grabbed her cup of doogh, a cold yogurt drink, from her hands. "Tell me a favorite or I drink it all."

"Give it back, you jerk!" She was smiling ear to ear.

"I'm waiting," replied a persistent Jalal, continuing to hold the doogh away from Zia, desperately hoping she would come near enough to take it from him.

"Okay, fine. My favorite poet is Rumi."

"Now, was that so hard?" He handed her drink back, releasing it slowly as their hands briefly, and gloriously, touched.

"I know what you're thinking," continued Zia. "Everybody likes Rumi."

"No, not at all…" He paused. "Actually, he's my favorite, too."

"What?! You're just saying that to make me feel better."

"No, I'm not!" It wasn't the only protest of the morning for Jalal, but definitely the most enjoyable. "So you think I would just tell you what you want to hear even about something as important as my favorite poet? You must think highly of yourself, Zia Tehrani."

She pushed him sideways, suppressing a laugh. "Okay, if you're so into Rumi, let me hear your favorite poem!" She called his bluff.

"I don't want to do that here. We're supposed to be part of a demonstration." He managed a sheepish smile as he grew red with embarrassment.

"I'm not buying it. Quote it now or we both know you're lying."

Jalal's face revealed an admission of defeat. He moved closer to her and lowered his voice. After a few deep breaths and awkward attempts to start, he began in full earnest.

It's not Me that's glorified in acts of worship.

Zia immediately recognized it as Moses and the Shepherd. The part he was quoting was written as the voice of God. Her heart grew strangely warm.

> It's the worshippers! I don't hear the words they say I
>   look inside at the humility
> That broken-open lowliness is the Reality, not the
>   language! Forget phraseology. I want burning,
>   burning!
> Be friends with your burning. Burn up your thinking
>   and your forms of expression!
> Moses, those who pay attention to ways of behaving
>   and speaking are one sort.
> Lovers who burn are another.

"You didn't start in the beginning," she said flatly.

"That's because my favorite part is in the middle! And you interrupted." He started to continue when the chants started. A television crew had arrived, evoking renewed focus among the protesters. To be sure, there were those among them ready to use violence, and clashes occurred daily. In fact, they had become so commonplace that distant explosions no longer caused so much as a hitch in the stride of the onward marchers. Even so, the greatest weapon wielded by the revolutionaries was more uniquely Iranian. Poetry, it turned out, was as equally potent in generating dissent as it was in wooing a young woman.

The memorized chant, performed with excellence for the camera crew, was screamed at impressive decibels. The topic of the lament was the Black Friday massacre, its aim to sway the young armed forces keeping watch over the city.

> Will you kill your brother?
> We gave you flowers, you replied with bullets Rise, O,
>   soldiers
> Your brother is killed. I will kill, I will kill

> Those who killed my brother no nation has ever seen
> Our armed forces can be so mean!

Dilruba and Kamran returned to find their friends shouting more loudly, their countenance more fierce than ever.

"Quite impressive for someone who had to be dragged out of bed." Dilruba had to practically yell directly in her left ear to be heard above the crowd, the loudest of which was the girl in whose ear she was shouting. Zia was startled and her voice embarrassingly cracked when she finally heard Dilruba. She looked up to see that her friends clearly heard it and responded with daggers aimed at her roommate. Her face now a darkish pink, Zia had little to say and knew she was at her mercy.

Shots rang out about two blocks away, a little too close for comfort this time. No one ran or screamed, but most of the protesters walked briskly in the other direction as shouts in the distance were clearly discerned. Flirting and taunting quickly turned to sobriety as the guys escorted the girls to a safer venue. The party was over, for today, at least.

Word spread throughout the city someone had been shot and that soldiers had used tear gas. As usual, rumors piled onto the truth, sending citizens into a calculated rage. Zia went to her family's house to watch the news with Ali. Technically, they had little reason to expect to see the reporters show anything incriminating about the government, but the media had shown a surprising amount of public sympathy with the movement, eliciting an increased viewership among hopeful Iranians.

As the evening news began, both Ali and Zia saw something in the newscaster's countenance hinting that this may not be the usual slants and myths from state-employed talking heads. He began by describing the protests of the day with no particularly remarkable details. As he proceeded to talk about the soldiers using tear gas and firing shots into the air, however, his voice began to betray his emotion.

What happened next wasn't just another report for the evening news. It was outright rebellion, not only by the man on the screen, but by everyone on all levels of production. With tears in his eyes, he told millions of viewers that a high school student had been heartlessly shot dead by the soldiers. It was immediately followed by footage of armed soldiers wearing gas masks and automatic rifles chasing young men wielding nothing but stones into a corner of Tehran University.

To be sure, this was not even close to the greatest atrocity committed by the Shah's soldiers during the revolutionary protests. Seeing truth on television, however, practically crumpled Zia and Ali into a puddle in the middle of the living room. It wasn't the revelation of this particular young man losing his life. It was the catharsis of finally knowing that everyone in Iran also knew the truth about this particular young man. And the Shah, slinking somewhere in halls of his great palace, knew that everyone knew. November 4 was a game changer.

9

STANDING ALONE

Three simultaneous explosions jarred Arman out of his short-lived rest. Glass spewed from the north side of Tower 2 as he looked across the empty space between the newly- disconnected buildings. The towers were still identical, but now stood alone. Like Siamese twins recklessly ripped apart, each seemed precariously vulnerable and naked without the support of the other.

Arman had no idea how the latest explosions were happening or who was behind it, but he didn't need to wait around to find out either. After the bridge fell, he'd assumed that was the end of the immediate danger, but now it was obvious there were more assailants and he needed to get out of the building as soon as humanly possible. As he ran to the stairs he realized he was the only one still on his floor, prompting him to pick up his pace even more. He also realized he didn't thank the guy who had helped him, but it was too late now.

Just run.

A look down the staircase revealed a whirlpool of tourists and resident workers streaming their way toward the bottom. It was fairly smooth until the man in front of him lost his self-control and ran into the line in front of him, creating a domino effect of tumbling Malaysians slamming into the walls and steel arm rails. Arman reflexively jumped over them and approximately nine stairs, gaining his balance against the wall and avoiding the pile-up behind him. He would do this several times more before it was over.

It still didn't seem real. In his dream-like state, he bounded over more unfortunate people even as he pictured Farzin and Banu reach for their belts. It was a scene he couldn't get out of his head, as if Dahag himself had cruelly placed it on a permanent loop. It overlaid with the real images before him as if he were looking at two screens, increasing the challenge of avoiding collisions with the fellow refugees below.

He finally reached the ground floor and began to feel he was safe as he heard another explosion rock one of the towers. This time he couldn't tell which one. A crowd of people packed the enormous space in front of the exit to Jalan Ampang, so he quickly sprinted toward the other side. He sped around the central area of Suria KLCC, lucky red lanterns nothing but a blur as he ran past Parkson department store toward KLCC Park. Arman was relieved to see the crowd was minimal and he would soon be outside.

He felt safer as he burst through the double doors, but he then realized that he was entering another crowded area. Everyone in the stairwell was of the same mind, trying desperately to get down the stairs, but this crowd was a mix of hundreds of people staring upward, as if watching a fireworks show, and many others fleeing the towers altogether. The latter poured into one side of the enormous water fountain and out of the other like salmon swimming upstream. Arman decided instead to run around the edge of the pool, which turned out to be a fortunate decision.

More explosions rumbled from the towers, hurling Arman onto his face. He looked up to see fresh smoke spewing from Tower 2, again near the gaping hole previously connected with the bridge. This time, however, large swaths of the forty-first floor ripped apart, followed by the top half of the building lurching downward toward KLCC Park. Specifically, toward the newly populated water fountain.

Most of those unfortunate enough to be in the fountain

multiplied their problems by continuing to run east, directly away from the falling tower, but not out of its path. They would never make it, of course. Arman turned a sharp right and ran south as fast as he possibly could. He briefly panicked as the shadow of the falling building enveloped the walkway before him, assuming he would be crushed. He dove behind a short wall along the walking path and braced for impact.

He'd experienced earthquakes before, but nothing compared to this. Approximately thirty floors of Tower 2 thundered into the center of KLCC Park, crushing everything in its path and sending shockwaves blasting through the glass of the Convention Center behind him. He huddled as close to the wall as he could, covering his head to protect himself from debris that seemed to be coming from everywhere. An enormous cloud of smoke like a giant sandstorm enveloped Arman, mercifully preventing him from seeing the glass and steel beams slamming to the ground around him. All he could do was wait. And pray.

After the wave of smoke and ash subsided enough to uncover his face, Arman wiped his eyes and opened them to a frightening gray apocalypse. One by one, mounds of ash slowly rose and formed into erect, zombie-like humans, gasping for breath, aimlessly reaching for anyone or anything to grant them a semblance of stability, eventually attempting to wipe their faces with the insides of ash-covered shirts. A few moved more quickly, frantically screaming names of loved ones as they uncovered object after object in vain. Most of them walked nowhere in particular, half dazed, half mourning.

Distant sirens grew louder as rescue teams prepared to dig for the living. Arman grew dizzy with exhaustion, both physical and emotional, and knew he had to get away. He looked back one more time at the historic disaster he'd just witnessed and the loop with Farzin and Banu restarted, this time visually overlapping with the massive death and destruction they'd caused. It was too much to process, or even believe at the moment. Survival instincts again kicked in and he sped away, mostly in a vain attempt to push the truth out of his head.

He ran toward the space between the Convention Center and the mall and noticed a nasi kandar restaurant on the corner, still inside the park. He felt drawn in by the promise of both empty tables and spinning fans to clear the air, hopefully allowing him to breathe. As he slowed his pace to a jog, the men and women running past him no longer registered or made any kind of impression, even when they bumped into each other.

As he entered the open-air restaurant, he found an empty table and collapsed onto a row of chairs. He hoped to experience some semblance of rest, but then he remembered Yusuf, envisioning him clinging to the rail, and buried his head into his right arm.

It was a long and quiet sob. His tears mixed with dirt and ashes, inflaming the scar on his face. Finally having time for initial reflections, his pain over losing Farzin and Banu was now solidly mixed with hot anger over their betrayal. *How could they do this? Why would they do it? How could I be so stupid not see it?* It all sent him into a downward spiral, leaving him only faintly clinging to sanity. With everything he had already been through, it was difficult to imagine that he could ever grieve more deeply than this.

He was wrong.

10

UP ON THE ROOF

S cared young soldiers slunk into the shadows of link houses in
District 8. Throughout the neighborhood, families and friends
gathered on top their rectangular dwellings as a way to continue the
protests despite the imposition of martial law. "Allah-O- Akbar!"
was again the favorite chant as their cries successfully intimidated
the military below, most of whom were desperately hoping their
superiors would join the cause of the people. In the frigid December
air, cold smoke shot from their mouths and mingled together as a
blanket of incense rising to Allah, prayers for freedom on the eve of
Ashura.

The following day was the traditional time on the Persian
calendar for Shi'a Muslims to commemorate the tragic murder of
Hussein Ibn Ali - the grandson of Muhammad and the man whom
they believed to be his rightful successor - with rites of self-
flagellation and dramatic re-enactments of his bravery. In 1978,
however, traditions were overshadowed by two days of protests
which included approximately ten percent of the entire nation.

Ali, Zia, and Jalal joined the chorus side by side on the roof of
their parents' house. They joined cold hands, echoing the various

chants around them while aiming their gaze at the nearest soldiers. There were no front yards. Only sidewalks and streets, bringing the people closer together as their collective cries fell upon the boys with guns. It was psychological warfare at its best and it clearly felt like the people were winning now. Ali knelt on his prayer rug as he screamed into the darkness. The rug felt like a new appendage as the consistency of his daily prayers increased, along with his hope of a future.

A few hours earlier Jalal had entered the Tehrani house for the first time. After their parents, Yasmin and Davoud, briefly came out to meet Jalal, they mostly stayed in the back of the house and let the younger ones remain by themselves. Although they weren't overtly traditional regarding dating, they still required Zia and Jalal to stay with Ali when they were inside as a sort of chaperone.

While there were no signs of awkwardness with the parents, Jalal didn't get a warm and fuzzy feeling from the brother. Ali's first impression of Jalal wasn't entirely positive and he wasn't very concerned with hiding it. He'd grown tired of the flared pants and round glasses, along with most of the other trends that came from the West as well. He saw Jalal's smooth face as soft and weak as he peered down from behind his ever-thickening beard. Ali now preferred loose pants and khaki shirts with Chinese-style sneakers as he and untold thousands of other youth found ways to avoid identifying with America.

Now, however, as they stood hand in hand, equal in fervor against the Shah, Jalal was no longer a slick and shallow disco boy courting his sister. They were brothers in arms.

"I'm going downstairs for a minute," said Zia. "I'll be right back."

The chanting had temporarily died down and Jalal assumed this was an intentional exit designed to let her brother and boyfriend connect. He put his freezing hands into his pockets as he sat next to the taller and larger Ali, wondering what he really thought about him. Since Ali wasn't offering anything to break the sudden silence, Jalal decided he would take a chance.

"Zia told me what happened." He was nervous about how Ali would react to this, but wanted to show solidarity with the horrible injustice he'd suffered. Ali glanced at him briefly and nodded.

"She talks too much." The smirk on his face gave Jalal permission to smile. "You'll find out more about that soon, I suppose."

"Yes, I've noticed that," admitted Jalal with a grin.

"And you won't have to worry about knowing what she's really thinking, either," Ali added. Jalal howled in laughter.

"Actually, that's what I like the most about her. Truth is rare these days." Ali again nodded in agreement. They sat and quietly observed silhouettes of their neighbors walking across the flat rooftops across the street. It was difficult to tell if they saw their cold breath or if their fellow protesters across the street were smoking.

"What if everything's about to change?" Ali looked straight ahead, but his eyes were wide with earnestness and hope.

Zia re-emerged through the rooftop entrance with a mischievous smile, her left hand behind her back.

"What are you up to?" asked an unsurprised Ali. She pulled her arm forward in a deliberate fashion and revealed a yellow softball-sized water balloon. Jalal instinctively pulled his coat over his face as a shield.

"You don't need to worry about getting hit, Jalal," offered an amused Ali, who knew his sister well. "You should worry about getting shot."

Jalal tilted his head and narrowed his eyes, confused about what he could possibly mean until he saw Zia wind up.

"No! No! No!" It was a hushed plea for caution as he desperately wanted her to stop, but was even more desperate to avoid the attention of the two soldiers approximately fifty feet down the street. It was too late. They watched in slow motion as it crossed the road, a ball-shaped shadow streaking across the parked cars under the street lamps.

The young men with rifles across their shoulders had been freezing as they walked up and down the street. The fact that they sympathized with the voices of fury aimed their direction added to their chill. The one solace they could find in their misery was the occasional cigarette. They had carefully rationed them to last until the end of their shift and it was now time for a little pleasure and a hint of warmth. One of the soldiers, cigarette in mouth, leaned forward as his comrade held out a small flame from his lighter. The balloon slammed into his face like a ball of ice, dousing the flame and drenching his clothes. Instant frostbite. His cheeks flushed, freezing and in pain, and he stood still in stunned confusion for about ten seconds while his partner looked up to see where the water missile came from.

Ali threw Zia onto the flat roof beneath them and covered her mouth, scared she would shout in triumph. Jalal quickly followed his lead and put his finger over his mouth, begging Zia to remain quiet. Suddenly they heard muffled giggling from the house to their left. Jalal and Ali both froze, looking toward their neighbors like they were insane. The soldiers heard it and looked their general direction. Jalal was the only one who could see the scene below though he was safely out of view, so Zia asked him to describe what was happening.

"They're walking toward us," he whispered. Jalal's voice quivered, clearly panicked.

As the soldiers were about halfway to them, they heard more strained laughter from a roof across the street to their right. The soldiers stopped, aiming violent stares behind them. Then they heard chuckles from the house on their right, then across the street to the left. Suddenly, the pent up laughter broke loose like an avalanche from unseen neighbors in all directions. The indignation enraged the soldiers and they reached for their rifles.

Laughter subsided as they shot wildly at the rooftops, furiously determined to restore their honor. A bullet split through the edge of the roof next to Jalal, scattering bits of cement into their hair. They huddled together, hands over their heads, and prayed for the shooting to stop.

After twenty seconds, the shooting did, in fact, stop, but no one dared move. The neighborhood was intensely quiet as they anxiously waited for the bullets to return. Zia saw Jalal raise his head slightly, as if he'd heard something and was investigating.

"What are they doing?" she whispered carefully. Jalal again put his finger to his mouth, but he no longer looked frightened. He listened intently, as if to confirm the unbelievable. Then he looked at them with a hint of a grin on the left side of his mouth.

"Crying," he said, bewildered by the moment. "They're crying."

The rooftop snickering returned, but this time they morphed into open laughter more quickly than before. Then guffawing. Soon the unthinkable happened. The soldiers, swallowed up in shame and beaten down by months of being forced into the role of oppressors and enemies of the people, simply... ran away. They threw their rifles down and sprinted down the road until their long shadows were invisible.

The rooftop silhouettes multiplied in number as roaring laughter turned to dancing. Ali and Jalal hugged Zia and hurled her up on their shoulders, joining the revelry with triumphant shrieks of joy. They wanted to let people know who threw the water balloon, to literally shout it from the rooftops who the hero of the moment was, but they all knew how word would spread. Until the SAVAK no longer existed, it was classified information.

The traditional Ashura celebrations planned for the following day were swallowed up in unprecedented protests. Approximately ten percent of the nation of 9 million people flooded streets all throughout Iran. It was a climax that reached such a dramatic height that they not only believed the end was near, they believed it was inevitable. The Shah's control over the people was slipping through his royal fingers as he watched one institution and leader after another shift support to Ayatollah Khomeini. The last buttress delaying the total collapse of his house was the military.

General Azhari, the ultimate commander of the armed forces,

knew his soldiers were shaken by the eerie nighttime rooftop protests. Morale was low and troops were rapidly going AWOL. Perceiving the need to act, he tried to spread a rumor that the thundering shouts in the dark were nothing more than clever leaders among the opposition with cassette tapes and high-decibel loudspeakers. It was a last gasp lie that lent itself to mockery.

Ali and Zia marched with the throngs of hopeful Persians throughout the streets of downtown Tehran. They had planned on connecting with Jalal and other friends as well, but it was impossible to find them in the midst of the massive crowd, especially since they were two decades removed from owning cell phones. Unlike previous protests, however, Zia was singularly focused on the task at hand as she joined the collective voices of her people.

In response to General Azhari's smokescreen, the people wielded their usual poetic weaponry. This time it wasn't even a fair fight. The overwhelming size of the crowds now in plain sight made it ridiculous to doubt the source of the cacophony the night before.

"Azhari, you cow!

You think tapes can march now?

How?!"

It seemed appropriate for the protest of all protests to happen on the Day of Ashura. The hero whose life and death they celebrated on this day assumed the perfect guide for their struggle. Hussein ibn Ali refused to give in to his oppressors, but instead sought to live as Allah wished. More than a millennium after his death, he now led Iranian Shi'a Muslims to the victory they so terribly wanted.

Ali Tehrani alternated between joy and cathartic anger as he chanted and screamed alongside his people. He saw his captors urinating on him and believed he could taste their future justice, dreaming of private members of the SAVAK outed and dragged through the streets. He thought of how much he hated working at the movie theaters and remembered how he lost his career. And in the dry reaches of his soul, there was a strange whisper of hope echoing toward his heart. Zia watched him throughout the day in sheer delight. It was obvious this was the beginning of the end and she was elated for Ali and everyone else who deserved justice and a life released from being trapped underneath the thumb of tyranny.

A month later the military announced their neutrality, in effect no longer supporting the Shah. The King was gone and Khomeini had returned as the triumphant leader.

Exactly what they'd hoped for.

RUNNING TO STAND STILL

Arman laid in the same position for a half hour, grieving and engulfed in hopelessness. Eventually his mind cleared enough to think through further implications of the horrors he'd witnessed. For the first time, he finally wondered how family and friends in Iran would react. How would he tell his parents? And his aunt, Farzin's mother? His chest hurt as he rehearsed how he would retell such a heinous story.

And what if…? His eyes flew open in horror as he followed the trail of the last thought.

His attention was diverted to televisions on the wall as the Indian owner turned the volume up. A somber crowd huddled around the screens, one of which hung directly over a tandoori oven. He could discern that some were Chinese and a few were Malay, but most were just as covered in ash as he was. For this unique moment in their lives, they stood next to each other, not as members of ethnic groups or religions, but in the kind of solidarity that only comes when evil has clearly revealed its face against all of humanity.

A reporter for a local news station was conducting interviews with eyewitnesses to the tower's collapse when she was interrupted by a colleague. The young Chinese woman listened intently to what she was being told, then alertly announced, "We have an eyewitness to the escape down the stairwell of Tower 2 who is also a journalist for Reuters."

Matt! Arman hadn't even thought of his American friends who worked in the building, but he was immediately grateful to at least have one friend who survived. Matt had apparently chosen a better exit than Arman judging by his appearance. No dirt and ashes. His brown hair was too short to be messed up, but his clothes did look a bit disheveled. He closed his eyes as the reporter asked a question Arman couldn't hear. Matt shook his head slightly, glancing upward before speaking.

"There were a few people who fell, but fortunately everyone kept from panicking.

People were yelling 'No running!' Matt explained. "I didn't see anyone trampled."

"What floor were you on?"

"The thirty-second floor."

"Do you know if any employees on the floors above the bridge – the forty-first and forty-second – were able to escape?"

He paused and looked down, his face re-emerging with eyes covered in mist. "I was told the explosions blocked the stairwell from the thirty-ninth floor upward, so I ran up to see if I could help them get through." He choked on his next words. He looked at the camera as if he was talking to someone specifically. "There was no way. I tried everything I could."

"So you first ran *up* instead of down?" She was incredulous, but respectful. Then the right question dawned on her. "Did you have friends above the bridge?"

Tom! Arman held his hand to his mouth and looked away. His mind reeled as he considered the kind man from Houston who'd been his host, and the sweetest woman he ever met who was now a widow. The news faded as Arman slumped into a nearby chair. As each new revelation added another layer of sorrow, he became numb and unable to process the implications. Somehow everything just kept getting worse.

The men began pointing toward the television in anger. He couldn't hear it over the shouting and couldn't understand what they were yelling and cursing about in the Tamil, Malay, and Chinese dialects surrounding him. As Arman refocused on the nearby screen, it took a few seconds to realize what he was seeing. It was a black and white scene, played on a loop, of young men and women walking through something that looked like an empty door frame. As he looked closer, he realized it was the security scanner he walked through before getting in the elevator to the bridge. The three-second clip also showed a young man and woman taking off dark jackets and laying them in plastic containers.

"Shut up, lah!" The restaurant owner, clearly agitated, quieted the crowd and again turned up the volume. Arman could now hear the television commentary.

"Again, you are looking at footage from a security camera at the bottom of the Petronas Towers where tourists enter the elevator to the SkyBridge. Two eyewitness survivors of the initial explosions on the bridge report seeing a small group of men and women, believed to be Iranian, wearing black jackets and acting suspiciously just before the bomb exploded. All of them were on the side of the bridge that disconnected first, so it is believed that they are all dead. The young man and woman you are looking at now are believed to be a part of this group."

Arman knew now he was looking at Farzin and Banu. The video was grainy, but it was definitely clear enough for people who knew them to recognize their image. Soon the whole world will know who they are and what they did.

"We believe, however," the reporter continued, "that one of their friends may have survived. Look at this picture as they zoom in on the upper right hand of the footage. A man - it's hard to tell how old he is – with a short dark beard is looking away, so we can't see his face clearly. However, if you look closely, you can see a unique design on his t-shirt. On the left is either some kind of stone tablet or tombstone. On the right is what looks like a capital 'I' in an outline form. Or maybe it's supposed to be a pole. It looks like there's writing inside." As he continued to try to describe the shirt and the person wearing it, the camera switched to a completely different scene, again from security camera footage.

"It appears the same man I was just describing is here hanging onto a rail of the fallen crosswalk. As you can see in the looping video, he lets go of a baby stroller to save himself." The reporter stopped briefly, reaching for words until she eventually settled on mumbling her real thoughts under her breath. The men surrounding Arman in the nasi kandar became indignant. An older Indian gentleman with thin gray hair stood still, eyes red with anger, mouth hung in exasperation. A young Malay man with long black hair slammed his fist on the table where Arman was sitting. He screamed.

"Coward!"

Arman was already afraid. Now his cheeks flamed red with shame.

Gathering himself, the reporter continued. "Fortunately, a man above him, in the green shirt, grabs the stroller at the same time. A hero and a villain in the same moment." She concluded, "If you have seen the man in the white shirt, please report it to the police! I repeat, please report it to the police! He is a suspect and is believed to have information on the Petronas Towers bombing. If you see him, do not approach him. He is believed to be armed and dangerous. Just call the number on the screen and let the authorities handle the situation."

12

AFTERGLOW

The air was light on an unusually warm March afternoon. The students were back on campus and seemed to glide across the grass and sidewalks in between classes. Gaping smiles and exuberant greetings were more common these days, Jalal, who was busy putting off studying, sat lazily on a bench when he saw Zia approaching from his left. The sun danced through her brown curly hair as it shone from behind, the halo effect appropriately eliciting an inability to speak. Her light purple dress lit up underneath the wide smile beaming at the young man she'd fallen in love with. Jalal was dumbstruck that such a beautiful girl would look at him that way. He smiled beneath his thick new Stalinesque mustache, an open identification with his political party of choice, the Mojahedin. Hiding your political alliances seemed like a thing of the past.

It was the first glimpse of Spring in 1979 and all of Tehran University teemed with new life. No longer were the students laboring under the expectation that they would graduate only to enter a workforce dominated by Shah loyalists and pocked with secret police. They now truly believed they had a future worthy of embracing and celebrating. Only a month earlier a radio announcer, the first voice of the revolution to hit the air waves, tearfully read the triumphant message from the Ayatollah, their champion of freedom.

We are grateful to Almighty God and wish to express our gratitude to the army for responding to the call of the eminent ulama [scholars] to join the nation. I plead with the rest of the army commanders, officers and NCOs, who have not yet taken the big decision of their lives, to join the people. I would also like to ask the people to be vigilant and confront and crush any conspiracy. Please maintain law and order and safeguard state buildings together with all their files and documents, which belong to the nation.

His message was followed with shouts of joy and cathartic tears across the country. After it was over, news bulletins continued as one piece of good news after another slowly soaked in. Between news segments, they blasted their new anthems, songs of the revolution composed and recorded as sheer acts of rebellion the previous year. Exuberant Persians gathered around radios in tight-knit clusters, reacting with laughter and, of course, dancing. Much dancing.

The actual time Jalal spent staring at Zia in disbelief at his new life was only a couple of seconds. And yet the scenes which sped through his mind could have been woven together into an epic motion picture, the musical theme of which was already emblazoned into his memory forever. It was one of the first revolutionary songs publicly unveiled on the radio that great day.

> The air is now pleasant, the flowers have blossomed
> The dove, upon return, sang a song of hope
> Happy spring! Happy spring!

As the blossoming poppies echoed a theme of hope, Jalal and Zia talked in disbelief about how their parents had already agreed to let them be married. They thought it would surely be more difficult for this to happen in such a short period of time. Perhaps they were actually convinced it was right, or perhaps they were too swept up in the jubilation surrounding them to say "no." Either way, they were now engaged, in love, and filled with dreams.

13

DEEP WATER

Arman's scars shrieked as he tried to inconspicuously fold his arms over his t-shirt. Somehow it hadn't yet occurred to him that he would be a suspect. He had even envisioned going to the police to tell them everything he knows, but was honestly thinking he would walk away from that encounter a free man. He'd been so preoccupied with grief and the pain of losing those he loved that he just didn't think about it.

How stupid! Of course they'll suspect me. I'm Iranian. That means I'm a terrorist, right?!

Intense sadness turned to defiance and hot anger. And fear. Indescribable fear. He looked down at his shirt and was reminded that he was covered completely in ash and dirt. No one could possibly recognize him like this. He decided he needed to find somewhere to be alone and think. He had no idea what to do or where to go, inexperienced as he was at being a fugitive. Arman walked out of the restaurant with the intention of leaving the KLCC Park area and heading toward Jalan Pinang (Pinang Road). However, the masses of people pouring into the area – firemen, policemen, reporters, civilians, etc. – made him decide to take the easier path, southward on the walkway next to the Convention Center.

The large glass outer wall of the Convention Center revealed a long, tall, and attractively empty hallway. He slipped inside the double doors and quickened his pace, looking for a corner of the building where he couldn't be seen. The hallway was longer than he realized. There was a ghostly quiet following him as he looked back at the large glass wall and remembered the chaos still unfolding outside. He saw an escalator heading down into the aquarium – Aquaria KLCC – and promptly jumped on, guessing that everyone had lost interest in marine life. As he reached the bottom of the escalator, his instinct was confirmed. Everyone was gone. Even the workers.

Arman hurried through the empty food court, past the Starbucks, and jumped over the turnstile entrance, void of even a single ticket agent. He stopped at the seahorse display, peered through the enormous tanks, and listened for anyone who may be near. Nothing. Just Arman and the ocean.

As he slowed his pace to a walk, he found the narrow, dark, and glowing hallways both made him feel safe and calmed him enough to think. The jelly-fish display shone with iridescent purple and pink hues as he snaked his way down to the main viewing area. A large octopus, silhouetted by a soft blue light, hovered above him as he entered the tunnel.

Aquaria KLCC was one of the larger aquariums in the world, with innumerable displays and glass tanks encompassing 60,000 square feet of space within the Convention Center. The tunnel Arman had just entered was approximately 300 feet long and allowed visitors to feel as if they were immersed in the water, viewing the ocean life on both sides and just inches directly above them as well. A travelator circled through the aquarium, allowing guests to effortlessly gaze in wonder at stingrays, giant groupers, and tiger sharks without continuously bumping into a crowd of strangers. Well-placed rocks and the remains of a ship added an exotic feel to the underwater environment.

Arman sat down on the travelator with his legs crossed, looking up blindly toward the stingray drifting lazily above the glass. The longer he stared, the more it seemed to be smiling at him. Or was that mockery? He wondered if anyone would ever smile at him again. His mind searched through the events and tragedies of the day, detailing their personal implications and trying to see if he had missed anything. After all, every time he thought he had a grasp on just how bad his situation really was, another truth emerged.

Unfortunately for Arman, his mind landed on yet one more devastating reality. When he first realized he was a suspect, his main concern was whether or not he would be found guilty by association, which was why he sought a hiding place. The question immediately on his mind was, *"Should I turn myself in or run?"* His prospects of somehow escaping seemed dim at best, but his prospects of being heard in an unbiased way seemed even darker.

Now, however, he realized the hammer in the court of public opinion had not only landed on him, but it had most likely already slammed onto his mother and father as well. Across the Indian Ocean, the entire country of Iran would be filled with the news of young Persians bombing the Petronas Towers. There were some among the hardliners, no doubt, who would be privately pleased to hear that another materialist Mecca within a Muslim- majority nation was destroyed. Still others who would rejoice that Sunni Muslims were suffering.

The large majority of Iranians, however, would feel shame. Deep and abiding shame. And the weight of the great fog descending upon them now centered on the family and friends of the accused. Arman knew that his parents' lives were over. Even if they believed Arman, their reputations were shattered and they would live the rest of their lives under suspicion. They would lose friends. They would lose their jobs. Sure, they could find solace among those who actually support terrorism (and perhaps even jobs), but they would rather jump off of the peak of Mount Damavand than join their ranks. Less than a year earlier, Arman thought there was nothing he could do to cause more shame for his father than what he'd already done. The suffering this would cause them both, however, was worse than a thousand deaths, and Arman couldn't help but believe that it was his fault. Not because he was guilty, but because he was stupid. *How did I not see it?!*

As he felt the weight of both his family and, indeed, his entire nation upon him, the water above seemed to grow murky and heavier, like his own personal heavenly firmament preparing floods of judgment. His thoughts crashed and swirled around him until he seemed carried off completely, floating toward a nameless shore. He continued to beat himself up as he drifted alongside a tiger shark, unaware of the evil stare out of its left eye. Time was quickly running out, but he just couldn't make the inevitable decision that lay before him. He looked through the shark toward the surface above.

The water at the top of the tank rippled unnaturally, causing a school of bluefish to dart to his right and then his left, both erratically and in perfect unison. *Is the ground shaking?* Arman stood to his feet to notice the travelator seemed less stable than before. *Is this an earthquake?* It seemed consistent with an earthquake, but then he admitted that this was just denial. Completely frozen, he just stood there and waited.

The ceiling crashed inward with the intensity of Niagara Falls. Arman was thrown to the floor, his face landing on the still-moving travelator. He covered his head in a crippled fear, knowing there would be no chance of survival when the glass above him cracked. "*This is it,*" he told himself, briefly comforted by the thought until he felt the sting of Dahag. *What will it feel like to die? Will I immediately be in front of the judgment seat of Allah?* He remembered his sin and shame and laid still in terror.

But the rumbling stopped and he was okay. He looked up and saw that the glass ceiling directly above him seemed mostly intact. Waves were splashing over the edge of the top of the tank. Stingrays scampered around in both quick and halted motions like squirrels. The sharks propelled their bodies side to side in exaggerated motions as if in anger. But he was unharmed.

He jumped to his feet and tried to see where the most damage was. He wanted to run, but he didn't know which direction was safest. It quickly became clear the back of the aquarium had absorbed most of the damage, so he ran as fast as he could toward the entrance. Just as he began his sprint, the glass cracked directly above him. He looked up and held his hand over his face, expecting gushing water. There was none. Yet. The crack both deepened and continued to expand toward the entrance. No matter how hard Arman ran, the crack continued to emerge directly above him. Chasing him. Mocking him.

As he ran through the exit of the tunnel, where the largest tank was no longer directly above, he leaned his head and chest forward like a sprinter at the end of a race. The crack arrived at the same spot in a photo finish, quickly climbing up the side of the aquarium as Arman sped away.

The tank exploded into a million shards of glass, landing all around his path like jagged snow. An inescapable tsunami of tens of thousands of gallons of water rushed from behind, quickly overtaking him and slamming him into the glass of a reticulated python display. While chaos had broken loose in the rest of the aquarium, affecting all of the other creatures as well as Arman, the metallic-brown snake seemed calm and still. It just looked at him, casually flicking its tongue in and out, gauging its surroundings as if nothing abnormal was happening. For some inexplicable reason, and for a duration of time that lasted no more than a few seconds, Arman found himself simply wanting to gaze.

He came to and realized his feet no longer touched the ground. His head was submerged for another brief second, revealing an underwater view of the python, still looking. Frantically, he swam toward the entrance to the aquarium believing there was hope, for two reasons. The exit he was approaching moved uphill, making it more promising to find a solid foothold, and the continued force of the water was thrusting him in that direction anyway. *Just stay above water.* He said this partly to encourage himself to keep moving, but mostly to help himself pretend that drowning was his only concern. In addition to fear of what he knew was now swimming nearby, the combination of water and movement inflamed all three of his wounds, evoking panicked images of Dahag gliding through the temporary ocean underneath.

As he turned his head to the right, he noticed several sets of giant floating shark jaws, the vestiges of one of the aquarium's most popular displays. A set of smaller tanks, now floating upside down, gathered in front of him in the hallway, blocking his path. He climbed across one of them and, as he reached across the next obstacle, he realized there was solid footing to his right. He climbed onto a platform that previously supported a tank and briefly wondered if he should stay there until the rising water subsided. The rushing water behind him, however, seemed to show no signs of slowing and, as he looked ahead, he saw the food court. It was reachable!

He dove in hope and began swimming underwater. He risked opening his eyes and was relieved to see the water was still mostly clear, so he kept pushing forward. He noticed the various species of fish around him, but carefully focused on trying not to think about living creatures in the water. He followed the turns in the hallway, furiously pumping legs and arms like frantic propellers.

The hallway turned left and he met his greatest fear face to face, a tiger shark laying still in front of him as if in ambush. He screamed and inadvertently swallowed the strange mix of fresh and saltwater. Rushing to the surface for air, he was completely unsure if he wanted to keep his eye on the shark or if it was just better to not look. Initially, he decided to just swim, but then he couldn't help but to look back. As he did, the nine-foot monster lay completely motionless, and very slowly, but clearly, sinking.

This only encouraged him slightly as he transitioned to a flailing freestyle swimming motion. Suddenly he heard another crash, not a thundering collapse like before, more like an object of several hundred pounds falling next to him. A searing pain simultaneously ripped into his ankle at the exact place of his scar, sending him into a tailspin of hysteria as he waited for the shark to finish him off. Instead, he felt the shard of glass in his leg, pulled it out, and continued his escape.

He was only forty feet away from the food court now. The elevation was higher and it still appeared he might be able to stand and run in the surrounding area. If not, he knew the escalator would lead up and out of the water. Another sharp object hit him in the side – the corner of a table from the Starbucks he was now swimming past. As he looked back to see what it was, all he saw was the cloud of blood, oozing from his calf, floating in his wake.

Blood!

It was the only coherent thought he could form as he looked back to the space where he had seen the shark. It had vanished. He broke into an underwater Olympic sprint, using every ounce of strength and courage available. Thirty feet and still clear.

The shark appeared like lightning from his right, approaching at a speed humanly impossible to avoid. It approached with its mouth wide open like the tiger it was and clamped its massive jaws at the moment of impact. Arman was knocked sideways, but, unbelievably, was untouched by the shark. It was then he realized an enormous wall of glass floating vertically, and miraculously, between them.

Twenty feet until the food court. Fifteen feet and the force of the water threw him into the counter of a food stall. He grasped its edges with both hands and sprung upward to the safety of the table. Arman raised to his feet, heart thumping, completely out of breath. He looked up to find approximately twenty more feet between himself and the escalator. In between were floating orange chairs, long white tables, also floating, and a set of four high tables which appeared to be bolted to the floor. They lay out in a perfect pathway toward the escalator, which seemed to be an engraved invitation to jump forward, but his first instinct was to stay put until the water receded. The water, however, wasn't receding.

14

AZADI AND LOVE

Zia leaned back on both hands as her feet rested lazily in the calm of Azadi Lake. Jalal lay comfortably at her side as she bathed in the reflection, clear as glass, of the Alborz Mountains. Arid and brown in late Spring, she imagined them as a blank slate, ripe for pine saplings and all manner of vegetation in the wake of the recent thawing of snow. To her right the lake's mirror revealed the titanic image of Azadi Stadium, the centerpiece of the complex built nearly a decade earlier.

It was the perfect place to celebrate Zia's graduation. First because it was both peaceful and beautiful, but also for its name. Azadi, meaning "liberty," is surely what those who erected the stadium and dug the lake longed for as they labored in the era of the SAVAK. Having completed the first class venue for international competition, the engineers and laborers alike joined the rest of the nation in the struggle against the Shah. To Zia, this was incontrovertible proof of what their people could accomplish together. A towering stadium built to seat 120,000 people next to a man-made lake reflecting a sweeping vista of the Alborz. And now the sons and daughters of Cyrus had another vast and yawning cavity before them - their new nation - just waiting to be filled with streams of freedom and prosperity.

Jalal suddenly raised up and changed positions, crossing his legs and leaning slightly forward with his head and torso in a submissive posture.

"Teacher, I have a question."

Zia unsuccessfully pretended to keep a straight face as she played along with Jalal's nod to her future career. Her actual goal was to continue with her education so she could eventually teach history at a university. To her, the idea of teaching children seemed both overwhelming and academically unchallenging, which is exactly why Jalal liked to pretend that's where she was headed.

Zia let out an exasperated breath and rolled her eyes, playing along with hidden delight.

"Yes, child?"

Jalal shifted nervously and spoke in a higher pitch. "Why do we have to read about things that happened so long ago?"

"Well, ignorant boy," she said with as much condescension as she could conjure, "We study history because, as George Santayana said, 'Those who cannot remember the past are condemned to repeat it.'"

Jalal tilted his head to the side quizzically. "You mean, like, when I tried to put a booger under the desk and forgot that I had just put one in the same place?" His eyes were wide and innocent. She was amazed how much he actually looked like a nervous eight-year-old.

The left corner of Zia's mouth twitched slightly and she briefly looked away. "Perhaps," she eventually answered. "But it's probably more like when you forget that boogers are not actually food."

Jalal, who had a natural gift for acting, remained unflappable. He loved Zia's sense of humor, but it was a rare event for her to make him laugh against his will. Still, he hadn't elicited the desired reaction from her, so he pressed on.

"Is it true that Reza Shah had green boogers coming out of his ears?"

"Let's talk about something else, little one." She stared him down unflinchingly. Her thick black shirt and black pants assisted her attempt at intimidation.

Jalal shot his hand in the air. "Teacher?!" Zia turned her back and pretended to write on a chalkboard, effectively ignoring him. Jalal quietly rose to his feet and crept up behind her. With his right hand he pretended to scratch his nails on a chalkboard and with his left he poked his finger in her ribs.

"Screeeeeeeech!"

Zia squealed and jerked away, finally granting Jalal the acquiescent giggle he'd worked so hard for, but she quickly recovered.

"Sit down, young man!"

Jalal acquiesced and resumed his humble posture on the ground, eyes carefully focused on the dirt.

"Teacher!" he cried again.

"What now, little Jalal?"

His hands were crossed above his lap, his face anxious and red. "Can I go to the toilet?"

Zia finally gave up and cackled freely as Jalal continued with the act. He walked to the edge of the water, his back turned to Zia, and acted as if he would create a few ripples onto the still water. As usual, his mistake was underestimating the boldness of the young woman he'd fallen in love with. Her bright red lipstick glistened in the brilliance of the lake's reflection as she formed a devious grin. She slithered up behind him with both hands close to her chest, elbows bent like springs ready to fling her new fiancé into the abyss.

At the last split second, Jalal turned and caught a glimpse of his impending doom just as she uncoiled her arms and shoved him forward. There was no saving himself even as he reflexively reached back for stability. As he did so, he unintentionally grasped Zia's shirt, pulling her down with him. They slapped against the water like Cypress trees and quickly came up for air, arms flailing to the cement walkway. The lake was deeper than they thought and definitely more frigid.

"Oooh it's so cooooold!" Zia attempted to climb out when Jalal grabbed her arm, both gently and firmly.

"One last question, Teacher." His dark eyes were still playful, but a little softer and more sincere. Zia held his gaze and tried not to shiver.

"Okay. One last question."

Jalal leaned forward with an earnest smile. "Can I kiss you?"

Zia looked around to see if anyone was watching. She could only see a few distant people near the stadium as they floated near the walkway, but the concrete edge a foot above them shrouded their heads from everyone on their side of the lake.

"I don't normally give my students permission to do that. But… maybe just this once."

He leaned forward and pressed his cold wet lips against hers for a warm and fleeting moment. He pulled back slowly, looking deeply into her eyes. Zia blushed under the thick and slightly smeared make-up, then quickly reached up with both hands, grabbed his head, lifted her entire torso above him, and shoved him underwater. Having created space between them, she successfully pulled herself out of the lake before he could catch her again.

"That was wrong, Teacher!" He protested in vain and pulled himself out in time to give chase. Her pace was slowed both by her guffawing and by the obvious fact that she didn't really want to outrun him. He caught up with her just as they reached the parking lot and wrapped his arms around her, which she received with delight.

"Okay, so that's the last time I let you teach me anything."

"I hate to tell you, but I think that's the first of many painful lessons you'll receive from me, young man."

They continued to hug as they playfully tried to one-up each other. At first their eyes were closed, oblivious to the world around them. As he finally began to look around, Jalal noticed a family walking past them approximately thirty feet away. The mother and father rushed to stand between the flirtatious couple and their children as if to shield their eyes. He suddenly felt conspicuous and wondered about the perception of strangers.

"I think it's time to go home. I'm freezing, too," said Jalal. Zia agreed as they walked hand in hand to the other side of the large parking lot.

There was a sudden crowd as an event in the stadium had concluded. It eventually occurred to Jalal that there were more men with long and thick beards than normal. Not all the men, of course, but enough to make him take notice for the first time. Zia, for her part, observed more dark-colored chadors and fewer stylish dresses and blouses among the women. They both felt the weight of dark stares from both sexes as they frowned at her wet and suddenly form-fitting clothes. An older man walking alone - long grey beard, loose brown clothing, and white Adidas sneakers - approached from the front. At first he bored a hole through Zia with a stare somewhere between lust and paternalism. Then, just as they passed each other, he glared at Jalal with a look of contempt he'd never experienced.

Were they just imagining that this was worse than normal? There was always a difference between the generations, but the judgment here didn't appear to be restricted to age. Was it just the nature of those attending this particular event or was something more profound happening in Tehran? In the nation? There was very little conversation as they rode back to her house, quietly pondering these questions as they attempted to warm up. Their clothes eventually dried off, but in the coming months the chill would remain as they watched the subtle cultural shifts around them.

15

———

LEAP OF FAITH

As water crept up the side of the counter, the tiger shark emerged into the center of the food court. It circled the area in front of him, the scent of blood still lingering in its gills, biding its time until it had a clear line of attack. It was a horrifying choice for Arman, but in the end, it wasn't really a choice at all. If he stayed where he was, he would be killed. In this proverbial "Should I stay or should I go?" scenario, the waters were crystal clear. Garnering the courage to jump, however, was a different thing completely.

The problem with using the tables was that the first one was eight feet away. He could jump that distance while on the run, but not while standing still, so he hesitated. The water was now half a foot from the top of the counter and rising quickly. He watched the circling of the shark and waited to see if there was a pattern to its lurking. There seemed to be obstacles in its way preventing a perfect circle, but there was a general motion he could recognize as its tailfin wandered through the dining area.

The water now beginning to cover his black Adidas, the shark was at its furthest distance in its loop, approximately fifteen feet from the first table. *Now or never.* He jumped and covered the distance in seconds, pulling himself up while half-expecting his legs to be dragged backward. Without the slightest break in motion, he rose to his feet and sprang forward into a triple jump across the tables toward the escalator. Just before his foot hit the last table, the tiger shark appeared from his left, thrusting upward in full attack mode. They leaped simultaneously, the shark bursting out of the water and Arman flying horizontally above.

He landed hard on the escalator, using his hands to blunt the initial impact from its sharp corners. It quickly carried him upward and away from harm. He turned over and looked down at the frustrated shark, still circling below, and still unsatisfied with the offerings in the food court. Arman exhaled and shook his head. It reminded him of a conversation he overheard a week earlier, when Matt taught Farzin an American idiom, while critiquing Farzin's taste in movies, to describe what happens when a writer uses sensationalistic material to boost short-term ratings. It had something to do with a guy on water skis wearing a leather jacket. *What was that phrase again?*

Regaining his focus, he held his calf, still hurting though it was not a serious wound, and breathed deeply. There was no time for reflection, of course, with the urgent decision in front of him. As he ascended to the ground floor, he realized he'd already made it.

He would run.

Soaked and nearly hyperventilating from exhaustion, Arman jogged back through the Convention Center hallway toward KLCC Park. He had been looking almost straight down, his wet squeaking shoes already annoying him, then looked to his right and was quickly reminded of the chaos outside. There were more lights from fire trucks and the digging seemed to be more organized. He would've preferred to exit the building on the other side, but that wasn't possible. He would have to enter the central area of park again.

He pushed through the glass doors, walked outside, and began looking for confirmation of his theory of what caused the aquarium ceiling to collapse. It didn't take long to find it. Looking to his left, he saw the empty space left behind from the top half of Tower 1, smoke still gushing upward from its center. The Petronas Towers were twins again, two stumps smoldering in the middle of Kuala Lumpur. The top half had fallen southward and slightly east, landing between Jalan Pinang and the Convention Center, hitting the latter only indirectly, the reason Arman was still alive. He stood still and briefly considered how closely he had yet again come to being crushed.

Remembering the urgency of getting away from the scene of the crime, he turned around and walked in the opposite direction of the towers. Previously it would have been easier to get out of KLCC Park going south, but the latest building collapse pushed him to the east side of the park. He walked with haste, feeling conspicuous as everyone else seemed to have a purpose for being in the area. He looked at the ground to avoid eye contact with the authorities, then noticed how the dirt and ash stuck to his wet shoes and pants. For a moment he almost began to walk more cautiously to keep his pants from getting filthy again.

Another sudden wave of panic. *My shirt is clean!*

He looked up to see a uniformed officer walking his direction, eyes fixed on Arman. The policeman lifted up his arm and pointed at him with his thumb.

"Hey, boss! I need you lah!" He was now twenty feet away.

Arman crossed his arms over his chest to cover his t-shirt design. *Think, Arman. Think!* He was absolutely certain that, in a few seconds, his chest would be laid bare and it would all be over. He pictured himself being carried away with his hands cuffed behind his back. He dragged his feet to delay the inevitable. As he did so, he kicked a heavy iron rod hidden in the soot. His arms were crossed so tightly that there was no opportunity to balance himself, so he slammed to the ground much like the towers before him. He landed face first, covering the entire front side of his body in a fresh layer of ash.

"You okay, boss?" The policeman offered a hand to lift him up. Arman, suddenly realizing his shirt was again shrouded in obscurity, freely accepted the offer.

He rose to his feet and explained why he was there. "I'm sorry. I'm sure you only want workers in the area, but I was stuck in the Convention Center…" The policeman, obviously unconcerned with anything he had to say, interrupted.

"Hey, we need more workers on the east side of the park! Mostly diggers, but just look for the firemen or other emergency workers and they'll tell you what to do."

Arman quickly agreed and was happy to continue walking in the direction of the exit to the park. He saw a collection of yellow hardhats, along with excavation equipment, laying in a pile along the path. He promptly put one of them on and continued along the eastward path with purpose. Regardless of his legitimate reasons to be worried, it was clear that everyone around him were only concerned with trying to save just one more from the rubble.

As he reached the eastern end of the park, he saw workers of all stripes moving in and out of the area, so he simply filed behind those exiting and made his way to Persiaran KLCC, a road adjacent to KLCC Park. He tossed his hat over the wall next to the sidewalk and made his way to Jalan Kia Peng, going west past the Philippine embassy and then south toward Jalan Raja Chulan. He breathed a sigh of relief as he realized he couldn't see any policemen. Still, he knew he had to get out of the area as quickly as possible.

He saw signs for a train entrance and began to plot his escape from the downtown area. As he walked down the stairwell into the station at Jalan Raja Chulan, he was informed by others coming out that it was closed. They guessed that it was because of the collapse of the towers and the subway that went beneath it and that it had probably shut down the entire line. As Arman continued west on Jalan Sultan Ismail, their guess seemed to be confirmed as station after station was closed. Finally, after what seemed to be about twenty minutes of waiting to be pulled off of the street at any moment, he came across the Port Klang line and saw people descending underneath the street, so he swiftly jumped in line.

He didn't know how the rail system worked or how one line may or may not be affected by another, but he was certainly glad this one was open, whatever the reason. He sat next to an older Indian woman in a red sari and waited for the incoming train. He was still mildly wet except for his socks and shoes, but the walk had mostly dried his clothes and the ash almost appeared as a natural part of his shirt. Finally, the first train arrived. The screech of metal had never sounded so sweet as the north-bound subway grounded to a halt.

The windows speeding in front of him revealed quick glimpses of men and women dressed in the brightest array of clothing he had ever seen, like peering into a twisting kaleidoscope on a clear day. The train looked completely full with a crowd of mostly Indians. Arman jogged down to see the other cars only to realize they all seemed impossibly packed, so he sat down to wait for the next train in the line. Undeterred, the old lady in the red sari slammed her body into the crowd as soon as the doors opened, prompting the passengers to make room where there seemingly was none. He'd heard the Indian adage, "always room for one more," but only now did he realize what it actually meant.

He let the train go only to realize that, somehow, he was the only one who didn't get on. *How is that possible?* A new crowd of men, women, and children in traditional Indian dress began to pile into the waiting area and he now understood what he would have to do if he ever wanted to get out of downtown KL. After the next train arrived, he braced himself as it slowed. As others crowded next to him, jockeying for first place in line as the doors opened, he employed his elbows, used footholds for leverage, and did whatever he could to stay in the front. If people didn't want to come into contact with his wet and dirty body, they would just have to deal with it. As the doors opened, there was no waiting for anyone who may need to get off, he immediately crammed his damp body into the crowd, wedging his right side into a crack between two people just enough to cause them to find the impossible space that he'd hoped would avail itself. The doors closed behind him and he found himself reaching across a woman in front of him for a balance rail, his face buried into the underarm of a young Indian man holding onto a handle above.

As the train lurched forward, he was overwhelmed by the aroma of incense and sweat. Huddled with peopled pressed in on all sides like sacred cattle, this would've normally been a very unwelcome experience for Arman. As the train moved swiftly northward, however, he was more than content to have some time to just stand and breathe, regardless of what he was inhaling. After a few minutes, it occurred to him that this was the most packed train he'd ever ridden in KL or with that high a percentage of Indian-Malaysians.

Where are they all going?

16

LOSING A BROTHER

Zia beamed as she floated down the stairs to await Jalal's arrival for the family dinner. Her clear brown eyes dancing underneath thick dark eyebrows, she descended to the living room to see her father, Davoud, behind a newspaper in his favorite black chair, as usual.

However, it was clear that he was cleaned up and ready for the first family dinner with Jalal since he became her fiancé. It was a time of celebration, of course, but it was also going to be a time of planning and negotiations for the upcoming wedding.

Although Davoud and Yasaman readily agreed to Zia's marriage to Jalal, the period of time between them meeting and getting engaged was relatively short, so Jalal was still getting to know his future father-in-law and they were still in a somewhat awkward stage in their relationship. It didn't help that both Davoud and Ali, the only significant men in Zia's life until Jalal came along, were similar in ways that were strikingly in contrast with Jalal. They were both trained engineers, preferring practical sciences and plain-spoken words. Jalal was finishing up a degree in journalism and naturally spoke in the theoretical, preferring metaphors and concepts to small talk over everyday affairs. The Tehrani men dressed casually and plainly, intentionally not trying to keep up with the latest styles. Jalal could've been an extra on Starsky and Hutch. The primary difference between Davoud and Ali, on the other hand, were the measured words and calm demeanor from the elder Tehrani and the tempestuousness of the younger. Previously this difference made Ali feel like he was a misfit, but the more Jalal visited the house, the more he saw himself in his father's chair.

"Mmmmm. The kebabs smell so good!" Zia closed her eyes and smiled as her father lowered his newspaper. His peppered hair and dark black eyebrows blended with the printed word in front of him.

"You've missed something. I'm a little disappointed." Davoud's playful smirk challenged Zia to test her senses again. It didn't take long.

"And tahdig!" The crunchy fried rice that tasted like a combination of potato chips and popcorn had always been her favorite and she was excited that Jalal would finally taste her mother's best dish.

Ali entered and quickly chimed in. "It's too bad Jalal won't be able to have any." His mouth was full and he had tahdig in his cupped hand.

"You're twenty-four and you're still stealing food from the kitchen before dinner?!" Zia both smiled and shook her head in disbelief.

Ali was clearly proud of himself. "And Mom didn't notice, as usual." He put the last of the fried rice in his mouth and licked his fingers. "I'm only half-kidding, Zia. If Jalal doesn't get here soon, I don't like his chances of having any leftovers."

"He is a little late," added Davoud. "And I'm not too sure how long I can be patient while smelling your mother's cooking."

Ali looked at Zia long enough to get her attention, then shifted to his father. "Well, it does take a long time to trim the corners on that new mustache of his." Davoud smiled weakly, resisting the temptation of joining in on the taunting of his daughter's fiancé. Ali had no such compulsion. "It's so long and has such perfect points. If we're out of skewers for the kebabs, he'll be just fine."

"You're just jealous he could grow it so quickly," said Zia. It was a less-than-subtle reference to Ali's wide, but sparse beard he seemed to have been working on since puberty.

"No, I don't think I'll ever be jealous of anything associated with the Mojahedin." He attempted a playful tone, but it was clear to Zia that he didn't like Jalal's recent involvement with a party that was critical of Ayatollah Khomeini.

The Mojahedin was an Islamic socialist party that saw most political problems through the eyes of class warfare. They weren't atheists, but they borrowed from Marx to criticize the capitalist West from an Islamic point of view. They were ardent participants in the revolution against the Shah and completely expected a seat at the table in the new Islamic democracy they were promised. Along with other political parties, however, they were beginning to see that Khomeini's Islamic Republic Party might not be too thrilled with the company of others.

Both Ali and his father were supporters of Khomeini, like most of the country, because it was he who led the movement against the Shah. Davoud, however, was more subdued in his support. He was ready to go along with the IRPs plans, whatever they were, but he was also willing to consider a dissenting opinion. Ali saw Khomeini as a savior and criticism as treason. After all, it was Khomeini who dispensed justice to those who tortured him and it was Khomeini who gave him back his future. Just a few months ago, he was stuck cleaning popcorn off the floor in a movie theatre. Now he was back in engineering. Just yesterday he couldn't imagine getting married. Now he had his eye on a young woman and was envisioning a future with a wife and kids. He would die for Khomeini.

Zia quickly processed the comment and decided not to respond. After all, if Ali knew what Jalal had been doing this very day, he might not have a mere political disagreement with her fiancé. They could become mortal enemies. While the Tehranis had been at work and home, Jalal had decided to stay at Tehran University to support the students and opposition parties who had formed a human chain around some of the campus buildings to protect them from a takeover by Hezbollahi gangs supportive of the IRP. It appeared that Khomeini and others in the party decided the university wasn't sufficiently Islamic and, therefore, had been engaged in a literal battle to "regain" control of them in order to raise a new generation that "understood what it meant to live in and support an Islamic Republic." Jalal and many others saw this as just one more action that proved the IRP had no intention of keeping their promise of a democracy. They perceived them as an encroaching monopoly, like a python slowly wrapping itself around every major institution and unseen crevice of Iranian society.

The fingers on her left hand curling into a tight and nervous ball, Zia changed the subject and kept the conversation light until it was okay to leave the room without being rude. She entered the kitchen and almost ran into Yasmine, bringing out the kebabs. The aroma of the lamb and beef minced meat thickened and helped Zia forget all about Ali's comment. She helped set the table and prepared the drinks, her usual job, but this time it was set for five.

Jalal knocked on the door and her heart raced as she considered what a significant step this was toward getting married. She skipped to the living room to see the door already open and looked up expecting to see his perfect white teeth and tight smile aimed in her direction. Instead she saw a wounded and scared young man.

His brown wavy hair was stylish and fastidious as always. His blue jeans and long brown cashmere sweater carried no hint of the young men with knives and clubs Jalal encountered only a few hours earlier. He obviously cleaned up and dressed for the occasion, but there was no hiding the gash on his left cheek, his reddened left eye, and the bulging circle over his eyebrow.

Zia raised both hands to her mouth in horror. "Oh my God, Jalal! What did they do to you?!" She rushed forward, hugging him with her left arm, gently placing her right hand on his left cheek.

"It's fine." He lowered her hand and attempted to move forward as if he were entering the house in a normal fashion. It was clear he wanted to downplay the situation, but he was woefully unsuccessful.

"Oh my dear boy! What in the name of Allah happened to you?!" Yasmine fought through Ali and Davoud, adding another wave of unwanted affection and pity.

Jalal continued to insist he felt fine, helplessly trying to deflect attention from himself. He occasionally cast involuntary glances at Ali while the women discussed amongst themselves, as if Jalal wasn't present, which home remedy was most appropriate for this situation. In less than a minute they had him lying on the living room couch, Zia caressing his hair while Yasmin went searching for aloe vera. Jalal was clearly embarrassed for this to be unfolding in front of Ali and Davoud, desperately trying to change the subject at every turn.

After fifteen of the most awkward minutes of his life, he shifted his tactics and began raving about the incredible aroma coming from their kitchen. When they finally felt as much pity for his hunger as they did for his wounds, they let him up and everyone, at last, gathered around the dining room table. They all agreed the kebabs were as delicious as they smelled, the men, almost in unison, making quick work of the tahdig, employing their right hands for the fried rice dish.

The evening conversation had already promised to be a potentially tense discussion regarding their future marriage, but Jalal's wounds complicated the matter exponentially. Yasmine, Davoud, and Ali knew about the possibility of a clash at the university, but neither Jalal nor Zia knew for certain they were aware of this. Meanwhile, everyone at the table were pretending to enjoy their meal while simultaneously planning how they would respond to a wide variety of conversational possibilities. Every crunch of the roasted red peppers sounded like a jackhammer in the silence.

Zia made the first attempt to break the ever-thickening ice. She used the sharp tip of her knife to carve a small hole in a piece of the minced meat and a small rectangular piece of red pepper, placed them next to each other with, holes aligned, and surreptitiously lifted them toward her fiancé, who was looking the other direction to see if there was enough tahdig for a second helping. By the time Jalal figured out what was going on, Zia had successfully placed both pieces of her kebab through the tip of the right side of his mustache, keeping them in place with her thumb and index finger.

"You were right, Ali." Determined to impress Jalal with her acting skills, she delivered the line naturally, feigning genuine surprise and delight. Her father roared with laughter, slightly choking on his fried rice. Everyone else cackled as well, even a confused Jalal.

"Wait a minute," Jalal protested, lightly. "What do you mean, 'You were right?'"

It was at this exact moment that Zia realized that by breaking the ice she had invited a flood. When she had the idea for the stunt, she was only thinking about Ali's mustache joke as funny, but now she kicked herself for somehow not thinking about where the conversation could go from here.

"Oh, he just made a joke about how you could use your mustache as a skewer." She downplayed it and began in vain to think of another transition as she disassembled her fiancé's mustache kebab. Jalal's laugh was less enthusiastic as he looked at Ali, trying to figure out if it was, indeed, just a joke. Ali wore a genuine smile, but the gleam in his eyes and his excessive grin suggested he was perhaps a little too proud of his joke and obviously unconcerned with how Jalal perceived it. Still smiling just enough to reveal the gap in his upper teeth, Ali looked across the table at Jalal and effectively ended the pretension.

"So… things didn't go well at our university today?"

A silence like death returned as Jalal heard himself chewing, trying to figure out how he would respond, thoughts spontaneously forming and colliding. *So he knows where I was. He doesn't like the Mojahedin and yet made a joke about my mustache. Is he really making light of my wounds? And what did he mean by 'our' university when he studied at another school?*

"No, I guess they didn't." He was angry but clear-headed enough to want to avoid a scene in front of his future in-laws. Zia grabbed his hand underneath the table and squeezed. He wasn't sure if it was because she was angry or making sure he remained under control. A glimpse at the color in her face would've revealed the answer, but he looked at his food instead, avoiding eye contact with everyone. He took another bite and looked up at Yasmine, smiling.

"Don't tell my mother I said this, but this is the best tahdig I've ever eaten."

"Well, that's quite a compliment, Jalal. I appreciate that very much." Jasmine hadn't quite finished the sentence when Ali, refusing to let him off the hook, interjected.

"What I don't understand is why anyone can openly oppose the man responsible for freeing our country from tyranny." He wiped his mouth, letting his words hang in the air, and stared at Jalal. "Perhaps you can help me with that."

A few beads of sweat appeared near the lump on Jalal's forehead. He had no idea how to respond. It wasn't as simple as being intimidated by Ali, although that was definitely the case. The main objective was to make sure he didn't do or say anything that would cause Zia's parents to lose face. Her complexion now a dark pink, Zia jumped into the fray.

"Why are you doing this?! Why are you trying to embarrass him in front of our parents?"

"It's okay, Zia. I'm not embarrassed." He lied. "Ali has been through a lot and has a right to ask this."

"That's exactly right!" Ali placed both hands firmly on the table. "I have a right to ask anything I want about this guy who wants to marry my sister. I have a right to ask about why he can't seem to remember who it is that gave us our freedom!"

"Ali, lower your voice." Davoud's tone was calm but firm. "You've challenged him in front of all of us and we all understand where you're coming from, but this is your future brother-in-law, so calm down and listen with respect." The crease in his eyes belied the stillness of his voice. Ali leaned back in his chair, both chastened and defiant. "Jalal, we're listening."

He swallowed and slowly wiped his mouth as a delay tactic, praying for the ability to speak without stammering. Every word he considered seemed as if he was choosing between standing up for what is best for the nation or securing the ability to marry Zia, so he began with as much deference as possible.

"Like all of you here, I gladly marched with our fellow Persians as we protested the Shah. I hated the secret police and the corruption of the government." He paused for a moment, considering how he could personalize his story, employing as much of his university training as possible.

"I don't know why, but I've always wanted to be a journalist. It didn't come from my family. None of them have any interest in it and none of my friends ever cared to hear about my love for writing about current events. No one prepared me for what I would discover when I entered Tehran University as a naive freshman, ready to begin studying to become some great truth teller to the world of politics. So when I began to learn how the Shah controlled the media and imprisoned his political enemies, I was devastated. Disillusioned. And angry. I felt completely helpless until the protests started. At the end of last year, though, I felt hope, just like you."

"Ayatollah Khomeini spoke about releasing political prisoners, an Islamic democracy where people can choose their leaders, a system that allows different political parties… But now I'm afraid he and others in our nation want to silence the political opposition just like the Shah."

Ali jumped to his feet. "How dare you compare Ayatollah Khomeini to the Shah!"

"Ali!" Davoud's voice had lost its calm this time. He didn't need to say anything else as his fierce dark eyes knocked his son backward in his seat.

Jalal was startled, but continued. "I believe in the principles taught by the Mojahedin, but I believe even more in the right for other political parties to exist. This is why I stood arm in arm with other students today. At one point we circled the 15 Khordad building in a human chain because that's where the opposition parties' headquarters are located. But they attacked us with clubs and now they've taken the university by force. They've probably taken all the universities by now."

Ali looked as if fried rice would explode through his nose any second. With all of the humility he could gather, he addressed his father while looking slightly down. "Father, can I speak now?" Satisfied with Ali's sudden self-control, he acquiesced.

"You speak of freedom and seem so unimpressed with the fact that we are now *freed…*" His voice began to rise and he paused to steady himself. "We are now freed from both the SAVAK and western domination."

"I didn't mean to minimize that at all," Jalal protested. "It's just that…" He wasn't sure what to say next, so Ali continued.

"Shouldn't we be loyal to the one who freed us? If someone risks their life to save yours, shouldn't you follow him?" He glared in Jalal's direction, unblinking.

"I guess that depends on why he saved you." This caught Ali by surprise, clearly confusing him. Zia again squeezed his hand under the table, encouraging the steady demeanor and clear thoughts that were now beginning to form.

"What are you talking about?"

"It's not always about what we're saved *from*. It's also what we're saved *to*. If a man saves you only to secure his own power and use you to dominate others, what good is that? What we needed is a leader who would save us in order to set us free. A few months ago I believed we had that, but I don't anymore."

"I don't care what you say," Ali countered. "I was tortured and shamed for days by the Shah's forces of Hell and Ayatollah Khomeini had the courage to point the finger at the person who was the real problem when no one else did. I was blackballed from ever getting another engineering job in all of Iran, and now I'm *free* to work."

"You have your wounds and now I have mine," said Jalal, pointing to his cheek. "That doesn't make either of us right or wrong."

Ali rose to his feet, wiping his right hand with his napkin. He stood still, staring intently at Jalal. Indignant and frustrated that his personal suffering failed to trump the flow of logic, he simply left the room.

~

Despite his own distaste for the Mojahedin and general support for Khomeini, Davoud understood Jalal's beliefs in freedom of political expression and was impressed enough with his ability to respectfully articulate his opinions that he never entertained any idea of trying to prevent their marriage. Besides, he loved his daughter and knew her well enough to know when to pick his battles. And this, in his opinion, wasn't one of them.

Yasmine, for her part, was mostly concerned with how this would affect Ali and Zia's relationship, a concern well-founded. From that day forward, things were never the same between them, bringing untold grief to their mother. Zia fully understood that, in choosing Jalal as a husband, she was losing her brother.

In the months immediately following the infamous dinner at the Tehrani house, the new government tightened its claws around all other political parties, especially the Mojahedin. During a massive demonstration in Tehran in the Summer of 1979, hundreds of Mojahedin were killed. Between this tragic event and student radicals taking Americans hostage in the embassy, Jalal and Zia believed their misgivings had been proven entirely correct. Within a couple of years, the number of the executed Mojahedin would rise to the thousands and they lived in constant fear that Jalal's previous association with them would be discovered. Would Ali inform on him? This kept them awake on more than one occasion. In the end, they eventually realized their assumptions that Khomeini would be just as oppressive as the Shah were actually radically mistaken. Compared to Khomeini, the Shah was merely an annoying hall monitor.

In 1981, Ali met and married a girl named Laleh Shirvani, an unassuming, quiet, and more subservient young woman than his sister. His support for the developing Islamic Republic only strengthened in the early years of the revolutionary government. Almost a year after marrying, he left the job he loved - the one made possible by his beloved leader - and joined the holy war against Iraq and Saddam Hussein. He became greatly admired as a soldier, truly possessing the sacrificial battlefield mentality which became such a revered trait among the IRP's armed forces. It was his ultimate glory. It would be his bitter end.

17

THE PIERCED ONES

The last stop going north on the Port Klang line was Batu Caves. Arman was determined to take it as far out of the city as possible regardless of the annoying fact that no one seemed to be getting off. In fact, at every stop more people somehow found cracks and crevices in which to wedge themselves, the air growing both thick and scarce. *Is there a single part of my body not touching someone else?* It felt like they were vacuum sealed into this speeding metal box charging northward.

Finally the train came to a merciful halt and everyone poured out of the railcar like a bursting dam. While Arman wondered if there would ever be an end to the people stepping off the train, he had a fleeting childhood memory of a clown he once saw pulling endless handkerchiefs out of his mouth. He really didn't have a clear plan for what was next, but decided against hiding in a crowd and was looking forward to just finding somewhere to be as alone as possible and hatch a plan, however impossible, to get out of the country. It occurred to him for the first time that his phone, which he hadn't even thought of since everything began, was most likely dead from the aquarium water. He pulled it out of his pocket, carefully avoiding jamming his elbow into the face an older sari-clad woman exiting the train. He quickly saw it wasn't on and tried the power button. Completely dead. At first he was angry with his continued poor luck, but then he realized that this was actually good fortune since the government was most likely tracking his mobile number by now. Just before stepping off the train, his thoughts were interrupted by the unexpected clamor of loudspeakers and crowd noise. Peering through an empty space of the queue exiting the train, his hopes of quickly losing the crowd were dashed as he saw a flowing ocean of people in every direction.

The mood was jubilant as he weaved his way through throngs of Indians spilling out of the railway exit. Families with young children slowed his movement as he searched in vain for a clear walkway. The women wore richly colored saris, most of them red and yellow. Some of the younger ladies wore traditional outfits with a tunic-like top made of silk, flowing downward to their knees, and loose pants narrowing just above their feet. They held hands to keep from being separated from each other in the midst of the endless worshipers. And because they were having fun.

The women were distinctively decorated with various patterns and charms, their shiny anklets jingling as they alternatively walked and danced past each other. Babies were tightly wrapped on their mothers' backs as they held the hands of the children who could walk. Arman tilted his head quizzically as he noticed the some of the children's heads were cleanly shaven. Men wore shirts also made in silk, mostly cream-colored and plain. Some wore traditional silky trousers hanging lazily downward, no space visible between the legs until all the way down to the calf. Others wore blue jeans and name brand sneakers.

Eventually Arman was able to discern an overarching gate, decorations similar to a Hindu temple, which seemed to be the destination of most of those around him, so he turned right to get away from them. After a couple of blocks the foot traffic didn't seem to let up in the slightest. Despairing he would ever find any space to himself, he stopped to take off his socks, something he'd put off since leaving KLCC Park. As he removed the disgusting mix of ashes, sweat, and saltwater, he cast a few glances around him, hoping no one would see him leaving them on the ground. As he did so, he saw the beginning of a long line of makeshift shops, consisting of nothing but tables and clothes, and food stalls similar to the night markets he had become used to seeing in recent weeks. One of the vendors sold cream-colored shirts, like many of the men around him, and he quickly realized the advantage of blending in, not to mention the practical need to hide his t- shirt.

Arman walked up to the young Indian vendor with clenched teeth, bracing himself to haggle. He bartered in Iran occasionally, but it seemed a bit different in Malaysia. He'd watched Yusuf negotiate a good bargain weeks before and taken some mental notes. It worked beautifully for him, but Arman wasn't so sure it would work the same way for a foreigner. It finally dawned on him that, while he was fortunate to at least have some cash, the one hundred ringgit in his pocket would dry up very quickly. *Can I even use my ATM card anymore?* Perhaps he could, but he knew that using it would give away his location, the last thing he wanted to do. He'd work through that later. For now, he just needed to focus on getting the lowest price.

Trying to sound as Malaysian as possible, Arman reached for his shirt of choice and asked, "How much for this one lah?" The young man, dressed in jeans, a black t-shirt, and fake Ray-Ban sunglasses, smiled broadly, his white teeth shining against his dark brown skin and black mustache.

"For you, boss… eighty ringgit."

Arman had absolutely no idea whether or not this was a good price. Regardless, he decided to respond with indignation. "Eighty ringgit?! Aiyo! Cannot lah!"

The young merchant continued to smile, completely unfazed. Arman continued the charade, much to the delight of the salesman.

"Thirty ringgit!"

"Can't do thirty ringgit." His smile faded slightly. "Seventy-five."

This is the part Arman knew he couldn't mess up. He looked straight at his nemesis, held his gaze for a full five seconds, and walked away.

"C'mon, boss!" Arman felt a pull on his left arm. "Okay lah. Sixty-five."

"This is my last offer," said a steely-eyed Arman. Holding up four fingers, his voice became lower and slower, enunciating each syllable as if he were uttering a death sentence upon a bitter enemy.

"Forty ringgit. And not a single ringgit more."

The young man paused, holding a slight grin on his face. He shook his head slightly back and forth and put out his hand. Arman, unfamiliar with the Indian head bob, interpreted it as a "no" and thought he was just pushing to get his sixty-five ringgit. Incensed, he slapped the young Indian's hand to the side and walked away. Only a few seconds later he felt yet another tug on his arm.

"I told you forty ringgit, okay?"

Arman jerked his arm away and glared at him. "Just leave me alone!"

"You told me forty ringgit and I agreed!" The young merchant's grin had vanished, and he was now fuming.

"You agreed?" Arman was baffled and starting to feel a little afraid as other Indians were now watching. He searched back through the encounter, trying to figure out how he misinterpreted things. His cheeks flushed and the scar underneath his beard sizzled. *Maybe he's just lying.* Either way, he needed the shirt and desperately wanted the attention to dissipate as soon as possible. He reached into his pocket and unfolded a wet hundred ringgit bill. The young man handed him his shirt and his change, followed by again nodding his head back and forth. This time it occurred to Arman there was something he didn't understand about this gesture. He smiled sheepishly and slithered into the crowd, quickly invisible.

A few blocks down the road, Arman could finally see a pathway out of the crowd when something caught his attention. In between the buildings on his left, he saw an ornate golden structure bobbing up and down. From where he was standing, it seemed to be floating mid-air and a great commotion surrounded it. Practicality demanded he continue on his path, but curiosity got the better of him. He darted around the side of a Seven- Eleven, more than a little tempted by the cold drinks and ice cream snacks inside, and squeezed into the thick line of people huddled along the road, trying to get a glimpse of the same thing he was chasing.

The golden structure had two poles on either side of it and was carried by four men on each corner. It consisted of a small house, or a temple, for a Hindu god. As it was still fifty feet away, a young woman next to Arman, silk Punjabi suit with loose pants, suddenly clutched his arm. Only slightly startled, he looked to his right at the young woman and proceeded to become genuinely frightened. Her eyes rolled into the back of her head and she grasped him even harder. For the second time in only five minutes, he again violently jerked his arm away from a young Indian. Her hand remained where it was as she let out a deep sigh, slowly reaching both arms upward, and gently rocked back and forth, her movement slowly progressing until it reached a slow dance. Eyes transfixed on the strange woman, Arman looked around expecting to find everyone else cautiously backing away from the bizarre spectacle, but, amazingly, they completely ignored her. As he continued to move away from the bewildering scene, he unwittingly inched closer and closer to a small tandoori oven on the sidewalk just outside of a nasi kandar restaurant.

An older voice to his left cried "Watch out lah!" as he felt yet another tug on the arm. This time he immediately realized it was a helpful hand, and he was saved from a nasty burn.

"Thanks." Arman looked down at the oven, then timidly up at the man who helped him. He had grayish hair, a white flowing beard, and a shirt similar to the one Arman acquired earlier. Ash covered his forehead, a red mark dotted in the middle. As his eyes narrowed, the lines across his face widened and his kind smile stretched to his ears.

"I can always tell when it's someone's first time." He didn't mean this as an actual critique. It felt more like a sage welcoming a young man into his home.

"I guess it's obvious, then." Arman kept both eyes on the

entranced woman even as he answered the older man in front of him.

The man chuckled and put his left hand on Arman's right shoulder. "Yes! Yes, it's obvious, my friend."

"Well, if you find that funny, you'll love my next question." The Indian gentleman bobbed his head slightly back and forth, causing Arman to hesitate as he continued to ponder the meaning of it. He looked at his feet, then to the queue and the golden structure now passing by. "What is all of this?"

"You mean, this chariot or the entire celebration?"

Arman grinned, knowing how weird it would sound. "The entire celebration."

His new friend, now with both hands on Arman's shoulders, tilted his head back and let out a belly laugh. "You're in the middle of nearly a million people and you don't know that today is Thaipusam?!" He laughed again, but Arman felt he was laughing more with him instead of at him. "Where are you from, my friend?"

He almost revealed he was from Iran, but alertly switched his origins to a country that didn't just have its citizens blow up the Petronas Towers. Not that it currently seemed to be a major concern. It finally dawned on Arman that everyone was too consumed with the celebration to be distracted by the fact that the most iconic symbol in all of Malaysia had just been destroyed.

"Germany. My name's Kamran." His intention was to simply throw him off a little, knowing the man would assume he's an immigrant, not pretending to be a native German. He prayed there would be no follow-up questions.

"I'm Kumar." He pointed to the procession. "Do you want to know what this is?"

"Sure."

"This is the chariot carrying Lord Murugan back into his shrine in Batu Caves." Looking more closely, Arman saw an idol of a man holding a spear inside a structure resembling a temple. "Thaipusam celebrates the day he was given the vel - his spear - that enabled him to defeat the powers of darkness in the world."

After the procession passed, Kumar stepped into the road just behind them. "Come on, Kamran. You have to go to Batu Caves for the real experience."

Arman was about to decline when he noticed Malay police officers on both sides of the road. His need to blend in suddenly escalating, he took up Kumar on his offer. He stood close to his new friend, keeping his head slightly down as they moved with the flow of Hindu worshipers.

His gaze was drawn upward as he noticed a group of Indian teenagers standing on an embankment overlooking their path. Most of them wore blue jeans, black leather jackets, even in the heat and humidity, and an assortment of jewelry around their necks and on their fingers. They shouted something in Tamil at the worshipers in front of and behind Arman, looked back at each other, then cackled and gave each other high fives. Kumar looked annoyed.

"Who are they?"

"Gangstas. They show up every year making catcalls at the women and yelling insults at all the devotees. They try to emulate western films and their favorite Bollywood heroes." He stared at them, eyes narrowing in contempt. "They're a nuisance. I don't envy the judgment waiting on them in the next life." His face softening, with perhaps a hint of pity, he added, "They'll be lucky to return as monkeys."

Three women in front of them stopped abruptly, arms shaking, fists clenched. Arman mistakenly believed their wide and wild-looking eyes were focused at him.

"What's wrong with them?"

"They've entered a trance." Kumar said this without the slightest alarm. "They're possessed either by Lord Murugan or another deity." He casually walked around them, neither fearing them nor wanting to disturb them.

The noise grew significantly louder as they approached the gate Arman saw earlier. Loudspeakers playing a combination of religious chants and Tamil pop songs competed with each other in the increasing heat and humidity. The vendors, displaying curried chick peas, noodles, coconut juice, and water, grew louder and more aggressive toward those entering the holy area at the base of the caves. Saris and Punjabi suits of all colors formed a dizzying mosaic as they progressed underneath the Batu Caves entrance. Incense and camphor mixed with the pervasive smell of chicken curry to make the sensory overload complete. Arman decided in that moment that he'd never experienced anything so completely cross-cultural as the unfolding scene before him. Little did he know it was all just getting started.

The area at the base of Batu Caves was long and wide, several football fields in size. The mountain in the background was mostly gray with interspersed trees and brush, pocked with black indentations with moss growing around them, like the eyes of the gods peering through a stone temple. The charged atmosphere steadily increased the further they pushed their way toward its base.

"Do you see the stairs leading into the caves?"

Arman looked up and easily saw the worshipers ascending and descending, but that's not what caught his attention. *How did I miss that?* At the base of the stairs, a giant golden statue soared into the air, dominating the landscape and making the worshippers in its background appearing like ants. It was easily the largest idol Arman had ever seen. Until now, he was uncomfortable for sure, but hadn't felt the kind of dissonance that was beginning to set in.

Sure, the Prophet Muhammad had clearly condemned idol worship, but Arman had grown up with imams and sufis alike. Poets and prophets revered equally. Rumi and the Qur'an both quoted as definitive sources of knowledge. While the religious government in Iran demanded absolute allegiance to Allah, zealously punishing apostasy with firearms and fatwahs, Arman's family quietly pushed back and embraced a more accepting view of the wider world, seeing no incongruence with their own convictions and what they considered to be "real Islam." But there was something about the size of the idol that challenged him to envision the founder of his religion desiring to do anything but smash it into a million pieces.

Kumar continued. "There are exactly two hundred and seventy-two stairs to get to the shrine of Lord Murugan. That's where the kavadi line is going."

"Is that statue also Lord Murugan?"

"Oh. Yes, of course. I forgot the most important part, didn't I?" His courteous smile and humble demeanor continued to be the only thing that kept Arman moving forward. That and the presence of Malay police officers. Perceiving the uneasiness in Arman, Kumar asked, "Are you Muslim?"

Good question, he thought. He had many frustrations and questions about the Shi'a Islam he grew up with, seemingly growing stronger by the day, but to reject being a Muslim was a rejection of both his family and his cultural identity as well. He saw what happened with his sister and had no intention of hurting his parents like that.

"Yes, I am."

"It may help you to know that the more educated among us aren't actually worshiping the idols themselves. We're worshiping the god the idol represents. We're a visually- oriented people and representations help us to focus."

Of course, Hindus still believe in many gods. Millions, in fact, and this was anathema to the monotheistic teachings of Islam. Arman knew that all arguments about needing a visual representation of Allah were vehemently rejected in Islam, but he saw no need to get into a dispute with his host. Kumar, sensing Arman's quietness represented some struggle within him, decided to end this part of their conversation. He would use the simple but potent phrase used so effectively in Asia when one is challenged with religious questions.

"Same same."

Not everyone was Indian at this massive festival. A smattering of Chinese Malaysians and internationals of various stripes and shades sprinkled the crowd. White westerners were the most visible of the latter, the majority of whom respectfully observing the unique religious rituals. Others, however, were clearly there for the sideshow aspect of the kavadi line, which Arman hadn't seen yet. He noticed a young western couple next to him taking pictures of themselves with Hindu worshipers and Lord Murugan in the background. The guy wore ragged tan shorts, a white t-shirt, sandals, and the ubiquitous frazzled cornrows in his hair, giving him that carefree bohemian look western travelers are so careful to cultivate. The girl had squeezed into short white shorts and a spaghetti strap top that stopped at her midriff. As they uploaded proof of their tolerance to social media, Arman noticed two older ladies in yellow saris casting sideways glances at the girl as they pushed their way past the immodest intruder.

"Over here!" Kumar motioned excitedly for Arman to follow. They swiftly arrived to a group of about twenty people surrounding a religious leader and a man who looked to be in his forties, shirtless and wearing a silk cloth wrapped around his waist. As the priest waved lime juice through the air, the man's eyes suddenly widened in what was either fright or anger, arms shaking as he danced wildly into those surrounding him. A few men grabbed the devotee, stabilizing him to keep him from hurting himself, then encircled him, chanting loudly while one covered his ears. Drums pounded as they held him still for the priest. The religious leader took a skewer, about a foot long and resembling the spear held by Lord Murugan (the vel), pinched his left cheek, and proceeded to slowly but steadily slide the vel into the spot on the cheek he had just pinched, then through the other cheek until it protruded from both sides of his mouth. The crowd around him screamed "Vel! Vel! Vel!" as he proceeded to dance in the middle of them. The intense energy, combined with the disturbing act he'd just witnessed, overwhelmed Arman, his heart racing, body covered in a fresh layer of sweat. He gathered himself just enough to inquire about what he was seeing.

"Why is he doing this?"

Kumar was still smiling. "Sometimes they are wanting Lord Murugan or another deity to grant them a job, money, a wife… the types of things everyone wants in life. In this case, this man has entered a contract, if you will, with Lord Murugan, to reverse his bad karma. He'll wear the vel in the kavadi line all the way up the stairs until he reaches the main shrine. When it's all done, he'll feel a beautiful sense of illumination."

"What's the kavadi line?"

"*Kavadi* means burden. Worshipers are suffering their chosen burdens for their deity. They walk, march, or dance in this line as others encourage them to keep going." He looked behind Arman, eyes glistening. "Look! Here it comes."

As the people around them spontaneously spread out to make way for this year's devotees, Arman's jaw dropped in bewilderment as he finally saw the worshippers in the line. A young clean-shaven Indian man, thin and shirtless, was somehow pulling a chariot similar to the one Arman had seen carried by four men earlier. When he first saw him leaning forward, he assumed there were ropes around his waist connecting him to the chariot. Then he saw it. Approximately 30 small ropes reached from the mobile structure toward the man's back, connected by hooks. The hooks were firmly entrenched into his body, stretching his skin outward at all thirty points of entry like traffic cones as he lurched forward. One look into his eyes revealed the same entranced expression that had suddenly become oddly familiar. However, something had been placed on his tongue that turned it a deep crimson, as if the god he petitioned was hungry for war.

Culture shock turned to nausea as Arman looked down to gather himself. The crowd on both sides offered ear-splitting encouragement to the devotees as they bore their excruciating burdens toward the stairway of the gods. Kumar, no longer playing host, burst into a ferocious chant as he did his part to pray for them. Arman was just as taken by the fervor of those observing the kavadi line as those who were actually in it.

Looking back to his right, he noticed two Malay police officers standing on a slightly elevated platform overseeing the festivities, both stonefaced and clearly disinterested in taking part of the idol worship. One was more detached, but the other officer's eyes conveyed both contempt and helplessness, like a fundamentalist preacher forced to chaperone a teen keg party. Unfortunately, as Arman was the only one looking backward, he caught their attention. He immediately looked away, keeping his head down as he moved closer to Kumar. Sweat inflamed the scar on his sockless foot, now rubbing harshly against his shoes. He wanted to ask Kumar to look back and see if they were still standing on the platform, but the man was clearly occupied. Finally, he decided he had to know where they were, a quick glance revealing what he feared. They were gone. Looking more closely, in between himself and the platform, he saw movement as if the crowd was parting to let someone through.

Arman was hemmed in on all directions. To his right, left, and behind him the crowd pressed in so closely that he was certain there was nowhere to go unless he was prepared to throw people to the ground. In front of him was the kavadi line, an almost unbroken chain of devotees passing through with thousands of eyes on them.

Kumar suddenly stepped into the line, drawing Arman's attention to a situation he hadn't noticed. A devotee with hooks in his back was followed, not by a chariot float with a god on it, but by a teenage boy holding the ropes connected to the hooks, pulling firmly as the pierced one in front of him moved steadily forward. The heat and the emotion of the moment, however, was overcoming him to the point of exhaustion, finally spilling him into a puddle on the hot asphalt. Kumar, along with several onlookers, knelt down to assist him.

Unconcerned with the drama unfolding in front of him, Arman looked back to his right to see how close the police officers were. At the moment, he could only see one of them, but he was about ten feet away now, so one fewer policeman wasn't exactly a comforting sight. A surge of fright pulsed through his veins until, finally, he felt yet another violent jerk on his left arm. Just when he was convinced he would spend the evening in jail, he spun around in a daze to find something had been placed in his hand. Who put it there, he never knew. He looked down and saw that he held what looked like a mashed ball of yarn, except there were strings coming out of it in another direction. His mouth gaped when he realized the strings were attached to the hooks in the back of the entranced man in front of him. He started to protest, but he was too frozen and lacked the presence of mind to just let go and flee the line of devotees. Just as he had gathered himself, he wondered if staying in the line and holding the ropes for this worshiper could actually be the best means of escape. So instead of choosing to reject participation in Thaipusam, he paused, leaving the door open while he tried to make the best decision. His hesitation, however, made the decision for him as the march toward the stairs suddenly resumed. And like a man unwittingly grabbing the leash of a Golden Retriever ready for a run, he held on for dear life as a man possessed by Lord Murugan yanked him helplessly down the kavadi line.

Easily the most reluctant worshiper among the hundreds of thousands present that day, Arman felt a genuine revulsion as he saw hooks pulling skin toward him only a few feet away. His immediate response was to ease the tension, but the supplicant had no tolerance for such feeble devotion to his task. Like a horse that actually wanted to feel the spurs, he whirled around, boring a hole through Arman with his bulging eyes, opening his mouth to reveal his reddened tongue for added effect. Arman got the message and pulled back until his skin again stretched several inches from the embedded hooks.

After about thirty feet of feeling like he was driving a chariot for the enemy's general, Arman now thought he was most likely a safe distance from the policemen. He glanced back and confirmed that he was right, seeing no one following him through the line and believing it would be impossible to keep up by weaving through the crowd. The irony of being saved by his participation in idolatrous worship wasn't lost on him. Even in the midst of the most surreal moment of his life (or was it?), he managed a smirk, deciding he would take this ride for as long as it led to anything that looked like safety.

A few feet in front of the man whose hooks he was pulling, another devotee carried a large and ornate temple-like structure about four feet wide, rising several feet above his head. It was attached by a belt of sorts wrapped around his torso, decorated in ribbons, peacock feathers, and flowers. The enormity of it made Arman wince at the thought of this guy trying to navigate the 272 steps ahead of them. Inside the cavity of his kavadi was a statue of a god that Arman thought was different than Lord Murugan.

Resembling a man's body with an elephant head, the deity gazed over the pierced devotees below. As Arman recognized the position of authority of this god before him, and his position of servitude, he felt the sting of Dahag under his beard. Was there any way out of this? Had he committed yet another grave sin, insurmountable even if he had two hundred years left to do good works?

He reached out for other voices to speak his desired truth into the chaos, eventually finding them. *There's nothing wrong with this*, they comforted. *After all, if it's wrong for you, then it's wrong for them, right? And you know better than to think there's one narrow way! Haven't you had enough of that kind of thinking among your leaders in Iran?* Arman was slightly calmed as he continued to apply pressure with the ropes. Still, he needed more assurance, so his mind searched further until he landed on the words of Rumi.

> I have given each being a separate and unique way
> of seeing and knowing and saying that knowledge.
> > What seems wrong to you is right for him.
> What is poison to one is honey to someone else.
> > Purity and impurity, sloth and diligence in
> > worship, These mean nothing to me.
> I am apart from all that.
> Ways of worshiping are not to be ranked as better or
> > worse than one another
> Hindus do Hindu things.
> The Dravidian Muslims in India do what they do.
> > It's all praise, and it's all right.

18

THE COVER-UP

Zia sat on a dark living room floor preparing a history lesson for seventh graders at the end of a beautiful Tehran afternoon. A sliver of light through the curtains made a thin line across her notebook as she furiously scribbled notes for the following morning. Aside from a slim ray of sunshine inadvertently allowed through the curtains, the only other light was the glow of the television. It was late Spring, 1988.

"Do you like the frame?" Jalal emerged from the hallway holding a small hammer and a picture of Farzin - Ali's newborn son and Zia's first nephew. He had sparse, but dark hair and a comical smile that made this one their favorite. She only turned around halfway and briefly viewed the photo out of the corner of her eye.

"It's beautiful. Thank you." Her tone was sullen as she forced a smile and looked back down at her work. The sound from the TV helped to ease the awkwardness of her response, but that was only because they weren't paying attention to what was was playing.

"When was the last time you talked to him?" Jalal asked. He knew there was no use in pretending she wasn't heartbroken over their estranged relationship and he was already wondering why he'd thought the picture would cheer her up.

"I called him about two months ago when he was home from the war for a few days." She wasn't offering more information and Jalal decided he wouldn't ask for it. He stood there holding the picture in his left hand and looked at his wife. The faint light coming through the curtains lit up her curly hair, reminding him how much he was still attracted to her.

Ali's allegiance to Khomeini would have caused problems with Zia regardless of whether or not she was married to Jalal, but he still sometimes felt that the strain in her relationship with Ali was his fault. His Mojahedin mustache was long gone now, primarily out of fear of retaliation, but his smooth face did nothing to earn Ali's acceptance.

Zia stopped writing and looked at the television. It was at this point that Jalal finally realized what was on. *Ten Days of the Revolution.* The Islamic Republic's official version of the fall of the Shah. Jalal knew what was coming next, but he waited a half second too long to make a move out of the room.

"Do you see what's missing, Jalal?" The film was showing a crowd marching through a wide street. Jalal knew the answer because they had the same conversation every time the state-run TV station showed the government's carefully edited propaganda. He remained quiet nonetheless, knowing good and well this was no longer a two-way conversation.

"Look at the female protesters. Do you see any mini-skirts? Colorful dresses? Do you see Dilruba's beehive hairdo? No! Just long black chadors! Just like what I have to wear to work every day now! And what about the other political parties and militant groups who also opposed the Shah? Where are they?!"

Jalal let it breathe. He knew the only helpful thing he could do at this point was sit and lament with her. Words were dangerous. He had planned to ask her where she wanted him to hang the picture on the wall, but for now he rested the hammer and the frame on the coffee table.

"They promised freedom. Opportunities. And now I'll never teach in a university because I'm a woman!" She looked at Jalal for the first time since he walked in. He noticed something different in her eyes this time.

"They said they saw his picture on the moon…" She shook her head in frustration, half laughing. "How could I have gone along with that? Why didn't I immediately see what was happening to my country? Why didn't I spend every ounce of persuasive energy I had convincing Ali that he was following a dictator in the making?"

Jalal noticed that she had both hands on her pencil now and wondered if she was aware that she had almost broken it. Helplessly folding his arms over his white dress shirt, he searched for soothing words that might calm her down but found none.

"Now he's this revered soldier in a war with Iraq where our young men are dying like flies! And for what?! To build Khomeini's land bridge to Jerusalem? They haven't even gained an inch!"

Zia wiped away tears on her cheeks as if she was angry at them. Her pencil was now split in half and her eyes were fixated on the television again. The scene zoomed in on a group of chador-clad women and their daughters. Jubilant. Wide smiles and arms in the air. One of them held a large sign saying, "Death to the Shah! Long Live Khomeini! Long live freedom!"

Zia looked away as if in torment when her eyes landed on the coffee table. Jalal saw her staring in that direction and flinched. As Zia unfolded her legs to get off the floor, Jalal pleaded, "Don't do it, Zia. Please, don't do it." She never hesitated. Within two seconds the hammer was firmly in her right hand.

"Zia, it's not going to help anything!"

"I'm not so sure about that," she replied. Her voice was calmer than he expected.

Zia turned sideways next to the TV screen and grasped the wooden handle with both hands.

"Don't, Zia!"

She plunged the metal head inside the screen and let out a primal scream. Jalal's mouth gaped as he reflexively put out his hands to protect himself from flying glass.

Amazingly, it didn't shatter as Jalal expected. Instead, it just stuck in the middle with the handle pointing directly forward. At first Zia stood still, just staring at it. Jalal didn't know if she was waiting for the hammer to fall or if she was going to grab it and take a few more swings. Finally, she looked back at him as if waking from a dream. She put her hands to her mouth, then hurried to the couch and crumpled into his arms in tears.

Ten days later, Zia received a phone call from Ali's wife, Laleh. She called to tell Zia that Ali had died in battle. Though Laleh was obviously mournful, she swelled with pride at the same time. "Your brother's a martyr, Zia."

Jalal stood silent, hands in his pockets, as he surveyed the destruction of yet another building in the city of Isfahan. During the "War of the Cities" - one of the final events of a devastating war - Saddam Hussein hurled scud missiles at will toward the major population centers of Iran. Ayatollah Khomeini replied in kind, yet they lacked the resources to inflict damage equally. In the midst of Iran's lost cause, Jalal was dispatched to one of the damaged cities to craft a "favorable report" for the government. He was told to write about the attack with enough accuracy to stoke the anger of the people against Iraq, but not so much detail as to discourage their will to continue supporting the war.

It was a game that had become second nature. Jalal would find a couple of victims to evoke sympathy, tell their individual stories in emotional and agonizing detail, and gloss over the extent of the destruction. In his earlier days he would protest such instructions and appeal to his boss's original ideals for getting into journalism. After a few legitimate threats on his life, he changed tactics and, instead of giving them *exactly* what they wanted, he would give them *almost* what they wanted. An unwanted detail here… A higher number of Iranian war dead there… It was his way of not completely giving in to the new regime, a strategy to maintain a foot in the door of dignity and honor. Then he would watch to see if they noticed. They did. Eventually his quiet subversion submitted to the overwhelming reality that he would either play the game or he wouldn't have a single job in the country.

It was an excruciating reality for a man who had committed as a youth to the ideals of reporting the truth objectively and accurately regardless of the cost. It was a humiliating assault on his honor that affected him in all areas of life, even with Zia. Sure, she had to deal with the same reality with her job as a teacher, but it didn't have the same impact on her as she seemed to be able to find creative ways of smuggling the truth past the watchful dragons of the IRP. So Jalal would return home after days or weeks of reporting in another country and lack the desire to look his wife in the eyes. And, of course, it didn't help that they had been trying to have children for at least four years.

Is it because of me?

He stared blankly at the flattened houses lining the street, not so much considering the disaster laying before him as much as the rubble of his former manhood, cruelly haunting him as he traveled across the nation.

"Jalal!" A man in uniform called from behind. It was Kamran, the soldier assigned to escort him to the most strategic parts of the city. He continued toward Jalal with a determined and mischievous smile. "Look, you've been working hard all day and I'm pretty sure you've seen the worst of the destruction. You can find some stories at the hospital tomorrow, but tonight…" He paused and looked him in the eye. "Tonight you're joining the men!"

"Sorry, but you know who I am, Kamran." They'd been through this before and he didn't want to talk about it again.

Yes, Kamran knew who he was alright. He knew that, underneath the veneer of fidelity and altruism was a desperate man seeking something else.

"Hey, we all admire your devotion to your wife. And, of course, we respect your desire to follow Islam. But mutah isn't adultery!"

He was referring to Nikah Mut'ah, or "temporary marriage." It's a practice first allowed by the Prophet Muhammad while traveling with soldiers weary from being away from their wives. Instead of engaging in prostitution, he allowed a brief contract of marriage and divorce in which the woman seemed to have more protection than normal, and a fair compensation for the time in which they were "married." Sunni Muslims officially rejected the practice and, although it never enjoyed widespread public approval, it was practiced more often among the Shi'a.

"Tell that to my wife." Once again, Jalal was forthright and convincing.

"No one's going to talk to your wife. I can promise you that much!"

At this point in the conversation, Jalal decided to remain silent, maintaining the semi-detached demeanor that had possessed him for so much of the day. Unfortunately, he didn't have another way to get to his hotel other than Kamran and his friends waiting in the armored vehicle, currently serving as his personal taxi. Somewhere in between the destruction and his hotel, in the midst of the smoke and illegal beer in the back of the truck, Jalal experienced a tragic change of mind.

He woke up the next day in misery. His crude attempt at recovering his manhood for a few hours dug a cavernous void inside him. Or did it simply uncover the void? It created a space for a shame and guilt to dwell on a scale he never thought possible, causing him to spend years finding ways to calm himself in the face of the oncoming judgment. While he never believed mutah was right, every time he replayed the act in his mind, he would find himself retreating into the legalistic "but it wasn't adultery" logic. It was the only choice he had, really.

Jalal soon realized his relationship with Zia was fundamentally impaired. He felt horrible about it and dedicated his life to repaying the debt he owed, repented in a thousand little ways, and many things that did, in fact, please Zia. His habits of faithfulness helped him to avoid further infidelity, but his affections were the true casualty of their marriage. His unfaithfulness, his hidden shame, and awareness of his own brokenness put an emotional wall between them. Zia eventually sensed this and their marriage devolved into a contractual, although congenial, relationship. It became about duty and Jalal performed, well… dutifully. Always trying to follow the rules, but never with delight. Always trying to atone, but rarely out of joy.

There was only one thing that really gave him any measure of comfort as he replayed his indiscretions to himself. It was his one saving grace that made life bearable. He repeated it as he wrote newspaper articles about the war and rehearsed it during the silence of the night while lying next to his wife.

No one will ever know.

Khina Ahura lay curled in a fetal position in the back of the bus, arms wrapped around herself as if to suffocate the pain of the last few weeks. She never remembered how it all happened. One day she was having a great time with her latest secret boyfriend, carefully avoiding any mention of him to her family, and enjoying a secret night life with a new set of friends. The next day she was standing next to a solder in a dark room in Isfahan as they signed a temporary marriage contract. Sure, she remembered getting drunk before the nightmare began, but someone must have been giving her some strong drugs to block out so much of the recent days. Her "boyfriend" had become her abuser, carefully striking her in less visible places every time she refused to go along with a mutah.

Finally, she summoned the courage to climb out a window of the Hell house in which she had been imprisoned and found a sympathetic bus driver who actually believed her story. He took her back to his station, showed her the bathroom so she could make herself as presentable as possible, then got her on a bus to return to her family in the city of Saveh. On arrival to her parents' house, she performed a well-rehearsed story that was received with shock and compassion. A few months later, Khina recognized the unusual bump in her stomach and panicked. She finally decided to call a distant cousin in Arak and confide in her with the truth. They had met a couple of times at large family gatherings in Tehran and immediately connected, though their parents didn't really know each other well at all. It was really her only idea and her only hope.

Afari and her husband Amir were never sure what to make out of Khina's story about what happened in Isfahan, but they knew better than to try to investigate a world they didn't know. If soldiers were involved, there was no hope for anything that resembled justice, but they believed her and wanted to do what they could to help. As it turned out, they had already been talking about having children, so after careful consideration while helping Khina through months of difficulty, they offered to raise her child as their own. Khina readily agreed and, for the first time in what seemed like forever, began to feel a glimmer of hope for her future. She imagined herself returning to her Saveh, reuniting with her family, and getting a normal job. After the birth of a baby girl, all of these things came to pass and, to her surprise, no one ever suspected anything close to what actually happened.

Afari and Amir were smitten with their adopted baby girl regardless of the annoying questions they sometimes had to answer. On the day she was born, Afari held her in her arms and looked up at Amir, eyes moist with joy.

"What do you want to call her?"

"I like Afari." She laughed loudly as his straight face gave way to a grin.

"We're not naming her after me. Seriously, is there a girl's name you like? I'm completely out of ideas for this beautiful creature."

"Okay, there is one I like," admitted Amir. "Well, just say it!"

He walked to Afari, gently placing one hand under the little girl's head and another under her tiny body, lifting her into his arms. His eyes lost in the innocence of her wondrous stare, Amir almost blushed.

"I like Banu."

~

Zia slipped mascara and lipstick into her pockets and put on the black chador expected of her. When she arrived to her destination, she would put on heavy make-up and rip off the horrendous tablecloth to reveal blue jeans and a pink blouse. This was now a way of life for her. But not just her. Zia and millions of Iranians had learned by now the art of living a double life underneath the thumb of clerical extremists. She watched her students faithfully chant "Death to America!" during the day and found ways to listen to Michael Jackson at night. "Death to the enemies of Islam!" in the public arena and Top Gun with friends at private video parties. It was the latter that would be Zia's indulgence for the evening. A friend with a VCR had just received a cassette of one of their favorite Iranian films made before the revolution - now banned by the IRP - so they quickly organized a party, replete with food, drinks, and someone to watch the door.

Before stepping outside, she carefully pulled out a single strand of hair, as usual, and let it lie freely outside of the covering on her head. It wasn't for the look, of course. She had tried pulling out a full tuft of hair before and was fortunate she wasn't beaten by the religious police, the Basij, who increasingly dominated the everyday lives of Iranians. No, it wasn't for appearances. She pulled out the single hair for her sanity. It was one of a thousand ways she found to silently remind herself she was resisting. While all appearances pointed to defeat, she let an invisible sliver of hope blow freely around her face as she defiantly walked past the men in uniform.

Black clothing dominated the streets, especially among the women. The birds of spring mocked her as she tried to envision the colors underneath the other women's chadors. She imagined a sudden burst of wind yanking them all off, revealing a mosaic of bright pastels underneath joyful faces. What she would give to have the power of that wind!

As she made her way to her friend's house, she wanted to do something useful with her time, which usually involved thinking through some issue at school. This time, however, she decided to settle her mind on the next day's lesson. After careful consideration, she decided the best way to influence a future Iranian generation to move forward is to point backward - to Rumi. Moses and the Shepherd, still her favorite after a decade of oppression, was even more meaningful to her now than it was when she met and fell in love with Jalal. In fact, it seemed to her a key to unlock the hearts of children daily fed a regimen of inflexible religious rules by clerics who believed that their way was the only way. After all, anyone who objected to the reading and memorization of Rumi would run the risk of being considered "un-Iranian." Yet it was fairly obvious to Zia that the ancient poet wouldn't have been on board with the current radical leadership. And even though it was fairly common for teachers to have their students memorize a poem from Rumi, for Zia it was about resisting oppression. She settled on one particular section of the poem, turning over every word in her mind and considering how she would add insurgent commentaries as she taught it.

> What is poison to one is honey to someone else.
>   Don't impose a property tax on a burned out
>   village. Don't scold the lover.
> The "wrong" way he talks is better than a hundred
>   "right ways of others." Inside the Kaaba it
>   doesn't matter which direction you point your
>   prayer rug!

19

STAIRWAY TO DARKNESS

The chanting and beating of drums continued as Arman tightly held the reins connected to the hooks in the back of the worshiper in front of him. His felt need to defend his actions continued as well, and he thought of a Shi'a practice similar to what he was experiencing at Thaipusam.

At the annual Ashura festival in Iran, there were often religious adherents who commemorated the martyrdom of Hussein Ibn Ali by self-flagellating their backs with chains or other sharp objects. The more fervent participants would keep hitting themselves until blood poured down their heads and backs. "See, it's all the same," the voices in his head preached. Of course, he then had to reckon with the fact that he and most people he knew hated the extremes and abuses of the practice and, therefore, rejected it a long time ago. While there were still a few who garnered lots of attention by drawing blood, most festivals included adherents practicing a much softer version of self-flagellation. Even then, Arman didn't like the use of chains in any form, even if the result was only a severely bruised back. How odd that he had briefly taken comfort by a practice he despised and which few modern Iranians practiced.

The entire experience jolted him in a way he hadn't expected.

Why would he even care about religions and philosophies when he's being chased as a suspected terrorist? The police were literally a few feet from him just seconds ago and he's worried about Rumi, Muhammad, and Lord Murugan! Still, he couldn't shake the fact that his assumptions about reality were being challenged in such a blatant way. It was one thing for him to consider a Hindu worshiping an idol, or even another Muslim who wanted to take part in a Hindu religious festival, but while he was the one actively participating, it felt altogether different. He pictured the local imam at the mosque he grew up attending and looked up at the enormous 140-foot tall idol at whose feet he was now submitting. Many gods versus one God. Reincarnation or one life? Heaven and Hell or Nirvana? He admitted these ideas were fundamentally at odds. Arman no longer felt tolerant. He felt like a fraud.

Cheering and chanting continued as the line approached the base of the stairs. He was fairly certain the guards had no idea where he was and that they probably had lost interest in pursuing him by now. The idea of walking into a dark and crowded cave was actually attractive since he would be even less likely to be recognized.

Just as the pierced young man in front of him took the first of the 272 steps lying ahead, Arman finally realized the obvious strategic disadvantage of entering a dead end no matter how dark and anonymous it promised to be. Fear and hesitation slightly halted his forward step onto the narrow stairs. Only the top of his toes made it onto the step, demanding greater balance and exertion from the muscles in his foot and calf. The sudden adjustment inflamed the newly raw scar on his ankle, causing him to fall backward. Instinctively, he used the ropes to balance himself, setting off an incredibly unfortunate series of events.

He felt the tension in several of the ropes buckle as hooks ripped out of the back in front of him. Blood splattered on his face and shirt like an altar sacrifice as they spun to the ground. Arman hit the ground first, landing squarely on his back and knocking out his breath. The young Indian man's torso landed on Arman's legs, but his head whipped backward onto the concrete below. The nearby onlookers let out a collective gasp as everyone tried to make sense of what just happened.

Everything around him blurred into a slow motion nightmare that would last for the next two minutes. Arman rolled onto his left side, still laboring to breathe, and saw several people bending down to help the other guy, unconscious and bleeding. A few onlookers stooped down both to try to revive him and to stop the flow of blood. Arman's breath returned enough to sit up and move toward them to see if he was okay. He felt the weight of the stares from others in the crowd and was promptly reminded of his minority status. Sighs of relief spread through the gathering as the Indian man began moving. None were more relieved than Arman, who was beginning to be concerned for his own safety in yet another way.

Arman's former partner in worship sat up and looked around in a daze. His eyes darted around before finally settling on Arman. *Is he angry or just confused?* Arman, still on the ground, unconsciously scooted backwards with his hands and feet, oblivious to the gathering crowd directly behind him. Eventually he backed into someone's kneecap and looked behind him to see concerned women in saris of every bright color on the spectrum. Some held their hands to their mouths as they reacted in horror to the rips in the young man's back. Others closed their eyes in prayer. Arman scanned people on all sides and was relieved to see that only a few were looking at him, so he stayed on the ground and continued his backwards movement until he was both behind and below the first two rows of onlookers. Now it was time to get out of here as quickly as possible.

Arman glanced backward to catch one more glimpse of the injured young worshiper before heading toward the Batu Caves exit. He turned around to see a wide-eyed Malay police officer staring at him through the crowd, only six feet away. Arman could have run in several directions, but his instinct kicked in and forced him to cut a channel through the crowd in the opposite direction. Up the stairs to the caves.

The stairs to the Batu Caves are steep and shallow. Two rails created three rows in which people could ascend and descend more safely if they choose to hold on. Monkeys perched themselves on the side walls, wandering through the stairs and waiting for distracted tourists to leave an unguarded snack in an open hand. On this particular day, Lord Murugan's faithful carried their kavadis to precarious heights, some of them needing to occasionally stop and rest. Most of them had a friend or family member to encourage them to keep going and to take care of any needs they may have along the way. All of this created a perilous obstacle course that lay between Arman and any chance of losing the one trailing him.

He sped past older men with skewers through their cheeks and around women with jugs of milk on their heads, glancing back to confirm the policeman was still trailing him. Despite the rapid pace of the climb, the experience continued to slow and became almost dreamlike, his observations of the environment impossibly detailed for someone running for his life. A monkey to his right reached into the backpack of a camera-wielding tourist and pulled out a packaged cup of blueberry yogurt. A teenage girl took heavy breaths while mumbling chants to Lord Murugan as he ran past her on the never-ending stairs.

The stairs…was he even getting anywhere? He watched them pass underneath his feet like trees through a car window. Glancing to his right, Lord Murugan appeared to grow larger, as Arman had yet to climb even half of his height. Cold, enormous, and unmoving, Arman hopefully imagined the golden god turning around, using his mighty vel to vanquish his enemy. Then he pictured what seemed like a more likely scenario. The 140-foot god grasping his spear and throwing it directly at Arman, piercing his calf in order to aid the angry officer below.

The never-ending ascent seemed to mirror his lifelong attempts to please Allah. Trying. Working. Climbing. Always running from mistakes and indiscretions. A god with his back turned, refusing to look on him and smile. *Oh, if only he would turn and smile!*

One stair morphed into another until they all blended together as one. He half suspected they would flatten together, slanting and cartoon-like, causing him to careen into his enemy's hands. Or would the steps begin rotating downward as he's desperately climbing to the top?

Looking ahead, Arman saw smiling faces as worshipers left the holy shrine above. Their eyes widened, some with confusion and others with anger, as they clung to the rails to make way for the chase unfolding before them. Arman believed it was only a matter of time before he was the cause of more blood spilled among the unsuspecting.

Suddenly, in a dramatic shift of perception, he went from feeling like he would never reach the top to suddenly nearing the end. A red-eyed monkey, much larger than the others, was perched on the side wall, seemingly awaiting his arrival. It stared at him intently, but there were other things to be concerned about as Arman turned his gaze in another direction and flew past. Claws tore into his shoulders, jerking him backward down the steps, but it wasn't the monkey. His adversary had finally caught up. The policeman jumped on top Arman and grabbed him by the throat. *Is he trying to arrest me or kill me?* Pigeons escaped from underneath them and hovered above as if to watch. Arman gasped for air, tried to punch back, and used his eyes to plead for help. Nothing he tried seemed to work as unsympathetic witnesses distanced themselves from the madness.

The red-eyed monkey hopped off the side wall, landing next to the distracted men. It searched in vain for something to scavenge, beginning with their hands and then turning to see if anything was on the back of Arman's assailant. Seeing nothing to lose at this point, Arman jerked its tail as violently as his own arm had been pulled throughout the afternoon. Infuriated and unable to discern who did it, the primate jumped on top of the shocked Malay officer, sinking his claws and teeth into his back simultaneously. He shrieked in pain, fear suddenly shaking his countenance, and Arman used his legs to flip both the monkey and the attacker over his head and down the stairs.

Leaping to his feet, he again saw the top of the steps and sped upward with all of his strength when something caught his attention. The line of worshipers descending from the cave had been coming down steadily on his left, but when there was a break in the flow of this line, he saw a narrow path leading to something very different, and obviously smaller, than the primary destination ahead. Believing the policeman was still occupied with the monkey, he thought a quick change of destination would be the perfect way to lose him. He jumped through the empty space in the line and, just as quickly as it had parted, it closed behind him like the Red Sea, leaving a wall of colorful people between Arman and the man chasing him.

The path wound to the left and up a short set of stairs, leading to a grand view of both Lord Murugan and downtown KL. He peered through a tree and saw, to his great relief, his attacker reaching the top of the main steps to the shrine in the opposite direction. *I lost him.*

He walked to the side of the path and collapsed into a bench, lungs feeling like they would explode at any minute, and plotted his next move. No rest for the weary. He noticed a group of somber-faced people crowded around the rail facing the city. Indians, Malay, Chinese, and Westerners alike appeared to mourn and gasp in wonder at the same time. Eventually, he gathered his breath and walked over to see the cause of the emotional reactions. He should've known. Peering over a blonde head, he saw in the distance what was left of the Petronas Towers, broken and smoldering like joss sticks. Farzin and Banu's unholy offering to Allah. He pushed the anguished thoughts to the side and forced himself to think.

Is it safe to go back down now that the policeman was searching the temple area? Or would he hurriedly return to search the steps? And what about other police officers?

Looking back down the path he just climbed, he saw something he hadn't noticed before and quickly abandoned all thoughts of returning where he came from. Halfway up the 272 steps, two Malay police officers slowly ascended the path to the holy shrine, eyes searching in all directions for something that obviously had nothing to do with the festival.

Arman felt his energy rush back to him and alertly searched out his immediate surroundings for a place to hide. He then realized the trail which had taken him to the bench and then to the scenic view of the city had another purpose entirely. He was actually at the beginning, not the end. He flew up a few more stairs, following the trail as it wound to the right, turned the corner, and saw that it opened up to a cavernous gathering area underneath the rock. As he entered, he read a sign above him.

The Dark Cave.

20

A WAR YOU WON'T BELIEVE

Zia caught her breath as they curled around the latest mountain peak and peered into the valley ahead. Tiny houses with red roofs, immediately surrounded by rice paddies, lay at the center of a larger landscape of lush green forest, a rarity in the nation of Iran. Jalal smiled at her reaction. They had been driving through the Alborz Mountains for hours on their way to Shomal, or "North" as it translates from Persian. They had already entered the Mazandaran Province and he was fairly certain, from the experience of multiple business trips to the Caspian Sea, that the scenery was about to explode with delights as the roads continued to wind up one side of a green mountain and down another. It had been many years since the family had anything resembling a vacation and they knew they were long overdue.

Arman and Mahnaz rode in the back seat of the red 2005 Paykan, one of the last of the Iranian-made series, listening to iPods while occasionally noticing a waterfall or misty forest, but mostly they were killing time until they reached the beach house. Mahnaz had just finished her first year at Tehran University, continuing a family connection with the school that was now in its third generation. She enjoyed being there, but her grades weren't making her parents very happy for the time being.

"You need to decide on a career and work hard to get there!"

Mahnaz could hear her mother's words as if they played on a permanent loop from her shiny new Apple device. "And what good did it do for you?" she would answer, usually in her head only. "All your work in school, your participation in the Revolution… how did it help *your* career?" It was fairly obvious to Mahnaz that her career options as a woman were fairly limited, so why not just have a good time while you can? She loved her mother and their relationship was mostly warm, but it was always a matter of time before Zia's ideal of the driven young woman, ready to plow through anything that looked like an obstacle, clashed with her daughter's apathy.

Arman was seventeen and the desire to choose a career path was uppermost in his mind. His parents were always open with him and his sister regarding what they believed about the government of Ahmadinejad and the Supreme Leader. As things stood in the political climate of Iran, they were clearly on the liberal side and had been quietly resisting for nearly three decades now. Arman understood his father's choice of going along with what he was expected to write about current events, but making subtle observations or leaving out crucial information that would add ambiguity to the state's narrative. It was the best he could do given the circumstances and Arman admired him for taking the risk. His determined outlook on life made his mother happy. His choice to follow in his father's footsteps made Jalal proud, especially since he was so committed to his future at his age. And, unlike his sister, he was actually looking forward to this vacation.

The last few years had been especially difficult on Jalal and Zia, and to a great deal of the country, in fact. For those who had been inspired by the seemingly brief prospect of freedom experienced under President Khatami, his downfall and the rise of President Ahmadinejad was like a cruel bully sneaking up from behind, pulling the Persian rug out from under them. Khatami talked about increased freedoms of the press. Ahmadinejad wanted a return to the ideals of the Revolution. Khatami talked about peace with the West. Ahmadinejad shouted about developing nuclear weapons and renewed the vitriol against the "Great Satan."

When shifting sands in the desert gave up the corpses of dead soldiers from the Iraq War, Ahmadinejad ordered their bones to be buried in public spaces, such as parks in upper class neighborhoods and Tehran University, in order to remind a softer generation of both the ideals and the cost of the revolution. After a critical step forward in the country's renewed goal to establish nuclear weapons, he ordered the country's schools to celebrate the achievement with yellow cake parties. Yellow, of course, for the color of uranium. Perhaps the greatest embarrassment to the millions of Iranians who did not share Ahmadinejad's vision for the country was his denial of the holocaust. It felt like he was shouting to the whole world that Iranians were "bisavad," or "uneducated." These same Iranians had great reverence for the memory of King Cyrus, including the fact that he was way ahead of his time in showing tolerance to religious minorities, including the Jews. To make matters even worse, Ahmadinejad held a global conference on the Holocaust and invited as a guest speaker David Duke, leader of the Ku Klux Klan, causing millions such as Zia and Jalal a great loss of face on the world stage.

While the West focused on more outward actions such as these, they mostly missed one of the major theological underpinnings of Ahmadinejad's approach to government - the return of the Mahdi. One of the distinctives of Shi'a Islam is their belief that the Prophet Muhammad's grandson, Hussein, was the rightful heir to lead all Muslims. The annual celebration of Ashura celebrates his heroic martyrdom. A descendant of Hussein's, Muhammad ibn Hasan al-Mahdi, was the twelfth imam in the lineage of Shi'a leadership. In the ninth century, he went missing and was never found, eventually becoming known as the "hidden imam," who still lives today and is waiting for the right time to reveal himself and rid the world of evil.

After President Ahmadinejad addressed the UN General Assembly in 2005, he later told the press that there was a halo illuminating him and that none of the delegates had blinked during the entire speech. He saw this as a sign that the hidden imam was with him. Ahmadinejad regularly spoke about the Mahdi and emphatically declared that anyone who supports Islam must support the President who is ushering in the return of the hidden imam. Islam and "God's Government" were one. Many bought into this while others were uncomfortable with the complete lack of distinction between Islam and this particular government. Still others, believing that Islam and this government were, in fact, inseparable, would eventually question the whole thing entirely.

∼

Jalal decided to take advantage of the time "alone" with Zia to ask her a question he'd put off for over a year.

"I'm sorry I didn't ask you about this earlier." He hesitated and stammered over a few words in an effort to begin the next sentence, as if meaningful communication required a long-forgotten muscle memory. "The yellow cake celebration… You never told me what happened and I guess I just didn't want to bring it up."

Zia looked down, away from the beautiful evergreens lining the mountainous roads, and closed her eyes as if in pain. Jalal immediately regretted raising the issue.

"I'm sorry. I shouldn't have… "No, it's okay."

"Are you sure?"

"Yes, I'm sure." Her long pause made Jalal doubt the certainty of this last statement, but she eventually continued.

"I dreaded the party all day. I was determined my students weren't going to have any cake, but I knew I was being watched. When it came time for the teachers to get the cake for our students, I didn't go. I'd planned the best lesson of the year for that day so I could keep them distracted. Unfortunately, I couldn't keep them focused once they heard the other classes cheering when the yellow cake arrived. I told them I'd already had a piece and it was terrible, but that didn't stop them from complaining. Eventually, a few of them started crying and I knew I'd be in great trouble if I didn't do anything."

"What did you do?" Even though the answer may have seemed obvious, Jalal never underestimated his wife's tenacity and wit. He listened, half expecting the inevitable and half expecting an ingenious solution only she would think of.

"They ate yellow cake… And they loved it." Zia wiped a tear with her right hand and went back to staring out the window.

"Wake up, Arman." Mahnaz whispered into the dark room of the beach house at about 1am. Arman had gone to sleep looking forward to a long rest and sleeping late in the morning, but Mahnaz had other plans for him. He sprung up and let out a surprised grunt, then began rubbing his eyes. Seeing that the house wasn't on fire and nothing else appeared to be wrong, he quickly became irritated.

"What are you doing in here?"

"Waking you up for a little adventure."

Arman immediately laid back down, but Mahnaz just grabbed him by the arm and pulled him back up.

"Let go of me! I just want to sleep."

Mahnaz smiled and walked over to the desk on the other side of the room. She grabbed a cup and glided smugly back toward Arman's bed.

"Don't make me go to plan B. You won't like plan B." She quietly sang it as if it were an old joke. Arman recognized it and slowly shook his head on his pillow, eyes still closed.

"You won't do it."

"You know I'll do it."

"What is it this time?"

"It may or may not be sweet lemon juice."

"Where did you get that?!"

"I'm sure that won't be the last time you ask that question tonight. Get up now or you're about to be covered in sticky sweetness for the rest of the night."

Arman shook his head again, but this time he was smiling. He was completely awake now and curious about what Mahnaz had in mind. Finally, he acquiesced to his older sister.

"Fine. Now get out of here and let me put my clothes on."

"Okay, but if I don't hear any movement, I'll come straight in here and douse you." She walked out of the room, but kept her foot inside the door in case he decided to lock it and go back to sleep.

He emerged from the room and they sneaked out of the back door. They crept down the short street leading to the beach and tip-toed through the dunes, Mahnaz giggling as they reached the edge of the water. Instinctively, she kicked at an incoming wave, wetting Arman's shorts and t-shirt. His only reaction was to smile and wipe a few drops of seawater off of his face.

"I guess saltwater on the beach is better than being covered in sweet lemon juice in bed."

"Oh, it could've been worse than that."

"What do you mean?" It wasn't that he disbelieved her. Just the opposite. He knew her well enough to expect the unexpected. Mahnaz jogged away from the water to a space on the sand where they could be mostly hidden in the dunes. He followed her because he knew the dunes would be safer, but what he really wanted to do is walk out to the pier. He loved to sit on the edge with his legs dangling above the water, feel the ocean breeze in his hair, and look up at the endless stars. It was his favorite place in the world even though he'd only been there a few times. Arman had heard that Paradise included 72 perpetual virgins. That seemed attractive enough, but if it didn't also include a pier on the beach in Shomal, he would be disappointed.

Mahnaz slung off her backpack, pulled out a blanket, and hastily spread it on a darkened area of sand. Reaching back in the bag, she pulled out a six-pack of beer, smiling wickedly at her brother.

"I could've poured this on you."

"Where did you get that?!"

"I told you that wouldn't be the last time you asked that question tonight." She laughed at Arman as his eyes widened in disbelief.

"Are you trying to get us arrested?"

"Stop worrying, little brother. First of all, the police aren't going to be searching dark places on the beach past midnight. Second, if anyone comes near us, we'll hear them before they know we're even here. And third…" She pulled out some cash and let it wave back and forth in the wind. "If a policeman does somehow spot us, I know how to speak the language of the law."

She pulled the tab on a beer, making a noise just loud enough to make Arman squirm and look around them. "Loosen up, brother." She offered him the drink in her hand. "You know it's not the first time."

He reluctantly accepted, offering one last defense. "You know what the Qur'an says." Although Arman wasn't perhaps the best Muslim in the nation, he did, in fact, make sincere attempts to follow the faith of his fathers. While their parents rejected the ideals of the Revolution and the "government of God," with all of its extremes and injustices, they never rejected Islam itself. They just followed a more liberal version of it, interpreted by the ancient poets and modern society.

"And what does it say?"

"It says that alcohol is haram."

"How do you know, Arman?"

"What do you mean, 'How do I know?' Everyone knows the Qur'an forbids it!"

"Have you read it?" The faint moonlight was just enough to reveal that Mahnaz was no longer smiling. Arman could feel the weight of her stare even in the darkness.

"You know I don't read Arabic!"

"Exactly! The only thing you know is what our holy and righteous religious leaders tell you, right?"

Arman knew it was ridiculous to deny that the Qur'an forbade alcohol, but he also knew he'd lost the argument. He exhaled, relaxed his body, and leaned back on one arm, using the other to lift the can to his mouth and begin enjoying an adventure with his sister. He changed the subject.

"So how are your classes going?"

"You mean Mom and Dad aren't complaining to the good child?"

"Don't call me that, Mahnaz. It's not my fault."

She started to push the subject further, rubbing salt in the wounds, but decided against it. "You're right. I guess that's not fair."

"Did you just say 'You're right'?"

She laughed. "Don't push it."

"If only I had an MP3 recorder."

"I said…"

"Okay, okay! I won't push it."

"Wise move," she warned. "As far as school goes… You'll not be shocked to know I failed two of my classes." She was suddenly quiet and it was obvious to Arman she didn't want to talk for now. He looked at her with genuine concern, knowing she couldn't see his face well, her silhouette revealing strands of hair from her hijab-less head fluttering in the wind.

"You're a smart girl, Mahnaz. You shouldn't let yourself worry so much about your future. You've heard of a self-fulfilled prophecy, right?"

"Easy for you to say. You're a man."

"Yeah. An Iranian man who wants to be a journalist. Nothing but privilege here, right?"

"Well, if you weren't so set on following in your father's footsteps, you'd have a lot more opportunities than me, even in this economic black hole."

"I've never told you this. Or Mom and Dad. But…" Arman choked on his words. He gathered himself after a full minute, then continued. "I'm not planning on staying here."

Mahnaz chuckled. "You think that surprises me?" She looked at Arman, trying to gain eye contact. "Let me guess. You're going to join Farzin in Malaysia, graduate with a bachelor's degree, then move to Australia or another Western country?"

"Was it that obvious?"

"Yes."

"Just so you know, I'm not planning on forgetting about Iran.

Wherever I go, I'll write about the corruptions of our government and let everyone know what's really going on."

"Western countries already know our country's corrupt and that they control the media. How will that help?"

"It's not about letting them know, although that might help me actually make a living. It's about being able to write freely and getting unfiltered information back into Iran. Dad has to be so subtle that it's hard to know if he's making a difference or not. It needs to be more direct."

"And how are you planning on spreading unfiltered news into Iran?"

Arman smiled like a child who'd just discovered a hidden cookie jar. "Have you heard of Twitter?"

Farzin sipped hot teh tarik in a sweltering dorm room at 2 a.m. while watching First Blood, one of his favorite movies, on his laptop. He'd purchased it for a mere five ringgit somewhere on the streets of Kuala Lumpur, a perk from living in the land of pirated media. Blue light flickered above the ceiling fan, which would have helped a lot more if it hadn't been stuck on the lowest speed. He laid on the bed in his underwear, doing anything he could to remain as cool as possible. Anything, that is, except give up the pleasure of his new favorite drink.

He loved the Rambo movies, and pretty much anything else with Sylvester Stallone. Sure, he'd participated in the "Death to America!" chants just like all other high school students while in high school, but, like most of them, he would return home looking forward to a taste of the latest offering of Western music and movies.

As he watched the film, one of the scenes pushed his mind to a memory he hadn't expected. While seemingly hundreds of police officers and local volunteers hunted Rambo, the camera shifted from their movements along the embankment of a nearby stream. It appeared to the viewer that there was nothing there whatsoever until, suddenly, Rambo's eyes jolted open, revealing the mystifying presence of a man covered completely in mud.

Farzin had watched it over ten times, but this time it reminded him of the bodies of the Iraq War soldiers, hidden for two decades, suddenly uncovered in the desert by wind and shifting sands. Inevitably, it also reminded him of one of the worst experiences in his life, years earlier.

Farzin approached the new monument the way a daring teenager enters a haunted house. He crept forward gingerly, out of both fear and reverence for the dead, not knowing exactly where his eyes should focus nor completely certain the new grave actually contained the bones of the war dead. There was engraved writing on the stone in front of him, but he could never concentrate on what it actually said. It didn't matter, really. For him it was all about the possibility, however infinitesimally small, that a single bone of his father may be in this tomb of unknown soldiers. It made the hair on his arms stand at attention, a visceral response caused by his reverence for heroes of renown, his mouth dry as the desert, and his pulse racing. He had no living memory of his father, and simultaneously possessed both an intense desire to feel close to him and an overwhelming fear of such intimacy. Overwhelmed, he finally succumbed to his emotions and slunk to the concrete sidewalk, head in his hands, tears streaming down his smooth face.

At first he lay curled at the foot of the monument, heedless of those passing him on the sidewalk, eventually moving to the curb, legs in the road and eyes still moistening his palms. Two college students, both male, stopped to look at the oddly-placed tomb, paying no attention to Farzin's presence as they complained about their President's latest goading of the educated class. No longer feeling as if he was afraid of a ghost, he'd now apparently become one. Farzin paid little attention to what they were saying in the beginning, but eventually the voices behind him became annoying. They spoke in hushed tones as if not wanting to be heard, but somehow they had let their guard down enough to speak loud enough for a stranger to hear. Perhaps Farzin seemed so despondent that they thought of him in the same way they would think about a park bench. His eyes were still closed, so he never saw who was speaking as he eavesdropped.

"He's such an idiot! Does Ahmadinejad really think burying soldiers on our campus will make us want to follow him?"

"Yes, he is an idiot. But I don't think he cares if we want to follow him. He can make us do that. He just wants to shove our lack of loyalty in our faces."

"Yeah, but using the bodies of dead soldiers found in the desert to make a point? He's a madman."

"Again, you're right. What I think is insulting is the very idea that they actually died for some great purpose."

"750,000 soldiers dead. Not an inch of ground toward Jerusalem gained."

As Farzin listened, the idea of the soldiers dying in vain was not a new thought. Because of his father, however, it was the first time he heard anyone say it so emphatically in his presence. It angered him, but not enough to push him to any action. Not yet.

"They say the best soldiers were the ones who had the real 'battlefield mentality.' No sacrifice too great for the Supreme Leader!"

"I can't imagine what they were thinking. If they thought they were dying for some great purpose, they were as stupid as Ahmadinejad."

Farzin didn't remember too many details about what happened afterward. He vaguely recalled his fists flailing at two stunned young men; yelling, kicking, punching, pushing, loud cursing, and eventually a cloud of dust in the wake of the fleeing students.

Blood was splattered on the sidewalk, on his shirt, and across the tomb, the latter appearing as some kind of offering to the saints. The last thing he remembered is standing alone, holding a shattered lens from one of the students' glasses, wishing he could punch them in the face just one more time.

~

It was a painful memory for Farzin, but one of the more influential experiences of his life. Regardless of how much he still hated those two students, it cemented the doubt he had concerning the meaning of his father's death. Did he die for a purpose or was he just a tool of the state? Was he a savage or a saint? Hero or fool? The two sides argued with each other like the metaphorical angel and devil on his shoulders, except this pair changed clothes whenever he thought the angel was winning. They'd each land their blows and ultimately get nowhere, leaving Farzin exhausted in his effort to honor his father.

Ultimately the main frustration was the utter powerlessness of it all. Though naturally an extrovert, it drove him inward and, when he didn't have to study, he would spend long nights alone in his dorm room bingeing on old American action hero movies. Where the soldiers are good. Their cause is just. The good guy has the power to beat the odds. And he shames his enemies with one-liners in the wake of his victory.

Farzin snapped out of his despondent fog as he recognized one of his favorite scenes approaching. Rambo, the unjustly persecuted soldier, sprung out of his perfect camouflage to seize an utterly terrified Sheriff Teasle and shove him against a tree, putting a knife to his throat. Above the choking of the lawman, Rambo's threats are loud and clear.

Farzin silently mouthed his favorite line along with his hero. "Don't push it or I'll give you a war you won't believe!"

The faint blue light from Farzin's laptop revealed a satisfied grin. He had escaped, for a little while, at least. He went to bed later that night with dreams of being a hero. "One day," he thought. "One day."

2 1

HIDING IN A CAVE

A brief scan of the small gathering revealed a family of four sitting on a bench, a group of around 15 men and women talking to each other, and a smattering of others sitting in pairs, quietly waiting for something. They were all wearing hardhats with a light on the front. Behind them was a desk, currently unmanned, with a sign reading, "Cave tours, fifty ringgit." Next to the desk there were two waist high poles with yellow tape connected on either end, obviously the entrance. He knelt down in a dark corner nearby and wondered if it would be possible to slip through unnoticed.

"Okay, everyone! Make a circle around the benches so I can give you some final instructions!"

Arman caught a glimpse of a slender young Malay woman through a gap in the crowd now thickening around her. All of the people who were apparently getting ready for a cave tour now had their backs to Arman, and the men in the crowd were tall enough to completely block the view of the shorter tour guide just enough to where she had no chance of seeing him. Without hesitation, he slid under the entrance and sped down a dimly lit walkway into The Dark Cave looking for a place to hide, and maybe get some rest.

157

Very quickly the cave changed from dimly lit to utterly black, and yet he threw himself into the darkness as a four-year-old boy jumps into the arms of his father. He thought it was amazing how something so terrifying as complete darkness could so quickly feel like salvation. A handrail accompanied the concrete walkway through the cave, allowing him to slide his hand along the path, alternating between running and walking even when he could no longer see. At first he moved quickly, thinking about the group that would be right behind him, but when he considered that he couldn't be entirely sure the path wouldn't end, he slowed down and put his weight on his back foot in case the ground in front of him shifted or became unsteady.

The first half minute of walking felt okay, but soon his lack of any kind of a plan began to sink in and everything changed in a moment. The darkness suddenly carried an unexpected weight that seemed to press him to the ground. It was the silence, however, that made the hair on his arms stand on end. The vague idea he had while running into the cave was to find somewhere to hide. But now, with tourists wearing lights on their hardhats behind him, he had no idea how to find a hiding place. He couldn't envision his surroundings in the slightest. The walkway was solid and predictable, but what was on either side? How far away were the cave walls? Was the cave floor wet, muddy, or dry? Would he hit his head on stalactites? Were there crevices in the walls that would make a good hiding place? And what exactly might be crawling on the ground and the walls in here? It was the last question that suddenly froze Arman and made him regret entering this place.

Voices echoed through the corridors of the cave and forced Arman into a decision. Would he stay on the walkway and get caught, drawing undue attention to the fact that he has something to hide? Or… would he hide? He shuffled his feet to the opposite side of the walkway from the rail. Putting his right foot down first, he gingerly began walking on the cave floor toward the wall. A single headlight flashed in his direction and he realized he had less time than he thought. He placed his arms forward in the darkness like Frankenstein and shuffled forward.

After only a short distance, his feet skated onto a hard, wet, and slippery surface. His legs flew upward in front of him, causing him to land painfully on his back, and he slid downward into nothing. Because he couldn't see where he was going, it felt like he was falling for eons. Would he slide into a stream of water? Would he land on some unsuspecting cave-dwelling creature? Do scorpions live in caves? Would he slide off a ledge into some kind of an abyss from which he would never climb out? His arms flailed in every direction as he desperately sought some kind of an anchor. His stomach turned and flipped, and he felt as if he would wretch. Falling. Falling. Falling.

In what actually took just a few seconds in real time, his left side landed roughly into what felt like a rock. His shoulder hurt, but overall he was fine. The surface was still too slippery to stand by himself, so he reached out and, finding that it was, in fact, a large rock, used it to pull himself up. About five headlights now bounced off the cave walls, a cause for concern, of course, but it also provided just enough light for Arman to realize the rock was a perfect hiding place. He quickly climbed over it and rolled onto the other side, which, thankfully, was dry.

The voices became louder and the lights brighter as the happy cave tourists wound through the tunnel. He could see the silhouettes of over twenty people, all sizes and shapes, and even felt their footfalls as they approached. Children giggled. Adults used the lights on their helmets to point to the stalactites in amazement. Some spoke in Chinese and a couple of other languages Arman couldn't identify. Finally they reached the path next to Arman. Part of him couldn't wait for them to pass, and another part longed for their light to remain.

"I'd like to officially welcome you to The Dark Cave!" said an enthusiastic young woman at the head of the group. She wore black pants and a black t-shirt, no hijab. Headlights swung in her direction and gathered in front of her, illuminating the Malay woman like spotlights on an otherwise black stage.

It was at this point that Arman realized he wasn't hiding behind one rock. There were two large boulders in front of him and he could see the group through a crack between them. The tour guide had a clear light brown complexion and beaming white teeth accompanying her confident smile. Even from where Arman was standing, he could clearly see the gleam in her eyes as she guided them through the history and wonders of The Dark Cave. Millions of years old... Stalactites and stalagmites formed over millennia... Arman felt her awe of the cave wash over the group as their lights lay still, transfixed on their leader.

In addition to the wonders of the cave itself, she explained its ecosystem and the creatures which lived inside. She pulled out a booklet with pictures to aid her presentation. She started with the bats - their guano, more specifically - which provided the foundation for the creatures' sustenance, then enthusiastically watched their faces as she explained what else may be crawling somewhere close to them. Cave crickets, the cave racer slithering along its walls and floors, and the occasional python sighting. She especially lit up as she talked about the extremely rare trap door spider.

"The trap door spider hides under a door it creates with soil and other materials. The hinge of the door is made of silk. When an unsuspecting creature, such as a cave cricket, trips one of its spider webs..." She pulled her hands up in front of her face, curling her fingers, bared her teeth, and widened her eyes. "The spider leaps out and grabs it!"

When she said, "Grabs it!" she seized a man twice her size by the shoulders. He jumped backward, involuntarily letting out an "Aiyo!" The children squealed. Others jumped and then began laughing, including the man who had just been somewhat shamed by the tour guide.

Out of all the creatures discussed, the one that chilled Arman the most wasn't the trap door spider or even the snakes. It was the long-legged centipede. The *poisonous* long- legged centipede. He began feeling something touching his legs and arms even as he wore long sleeves and jeans. He felt the hair on his beard move and couldn't stop himself from brushing off imaginary centipedes with his hands. He couldn't see the picture shown to everyone else, but his imagination made it significantly worse than the reality.

The tour guide's countenance shifted into a frown and she pointed toward Arman. His stomach dropped and he quickly pulled his head out from behind the space between the rocks. Head lamps shone all around him now, scattering bright light across water trickling down the cave wall like strobe lights, forming large shadows from the boulders.

"Although this is the most researched tropical cave in the world, it was closed to the public for many years. In the seventies, there were parts of the cave covered with graffiti." Her voice carried an authentic grief as she said this. The crowd groaned. "They had to shut off access to the cave before irreparable damage was done. Of course, there was significant damage even through the careful removal of the paint." She paused and turned her headlamp off, causing the others to do the same. "As we stand in the silence, can you feel the pain this caused? Can you sense the Earth telling you what a crime this was?"

As they turned their lights back on, Arman began to sense something completely unexpected. On the surface, there were no idols in here, unlike the cave next door where throngs of worshipers honored Lord Murugan, so there was no official religious worship. It was also true that the tour guide was getting paid and the cave had been turned into a commodity for global tourism. And yet, the more he listened to her and watched how most of the crowd followed her, he believed they were experiencing something holy. Instead of idols or gods, the cave itself was the object of worship and the tour guide its faithful priestess, a mediator between sanctified nature and materialistic mankind.

She continued, "However, the most significant damage that can be caused by tourists and other careless visitors has to do with the limestone walls and floors. Whatever you do, don't step off of the walkway, especially if the floor is wet. It's not just that you would slip and fall, it's the damage that will be caused to the limestone. One touch in the wrong place on the cave walls can disrupt the flow of water that's been dripping for millions of years to form these stalagmites and stalactites we all enjoy so much."

The lights continuing to flicker above Arman felt like a search party chasing an escaped convict. He scanned the cave floor where he'd just slid on his back like a child at a water park to see if he'd left any permanent marks. Little did he know, when entering the cave, he would experience such an altogether different kind of shame. Whatever the religion, worldview, or worship practice, he would always be a hopeless transgressor. He was now convinced that, even if he encountered the most kind, loving, and forgiving god believed in by any human, he would find a way to utterly offend him. If there was a deity as innocuous as "The Goddess of Fuzzy Bunnies," he would be the first one to step on a tail, earning her eternal hatred.

Before moving forward, the guide concluded, "In The Dark Cave, as with all of life, our greatest aim is to leave as little footprint as possible so we can pass on the environment to the next generation unspoiled." As the group moved on, two of them pointed their helmets in the direction of the cave floor where Arman had slipped. He wasn't sure if it was his imagination or reality, but he could've sworn he saw a footprint matching the pattern of his shoes.

Arman lingered in black silence. He could no longer see even a faint hint of light from the tourists, but could still hear echoes from the children laughing as he contemplated his next move. Should he go back to the opening of the cave? During the tour guide's presentation, she mentioned a large opening in the roof at the end of the tunnel. Should he wait until they pass by on their way back, continue to the end of the path and try to climb out? Finally, the unbearable darkness, and the constant feeling that something was crawling on him, made the decision for him. He would take his chance with the police.

As he took the first step up toward the path, however, he heard a sound that froze him like a lion's roar, though it wasn't loud at all. In fact, it was a whisper. And it was probably less than fifteen feet away. Was he hearing things? Was it a ghost? Or a devil? Another whisper. Now it was clear there were two voices and they were speaking Chinese. Head lamps suddenly lit up, nearly blinding Arman. He alertly remained calm and slowly bent back beneath the rocks, but these tourists were off the path now and the angle was different. If they looked directly at him, they would see him, but at the moment, they seemed to be preoccupied with the floor around them. One of them would point at a spot on the cave floor and they would both inspect it, slightly digging under the earth as if looking for something specific. One of them, Arman noticed, carried a small rectangular glass object that looked like some kind of an aquarium. *Are they looking for a trap door spider? That would bring them a fortune in the black market.* They were now about eight feet away from Arman and he was wondering if he should say something. Maybe they would help him get out.

As the men bent over, one of them lost his helmet. It clanked on the ground, echoing throughout the cave, and scattered light in every direction as it rolled downhill. Arman, who was sitting on his rear end with his legs crossed, watched helplessly as it bounced in his direction. Even if he was in a more mobile position, he was backed into a corner and had nowhere to go. The head lamp turned, clanged, and bounced until it landed perfectly in Arman's lap. As it came to its resting place, the glow of the lamp shone directly upward under Arman's chin, illuminating his face in the same way a child would use a flashlight under a blanket to tell a ghost story. Half of his face was covered in shadow, the other half glowed in a dark reddish hue. His eyes bulged and his mouth flew open, only adding to his demonic appearance. He tried to speak, but before he could utter a word, one of them screamed.

"Yaoguai!"

Arman had no idea that meant, "strange devil," of course, but he wouldn't have been surprised either. The other man quickly joined the shouting and they flew toward the path, slipping and falling every few feet. Arman never saw their faces after that. He only saw the lone headlight between the two of them and it never looked back in his direction. It bounced up and down, lit the way down the path ahead of them, and occasionally went mostly dark for brief seconds as the man wearing it fell face down. Very soon he could no longer see any evidence of his Chinese visitors.

Arman sat there in disbelief, holding his shiny new toy, an incredible gift; the proverbial light in a dark place. After an entire day of everything going wrong that could possibly go wrong, something good happened. Impossibly good, actually. Yes, he understood his situation was still dire, but he felt a faint white lining developing around the black clouds. Finally, after processing his new situation, he thought about how he shocked the unsuspecting robbers; the fact that they were obviously trying to get away with something, and the odds the light would've landed in his lap in that direction. And then Arman did something he hadn't even considered since entering the Petronas Towers walkway. He smiled.

Before the last encounter he'd decided to go back to the cave entrance, but now he felt confident enough to stick around and see if he could climb out of the opening at the end of the tunnel. He put his hat on, scanned his surroundings, brushed off a couple of imaginary long-legged centipedes, and crept down the path in the same direction as the tour. He knew they would have to come back in his direction, so he relentlessly scanned the cave floor and walls for hiding places. Eventually he came across an indentation in the side of the cave that was deep and high enough both to stand in and to avoid being seen. The floor leading to this area was dry, so he decided he would take this opportunity while he had it. He walked in, scanned the walls for unwanted cave creatures, and held his hat in his hands so he could peek out for the ecotourists without being seen while having the comfort of a little bit of light at the same time. Soon they came and went without incident and Arman walked briskly down the path in the opposite direction.

Now that he had a light, the quiet was an unexpected relief and he was happy to be away from the cacophony of Thaipusam. Not having someone right behind him wasn't bad either. A breeze entered the tunnel, which was both refreshing and a good sign that he may be nearing the opening. He quickened his pace until, at last, he saw a faint hint of sunlight. He'd been unsure if there would be any sunlight left, but then again, the entire day felt like something of a time warp. The collapse of the towers already seemed like a week ago.

Reaching the end of the path, he found the enormous circular opening overhead was just like he'd pictured it. The sunlight was dim, but it was incredibly welcome all the same. Arman walked around the edges of the open ceiling and looked for the best place to climb out. Trees and brush were scattered along the enormous cave walls, but it was mostly a mixture of black and grey rocks. The longer he searched for a path to climb, however, the more he became discouraged. The edges of the ceiling were austere and concave, a challenge for even experienced climbers - and he was not an experienced climber. After at least ten minutes of discerning the easiest path, he finally saw one that seemed to have just enough trees to grab and use as footholds that he believed an escape from the cave would be possible. He climbed over the first few rocks easily enough and was able to get a closer look at his chosen passage. Not only was it more steep than he realized, it was also pocked with crevices all along the way. He considered the cave racers, pythons, and, of course, the long-legged poisonous centipedes. What would happen if, when his hands were completely occupied with climbing, his head lamp revealed a snake in front of him. And what if centipedes crawled over him?

As the dim sunlight escaped the cave, he reconsidered his situation. He was hungry and exhausted, but probably more exhausted than hungry. He had no real plan even if he was able to climb out. And despite the eerie nature of hiding in a cave, he was at least safe for now. Finally, he decided to find a place to rest. He jumped down from his short climb and went back to the concrete pathway, which ended exactly in the middle of the opening in the cave ceiling. The sunlight was gone, but there was a slight haze from the city lights that at least enabled him to see the edges of the opening. No stars, of course, and he couldn't see anything directly around him without his helmet lamp. He laid down on the walkway and rested his head on his helmet, light still turned on, of course. It would've been more comfortable on the dirt next to the path, but he wanted to feel as far away as possible from anything that crawled.

Arman was confident the tours were shut down for the evening, so he knew that, for the first time all day, he actually had time to think. He lay there, eyes closed, his mind spinning in a million directions, trying to figure out what he should do next. Rest for a few hours and then go back to the entrance? Perhaps there would be a restaurant open somewhere nearby. After all, it's Kuala Lumpur. And what then? How would he escape the country? Perhaps he could find a bus to a city just south of Thailand and sneak across. And what then? He processed about ten other dead end plans such as this until he could no longer concentrate.

Instead of planning his escape, hopelessness seized him and he lost control of his thoughts, numbering his personal tragedies like an army captain counts dead bodies. He thought of his father and tried to picture him smiling, but could only imagine disappointment in his eyes. He wished he could talk to his mom, but wasn't even sure if she would believe him. The scar on his chest cracked and flared. Had it been that way for a long time or had he just been too preoccupied to notice? Then he thought of the Marburys.

Only a few weeks ago, Arman was overwhelmed with their kindness and had a strong sense of joy just being in their presence. Now Tom was dead because of his cousin and Banu. Worse still, Barbara had every reason to believe Arman was complicit. His soul splintered into fragments as he imagined the sweetest woman he'd ever met hating Muslims. Hating him. He imagined her moving back to America with a new mission in life. "Don't ever let Muslims into your town," she would warn everyone. "Especially Iranians!" He envisioned the specifics of conversations she would have in the future as she explained to her family and friends how it all started with letting the wrong kind of people into her home.

With anguished labor, he forced himself to find something else to think about. *Or better yet,* he thought, *I need to just think of nothing at all.* This was impossible, of course, but he did, however, manage to create the desired void for approximately two seconds. With all the effort of a champion weightlifter attempting a personal record, he heaved his burdens just above his head, claimed victory, only to watch them crash down with greater intensity than ever.

He'd pushed the greatest question out of his mind all day because he just didn't know what to do with it, or how to even begin understanding it. Also, he had the advantage of being consumed with mere survival. But here he was, with time on his hands and a sudden inability to think of anything else.

Farzin… Why?

His older cousin; his hero; his protector… The brave one who was never afraid to stand up for those he loves; now their entire relationship felt like a lie. The fact that Farzin apparently went out of his way to make sure Arman survived on the bridge meant nothing. Surely he realized Arman would be a suspect and wouldn't be given a fair trial, especially in the court of public opinion. Was it his cruelty that led him to keep Arman alive? At this point, dying on the bridge seemed a greater mercy than the future lying ahead of him. Public scorn, rejection, and imminent punishment, probably execution, is all that awaited. Even worse, the shame of his alleged actions, both the association with terrorists and video footage of him letting go of a baby stroller, would stay with them forever. His parents were probably disowning him even as he lay in this desolate cave.

He thought of Banu and his mind turned to hatred and regret. Surely it was she who corrupted him. Surely she used her beauty and charm to play on Farzin's pain of never knowing his father, convincing him that Ali would've wanted him to blow himself up on the bridge - that he would join his father as a hero if he did. Yes, that must be what happened. How could he have thought of her like a sister just because she looked like Mahnaz? How foolish!

Finally, he broke. He burst into tears, body convulsing violently, and curled his knees to his chest. Wails echoed off the cave walls, down the tunnel, and returned to taunt him like a cruel prison guard. Tears streamed through his tightly closed eyes as he tried to stop his body from shaking, but to no avail. Light from his headlamp scattered moving shadows in front of him. He laid in the same position, on the path and in the center of the bowl-shaped opening in the cave, longing for a pier on a beach in Shomal. He continued to let these thoughts torment him until, mercifully, he cried himself to sleep.

With his battery-powered headlamp still on.

~

Half-conscious, Arman wiped a few raindrops from his face. A flash of lightning caused him to open his eyes, the brightness of which caused him to see hazy white light even after it was gone. The thunder jolted him upright and caused his helmet to fly from his head, tinkering off the path. The slight haze from the city lights was completely swallowed by storm clouds, leaving him again trapped in utter darkness. He immediately followed the imagined path of the helmet and felt his way through the dirt on his hands and knees like a blind beggar. Rain steadily increased, turning the dirt to mud, and his search seemed useless as he considered going back to the path and using the rail to find his way to the tunnel.

Lightning struck the Batu Caves, both shocking him and illuminating his surroundings for a fleeting moment. He saw something to the left out of the corner of his eye and he quickly shuffled his way over to find that it was, in fact, his helmet. He sighed with relief, placed it back on his head, and stood up, pressing the power button to light his way back to the path. Nothing. He pressed it again. And again. He pressed it harder. Then slower. He took it off to see if he could feel for a place to remove the batteries, think that perhaps they fell out of place when it came off of his head. Lightning struck again, this time immediately followed with such violent thunder that it knocked him to the ground, much like the bombs on the Petronas Towers crosswalk. He clung to the helmet as he fell and quickly resumed his vain attempts to turn it back on. Then he remembered.

I never turned it off.

He had no idea how long he'd been sleeping, but suspected that it was several hours at least. Finally, he admitted the battery was dead. Regardless, he put it back on as he approached the concrete, hoping it would generate some hint of comfort as he journeyed back into the tunnel. He grabbed the metal rail and slid his hand along its side as he quickened his pace, but then, realizing the terrible combination of lightning and metal, he shifted his strategy, tapping his hand back and forth on it instead. Rain fell in sheets now, beating on his helmet like tiny hammers until he reached the tunnel. Another flash of lightning both confirmed his location and shook the cave around him, an ear-splitting thunder like he'd never experienced. It punched him in the chest and bounced around the tunnel, continually shaking him with each echo.

Previously he wanted to stay at the end of the tunnel because of the light it had offered, however dim. Now he was torn between wanting the occasional glimpse of the cave through the lightning and desperately wanting to get away from the thunder. Eventually he considered that he'd also been waiting until the police were less likely to be near at the cave entrance, and realized that it was most likely safe for him to leave down the stairs of the Batu Caves. Not only had many hours passed, but it was nighttime and there was a thunderstorm. The more he thought about it, the more he realized it was the perfect time to escape. He tapped the rail again to make sure he knew where he was, turned away from the end of the tunnel, and stepped forward with renewed determination to leave this nightmarish place for safety. Another bolt of lightning, another glimpse of the cave tunnel ahead. But this time it was different.

Something moved.

Something large moved. A serpent tail larger than anything described by the tour guide, even a python, seemingly emerged out of the cave wall itself for the ever brief split second he was allowed to witness it. At first he was immobilized, but then decided to turn and run. He slid his hand along the rail, heedless of the lightning and metal combination, and flew toward the cave entrance. He decided he would find the first potential path to the cave opening and run, climb, jump, and grab whatever was available to get out of there as fast as possible. If he fell, he fell. After a few more steps, and well before he reached a path, unfortunately, he fell. He'd slipped on the path right at the point where it changed from dry concrete to a wet and muddy surface on top of the walkway. Lightning struck again and his worst fears were confirmed.

A mere five feet in front of from him he saw a three-headed snake, its cavernous wings wide open, lifting its body well above Arman. Its tail was coiled on the floor as if ready to strike while its recognizable steel tip rattled in the middle. Each head was slightly different, but mostly the same. The brevity of the light mercifully prevented him from seeing all of beast's features, but its six red eyes continued to glare in the merciless darkness that followed.

Dahag!

Instead of thunder, Dahag's three-pronged voice, like the shrill of a table saw cutting through iron combined with the angry chanting of a tribe going to war, roared and shrieked just inches from Arman's face, knocking him backward onto the pavement. His chest felt like Dahag's tail had already struck, but he knew that it hadn't, and since the predator had changed directions on him, he fled back toward the cave entrance. Sliding his hand along the rail, nearly falling every twenty feet, legs flailing behind him, Arman ran with reckless abandon. Wind whipped through the tunnel with great force, further knocking him off balance. He knew the creature could reappear in front of him with ease, but it didn't matter. He fled on pure instinct until, finally, and surprisingly, he reached the entrance to The Dark Cave.

As he suspected, everyone was gone. It was still nighttime, but the rain had let up and there was enough light from the city for him to easily see where he was going. He kept running until he was well outside of the cave, collapsing on the bench he'd found the day before. His chest still heaving, one eye still fixed on the cave entrance, he slowly began to recover. The image of Dahag still burned into his mind, but he now considered another interpretation of the horrifying incident.

I'm going insane.

The more he recovered his breath, the more he believed he was just seeing things. Dahag wasn't real, of course; he was only able to torture him in his dreams. He was just under too much stress and, after all, it's not uncommon for people to see things in the dark, right? Arman looked down at his white shirt, only slightly comforted by the thought that he was crazy instead of being hunted by a snake-dragon, and saw the splatters of blood from the kavadi worshiper the day before. Since his outer layer was now both soaked and bloody, he decided he'd take his chances with his now-infamous t-shirt underneath, seeing that it was still too dirty to be easily recognized.

He walked over to the 272 steps leading to the Batu Caves, looked down, and saw that he and Lord Murugan were alone. Relieved, he began to take his first step down when he heard a voice on his right next to a few trees. It was a voice he immediately recognized, and one he hated almost as much as Dahag's.

"I didn't know you had it in you, Arman." His words were thick with arrogance, a tinge of mockery in his voice.

Stunned by his presence, all Arman could say was, "What are you doing here?!"

2 2

BLOOD OF THE MARTYRS

Dusk had fallen on Sattar Khan Avenue in western Tehran during the Ashura celebration of 2008. The mourning of the daytime had gradually given way to the nighttime celebrations which had frustrated conservative Muslims for years. Earlier in the day, the scenery prevailing in the streets consisted of black sheets of cloth covering the storefronts, black flags with religious calligraphy waving from every building, and tents erected for those properly mourning the slaughter of Imam Hossein and his seventy-two loyal companions in the seventh century - the first century on the Islamic calendar. The extreme ascetic practice of Shi'a followers cutting their heads and bodies with knives until blood ran down their head and torso, as a way of identifying with the suffering of Imam Hossein, no longer dominated the festival as in days past, though there were still a few of them on the streets that afternoon. Regardless, there was enough self-flagellation through the use of chains and other blunt objects to effectively carry on the spirit of the tradition. Carrying on the spirit of the tradition, however, was not uppermost in Arman's heart.

He sauntered down the street after a healthy meal of sheep stew and nan-e-taftun bread with a friend from school, Habib

Mahmoud. Habib was Arman's age and almost his height, though significantly skinnier, and was currently undergoing a bit of a revival and rediscovery of his Islamic roots, including a new and deep appreciation for Ashura. His parents had raised him to pray regularly, observing the five pillars as well as routine attendance to the mosque on Fridays, but it wasn't until the previous November that his worship became more intrinsic rather than just obedience to his parents.

It started with a simple observation from his father - a spontaneous lament a few months earlier while walking the last few blocks to the mosque. As they passed sign after sign pleading for passersby to enter a rather large building full of Western clothing stores, restaurants, arcades, and a movie theater, he stopped, breathed a heavy sigh, and looked at his feet.

"The malls are full. The mosques are empty."

He looked up, swallowed hard, and continued his family's mini-pilgrimage down the street. He never mentioned it again, but the comment hit his son like a sledgehammer. A mustard seed implanted in his soul, it grew from his trunk to his limbs until all he could see was the spiritual compromise of his generation. Drugs. Pornography. Prostitution. The worship of Western movie stars and musicians. As he studied the Revolution, he heard Khomeini's warnings of Western infiltration and social corruption with new ears. He studied the Christian West and saw how the places that gave birth to its greatest religious movements, such as the Protestant Reformation in Germany, were littered with prostitution and homosexual practices. He read about the private lives of self-professed Christians in Hollywood, the most prodigious exporter of immorality in the world, and vowed to do everything possible to keep this from happening to his beloved country. While many of his friends silently dismissed Ahmadinejad, Habib's appreciation for the president's efforts to renew the Government of God increased by the day.

And so it was the gentle but consistent prodding from Habib which brought Arman to observe the more sincere worship in their country's great Ashura festival. He'd noticed Arman's lack of fervor and heard rumors about his involvement in underground parties, but had a soft spot for him nevertheless, ultimately blaming it on his father. Jalal rarely brought Arman or Mahnaz to the mosque and Habib saw no real effort on his part to teach his children to follow the ways of Shi'a Islam with any sincerity. He was quickly growing to hate such compromise and, although he was fairly close to Arman, he wasn't sure how much longer he would be able to hang out with him if his life continued in the same direction.

"I think that was the best stew I've ever eaten," gushed Arman.

Habib revealed a satisfied grin. "It's my new favorite. But as much as my stomach is full, I have to say that my heart is even fuller after a day like today."

"Yeah, it's been a good day. Thanks for asking me to come." Arman was being polite. He had no problem with celebrating Ashura, but no amount of sincerity on the part of Habib could diminish his skepticism of the government, a constant awareness which threw the same cloud of skepticism over all religious gatherings. He was a Muslim in his own way. Like his parents.

"Perhaps you can join me at the mosque next Friday?"

"Sure. I think I can." His mind searched for excuses to be unveiled on another day, probably through a text message.

"Great! I'll let you know where to meet later." Habib smiled broadly as they continued down the road to rejoin his family before returning home.

Loud dance music pierced the nighttime air ahead of them. Further down the road, a large group of older teenagers exited five different cars, now parked along the side of the road, and joined the thickening crowd on the streets. The mood was jubilant, very much unlike the daytime mourning they had experienced earlier, and the sparse street lamps now revealed to Arman and Habib that the music was coming from the cars. Arman saw Habib stop and frown, gravely observing the scene. The young men were dressed in black, the appropriate color, but it was a stylish black that was obviously Western, most of them wearing long wavy hair with no beards. Worse still, Habib thought, the girls were dressed in form-fitting black dresses, wearing loud make-up, and both sexes were freely mingling in the dark corners of the street.

Arman saw Habib's indignation and tried to redirect him. "Let's just keep going. We're not far from your parents."

"They've turned the day of mourning into a street party," said Habib. He had to raise his voice to be heard over the music and laughter. Arman stared blankly, with no real idea what to say next. Habib sighed deeply and stared down the road.

"The malls are full. The mosques are empty," said Habib. Arman's heart skipped a beat, nervous about what might come next. Habib looked up to see a young man and woman in each other's arms, just behind one of the cars, partially hidden by the shade of a tree. He looked at Arman to see if he noticed it as well. He did. Anger welled deep within Habib, his eyes bulging as he was clearly considering some kind of action.

"We can't do anything about it, Habib. Let's just go, okay?"

"Are you sure about that?"

"About what?"

"That we can't do anything about it?"

"Yes! He's bigger than both of us put together and he has friends."

Habib dismissed Arman's pleas like a father ignores a child's cries to stay home from work. Someone had to be the adult here. With clenched jaws, easily visible through his adolescent beard, and his head upright, he left Arman on the sidewalk and marched straight through the sea of teenagers like he was armed with a machine gun. Except he wasn't.

Arman watched from a distance as his skinny friend tapped his index finger heavily into the back of the young male lover under the tree. Unsurprisingly, he turned around angrily and the two began having heated words, the girl's eyes wide with emotion, hand over her mouth. Arman wasn't sure what to do. At first he just stood there hoping against all hope that it would soon be over and Habib would be back, probably a little wiser. When two other boys joined the guy Habib had foolishly confronted, he knew he had to do something.

He ran over to the group and grabbed Habib by the arm, pulling him away. "I'm very sorry, guys. Come on, Habib!"

Habib jerked his arm away, briefly glaring at his friend before returning his animosity to the nighttime revelers. One of the guys, taller and more muscular than Arman, looked down on them in contempt. Staring at Arman, he blurted, "You'd better tell your friend to stay out of other people's business or he's going to get hurt one day."

"It's not just your business," replied Habib, "when you're practically making love on Sattar Khan Avenue on the evening of Ashura!"

"What are you talking about?!" the accused boy replied. "I was barely touching her!"

Arman, sensing their anger and a few more guys beginning to surround them, pulled Habib close and whispered in frustration, "Just let them choose, okay? Let's get out of here."

The words "let them choose" echoing in Habib's mind like bitter poison, he turned his gaze to Arman. "So you're with *them*? You just want to let our great Ashura festival be desecrated by these immoral Westoxified swine?"

Less than a second after the words left his mouth, a fist came from nowhere and flattened Habib, leaving him lying on the ground, blood gushing from his eye. Arman looked up to see who had hit him, but whoever did it was gone. The other guys, except for one, wore stunned expressions, overwhelmed by what just happened and suddenly beginning to wonder who Habib's father is. Or what religious leaders he knew. The bolder nighttime partyer stepped forward, clenched jaw and slight grin, and put his foot on Habib's stomach as he was still holding his head, writhing in pain. He spat on Habib's face, glared at him one last time, and slowly walked away. The others, shocked and fearing retribution, fled the scene as quickly as possible, disappearing into nearby cars like rats in a hole.

Arman knelt down next to Habib. "Are you okay?"

Habib wiped the spit off of his face and looked up at Arman. At first he was angry, but as he looked around at the empty street, his eyes opened in wonder and, amazingly, he grinned with victory instead. He pushed himself up with his left hand, the other holding onto his wound. Slowly returning to an erect position, he walked a circle around the area where partygoers had stood just moments earlier.

"You say we can't do anything." His tone was smug and condescending. "You say we have to let them choose, regardless of what they do to our faith and our country!" He was angry again.

"Look at this, Arman! Do you see anybody dancing out here?!" His nostrils flared and his eyes narrowed. "Do you see anyone profaning the name of Imam Hossein by openly cuddling a woman he's not even married to?!"

Arman wasn't afraid of the slightly shorter and much smaller Habib, but like the muscular guys who just fled the scene, he was absolutely terrified of the people Habib knew. He stood still, afraid to move, completely unknowing how to respond. Habib walked over, grabbed Arman's arm, and pulled him closer, much like Arman had done to him earlier. Mocking the previous gesture, Habib whispered with rage in the ear of Arman.

"I'll remember the face of the guy who spit on me. And I'll remember how you took his side."

"But I was just trying to save you!" Arman protested.

"What, you mean 'save me' from a little blood?" He took his right hand, soaked with blood from under his right eye, and stared at Arman. Unblinking, he took two fingers and drew four lines down his face, a nod to the more extreme Ashura celebrants earlier in the day. His face fell, as if in sorrow for what lay ahead, and his tone changed to one of resignation as he walked away.

"Perhaps a little blood is just what we need."

Jalal sat at his desk in the living room staring at a computer screen. Zia, lying on a brown couch on the other side of a lush oriental rug, was lost in a novel somewhere in the Swiss Alps. Arman sat in a chair next to her, texting a friend on his cell phone, when Mahnaz entered. She walked lightly across the rug, slowly sitting down on the end of it, allowing her to see all of her family, crossed her arms around her knees, and pulled them tightly to her chest. Her jet black hair hung across her left shoulder, slightly covering her face, which had conspicuously less eye shadow than normal. Her head tilted slightly downward as her eyes looked up at her parents, as if in submission, waiting to gain their attention.

"Are you okay?" Zia was the first to snap out of it and engage her daughter.

"Yes. I'm okay." Mahnaz grinned widely, seemingly at peace and nervous at the same time.

Jalal and Arman were now alert, no longer staring at the glow of a screen. It was obvious that Mahnaz was calling some kind of a family meeting. They were used to drama when it came to the older sibling, but this appeared altogether different. Gone was the depressed and brooding countenance they were used to lamenting whenever she created a scene, and there were none of the usual warnings of irrational anger that could explode whenever she thought a family rule was unfair. Instead, she carried herself with composure and respect.

"Mom. Dad. I wanted to start by telling you I'm sorry." Tears formed in her eyes as she continued. "I'm sorry for not listening to you. I'm sorry for being such a brat when I don't get my way." She looked directly at Zia. "I'm sorry for letting myself lose hope and not working hard; not studying hard; and acting like you've been foolish your entire life for believing things can change." A single tear ran down Zia's cheek. She sat up and leaned forward, gently placing a hand on Mahnaz's shoulder. Taking a moment to gather herself, she comforted her daughter.

"It's okay," Zia assured. "We live in difficult times. Sometimes I lose hope, too."

Jalal and Arman exchanged a quick glance, as if to ask each other what they should do. This was new territory. They unanimously decided to let things unfold between the women. Mahnaz covered her mother's hand with her own, looking at her with eyes so clear and bright that Zia felt as if she had gone back in time. She saw her five-year-old daughter jump off a swing, mid-flight with limbs extended and arms flapping.

"Mom… it's hope that I've found. The source of life. I feel like I've had a completely new start."

"Source of life?" Zia's smile was only half-formed, restrained by caution of the unknown. "I'm happy that you've found hope, sweetheart."

Unable to think of a better transition, Mahnaz launched into her story.

"You won't be surprised to know I've been depressed and angry for years. When I started going to underground parties, it was for fun." She looked away as she said this, unknowing how her parents would respond. "But eventually it was just an opportunity to numb the pain."

Jalal and Zia knew that this meant alcohol, drugs, or perhaps both. They didn't want to know what else. Voices swirled inside their heads, accusing them of being bad parents, convincing them to act with self-justified anger, and arguing for a more gracious approach all at the same time. Arman's skin felt as if were burning as he wondered how long it would take for his parents to realize that he was surely with her in some of these places.

Mahnaz continued. "A few months ago I'd completely given up. I felt ugly, stupid, and dirty. I realized most of my problems were brought on by myself and I felt horrible about how much I'd disobeyed you." She looked back up at her mother, insecure eyes pleading for understanding. She slowly rolled up the sleeves of her yellow blouse to reveal her forearm, palms upward. "I don't know why I started it. It seemed like the only thing that would stop the pain."

Jalal gaped in horror, briefly picturing his daughter's soft and perfect skin the first time he held her in the hospital. Zia burst into tears and clutched Mahnaz's arm in disbelief. Arman sat still on the couch, sad yet unmoved. He already knew. About six months ago, he'd heard her crying in the middle of the night and walked in her room to see her suddenly throw her sleeve down and hide something in her pocket. She'd reacted angrily at his intrusion, much more than her usual irritability. She barked at him with a possessed fury, causing him to practically jump out of the room, but not before he saw traces of blood.

Jalal had heard about the practice of cutting much in the same way an American may hear of a Tibetan Buddhist monk's self-immolation in the midst of a protest. Sure, the practice existed, somewhere in a far-away land called "America," but not here. Zia, on the other hand, had never even heard of such a thing and, together, she and Jalal quickly decided she was crazy. Jalal bent to the floor next to his wife and daughter and looked Mahnaz in the eye. "We're going to get you some help, okay?"

"You don't understand. I've already found help. Jesus has healed me!"

The very words Mahnaz thought would strike a chord with them, possibly eliciting anger over her conversion but at least making them take her seriously, only served to further convince them they were right and she needed a psychiatrist. She tried to tell them a story about a teacher she heard while watching satellite TV, how she contacted the people at the station for more information, and how they eventually connected her with others like her in Tehran. But her parents literally wouldn't hear it. They kept interrupting with words of "comfort," telling her she's going to be alright and that she would be able to talk to a professional soon. Mahnaz, who began the conversation with such grace and confidence, was reduced to tears and eventually became so frustrated that she left the house. Arman followed.

He caught up with her after a couple of blocks. "Mahnaz! Wait!"

She turned around and glared at him. "Did you follow me so you could tell me I'm crazy, too?"

"No." He stood there, hands in his pockets, unsure what to say next. He'd never had much success calming her down when she was angry. Fortunately, the concern and helplessness on his face communicated enough to soften her defenses. She exhaled, wiped a few tears, and walked over to give him a hug. He gently, and awkwardly, hugged her back. They never hugged at home, much less in public. She released him and pulled away slightly, leaving both hands on his shoulders, and looked at him with love.

"Arman, I want you to come with me." "Where?"

"The home of a new friend of mine. I want you to meet some of the most amazing people I've ever known."

Unlike his parents, Arman was listening when Mahnaz talked about the teacher on TV and Jesus healing her. Sure, all Iranians had great respect for Jesus. In their eyes, he was a great prophet and their poets spoke of him more than Muhammad. But Iranians didn't usually speak of Jesus healing them.

"It's a church, isn't it?" He took a step backward as if in self-protection. Mahnaz paused and closed her eyes. Arman wasn't sure if she was just searching for words or praying. As she looked back up, the brightness had returned and Arman briefly remembered how beautiful his sister was.

"I had no hope, Arman. I was horrified at what I'd become. I didn't think God could ever love me or forgive me. What I've learned has changed me forever."

"You can't go back there, Mahnaz!" Arman's timidity completely left him as he looked into her future. "Don't you know what they do to people who leave Islam?! To the infidels?! You'll be in Evin Prison! They'll torture you!" His mouth quivered and his voiced lowered. "And who knows what else they'll do to you…" He grabbed her right hand firmly. "Let's go home. Please… Let's go home and forget about ever going back to this group."

Mahnaz squeezed his hand, affirming his sincerity and love, then pulled it away. "This is who I am now. I have a new life." She looked around them, peering down the restaurant- filled street as if weighing its worth. "I'm ready to die for what I believe."

"And what about Mom and Dad?! Have you even thought about what that would do to them?!" She looked away and again closed her eyes. Arman grabbed her by the hand and jerked her forward. "Let's go, Mahnaz!"

She pulled away, eyes filled with both defiance and love. Words were no use. She gazed at him for several seconds, then turned and walked away.

∼

The next few months were difficult for the Javadi family. Mahnaz refused to see a professional counselor and had several heated arguments that shrouded family meals in an unbearable tension. Arman continued to try to persuade her to stop going to the home gatherings, though he did so privately in order to preserve their relationship. Eventually all three of them had to admit that she was a changed person and that these changes were for the better. She talked to her parents with more respect. She smiled more. She was more focused on school. It was clear that her entire outlook on life had changed, her outward beauty was finally matched by an unmistakable inward glow that seemed to reveal more of who she actually was. In fact, she was more herself than she'd ever been.

This eventual recognition paved the way for deeper conversations with her parents, who finally took her conversion seriously. They discovered how she learned about Jesus, how she got connected with a home group of Christians, and what their meetings were like. It terrified them to think about what could happen to her, but they knew they couldn't stop her from going. For their entire adult lives, one of the primary convictions they shared about religion and government was that people should be free to choose, not coerced to follow any one belief - a truth Mahnaz had gently reminded them of on more than one occasion. In the end, it would have been the height of hypocrisy for them to force Islam on their daughter.

After this period of time, they were finally supportive of her decision, at least outwardly. They said they were happy for her and tried as much as possible to actually believe it. The reality, however, was much different. Try as they might, they couldn't help themselves from feeling ashamed. It was as if Ali taunted them from the grave, telling them "I told you so" for their refusal to embrace the Revolution.

Arman observed a significant difference in how his parents thought about her, though it was more subtle than anything that was said. When he was with his parents in public or with family friends, he noticed that Zia and Jalal no longer talked about their daughter. Previously, he would hear them talk about how she was doing, the good, bad, and the ugly, but now it was as if she didn't exist. Or maybe they were so afraid someone would find out she was a Christian that they avoided talking about her altogether? He was skeptical of that last thought, but held onto it as a possibility just the same.

Mahnaz wasn't the only person in Arman's life experiencing a dramatic change. Much to Arman's horror, Habib had begun the strict training involved to become part of the Basij - the religious, or "moral," police. In addition to learning about the Qur'an, they were given guns and authority to arrest anyone they catch drinking alcohol, doing drugs, being alone with the opposite sex, or anything else they deem to be morally inappropriate. They were just as hated as they were powerful, but there was little anyone could do about it. Arman, who was bigger than the skinnier and slightly younger Habib, found it incredibly frustrating that he should have reason to fear someone who'd always been just another kid in the neighborhood.

He occasionally reflected on the similarities and differences between Mahnaz and Habib. Both of them avoided the moral vices plaguing most of the youth around them, and both were sincere followers of their respective religions. But one seemed to have joy and the other one had anger. His sister was humble, admitting her embarrassing failures of the past and honest about her present imperfections. Habib claimed a personal righteousness that gave him the right to punish transgressors like Arman. And the more he actually did this, the more he learned to love the power that came with belonging to the Basij.

Unlike Arman, who was more concerned with his own safety and general enjoyment of life, they'd both chosen a very different path. In a way, it was very similar. They both could be described as "the way of blood." One, however, was much more likely to become a martyr than the other.

2 3

ESCAPE TO A DUNGEON

The sudden rage Arman felt at the mere sound of Habib's voice joined forces with his extreme exhaustion and hunger, almost causing him to faint from dizziness. Habib, still as skinny as ever, looked down on him with a broad smile creasing his pimple-covered face, arms folded casually over his white long-sleeved shirt. It was similar to the one Arman wore earlier to fit in with the Thaipusam crowd. His beard had finally grown in a little, though it was still pocked with unsightly patches, and he had a gray backpack slung over his right shoulder.

"What am I doing here?" Habib looked back toward the city. The center of KL was perched over the right shoulder of Lord Murugan. The lights were still bright in the early dawn, and the twin towers, in spite of the thunderstorm, continued to smolder.

"I'm admiring your work." He laughed wildly, like he thought of himself as the evil villain in a superhero movie, but it came off awkwardly and only solidified Arman's determination to hit him. A past encounter with Habib flashed before him and, losing all control, he screamed and ran toward Habib, ready to tackle him and pound his fist into his face for as long as his energy would allow. Perhaps this would be the last pleasure he experienced in this life, he thought, so he was determined to make the most of it. He thought of how incredibly fortunate he was to encounter Habib alone and in a foreign country, far away from the people and structures that gave him his power. Sure, he was afraid to let Habib see him at the Marbury's house, but that was because he could inform on him back in Iran. That didn't matter anymore. In this deserted place in Malaysia, with no witnesses in sight, he was just another skinny kid.

Habib neither flinched nor lost the smirk on his face. He simply waited until Arman was about ten feet away, unfolded his arms, and pointed a pistol straight at his face, stopping Arman in his tracks. Guns were illegal in Malaysia and violators were severely punished. Arman realized it was unlikely that he acquired a gun on his own, so perhaps Habib wasn't far from his power base after all.

"I don't know what you're doing here, Habib, but I wasn't involved with the attack. I didn't even know about it!"

"Oh, trust me. I have no doubt that you didn't do it. You would never have the same courage as your cousin."

The offhand comment about Farzin stunned him. He stood there, speechless, head spinning. Habib smiled arrogantly, enjoying the moment.

"What? Are you surprised to find out Farzin and I were on the same team?"

Arman tried to come up with some kind of an argument against it, but he had none. Farzin obviously had joined a group of radicals, so anything was possible now and he knew he couldn't win the argument, so he changed the subject.

"Why are you here?"

"That's the obvious question, isn't it?" He used normal hand gestures as if he wasn't carrying a gun. "Well, I hate to admit it, but I'm not the man in charge of my operation."

"What operation?"

Habib ignored the question. "Farzin somehow convinced them that you were in on it, but, for some random reason unexplained to me, you would need to stay alive. I tried to convince them you were way too much of a coward to put your life at risk in the slightest, especially for something bigger than yourself, but they didn't listen to me. They listened to your dead cousin instead."

Arman was infuriated. He inched closer, waiting for the slightest lack of concentration; a turned head, closed eyes, belly laugh… anything. He was ready for the risk.

"So I'm here, believe it or not, because they want to protect you and take you safely back to Iran." Habib paused and gently shook his head in bewilderment, a slight look of defeat in his eyes. "I'm here… to take you to a group of people who are ready to welcome you as a hero."

Arman cursed and spat on the rocky ground. "Do you really think I'm going to believe you?! You think I'm just going to willingly walk down these stairs and go off to God knows where? With you, of all people?!"

"Yes, I do," said Habib unflinchingly. "One. Because I have a gun. Two. Because if you don't, you'll be in jail within hours. It's not just your association with Farzin and Banu, by the way. The unfortunate clip of you letting go of a baby stroller to save your own life is the most popular video on the planet right now. YouTube, Twitter, Facebook… man, you're quite the rock star!" Habib fixed his eyes on him with a smirk to see if he was getting the desired reaction. He was, so he continued to taunt. "I'm sure your parents are proud, right?" He unleashed his horrendous laugh again, but kept his eyes straight ahead. Arman looked down, too ashamed to even show Habib how much he hated him. His mind reeled as he considered the implications. Even if he escaped, where could he go now? How could he ever have his old life back? Would all of his friends and family shun him?

"So unless you want to starve yourself to death in a cave first," he motioned toward the city with his gun, "You really don't have any choice. Look closely, Arman. Do you see anything interesting?" At first, Arman only noticed the dim light of buildings in the early dawn light, but the longer he stared, he began to discern police lights faintly dancing off of tall buildings in various parts of downtown KL. They were everywhere. How did he miss it earlier?

"Police. CIA. Malaysia's army…. They're all looking for you

and they'll find you quickly. You and I both know you'll be guilty by association. They won't believe you. As a matter of fact, I'm actually the one person on this entire planet who actually does believe you!" He launched into his annoying laugh again, this time almost closing his eyes long enough to allow Arman a chance to attack.

"Hey, I realize this is a lot to take in, so I'm going to give you one minute to think it through and make the smart choice. I've got to take you in either way and, as much as I'd love to shoot both of your legs, I don't really feel like dragging you all the way down these stairs." Habib stood there, silent and smirking, amused as he waited for his childhood friend's next move.

Excruciating. Soul-tormenting. Of his three scars, his chest hurt the worst as he remembered how he acquired them; and how Habib was there, mocking his anguish. He despised the Basij, what they routinely did to the citizens of Iran, and what they did to young men like Habib. Now he was apparently involved in something on a much larger scale than the local religious police and actually knew about the Petronas Towers attack before it happened. He still didn't know why they bombed the KLCC. Perhaps they were too Western for a Muslim country? Either way, he'd probably never know. Arman loathed him for it and, somehow, even his hatred for the hardliners in his home country found room for growth in this horrible moment of decision.

The question before him, however, was becoming clearer by the second. *Do I want to go to jail and then be executed for something I didn't do?* Sure, he knew Habib could be lying, but Arman believed the chances Habib was telling the truth were greater than his chances of being found innocent in a court of law in Malaysia. He knew what he had to do in order to live, but the very thought of it made him queasy. Up until this point, he could honestly tell people that, not only was he not a terrorist, but he'd never had a single interaction with a terrorist group. If he went with Habib, he would be officially joining them.

On the surface, it seemed the he may not have a choice at all since Habib was holding a gun. One of the options running around in Arman's mind, however, was to pretend to go along willingly, but look for every opportunity along the way to either attack or escape. The longer he thought about it, the less this seemed like a real option. The fact of the matter is that he'd been running for less than a day so far and, regardless how much he racked his brain trying to come up with a plan, he had none and he knew it. What tragic irony that his only salvation seemed to be joining the very people he believed were destroying his country. But in the end, at least they were Iranian. Perhaps that would be enough motivation for them to smuggle Arman back home, where he would be more likely to get a fair trial. Or even better, a biased one.

His hatred for Habib still simmering, he could neither look him in the face nor speak to tell him he was coming willingly, so he just turned around and walked toward the stairs.

"That's the first smart thing you've done in your meaningless life." Habib was hoping for a reaction, but received none. "We don't have a long walk ahead of us, but you might want to put this on." He reached into his backpack and pulled out a cream-colored silk shirt similar to his own and the one Arman had purchased the day before. He quickly put it on, understanding the need to fit in as much as possible.

Arman had no plans to pretend they were on the same side and the last thing he wanted was a friendly conversation. Before they started down the steps, however, he had to ask a couple of questions.

"Why did you and your group - whoever you are - bomb the towers?"

Habib offered a condescending smile, but no response. Arman hesitated to ask another question, but the second one was burning.

"When did Farzin turn?"

"Turn?" Again, the annoying cackle. "You're such an idiot, Arman." He looked at him with smug disbelief, paused, and delivered the blow.

"He was always with us."

∼

They made their way down the stairs and out of the main gate to find an Indian taxi driver waiting on him outside of his cab. No one exchanged words. The driver gave Habib a knowing look, an abbreviated head bob, and got into the driver's seat. Arman and Habib climbed into a back seat with tinted windows, tilting their heads downward.

Habib didn't give him an address or a single direction, yet another sign this was well-planned. The only sound inside the car was a faint squeak coming from the driver's Lord Ganesha idol on the dashboard. Its head was set on a barely visible spring like a bobble head doll, something Arman would've found amusing under different circumstances, and creaked every time they hit a pothole or quickly turned a corner. Twice while driving through downtown, they drove past a set of police cars, lights flashing, but the officers were standing outside their vehicles, concentrating intently on the unfortunate pedestrians who happened to be available for interrogations. Arman clutched his chest each time he saw blue lights. When it was all over, he would wonder if he took as many as four breaths during the entire twenty minute journey.

Finally they turned into a side road in the middle of the city that would have felt like they were in a completely different town if it weren't so close to the KL Tower. Not to be confused with the Petronas Towers, the KL Tower wasn't quite as tall as the twins had been, but its placement on a hill had made it the highest building in the city nonetheless. Similar to Seattle's space needle, tourists could ride up an elevator to the top for a breathtaking view of the city. Those willing to spend more money had the option of eating dinner in a restaurant that slowly and continuously spun in a complete circle.

The immediate view in front of them included a two-story shop lot on the left with an Old Malaya restaurant resting under beautiful black awnings, designed to give its customers both shade and protection from the oppressive Malaysian sun. Banana-leafed plants lined the side of the road in front of the restaurant and all of the other shops as well. On their right were various species of trees, both short and tall, standing in between them and another shop lot.

Directly in front, at the end of the short road, was a small building, next to a closed gate, leading into an area that Arman could only describe as a forest. Of course, that didn't seem possible since they were in the middle of the city, so his mind searched for other ways to understand what he saw.

It was the KL Forest Eco Park, in fact. Although it was technically a tourist destination connected with the KL Tower, it wasn't very well-known or highly promoted within the city, so he'd never heard of it. It was a lush rain forest in the middle of a large and congested city, providing visitors with brief escapes from their concrete landscape, if not the heat.

The gate opened sideways, automatically closing behind them after they entered, and they drove up a narrow pothole-filled road until they reached a small building that looked like a maintenance shed. The larger part of it was under a roof without walls, but there was a garage large enough for two cars attached. After they pulled in, the driver quickly exited the car, walked just outside, and closed the windowless garage door. Arman saw him briskly walking away through the window of a smaller door on the side of the building.

"It's time to do a little hiking, Arman." Habib motioned with his gun for Arman to exit on his side, so he slid out, following a series of wordless orders. They walked out of the side door of the garage and into a world covered in deep dark green. The morning sun was out now, but the trees were so tall and the forest so lush that it felt like their eyes were attempting to collect light from the bottom of the ocean. Arman could see open trails about thirty feet away, but they were avoiding the clearings, trying to make as little noise as possible as they brushed past enormous banana leaves blocking their way. Looking up, he noticed wooden walkways suspended about fifty feet above. The bridges wound around the park and were connected by tall structures with spiraling staircases and red canopies, beautifully woven into the environment. As inviting as they were, he knew they weren't going anywhere near them.

They crept past a collection of rain trees and it reminded him of the dream when he took a bad shortcut and ran into Dahag, causing him to carefully avoid touching the low-lying branches regardless of the available light. Spiderwebs were visible in just about every direction, some inhabited by wolf spiders the size of his hands. Various species of birds sang cheerfully near the top of the trees, but by the time it was filtered through the thick brush it sounded almost like a funeral dirge.

Habib spotted an older Chinese couple on the walking path about fifty feet away from them. He motioned for Arman to sit next to him behind some brush, covered by banana leaves, until they passed. Exhausted and hazy, Arman stared at the forest floor as they waited for the couple to pass. In between the leaves where they sat were patches of dirt and a collection of shy plants, whose leaves looked like tiny ferns. He stared at them until he became mesmerized, eventually feeling compelled to touch one. He reached out with his right index finger and then pulled it back reflexively, shocked to see that it closed at his touch. Again amazed to see it open back up, he touched it again, then again as he allowed himself to feel a faint sense of delight at the goodness of the created world. Eventually, however, he saw himself in the center of the plant, the world closing in on him by some unseen touch above.

The intruders were now at a safe distance away and Habib motioned to follow him. Soon he walked into a patch of brush and banana leaves that no one would intentionally enter unless they knew something was there. By the time Arman moved branches and leaves out of his way to join him, he saw Habib lift up a door, completely covered in moss, with a handle that looked like a tree root. He could've searched the area for months by himself and wouldn't have had a chance.

It was a small round opening with a ladder leading straight down into a deep and dark emptiness. Habib looked intently at Arman, making it clear he was to go first. He took a deep breath, glanced upward one last time, and began a climb into the darkness that reminded him way too much of the cave he just escaped. Habib followed, closing the door with a click that sounded like it was now locked from the inside. Arman continued to climb down, hoping against hope he was doing the right thing, but knowing full well it would most likely all go wrong, and very soon.

Habib turned on a flashlight, much to Arman's relief, and he could now see a floor thirty feet below. Light and shadows bounced around the narrow stairwell as the flashlight swung from Habib's wrist. His rings, large and gaudy, occasionally met the iron ladder directly, echoing up and down the opening. Arman's heart beat wildly and he was beginning to have trouble holding onto the ladder as the rungs seemed to pull away from his sweaty palms, but soon his feet touched solid ground.

He turned around to see a wide, but poorly constructed tunnel approximately four feet wide and five feet tall. Habib reached the floor behind him, pouring light into the new opening with his flashlight, but failed to make it more attractive. Arman bent over and began walking through the hastily carved-out hollow of earth, without a single block of cement to secure its opening. They continued the walk for about three minutes until, at last, they reached a steel door matching the height of the tunnel. It was clean and appeared well- constructed, perhaps a good sign for what lay ahead. Habib pushed himself in front of Arman, pulled out a key, plunged it into the latch, quickly opened the door, and, unlike Arman, wasn't surprised to see there was another door, this one possessing a long lever attached at its center. Habib pulled out another key, turned the latch, and proceeded to pull down counterclockwise on the lever with all his might. It moved downward slowly, eventually ending its course with a loud click that startled Arman as the door swung open. He drew his hands in front of his face as the sudden brightness of the room nearly blinded him, then Habib climbed through the door and jumped about five feet down into the fluorescent-filled room. Arman could only see Habib and an empty space from where he was standing.

"Come down, Arman."

Not seeing the point of checking things out first, he jumped through the opening, slipping and falling as he hit, and was fortunate to catch himself with his hands. He grabbed the scar on his ankle and held it for a few seconds, intentionally delaying getting up and moving forward, then he saw something out of the corner of his left eye. He looked up to see nine young men, most of them much larger than Habib, AK-47s strapped over their shoulders. All of them looked Iranian and wore various lengths of beards, a fairly plain assortments of jeans and t-shirts, name brand sneakers, and most of them were smoking. Arman was relieved to see that most of them also wore relaxed smiles.

The room was wide and round with weapons of various kinds hanging on the walls. Pistols, rifles, knives, and were those bombs of some kind? Long fluorescent lights hung from the ceiling and would've been bright enough to make it feel like daylight if it weren't for the dark-colored ceiling. Across from the circular room where they entered was a long straight hallway which seemed to get darker the further back it went.

One of the men, about six feet tall with wide shoulders and muscular arms protruding from his tight black shirt, stepped forward and looked directly at Arman. His hair was as light as was his skin, though it was curly and disheveled. He pulled a cigar out of his mouth, smiled at Arman, then addressed Habib.

"Not bad, Habib. I admit it. I didn't think you'd find this coward." His face curled into a snarl and Arman lost what little hope he had taken with him into this underground tomb. "Throw him in the cell until I figure out what I want to do with him."

"You said I'd get to kill him right here in front of everyone! I'm the one who convinced you Farzin was lying to protect him! That he'd never join the attack! Imagine the information about Farzin and Banu they could've pumped out of him!" Habib's angry protest unwittingly pulled him within about a foot in front of the big guy, who was apparently in charge. He grabbed Habib by the face and threw him to the floor with one arm.

"You're lucky to even be with this team! Get in my face again and I'll slit your throat and we'll watch you bleed while we smoke cigars!"

That was the last thing Arman remembered about his encounter with the team of terrorists that morning. He was vaguely aware that some of the guys were laughing and that Habib was angry, but his world became strangely silent, and he didn't really hear anything. His body went limp, head whipping to the floor, and soon he was staring at cracks in a makeshift ceiling passing above as someone dragged him down the dark hallway by his hair. He knew the guy pulling him by the head was also mocking him, but he only saw the his lips moving, occasionally forming a smirk while he looked down on his victim's pathetic state. The only thing Arman heard with clarity was a cell door slamming shut. It briefly jarred him out of his haze, cementing in his mind that yet another worst nightmare had come true, then he passed out where he lay.

24

FIRE AND SHAME

Arman was doing a good job of playing it cool, but inside he was exploding as he walked through Pardisan Park, in northwestern Tehran, with his new friend, Reza Kazemi. It was Chaharshanbeh Suri, his favorite night of the year, and in every direction either the sky was either lit up by multi-colored fireworks or the ground was glowing with bonfires.

Walking west through the park, he smiled as they came across a group of families with a string of campfires small enough for the children. Small enough for the children to safely jump over, that is, since jumping over fire is the primary ritual for this celebration. There was just enough light to see the satisfaction on the faces of parents as silhouettes of their children, around three feet tall, successfully cleared fires comprised of only tiny branches and a small piece of wood. Each jump began with a mother holding her breath, a father urging his child onward, and the entire group of children squealing with joy at every leap of faith. His attention fixated on a little girl, dark hair with pigtails, who was standing five feet from the little fire trying to work up her courage, smoke pouring from her mouth and nostrils in the cold air. Finally, she launched into the traditional song, sung by Persians for centuries in the days

197

preceding their new year celebration, as they hurled themselves over the fire.

> "Oh Chaharshenbeh Suri, Give me your healthy
> glow. Take my sickly pallor."

Adults and children joined her for the last line as she leaped into the air and cleared the fire. As she landed, she tripped over a loose stone, light brown hair suddenly flying upward, and fell on her face. Her parents rushed to her, each simultaneously pulling her up by an arm, only to find her laughing.

Arman watched all of this with delight, but sensing that Reza was watching, he dropped the smile and tried to pretend he was only vaguely aware of this lame imitation of fire jumping. Greater things awaited and Arman didn't want to make a bad impression on his new friend. Even more than that, he wanted to avoid making a bad first impression on Reza's friends, who had reluctantly agreed to let Arman join the biggest party of the night for anyone associated with their secondary school.

Occasional explosions reminded Reza and Arman of what awaited. Hearing a flurry of blasts behind them, they turned around to see a sky of green, like thousands of light bulbs bursting over Milad Tower, which overlooked the park from the east. Reza's eyes widened, granting Arman permission to act impressed as well. As soon as he turned around to continue along their path, however, there was an explosion so loud and piercing the ground shook and they both jumped like frightened children, briefly stopping in their tracks. Gathering themselves, they both laughed and quickened their pace. Not away from the ear- piercing commotion, but toward it. They were close!

~

Chaharshanbeh Suri, or "Red Wednesday," is celebrated every year on the last Wednesday on the Iranian calendar. The main festivities are actually observed on the night before — "Wednesday Eve." The history of the celebration traces its roots for over 2500 years and was practiced by both King Cyrus and King Darius 1.

Predating the arrival of Islam by over a thousand years, its roots are firmly in the Zoroastrian religion as a celebration of the coming of Spring. The short poem, sung while performing the purification ritual of jumping over fire, expresses their desire for everything negative about the previous year - the worry, pain, sickness, and unhappiness - to be burned away in exchange for a new beginning. Many in antiquity also believed the spirits of their ancestors would visit during these last days of the year.

An ancient practice of Chaharshenbeh Suri, still observed by some, is called "Qaashaq Zani," or "spoon hitting." Children dressed up in clothes covering their entire body, sometimes using a chador, walked through nearby neighborhoods clanging spoons inside large bowls. They knocked on doors and waited for adults to answer and see their ghostlike bodies holding the dishes they hoped would soon be filled with treats. A bowl full of treats is a good omen - an empty bowl a curse. Whatever the roots of the practice, modern day Iranians practice it mainly for fun, ignoring certain aspects of its history much like westerners ignore the roots of Halloween.

Unsurprisingly, the leaders of the revolution and those currently in charge of God's Government didn't feel the same way. During the early years of the Revolution, they tried to eradicate the pre-Islamic tradition by force, leading many to find ways to enjoy it in private, and still others to practice it open defiance. Ultimately, the festival proved too popular to eradicate, eventually turning into an opportunity for youthful rebellion. Unsatisfied with merely jumping over fire while shooting off fireworks, they began throwing fireworks into the fire itself, creating delightful explosions which introduced the added element of danger. In the 2000s, they began making homemade firecrackers and then progressed to homemade "narenjaks," or "sound bombs," that can shake entire neighborhoods awake. Eventually a black market emerged, fueled by the internet, which allowed young people to acquire the goods to make the gravel-packed explosives. In response, the presence of

Revolutionary Guard and Basij forces multiplied along with the arrests of the more egregious offenders.

〜

"Remember," Reza reminded Arman, "this is my first time to be here as well. I only know a few of them and I've known them for less than six months."

"Okay, okay. You told me already. I'm going to be fine, alright?"

Reza stopped walking, exhaled, and briefly glanced up before looking intently at Arman. "Just do whatever everyone else is doing and don't embarrass me." Arman refused to respond and dismissed the warning altogether, feigning indignation and taking the lead toward the street party, like ancient nobility charging to battle.

The visibility of smoke, the smell of gunpowder, and the sounds of competing dance music, occasionally interrupted by thunderous explosions, led Arman and Reza to their destination with ease. Just a few blocks from Pardisan Park, the neighborhood he entered was a combination of three-story town houses and two-story stand-alone houses with small front yards. As soon as they turned the corner, the first thing they saw were three girls, bright lipstick and no hijabs, twirling ropes with thick sparklers tied at the ends through the air like cowgirls. Each spin left streaks of light in their wake, creating surreal mirages of stationary orange circles. Arman found himself quickly mesmerized, but it was probably less from the circles of fire and more because of the unique opportunity to meet girls. His eyes quickly fixated on one of them, dark curly hair and a bright smile, whose glowing circles looked to him like tangerine halos as they created just enough light for Arman to know she was attractive.

Bonfires were scattered throughout the edges of the street on either side. Like orange ghosts hovering over the asphalt, they danced in all directions, daring young men and women to pass through. Small groups mixed with guys and girls surrounded each fire, most of them dancing to both Iranian and western tunes blaring out of the nearest car. As Reza and Arman passed a blue sedan, a young man in a white long-sleeved shirt and black dress shoes rocketed through the flames of a tall fire, one that seemed too large, and crashed into Reza, sending both of them to the hard ground.

"Dariush!" shouted Reza, as he jumped to his feet, brushing himself off. As they hugged, Arman was greatly relieved they knew each other and, after a few words of greeting, Reza turned to make brief introductions.

"Dariush, this is my friend, Arman."

"Hey, nice to meet you," he replied, barely looking him. "Come inside! He spoke to Reza only. "I want to introduce you to my friends!"

Arman wobbled behind them as the third wheel he knew he was as they entered a home filled with smoke, alcohol, loud music, and a lot of young people committing khalwat - close proximity between males and females. He and Reza spent the first ten minutes being introduced to a wide variety of Dariush's friends, engaging in surface conversation while shouting over the dance tunes. But before long, Dariush and Reza escaped into another room, leaving Arman behind. His self-consciousness multiplied and his smooth face feeling a slight burn from the embarrassment of being alone in a crowd.

As he slowly walked in the direction of the door, he was pretty sure he noticed a few people taking drugs. *Probably ecstasy*, he thought. He was aware of the trend among certain circles inside Iran, but he hadn't been directly exposed until now. He remembered what Reza said about going along with what others were doing and regretted agreeing to such a thoughtless idea. As he was nearing the door, one of the girls he'd been introduced to, light hair and clear dark eyes, handed him a glass of homemade wine that seemed to be the drink of the evening. In terms of prohibited activities, he was more than happy to choose the more familiar one. The lesser of two evils. Much to his surprise, he wound up talking this beauty and hanging out with her for the most of the next hour.

After about fifteen minutes, he realized that he'd missed her name when they were originally introduced and it already felt too awkward for him to ask her again. While his mouth formed meaningless words and phrases, his mind swirled with ideas about how he could find out her name either without her knowing or in a way that seemed more natural than asking directly. The more he talked, the more he liked her. The more he liked her, the more he panicked.

They wandered outside to watch people jumping over, and sometimes through, the large bonfires on the street and to see everyone's reaction to the latest explosion of firecrackers and sound bombs. All the way down the roadway they saw dark silhouettes bursting through large flames, always followed by shouting and laughter. The shimmering fire shone in her straight and shiny hair, framing her face in a warmth like candlelight. He noticed that the normal fireworks, bottle rockets and firecrackers, made her countenance light up proportionally to their explosions. The louder ones did the same, but only after initially reacting like she'd seen a ghost. The cycle of fright and joy never got old as Arman and the nameless girl continued to journey in and out of the house for refills.

Soon it was clear that, although everyone was enjoying the homemade grenades thrown into the fire, what was really happening under the surface, at least for the guys, was nothing more than a competition for the loudest explosion. The guys held their narenjaks in their hands like a batter on deck, waiting for the perfect moment to step up to the plate.

One by one they seized the moment of glory, walking up to the fire, looking at the surrounding groups of people to make sure they were watching, then hurling their raucous creations into the flames. Their bombs would detonate, shaking the ground, and the ensuing cheers were generally equal to the blast. It was survival of the fittest at its finest and Arman was losing his inhibitions by the second. He yelled wildly after each explosion and, eventually, followed up his shouts with spontaneous dances of joy, most of which were joined by the girl in the bright red shirt and blue jeans.

Basij forces, the secret police, slowly emerged at the end of the street. They were dressed casually in order to fit in with the crowds, but at the moment they had chosen to wear AK-47s strapped to their shoulders, strutting down the street in an intimidating show of force and signaling to apostates that their reckoning had come.

Neither Arman nor the anonymous girl had any clue what was happening. In their drunken state, they didn't differentiate the quick and panicked movements of those around them from the dancing and jumping through fire taking place over the course of the entire evening. Backs turned to the gunmen, the sudden rush of movement around them just made them throw themselves into the blaring music all the more, thrusting their hands into the air and their hips in every direction possible. Meanwhile, guys scattered like roaches into nearby houses and alleyways, quickly followed by girls who had the double duty of flinging on hijabs and peeling off make-up while simultaneously fleeing the authorities.

Shouts came from the shadows of the rooftops. Arman looked up to see the faint outline of two young men yelling and pointing at the street. Oblivious to their warnings, he basked in the attention and was merely encouraged to refocus his energy into his dancing, even adding a song into his routine. Hands and feet flailed wildly and off beat, like someone trying to swat bees with a mop. The guys on the roof would've had to look away even if Arman wasn't in mortal danger. But he was. And now he was completely alone except for the ten young men with rifles approximately fifteen feet behind him. He would never know where the unnamed girl went.

Even if he hadn't been drunk it would've been somewhat understandable if he hadn't realized everyone else from the party was gone. On his right there was a car, still pumping out deafening music, on the side of the road. Directly in front of him and slightly to his left, the largest fire on the block covered over half the road and was high enough to make it difficult to see anything beyond it. His vision wasn't just impaired; it was limited. Limited, that is, until a vigorous hip thrust, as violent as it was awkward, caused him to do a 180, providing him with a view of the other side of the block. And angry young men loaded with beards and guns. There were less than ten of them, but there may as well have been fifty. His eyes craned open as the rest of him stiffened.

"No, don't stop for us. We were enjoying it," one of them taunted, followed by mocking laughter from the others.

"That was impressive!" added another. "I don't think this

country's seen dancing like that since before the Revolution. Who are you, John Travolta?" The others cackled, though most of them honestly didn't know who that was.

They continued with their lame insults, inching closer forward while Arman inched backward, trying not to faint. His heart sputtered, sweat dripped from his chin onto his tight black shirt, already soaked, and his hands shook with terror. There was no one to help him, no one to provide a distraction, and nowhere to run. Or was there? He glanced behind him and realized he was only about five feet from the fire. In the middle of it, he recalled, there was significantly less wood even though the flames from each side made it appear to be one large pile. Perhaps he could make it through and lose them in the chaos. It was his only chance.

Feeling a bit more sober, but not sober enough, he whipped around, took three quick steps, and launched himself over the lowest part of the fire. As his left foot rose over the jumble of wood, a nail sticking out of a two by four snagged the bottom of his jeans, pulling him back down just as he'd started to rise. He faced downward as he was yanked helplessly into the flames, shrieking as if descending into Hell itself.

He was right about there being less wood in the center, but while this helped him to survive the experience, he still landed on a flat, wide, and blazing piece of wood which quickly seared a hole through his shirt. He could smell his flesh burn as he instinctively rolled out of the flames. He kept rolling until he knew his shirt was no longer on fire, then stayed on the ground in a fetal position holding both hands to a horrific chest wound, howling and crying at the same time. He was in this position for about five seconds before he realized the nail from the two by four that tripped him up was stuck in his jeans and the piece of wood still attached, still on fire, was now burning his left ankle. He renewed his screams and shook his left leg violently in an attempt to quickly rid himself of the fire brander. To the Basij soldiers, it looked like a snake crawled up his pants, so they laughed all the more, callous to Arman's suffering.

He sat up to reach for the embers embedded into his ankle. Every inch of movement multiplied his pain, but he reached for it anyway. Multiple attempts ended in failure as his body instinctively prevented him from stretching the burn wound on his chest. Finally, he felt the flaming barnacle wrenched from him, the nail tearing open his blue jeans and scraping his leg. He collapsed on his back, gasping for air, again clutching his chest.

"Hello, Arman."

He knew the voice. He stopped breathing and closed his eyes. *It can't be. It can't be.*

A sharp-toed dress shoe cut into his side, jarring his eyes open. Standing over him, condescending smile and victory stretched across his countenance, was Habib. The neighborhood boy he grew up playing football with. The boy who had been in his house only a couple of years before. A guy whose parents Arman knew well. Obviously, none of these things mattered to Habib. Arman thought he was carrying a stick, but when he raised it up, he saw the end of a two by four on fire and Habib's eyes wide with delight. In one cruel motion, he slammed the torch into the right side of Arman's face.

He woke up somewhere in Pardisan Park as homemade wine splashed onto his chest. The alcohol exacerbated the pain, though it may have slightly helped in the long run. Regardless, this was not being done for medicinal purposes.

"Wake up, you swine!" A tall man in his thirties stared through Arman's cracked eyelids into his bloodshot eyes. There were only three of them now, Habib standing on the man's right. The other one was short, very stocky, thick beard, and a dull look in his eyes. As Arman slowly gained consciousness, he realized that he was handcuffed and laying on his left side. He was also immediately reminded of his excruciating pain.

"This is where we get to have a little fun, Arman." The other two cackled, but Habib seemed to be fawning more than laughing. He followed the lead of the tall guy and threw another glass of wine on Arman. They had confiscated quite a bit that night by the looks of the boxes behind them. They all howled again, Habib obviously enjoying the fact that he'd pleased the others. To continue impressing them, he reached into their contraband and pulled out a handful of firecrackers. Arman, eyes closed and teeth clenched, didn't see what was happening. The others saw Habib's grin and tried, unsuccessfully, to stifle their laughter. Habib lit the firecrackers and tossed them at Arman, hitting him in the stomach and landing on the ground only a few inches from his knees. They exploded just as Arman rolled away, saving some pain but providing a great show for his tormentors. They fell to the ground, practically in tears. When they were finally able to stand again, the short guy went into the boxes looking for more ideas and eventually pulled out a pack of roman candles. Habib and the taller one immediately lit up and ran over, beginning a playful fight for them. They began a race to see who would be the first to successfully unwrap one of them, light it, and shoot it at Arman. The tall guy was the first to get off a shot. He shouted in delight, revealing the crooked teeth underneath his scraggly beard.

Arman curled into a ball and faced away from them, occasionally feeling a quick burn through his white shirt, each followed by celebratory laughter. He was now fully sober and alert. He was also furious, terrified, and felt a burning sense of shame over his complete helplessness.

"Hey, I've got an idea!" Habib sounded very proud of himself. "Let's see who can hit him from the furthest distance."

"Oh, that's genius!" replied the tall one. This clearly pleased Habib, who took about ten steps back to take the first shot from a greater distance. After three tries, he hit Arman in the foot, prompting cheers and high fives, followed by the stocky one walking back ten more steps to try to set a new record. After five shots, a purple ball of flame slammed into the back of Arman's head, catching his hair on fire. It wasn't the heat that caused him to realize his head was ablaze. It was the smell of singed hair. He rolled his head around on the grass and put it out before any damage was done to his skin, but not before quickly becoming the highlight of the evening for the Basij.

After they had calmed themselves enough to talk, the tall one walked over to one of the boxes and pulled out a large jar of homemade wine. "I think it's time to celebrate, gentlemen!" The short one wholeheartedly agreed and reached for one of his own. They popped the corks, touched the jars together in a playful toast, took large gulps that were way too fast, then spewed half of it out. They slapped each other on the back and held onto each others' shoulders as if to steady themselves, then turned the bottle upward again.

Habib stood motionless, slack jawed at the clear violation of the laws of Allah.

"That is haram." His voice stammered as he found himself suddenly wedged between God and man. "That's why we joined the Basij. To make sure everyone honors the ways of Allah."

The tall one narrowed his eyes, briefly leering at Habib. The other one rolled his eyes instead, smiled, held his drink up toward Habib, and took another long swig as if in mock honor of the young and naive soldier.

"You see," explained the older one, "we will one day be martyrs. That is how we are fulfilling our duty to him. And when we die in the midst of jihad, we will immediately arrive in Paradise with perpetual virgins for an eternity of pleasure." He wiped alcohol off of his beard with his forearm. "In the meantime, we can indulge in a little pleasure-seeking if we want to!"

Arman turned around to see how Habib would handle this. Even in the midst of blinding pain, he managed to find a spark of happiness in watching Habib's world backfire. He also enjoyed the attention being taken away from him, at least for the moment. The tall and disheveled man walked over to Habib, put his arm on his shoulder, and held up his jar of wine.

"Don't worry, Habib," his voice was now cheerful but patronizing, "for people like us, it's okay."

The short guy started laughing. "Bottom's up!"

Habib refused to defile himself. Looking for a way to remain faithful to his vows and stay out of trouble with his superior, he walked away from him and to Arman.

"Get up, Arman. It's time to take you in."

Arman tried to stand, but since his hands were handcuffed behind him, he was like a roach on its back, moaning in agony with each effort to raise himself. Finally, Habib grabbed him by the shoulder and pulled him up, but he did so more gently than expected.

"The car's that way," said Habib, pointing forward with his rifle. They walked down a sidewalk and were soon hidden from the Basij revelers by a grove of palm trees, the top of their leaves glowing with city lights and fireworks. As they approached the car, an old white four-door sedan, Arman walked to the back door.

"Not there." Habib opened the trunk and motioned for Arman to lower himself in.

"So is this the grand plan?" Arman looked at Habib with disgust. "Is this how you're making a difference for Allah?"

To Arman's surprise, he didn't get punched. Or even shoved inside the car. Instead, as he lowered himself in the trunk, Habib never even looked back at him. He didn't even argue. As Arman looked out of the closing trunk, he caught one last glimpse of Habib from the side. *Was that remorse?*

Lines crept across Zia's face in the early morning light. Some of them were earned with age, merely serving to delicately frame the face that still attracted the attention of her husband. Others had emerged overnight as stress gouged crevices across her forehead. The police called at 1 a.m. to let her know her son was in jail and would need to be bailed out in the morning. The officer who called showed little emotion and even less empathy as he explained the situation. In a matter-of-fact tone, he spoke of Arman as if he was evil and made sure he indicted their parenting as well. She would later remember that the word "infidel" was used.

She woke up Jalal in a frenzy, the first time in their marriage he saw her in such a state. After the initial shock, they began planning for the court hearing. They discussed how much money they had in savings, but knew it wouldn't be enough. The economy had been hit so hard with sanctions that very few people would have the kind of cash on hand that would surely be demanded. They gathered documents - car titles, house mortgage, and retirement funds - and prayed they wouldn't have to use them all.

It was unusually warm on this Spring morning, but they were covered from head to toe. Zia still hated the chador and hijab and remained resentful of the Revolution's infringement on women, but today she was more than happy to cover as much of her body as possible, especially her face. Jalal wore a long overcoat with a wide collar pulled up as far as possible. It was common knowledge that the moral court was located on this part of Vozara Street. It was also common knowledge that it was inundated with rebellious youth the morning following Chaharshanbeh Suri and that their parents would be lining the street, waiting to be brought in for the shame-fest they called a court hearing. For busy-bodies, it was like Christmas morning. Traffic increased, both cars and pedestrians, as people chose the scenic route in hopes they would recognize someone and have a story to tell at work. Zia had already seen at least three people she knew, one of them a teacher at her school, but was fairly certain she didn't notice her. She was less certain her co-worker didn't notice Jalal.

For his part, Jalal had seen more people he knew than he could count, including a fellow journalist who hated him fiercely. At first he told himself that he hadn't been seen, but eventually he admitted this wasn't true. It was only a matter of time before he and his family would be trashed through email, blogs, and even in the local news. The cost in shame would surely surpass the financial difficulties. In addition to all of the other stresses pressing in on him, there was one thought that was always present. Another voice in his head that wouldn't be quieted, regardless of his efforts to concentrate on what lay ahead. It was Ali, half angry and half laughing. He could picture his late brother-in-law with folded arms and a smirk on his face, mystified by Jalal's obstinance in the face of Allah, frustrated that his sister married such a weak man who refused to teach his son to walk in the glorious ways of the

Revolution. "Of course Arman was drunk," he would say. And there were those three words he could hear coming from Ali's lips as if they echoed from the loudspeaker of the nearby mosque. "I told you so!"

The official name for the street where they were waiting was Khaled Eslamboli, after the Islamic radical who assassinated Egyptian President Anwar Sadat, who was now seen as a friend of Israel, in 1981. The name change was part of the government's efforts to remind people of the values of the Revolution. They changed names of other streets as well, but this particular revision never caught on with the people. Instead, they continued to call it Vozara and at this time it wasn't just a place for the moral court. Sure, today there would be young people convicted of such crimes as wearing make-up, taking off their hijab, drinking alcohol, and being in close proximity with someone of the opposite sex. But tonight, outside the courthouse, there would be hordes of young people enjoying themselves at restaurants, sitting down over cappuccinos, and finding the shadiest corners of Saei Park to snuggle with their special someone.

The door to the courthouse swung open, followed by a man in an olive-colored uniform and an impossibly thick beard complemented by a five-day stubble both above and below it. The soldier threw his cigarette on the ground and looked at his chart. Parents held their collective breath, both fearing they would hear their name and hoping with all their might to get off the street and get it over with.

"Jalal Javadi." The man looked up with a smirk, obviously enjoying the moment when parents had to own the sins of their children. Zia, who wasn't even addressed, was quick to step forward and leave the social vulnerability of Vozara Street. Jalal followed with his head down, shoulders slumped, and dread in his eyes. They were ushered into the courtroom with haste and, after a few short steps down the aisle of a small room, told to stand next to their son in front of the judge.

Zia expected to look at him and feel enraged. She was right, but for a different reason than she assumed. His previously white shirt was covered in ash, blood, and it looked like he had a hole in his chest. She saw that his right cheek was scarred and bloodied as well, even as he tried to cover his face with his right hand. His hair was disheveled, his pants were filthy, and dried blood was smeared across his hands. He'd clearly received no medical attention whatsoever. Arman's eyes welled with tears as he saw his parents. He was obviously in intense pain, but the shame on his countenance made the rest of his situation seem almost insignificant. Zia lost control.

"What did you do to him?!" She shrieked the words at no one in particular, which was probably the only reason she wasn't beaten. "Why hasn't he seen a doctor?!" Jalal grabbed her hand, squeezing hard, slowly started to pull her back to the exact spot they were told to stand.

"Shut up, woman!" The thick-bearded soldier with a thick chest pointed his rifle at her face, inching it forward until it rested on her nose. In that moment, Zia was more frightened than she'd ever been in her life, and Jalal knew it. In an emotional swap, Jalal took on her anger but managed to keep his head while he day-dreamed of a thousand ways to kill the man who held the fate of his family on his fingertip. Arman fell into a puddle, making unintelligible pleas for mercy in between his sobbing, his hands helplessly handcuffed behind him.

"We didn't do any of this to your son!" the soldier screamed, three inches from Zia's face. "He was so drunk, the stupid idiot fell into a fire!" He laughed as he finished the sentence. "And you can take him to a doctor yourself! We're not wasting a dime on this westoxified piece of trash!"

Zia breathed out heavily, hands trembling. The soldier glanced to his left to make sure Jalal wasn't getting any ideas about defending his wife. He switched his attention to the father for his last words, finally pulling the rifle away from Zia's nose. "You should thank us for not treating his burns. Since you obviously aren't pointing him toward the ways of Mohammad, we might as well prepare him for Hell."

"He's already been found guilty of drinking alcohol and public intoxication." The judge finally spoke. He wore a loose black robe, a long beard, grey and unkempt, and a stern and merciless countenance. He had apparently been fine with delaying his sentence, if for no other reason but to watch the Revolutionary Guard get in on the action of shaming the infidels among them. Like the other judges, he was also a clergyman, and the sentencing had taken place very quickly, less than a minute before the parents entered the room. Greater efficiency is possible when the man making the decision is an unholy trinity of judge, prosecutor, and plaintiff, all by himself.

"The only thing we need to discuss is how you're going to pay for his release."

Arman stiffened as the reality of financial ruin dawned on him. Until now he'd only considered his pain and the family's reputation, which were, in fact, the greatest tragedies. He buried his head in his hands, wetting dirt and dried blood with his tears. His Mom might forgive him, perhaps one day soon, after the anger subsides. His relationship with his father, however, was changed forever.

Vivid snowflakes with glimmers of moonlight shining through bright clouds danced all around as Arman first began playing the video game, Free Flyer. As hesitant as he was about going into the closet of an IT store, he was beginning to believe that this would be an enjoyable distraction as they waited to go to the SkyBridge.

The first thing that captured his attention was the breathtaking high definition quality. He looked up to see highlighted cracks in the clouds, providing light for the gorgeous scenery. It felt so real, he put out his hand thinking he would see something that represented his outstretched arm, but there was nothing. He looked down and his heart skipped at the illusion of hovering a hundred feet above the white blanket below.

He experimented with the touch screen controller by swiping up with his thumb, quickly bouncing him upward toward the heavens. He was holding it erect, so the upward movement made sense. Continuing to hold it in the same position, he swiped down a couple of times, eventually "landing" him on the ground. He went up and down a few more times to get the hang of it, then attempted to go straight ahead. After a few failed experiments, he intuitively held the controller horizontally to the ground and swiped forward, sending him gliding through a landscape of snow-covered pine trees below. *That's why they call it Free Flyer!* The shady salesman was right. In less than a minute he'd mastered the controls and the feeling of freedom had gripped him.

There didn't seem to be any real objective to this game so far, but the brilliance and realism of the landscape was more than enough to entrance him. He noticed footprints in the snow leading to a trail through the tall pines and decided to follow. The lowest branch among the trees was around 20 feet high, providing a clear view for long stretches of the trail, which was now distinctly visible. There was a soft and calming quietness, incredibly similar to the effect of walking through real woods in real snow. *How can the headphones block out noise like this?* This both thrilled and threatened Arman in ways he couldn't fully articulate in his own mind. He lingered a moment more in gaping wonder, but a quiet discomfort quickly moved him along.

He sped up the trail until it opened up onto a pathway along a river illuminated by cast iron Victorian style lamp posts, then decided to hover from around thirty feet above to fully imbibe the new scenery. A red and silver steamboat moved along the water while the landscape included horse carriages with men in black top hats and women in long white dresses. The first sight of people excited him, so he descended nearby to see how realistic it felt. At this point he wasn't too surprised to find that the scene was authentic, but eventually it occurred to him that he could walk completely around the horses and the people and see everything from the expected point of view. Likewise, the sound again amazed him. The closer he was to the people, the more clearly he could hear their conversations. *Wait, they're having conversations?!*

Intrigued, Arman focused on a particular young boy weaving dangerously through traffic in the cobblestone road below. He could've only been about seven years old and wore a threadbare black cap and green jacket with fraying coattails. Arman sucked in a fearful breath when the youngster was nearly trampled by a massive black steed.

"Watch your feet, ratbag!" the driver of the carriage barked in a clipped British accent.

"Sorry, sir!" the boy squeaked, diving back into the crowd.

An elderly woman sat on the side of the road, bundled up in a million wool shawls. Beside her was a rickety wooden stand displaying copious amounts of flowers with colors that looked odd in this winter scene.

"Magic winter flowers for sale!" Her wobbly voice made her advertisement sound more like mourning.

"Missus Greenfingers!" Arman realized the young boy he'd seen earlier had stopped to inspect the vibrant blooms. "I don't think no one's going to believe they're real flowers. You might as well pack up."

Miss Greenfingers craned her neck around slowly to look at the boy.

"That's where you're wrong, young man," she wailed. "My mother always told me to not underestimate stupid boys in love."

The kid in the green coat looked at her quizzically for another few seconds. Before he could open his mouth again, an opulently dressed young couple strode up to the stand.

"Oh George, look!" the young woman squealed. "Flowers this far into winter? They must be magic!"

"Hold on." The pale man next to her bent closer to inspect the yellow marigolds. "I'm not sure…"

"Aren't they lovely?" the woman interrupted, and tugged playfully on his elbow.

"Oh, all right," the young man consented. He rang up a bouquet of fake flowers and was on his way before the lady could ask for more.

"What did I tell you?" the old hag croaked. The boy in the green coat watched the couple disappear in a sort of horrified awe. The flower-seller suddenly took on an annoyed expression. "Now shoo," she said pointedly at the seven-year-old. The boy nodded and disappeared once more.

Arman laughed at the script and again marveled at the technology. He was curious about what might happen next, but he remembered that his time was supposed to be fairly short, so he decided that he should get an idea just how large this snowy virtual landscape actually was. He swiped up a few times, then forward a few more to discover he had just begun exploring.

The landscape changed from a snowy river on the horizon to white sandy beaches and crystal blue water. The nearby buildings looked modern, aqua blue and green beach houses mixing eloquently with eggshell condominiums. Groups of men and women gathered under straw-thatched huts for drinks while others surfed on the clear water. Because he could "fly" over the ocean, he began his inquiry into this world above the water. Schools of bluefish darted back and forth, their scales reflecting the sunlight in perfect choreography. Dolphins closely followed them, explaining the multiple and sudden changes of direction.

Further along Arman saw stingrays floating along the surface and decided to get as close as possible. Again his instinct was to reach out and see his arm gliding along the stingray's back, unafraid of any painful consequences, but was quickly reminded of the discarnate nature of the experience. As he pondered his lack of ability to touch anything in this world, a bull shark lurched upward violently, upending the stingray a mere two feet in front of him, sending Arman both backward and sideways as he momentarily lost command of the controller. In the real world, his foot became temporarily entangled with one of the many loose extension cords and almost sent him to the ground, but he caught his balance and continued his exploration.

He wasn't sure how much time he had left. It had only been five minutes, but he was quickly losing track of time. He floated back toward the beach to find a crowd of people holding drinks gathered all around an oval-shaped stage. He could hear the band playing louder and louder as he approached from a ground view. It was a fairly generic rock band (all white male musicians with drums, guitar, bass, keyboardist, and a lead singer), playing a tune he didn't recognize. Although the concert was loud, he could also hear faint conversation from those talking to each other within a few feet of him. Again, he marveled at the realism as he was able to look closely at all angles of the people in the crowd. This is where the line between delightful observation and voyeurism became obscured.

He kept telling himself that it was all harmless and inconsequential, though the very fact that he was now having a conversation with himself should have clarified the truth. A group of gorgeous young blondes and brunettes in bikinis looked directly at him, signaling with curled index fingers for him to follow. Their lighthearted and vibrant smiles enraptured Arman, who willfully followed with the relief that they wouldn't see the scar on his face. They passed under a grove of tall palm trees, providing shade from a sun he couldn't feel and a pathway toward an enormous bright red beach house teaming with large windows, three floors of ornate wooden decks, and clear sliding glass doors. Curtains closed, Arman's curiosity about what was inside was piqued beyond measure. His heart pounded as he followed the mirages in front of him. *"You really shouldn't go in there"* was quickly followed by, *"It's just a game."* This basic argument repeated itself approximately fifty times as he made his way to the only open door. A bathing suit twirled to the floor in front of him. He hesitated only briefly, then floated inside.

Dopamine rushed to his brain as he considered his freedom to go wherever he wanted in this fictitious brothel. At least that's what he thought it was. He was mostly right, except for the fact that in this virtual replica, all the women were happy and delighted to be there. This wasn't his first time to swipe a touch screen in order to see similar images, but it was by far the most lifelike experience. He continued to suppress opposing voices, gleefully exploring one debauched room after another, each one playing unfolding scenes of wicked glory on a loop.

He knew that he must be well past the requested ten minutes. Perhaps Adrian, the salesman, didn't care how long he stayed, but his friends would eventually miss him. Or perhaps Adrian was now with his boss and couldn't come back to tell him his time was up? Either way he knew he wasn't going to stop on his own. In fact, he was beginning to become conscious of the incredible pull this virtual Hell-house had on him.

His thoughts vacillated between justifications for staying and intermittent bursts of illuminated reality. Previously the women seemed to acknowledge him and invite him in. Now that he was inside, he was again nothing more than an anonymous, disembodied observer. The images excited needs in him which the game itself couldn't possibly meet, but it wasn't just the physical desire for sex. In the midst of the moral void, he realized he felt a longing to be seen. To be heard. Felt. To be… known.

Finally the worst thought of all entered into the clouded confines of his mind. Only minutes ago he was enveloped in a good, wide, and beautiful world, indescribable majesty surrounding him, and he even had the ability to simulate flight. He now realized there were probably more worlds to explore. Could he enter vast underground caverns? Were there blue lakes surrounded by mountains the size of Mt. Everest? What other wildlife might he find? Could he have gone underwater and plunged the depths of the ocean? In the end, however, he knew it didn't matter. The weight of the gravitational pull toward the depravity before him was too strong. Several times he started toward the door only to find that he couldn't make himself leave.

So many choices. So little freedom.

"Arman, are you in there?!" Banu called out more loudly than necessary since the dark hallway seemed much longer to her than it actually was. The voice of the girl who reminded Arman of his sister provoked a startled shame and sent pulses through his chest. His left foot stepped on two loose poles, sending both feet flailing above him until the back of his head whipped toward the ground and struck the cement below. It was lights out for Arman until the confrontation between Farzin and Adrian would wake him up.

THE AMBIGUITY OF FREEDOM

The rattling and clanking of the steel door jolted Arman awake, plucking him out of one nightmare and into another. He heard a laugh, the one he hated more than any other, through the hands he'd sealed over his ears.

"Get up, dog! Don't expect to sleep anytime soon!"

Habib continued his mockery and guffawing after every attempt at a cruel joke, but it all blended into the background like clanging white noise in Arman's haze. He wasn't sure if he'd been asleep for hours or mere seconds, but he knew one thing. No matter how long it was, he needed more. He rubbed his eyes, lifted his torso off the floor with his hands, and surveyed the room. Maybe he'd find a bed to relieve his aching back. Or perhaps there was something small lying around on the floor he could use to pick the lock. Or a rope he could tie into a knot to hang himself. Any of the three would do and he wasn't sure if he had a preference. Unfortunately, the only light available came from down the hallway where all of the brutes stood guard, so he could see almost nothing except for the faint light reaching the steel bars of his cell and, of course, Habib himself. Finally, he saw him lift his rifle and realized that he'd been shouting the same sentence repeatedly.

"I said, 'Give me your wallet or I'll shoot your legs off and get it myself!'"

"Okay, okay." He had instinctively raised his hands when the gun was pointed at him, but now he quickly reached for his wallet. The thought of handing over his identification card frightened him. But then again, what did he have to gain by hanging onto proof that he was a suspected terrorist? He hesitated slightly too long, leading to a volley of curses, followed by a single gunshot fired over Arman's head.

He slid the wallet underneath the cell door and looked up at Habib, his only pleasure found in the fact that he could shoot daggers with his eyes without being noticed in the darkness.

"So what happens now?"

"First of all, you can expect to be even more sleep-deprived in the next few days. That's why I woke you up as soon as I closed the gate. I can't see your face in there, but I can see if you're lying down. If you let me or anyone else catch you on the floor, I promise that you'll quickly regret it. As far as your future, I'm guessing they'll either kill you or sell you into a trafficking ring. One thing's for sure, it certainly doesn't help you to be carrying proof that you're Arman Javadi."

He was right, of course, but that didn't keep Arman from hating him all the more for saying it. As Habib walked away, he again scoured the dark room in vain for some sharp object to throw. Soon, however, he was able to find a small amount of satisfaction as he heard Habib's leader lay into him for firing the gun unnecessarily.

It was actually quite pathetic, he thought, to see what had happened to Habib. It was only a couple of years ago that he was a sincere seeker of Allah whose primary burden was to see people in his country go back to the mosque and live moral lives. Even though he strongly disagreed with Habib's decision to use force to accomplish it, there was a small part of him that admired his willingness to give up so many worldly pleasures. But something had happened since then. Now he just seemed like an awkward young kid trying in vain to impress these thugs, just as worldly as the

Westerners they hated, in an attempt to gain only the slightest hint of power and prestige. And what surprised Arman more than if he'd woken up with three working legs was an extremely brief and fleeting emotion which, at first, he couldn't even identify. Then he realized… It was pity. Somehow, against all nature and everything he thought he knew about life, he actually felt sorry for Habib. As soon as he gained clarity of this emotion, however, he pushed it aside as utter stupidity and returned to his hatred. *No one who's caused so much suffering should receive even the slightest bit of concern from those they've tortured.* He successfully repositioned his thoughts to consider the various ways he would gain his revenge.

"Can I have a drink of your water?"

The voice was calm and even courteous, but as it emerged out of utter blackness, he may as well have shouted through a bullhorn. Arman jumped to his feet and faced the direction of the voice, walking hastily backward until his head hit something hanging from an unseen wall. Chills assaulted his legs, goose bumps formed across his arms and side, and his arm hair stood on end. The very thought that someone he couldn't see had been with him the entire time, however long or short, was terrifying. Still disoriented, he finally came to himself and considered the question he was asked. *Why would he ask me for water?*

"They left a little bit of food and a water bottle next to the gate," explained the disembodied voice only about five feet from him. "I promise I won't drink too much." Still too unhinged to talk, Arman lurched to the gate where he could see the top of the bottle in the hallway light. Suddenly aware of the damp and musty air assaulting his nostrils, he became slightly dizzy as he walked.

He second-guessed himself as he reached for it. *Who is this person? Why should I trust him? What if this is the last water I get for days?* Regardless, he decided he believed him and guessed that, whoever this was, he may have been in here for a long time. He picked up the bottle and walked toward the unseen voice. Eventually he realized that trying to hand it to him in the darkness was probably futile, so he sat down and slowly slid the bottle until it appeared to touch him.

Whether it touched his knee, foot, or slid into his waiting hand, Arman would never know. He heard the seal of the bottle cap broken and a complete stranger, an invisible one at that, drink from a bottle that he would soon put his lips on as well. *What if this guy is excessively dirty? What if he has a beard with yesterday's dinner in it? Or what if he's sick?* His thoughts ran wild as he heard the bottle cap screwed back on and his water sliding back to him. He reached for it and knocked it over, eventually finding it nearby to his right. None was spilled and it still felt full.

"I'm sorry I startled you."

"You didn't startle me." In his vulnerable state, Arman didn't want to begin a relationship with someone he was locked up and alone with by admitting weakness.

"Are you sure about that?" The stranger stifled a laugh as he spoke. It wasn't a mocking tone, but more like a playful jab from a friend. It was disarming to Arman, who allowed himself to crack an unseen smile, okay with laughing at himself a bit if it meant potentially having a friend in this hellish place. After all, this guy was obviously a fellow prisoner and he spoke in Farsi as well. There was no reason to be unnecessarily rude to someone who presented Arman's first opportunity for a conversation since he was chased into a cave. *Was that yesterday or two days ago?* There was no way he could tell for sure.

"My name's Arman."

"Yes, I know. Habib shouted your name a few times in between cursing and rattling the door. I'm Atrin."

"Atrin? I'm not sure if I've heard that name before."

"It's Iranian, just not very common. It means 'fiery,' or 'full of energy.'

Arman thought it was an odd name, but he liked it. Of course, he could only be so interested in names and random facts at the moment. His disoriented mind wandered in and out of the conversation for about half a minute before he came to and fully realized where he was, and that he was talking to a complete stranger in a dark cell. The disturbing nature of this blind discussion returned to him, but he would hang onto the picture of someone who looked energetic and alive. It made him feel better than the other images that came to mind. Suddenly realizing his new cell mate may have helpful information, he began asking questions.

"How long have you been in here?"

"Only a few hours before you."

"Is it true that he woke me up right after the door closed?"

"I'm afraid so."

Arman knew it was true and yet it made him feel a new level of exhaustion all the same. He buried his face in his hands and left it there, knowing there was no need to try to make eye contact with Atrin. He could turn and face the opposite direction and it still wouldn't be rude. He decided to skip the pleasantries and asked what he really wanted to know.

"Is the way I came in the only way out?"

Atrin answered after a brief pause, lowering his voice. "That's what I was told, but I don't believe it. I saw someone I hadn't seen before approach from the other direction, the opposite end of the hallway from where you and I came in. When a couple of the others saw him, they berated him for being late. If he had just arrived, and he apparently did, then he must've entered from a second stairwell." Atrin's voice was deep, but clear and deliberate. He came off as friendly and intelligent.

Arman paused the conversation to consider this insight. He crept over to the gate, scooting across the damp cement floor on his rear, looked down the hallway for the silhouettes of anyone watching, and attempted, ever so gently, to see if the gate would slide open. It didn't, of course, so he slunk back to the place where he'd been sitting. Or, at least the place he thought he'd been sitting. As he resettled into his resting position, arms around his knees and head down, it dawned on him that this was the first time in days that he was no longer running. Sure, he would keep trying to think of a way out, but for now there were no real decisions to make, no weighing the odds of survival between two bad options, and no running possible. It was almost a relief.

"So how did you end up on the wrong side of Nahuel and friends?"

"I didn't hear anyone say his name,' Arman answered, "but I have a feeling I know which one 'Nahuel' is."

"If you're guessing it's the huge guy who threatened Habib's life and had you thrown in this cell, you're right."

"No surprise there." Arman paused to consider the original question and wondered how much information he should give. Eventually, he decided he couldn't imagine his situation getting worse, no matter how much information he gave out. "My cousin and his girlfriend were part of the group who bombed the Petronas Towers." This was the first time he'd said it out loud. It felt like punching himself in the temple. "I was on the crosswalk with them, but I wasn't part of it. I had no idea."

Atrin let out an empathetic groan. "I'm sorry to hear that. Were you and your cousin close?"

Arman had been in survival mode for so long, he'd almost become numb to the real nature of his loss. Hearing someone recognize it brought tears to his eyes. He covered his face again and waited until he could answer. In the meantime, he used his dirty white shirt to wipe his eyes, suddenly thankful for the darkness. The heat, humidity, and putrid air, however, was beginning to choke him. He took his shirt off, used it to wipe the sweat off his forehead, and set it next to him. "Yes, we were close. Close for our entire lives. I only met Banu about a month ago, but… she was almost like my sister." He choked on the last few words, causing Atrin to refrain from asking further questions. He gathered himself and continued. "I ran after the bombing because I didn't think anyone would believe I'm innocent. It felt like my only choice. Habib found me at the Batu Caves and told me - at gunpoint - that the boys in here would welcome me as a hero and smuggle me back to Iran. I knew it was most likely a lie, but again, it seemed like the best of two terrible choices, so I didn't try to run. From what I heard from Nahuel and Habib's argument when I arrived, my cousin had convinced everyone but Habib that I was actually with them, but that I needed to stay alive for some reason. Eventually Habib convinced them otherwise and they decided that they didn't want me to be interrogated and give away any information about Farzin and Banu." He let out a bemused laugh and shook his head. "And that's easily the most believable part of the last twenty-four hours."

"I can't wait to hear the rest," replied Atrin. He was playing along with the lighthearted nature of Arman's last comment, but it was apparent by now that he was genuinely interested. For some reason Arman couldn't completely explain, he felt comfortable talking with him. Perhaps it was because he didn't have to look at him in the dark, or the way that he made it obvious he was listening and sympathizing. Or both. Either way, Arman just started talking. Unloading even. He started with the events following the collapse of the towers. Running down the stairs, the aquarium, the shark, getting caught in the kavadi line at the Thaipusam celebration, The Dark Cave... He occasionally paused to see if he thought Atrin was still believing him and, so far, it seemed like he was. Regardless, he decided to leave out the more outrageous details such as jumping over the shark and, especially, nothing about a three-headed dragon. He also left out the part about letting go of the falling stroller.

After the events of yesterday, last night, and the morning were well-covered, Atrin asked him questions about his background, especially about his family and his relationship with Farzin. To Arman's surprise, he shared intimate details and insights, some of them for the first time, about his mother, his father, and even some of the history of his Uncle Ali. He lamented his ruptured relationship with his father and the unfairness that impacted so much of his life. Of all the heartaches he shared with Atrin, however, the one that seemed to impact him the most was the problem with his father. "I love my father so much," Atrin sympathized. "A disruption in our relationship is the worst thing I can imagine."

All throughout the conversation, Atrin found such subtle but clear ways to communicate his empathy that Arman almost tried to comfort him in return. As he thought about this later, he would say that it was as if the man in the cell had experienced his pain with him. On several occasions, Arman heard Atrin whisper a sentence or two and assumed he wasn't paying attention, only to realize that, not only was he listening, but he was praying for him. *So he's religious?* This threw him off in more ways than one. At first he couldn't put his finger on why this suddenly made him uncomfortable. Perhaps it was the shame he felt over a multitude of events, knowing he was facing a lifetime of rejection. Or maybe it was because most of the religious people he knew were too busy telling him what he was doing wrong to ever listen to him. *But this guy seems to actually… like me.*

It wasn't until about thirty minutes later, when Arman brought up his groaning for freedom, a topic he assumed would gain quick agreement, that Atrin offered any of his own thoughts. While Arman was in mid-sentence, Atrin abruptly asked, "What is freedom, Arman?"

He stopped, confused, and tried to retrace the conversation to figure out why Atrin would ask that. "What do you mean?"

"That's what I was asking, really. 'What do you mean' by the word *freedom*"?

Arman thought this was obvious and really didn't feel like explaining something so basic, especially if his new friend - he thought of him as a friend now - was going to split hairs over a random definition. However, he realized how long he'd monopolized the discussion and decided this was the least he could do. "It's the ability to choose what you want to do instead of having someone else decide for you. It's more like democracy and completely different than the government of Iran." He was proud of the clarity of his answer and, since this seemed to be a sane person who, by the way, was imprisoned by religious extremists from the "Government of God," Arman waited for his due applause.

"But what about people who are free to choose, yet they continue to make choices that hurt both themselves and others? What if they use their freedom as a cover-up for evil? After all, there's a great many sins that are birthed in a kind of freedom but are eventually revealed to be nothing more than slavery. And there's other life situations that can't possibly be changed simply by a government letting us choose."

"So you're saying you think it's a good idea to let a government or dictator make all of our choices for us?" Arman was indignant.

"No, that's not what I'm saying at all. I'm not questioning your assessment of our government. I'm questioning your belief that simply having freedom to choose will solve your problems."

"I happen to disagree." Arman was suddenly becoming less interested in talking.

"Here's just one example of what I'm talking about. You could have the freedom to choose to leave this place, but you'll still be hunted as a terrorist. Even if they let you live and, for the sake of theory, even if they let you out of prison, you'll still live the rest of your life in shame because of what people think you did."

The truth of his words was like a hammer to the forehead, infuriating him. This conversation was supposed to be about him venting about his problems and, hopefully, feeling some small measure better than before. Not worse and even more hopeless.

"Okay, so you've established the fact that my life is over. But what is *your* solution for government? Do you want people to be free or not?"

"Are you asking about my opinion of the best possible government in this messed up world or my theory of a perfect government?"

"Those should be the same thing, right?"

"Not at all. My idea of a perfect government involves a perfect king."

"A king!? You mean, a dictator?"

"Not what you're thinking of, even though there have been a few kings in history who have had some admirable traits."

"I have a feeling you may be a fan of King Cyrus, right?"

"True."

"I'm partial to King David," replied Atrin, "though he was far from perfect himself."

"You're right to protest since dictators in our world eventually become abusive leaders interested only in their self- preservation."

"But even if a perfect king existed, wouldn't there still be problems? After all, you just talked about the result of people making bad choices."

"Remember, I'm still talking theory, at least as far as this world is concerned. So you're right. Even with a perfect king, the hearts of the people would have to somehow be changed." Arman nodded his head, feeling somewhat justified. "The reason our 'Government of God' fails is that it's not really run by God at all, but by extremely flawed humans claiming to represent him. So sinful leaders who primarily love their own comfort and power spend their lives enforcing morality on people whose hearts are also not primarily inclined to follow God and his ways."

"You think most of us don't want to follow God and his ways? I have to disagree. Most people I know are good people. Regardless of religion, they try to do what's best most of the time."

Atrin was silent for a minute after this. At this point Arman wasn't sure if he was conceding the point or waiting for the right time to deliver the next blow. His suspicion was the latter, and it was confirmed soon enough.

"How did you get your scars?"

Arman's mouth gaped and his tongue dried like salt. A hundred thoughts flew threw his mind. *It's completely dark and I just took my shirt off. My left ankle is covered and the burn on my face is barely visible in the light. How could he know? And how could he know to ask this question while we're talking about morality anyway?* His heart quivered as large droplets of sweat fell from his nose onto the floor below. Eventually, he settled on the theory that a light must've been on when they threw him in the jail. How Atrin saw his chest scar was still a mystery, but nothing overwhelming in and of itself. He tried to play it cool and keep it simple. "I fell in a fire."

"Yes, it's true that you fell in a fire. And that it happened on Charharshenbeh Suri."

Arman's mind reeled again, this time quickly settling on the conclusion that it was just a logical guess. Either way, he really didn't appreciate the game Atrin appeared to be playing. "So you guessed that it happened on the day when half of the nation was playing with fire. That doesn't mean anything."

"It's also true that you had way too much to drink that night." He said this with such a matter-of-fact tone, it was almost pleasant. It wouldn't have felt judgmental at all except for the content of his damning words. While it was extremely confusing, it was the only thing that kept Arman from finding him in the dark and choking him.

"Again, a fairly obvious guess. It proves nothing."

Atrin offered another lengthy pause, this time it making Arman more nervous than ever. He had no intentions of telling this stranger - it was back to 'stranger' instead of 'friend' - the excruciating details of the most shameful event of his life. Earlier in the conversation, he earned a small level of trust, but Arman would trust no one with this part of his past. In the silence, he tried to guess what may be coming next from this glorified fortune teller and how he would respond. What Atrin finally said, however, was something that would've caught him off guard if he'd prepared for a thousand years.

"Tell me about this three-headed dragon, Dahag."

Arman leaped to his feet and shuffled backward, away from Atrin, again smacking into whatever hung from the ceiling on that side of the room. He grabbed the back of his head, yelling in agony and frustration. The thud followed by a scream evoked laughter from down the hallway. Arman wiped his balmy hands on his pants, then put his right hand over his mouth. Hands trembling, breath labored. Arman had never shared this with anyone. Mahnaz, Farzin… nobody knew about Dahag. The idea that someone finally knew produced a myriad of thoughts and emotions.

Surprisingly, one of the feelings was a slight relief. If someone knew, then he was slightly less alone in the world. But mostly, this simply terrified him as he now had no logical explanation for Atrin's knowledge. *Who is this?*

"What do you want from me?" Arman's tone was no longer angry, but respectful. Even fearful. While he waited a response, he was overcome by a sudden wave of peace. He didn't understand it then and was never able to fully explain it later. The closest he ever came was by telling others that it was as if he could hear Atrin smiling at him, if that's possible. Atrin's reply was voiced in the most sincere, humble, passionate, and even joy- filled words any human being had uttered to Arman.

"I want to set you free."

2 6

THE COLOR GREEN

She jumped out of bed only seconds after the alarm went off on her new iPhone. Just over thirty years after her mother was dragged out of her Tehran University dorm-room to reluctantly take part in a government protest, Mahnaz needed no prodding from a boy- crazy blonde to manipulate her in order to get ready.

By her parents' request, she was living in her mother's old room. Same bare walls, same window looking out over the center of campus, and the same cracks in the ceiling, only now they were outlined in streaks of dirty brown. But there was no roommate, no loud make-up to paste on, no mini-skirts to straighten, and no beehive hairdos. Just a young woman who, like millions of others throughout her nation, was angry about the fraudulent elections and determined to be part of a solution. Zia used to criticize Mahnaz for her blatant apathy toward life, yet here she was, heart ablaze for justice, eyes focused on her task in such a way that it made her mother's participation in the Revolution decades earlier appear lethargic. She pulled up her blue jeans and slipped on her green chador, effectively covering the faded denim, and threw on a newly purchased green hijab. The chador and hijab were to keep her from standing out for the wrong reasons, knowing the Basij would be present. Still, she chose green, the official color of what would become known as the Green Movement, to identify with the cause of her people and to make a stand for freedom. She slipped on her Nike shoes, shoved her cell phone in her pocket, and walked down an empty hallway toward the double doors leading out into the heart of the campus.

Most of her time in the last year was spent studying and talking about the *kingdom* of God, not the Government of God. But ever since she had been taught to pray, "Your kingdom come, your will be done, on earth as it is in Heaven," she had developed a greater desire to do whatever she could to make a difference on this earth, however long she remained in this life. And today, it was clear to her and two million other protesters on the streets that Amir-Hossein Mousavi, the candidate who had given them hope, was robbed. As were the people.

Hopes were high leading up to the election. The promises of Ahmadinejad had failed miserably, destroying an already fragile economy and leaving them under the thumb of a resurgent and oppressive government. Mousavi, however, represented a more progressive agenda and the people, yet again, had a faint taste of freedom. Polls leading up to the election showed him as the clear favorite in the four person race. The energy surrounding his rallies seemed to validate him as the one to beat. But the day of June 12, 2009, didn't go the way they had hoped. It went exactly how they feared.

The first concerns were raised when a state-run media outlet declared Ahmadinejad the victor three hours before the polls closed. It only got weirder and more brazen from there. Reports spread like wildfire through Twitter and Facebook, much of the information coming from Iranians outside of the country who had access to unfiltered news, about polling stations closing early even though long lines of people still waited to vote. Other stations ran out of ballots with no apparent effort to re-supply them. Three hours after the election, hardly enough time to count the tens of millions of paper ballots cast, the government announced that Ahmadinejad had won by twenty million votes. In spite of the great momentum carried by Mousavi, Ahmadinejad won the four way race by a two to one margin - the one representing the other three candidates. The official percentage of his vote was 62.63, a number that was suspiciously repeated in individual areas throughout the nation. Even in the opposing candidates' hometowns, Ahmadinejad claimed 62.63 percent of the votes. In other words, it seemed like they weren't even trying to hide their cheating.

As many as two million protesters flooded cities throughout the country, their individual shirts, hijabs, and chadors like scales of a green dragon surging through the awakened streets. They screamed for a recount, cursed Ahmadinejad and the Ayatollah Khameini, and held signs reading, "Death to the Dictator!" In some places, tempers boiled over into acts of violence. It was open rebellion on a scale unseen since the Revolution. On the surface, it seemed as if the government had miscalculated their actions. In the end, however, they showed that this was probably not the case. Instead, it seemed that they actually invited the anger, drawing out their detractors in a way that would allow them to unleash their own.

The blowback to the protests was brutal. Basij forces were unleashed like demons out of dark crevices of the earth. They fired guns into crowds. They threw tear gas indiscriminately. They beat them with rods, both men and women alike. They spit on them, cursed them, and relished in the pain of the rebellious crowds. The most notorious of the atrocities occurred when Basij forces shot Neda Agha-Soltan in the chest as she was walking back to her car. Her last breaths were captured on video and uploaded to the internet, spreading like wildfire among Iranians, both inside and outside of the country, and proceeded from there to capture the attention of the entire world. It galvanized the Green Movement and increased the fervor of the protestors, but to no avail. The Basij furthered their crimes on the people by what they did with the prisoners they rounded up. The infamous Evin Prison was again full and the ensuing weeks and months would reveal credible reports of torture, rape, and murder.

Evin Prison, however, wasn't the only jail full of protesters. The number of people arrested and set aside for "interrogation" created the need for more cells than could be found in Tehran alone. Just south of the city, Kahrizak Prison swelled with people piled on top of people. Prisoners dropped dirt-filled beads of sweat on each other as the smell of gas and urine was so pungent it made the strongest of them weak from nausea. Prisoners were interrogated, intimidated into signing confessions that they were part of a western conspiracy designed to infiltrate the country and spread the protests, beaten unconscious, tortured in a variety of ways, intimately violated in every way possible, and more than a few were killed without the slightest hint of a fair trial.

Some of these victims came from a student protest at Tehran University.

Zia arrived to Kahrizak in an angered panic. She'd called Jalal from the car to tell him that Mahnaz was arrested and was now in prison. His first reaction was a combination of rage and helplessness, scenes of his daughter as a little girl unfolding before him. When he heard that Zia was driving to the prison, however, his voice became calm and cautious, knowing his wife would need a counter to her own rage.

"Sweetheart, you can't help her by going to the prison." His words were measured and respectful, yet pleading and emotional. "I know you want to hit someone. So do I! But you're just going to get hurt!"

"They have my girl and I'm not leaving without her!" She screamed into the phone hoping somehow the Basij would hear her. Jalal pleaded with her for about ten minutes to turn around before she finally hung up. He immediately jumped in his car to find her.

She ran at the prison still screaming at whoever may be listening and banged on the door with both fists, demanding to be let in and for Mahnaz to be released. When they didn't immediately answer, she kicked the door with the heels of her shoes and shouted even louder, raining down curses from Allah. She continued this for more than ten minutes until she was exhausted, then collapsed onto the austere walls of the prison, head in her hands, sobbing.

The door clicked and she looked up to see a man quickly exit and shut the door behind him. Zia jumped to her feet and burst into his face, ready to unleash a flurry of insults and demands. She would never get the opportunity. He stuck the butt of his rifle into her stomach, knocking the breath out of her and sending her back to the ground. She landed on her knees and balanced herself with one hand, the other holding her stomach, gasping for air.

"Put your hair back under your hijab!"

Zia reached up slowly to find a couple of lockets that had fallen loose, some black, some grey. She looked up at the prison guard, staring him in the face. His eyes were bloodshot and cold. His mustache long and disheveled, eyebrows like dry bushes in the desert. He was tall with broad shoulders and thick in the middle, the buttons on his khaki shirt hanging on for dear life. Despite her immobility, he grew impatient with her lack of haste.

"I said, 'Put your nasty hair back in your hijab!'"

He turned his rifle around and pointed it at her, finger on the trigger. She instinctively pulled her supporting arm up to shove her hair back under her hijab and fell on her side, the other hand still holding her stomach. As she hit the ground, a cloud of dust formed around her body, slowly drifting off into the dry air. Undeterred, the merciless guard raised his rifle and peered down the barrel. Zia's heart raced as she realized his deadly intent and let out a scream. He smiled.

The door cracked open and a man Zia never actually saw began yelling at the man pointing the gun at her. His face was red as he screamed in the direction of the guard, ordering him inside to deal with an apparent crisis. They both ran back inside and she never saw them again. Zia laid in the same position in agonizing pain for the next thirty minutes until Jalal arrived.

~

Three days later the government released the names of those who died in Kahrizak Prison. The stories of the hellish conditions and torture had effectively spread through the internet and was the source of much outrage, so the authorities felt it best to throw this situation into the broader narrative they had created about the reason for the protests.

We regret to inform the people of the Islamic Republic of Iran that the same western spies who entered our country and stirred up the dissenters in the streets have now infiltrated our prisons, torturing many prisoners and even killing some. Many of the protesters don't understand that it was America and Europe who spread the lie that the election wasn't fair. It's very unfortunate that they fell prey to such deception and wound up in jail. Be on your guard! They are also causing rampant sexual immorality, fake mysticism, and are spreading house churches designed to overthrow our Republic. We urge the people to reject the ways of the West and follow the straight path which Allah has laid before us.

The story, along with the names of the dead, spread like wildfire through social media. Jalal, Zia, and Arman all read it on their phones, alone, via Twitter. Each stopped reading at the exact line in the article when they saw the name *Mahnaz Javadi*.

For a great number of Iranians, there was a moment in time following the 2009 election when their soul split in two. A time where they felt such a lack of hope that they lost even the ability to be angry and bitter. As people were eventually forced to publicly assent to the state's narrative, they privately decided they wanted no part of it anymore. Not just the government, but the religion as well. As for Arman, he became both numb and quietly determined at the same time. Numb to the pain and the incessant lies from which there was no escape. Determined to leave the country as soon as possible and never come back.

GREEN REVOLUTION

"So you can get me out of here?" Arman wasn't sure that's what Atrin meant by "I want to set you free," but he preferred to keep the conversation focused on the material, if possible.

"If you actually were able to get out of here and even leave the country, where would you go?"

"London."

"Let's say you made it to London without getting caught, somehow got a fair trial, and were found innocent of the bombings. Will you then be free?"

"Of course I'd be free! I could choose what I want to do and what I want to believe instead of having it forced on me by a monster government claiming to represent Allah. I could even say what I believe about politics openly without fear of being tortured. What else could I want?!" Arman was reacting instinctively and out of frustration, but the reality was Atrin had instilled a sense of awe. And yet, while he had a feeling that could only be described as fear, he wasn't afraid to show his anger. For some reason, he believed Atrin would be able to handle it.

"There's a kind of freedom beyond what you can imagine. You think getting to the West will truly set you free. It's true that you'll be able to choose your own beliefs and much of what you do from day to day. You might be happier as well. Some in the West use their ability to choose wisely, but many others make themselves servants to the selfish choices they make. Many of them freely take part in pornography and whatever sexual practice they choose, value possessions and entertainment over relationships, and never connect their addictions, loneliness, and lack of meaning to their choices. They decided that truth is whatever works for the individual and wonder why there is so little community. They're exhausted from trying to craft their own personal religious beliefs to provide some semblance of meaning while allowing them to do whatever they always wanted to do in the first place. Many of them say they believe there is only one God, but if every version of him in the West were given a name, they would rival the number of idols in India. In the end, everyone is controlled by what they love the most, and loving anything more than the actual source of life creates its own kind of captivity." Atrin paused and his voice dropped to a lower, more mournful tone. "This isn't just true of the West, of course. You know what I'm talking about, Arman."

There was no use pretending. Atrin already made it clear that he was somehow intimately familiar with his worst choices. If he knew about Charharshanbeh Suri and Dahag, what would he not know about? His mind reeled for what to say next, with silence quickly presenting itself as the most attractive option. Eventually, he did what most people do when confronted with their wrongdoings. He changed the subject.

"I can see that you're a prophet. So… can you answer a question for me?"

"If there's an answer to it, then yes."

"Our religious leaders say that Islam is the only way and that the infidels are damned. But our poets, who are also Muslim, believe there are many ways to Paradise. Personally, I like our poets."

"Moses and the Shepherd is your favorite, right?"

"Yes, it is. It's the earliest poem I can remember my Mom teaching me."

"What does it mean to you?"

"It means that we can't say that we're better than people in other religions."

"You're right. It's true that people in one religion shouldn't think they're better than those in others. It's also true that, just like the 'coexist' symbols on your shirt imply, people should show love and tolerance to those with different religions and ways of viewing the world."

"So you agree when Rumi says, 'Hindus do Hindu things. The Dravidian Muslims in India do what they do. It's all praise and it's all right?'"

"Arman, what was it that bothered you when you carried the kavadi?"

This time Arman wasn't shocked by Atrin's supernatural knowledge. Oddly enough, he even welcomed the enquiry. "I joined the kavadi line to escape the police and I stayed in it because I have believed for a long time that all religions are an equal path to God, so it wasn't wrong for me to be there. But the longer I stayed in the line, the more I felt like the differences between Islam and Hinduism were greater than I wanted to admit." He said this because he knew that lying was of no use anymore, but he still didn't want to let go of the argument.

"I've known Christians, Hindus, Muslims, and Buddhists," Arman insisted, "and I don't see that any of them are better than the other. Why can't we believe that they're all a path to God?"

"You said earlier that people from one religion are no better than others and I agreed. That may seem like good news, but it's not, really."

"What do you mean? How does that not prove my point?"

"What if human sin goes deeper than you understand? What if 'equally good' just means 'equally fallen'? Men and women were created to love God and love people. Whenever someone is impatient, unkind, easily angered, envious, arrogant, rude, or simply unwilling to do the good thing they should be doing, it falls short of the holiness of God. What if the everyday selfishness of men and women was more offensive to God than you ever realized?"

This question possessed both the ring of truth and a thunder of terror. Arman answered as honestly as he could. "I guess we would have to work even harder." His breath felt diminished as he uttered these words. He already had so much to do to earn Allah's favor. And so little power to change.

"Arman, you could pray five times a day for the rest of your life. You could give millions in alms to the poor. You could go to Mecca thirty years in a row… and you still wouldn't pay for the offenses against a holy and perfect God. Not only that, but there's not a single religious act of devotion that can get you out of the mess you're in right now. If you performed every prayer to perfection, you'd still be wanted as a terrorist. You'd still have the sting of shame hanging over you."

Arman put his head into his hands and quietly wept. Atrin's words were as real as the darkness that separated them. There was a part of him that hated Atrin for saying it, but there was another part of him that was tired of playing games. In a way, he embraced the despair.

"It's not hopeless, Arman." Atrin's voice was lighter now. Still somber but tinged with hope. "The problem may be worse than you ever thought, but the grace of God is greater than you can possibly imagine." Arman lifted his head out of his hands, confused about what he meant. "At Thaipusam, you saw people carrying kavadis designed to punish themselves and earn merit with their chosen god. The bad news is that the real burden of guilt and shame is much too great for your shoulders. The good news is that there's someone who already carried it for you."

Finally, Arman knew who Atrin was talking about. His reaction was visceral.

"My sister believed Jesus was God and it brought her suffering and death! Sure, there were other protesters, but the Basij knew who she was and they just waited for the right time to torture and kill her! Tell me, Atrin, what good were her beliefs?! What good is a religion whose hero died on a cross? It made no sense to me when my sister was killed and it makes no sense to me now! Tell me, since you seem to know everything, why would Jesus allow that?!" Arman was so angry that spittle leaped from his mouth and onto Atrin's legs. "Why?!"

His voice quaked, both from fury and exhaustion. He didn't know if he was about to be struck dead or if he would get an answer, but he was perfectly ready for both. What followed, however, was bitterly disappointing. He'd wanted either anger or an answer. A consequence or an explanation. What he received instead was… silence. Ear-splitting, soul-wrenching silence. He waited for several minutes, desperate to hear some type of a response, even if it didn't make sense. At least he could then have the satisfaction of proving Atrin wrong. But silence, and only silence, filled the darkness.

Having no idea how to handle it, he replied, "That's what I thought. There's no answer for this." Arman returned to his crying, but this time it was a long, slow wail. He sobbed at the thought of the wretched world responsible for torturing and killing his sister. He cried over his own actions and for their consequences. He wept over being falsely accused for something he hadn't done. And most of all, he despaired for his great loneliness and the hopelessness of the dead air filling the room.

A hand touched the back of Arman's left shoulder, causing him to jump sideways. When he realized it was just Atrin trying to comfort him, his first instinct was to grab his arm and push it away, cursing him as he did. For some reason, unknown to him at the time, he let it stay. And he was glad he did. For all of the bitter silence that had plagued him, there was something communicated, physically transferred even, that could not have been expressed if Atrin had the advantage of a thousand years. A sweet empathy radiated from Atrin's hand into his shoulder. In complete defiance of his desperation, he somehow felt hope. The inner sea of turmoil was calmed into peaceful tranquility. Where he felt hatred he now felt love. In contrast to the bars that closed him in and the public accusations ensuring a life of captivity at best, he felt a soft and faint whisper of the thing for which he longed the most.

An explosion rocked the underground bunker, shaking the ground in their cell and blinding Arman as a flash of light ripped open the darkness. The gunfire which quickly followed was so loud Arman instinctively grabbed his ears and fell to the ground. He rolled away from the front of the cell to avoid stray bullets and closed his eyes to keep from being blinded again. He risked a glimpse and saw the silhouette of Atrin next to the cell bars, leaning forward, heedless of the bullets, and looking to his right.

"What's happening?!" Arman screamed.

Atrin scooted back toward him. "It's the police. I have a feeling they're looking for you."

Arman's mind swirled as he tried to quickly process the situation. Machine guns continued to spew bullets. Bursts of light streaked down the hallway. Policemen and terrorists were apparently fighting… over him. And in a twist of fate so ludicrous it was comical, he was rooting for Habib.

Arman caught another glimpse of Atrin and saw that he was putting on his shirt. He barked at Arman, "Get your shirt on! This is our chance!" Arman never saw how this happened, but before he knew it, Atrin had opened the cell door, slid it wide open, and looked back at him. "Quick! Follow me!" He ran to the left toward the end of the hallway, away from the fighting and toward the area where he believed there was a way out. Bullets bounced off of the concrete floors and walls, spinning around them like hornets, but there was no hesitation. They ran as fast as possible. The intermittent light was just enough to confirm where they were going, but some of the sprinting took place in the dark as they had no choice but to operate on faith in what they had seen before. The gunfire was like lightning at night, revealing the contours of their surroundings. Arman stayed tight on the heels of Atrin, praying he knew where he was going.

Finally they reached the end of the hallway and realized that it turned a corner to the right. They practically dove into the open space, desperate to get out of the direct path of bullets. Looking up, they saw that the new hallway was very short, only about six feet long, but there were several doors. Arman jerked on the door nearest to him, but it was solidly shut. He tried the one next to it, but it was just as immovable. Atrin yanked on another door, one with a window, but it wouldn't open either. "The stairs are in here," he said, looking through the window. He took a deep breath, wrapped both hands tightly around the knob, and practically ripped the door off its hinges. Arman rushed in, ready to fly up the stairs, when Atrin did something so unexpected, it left him stunned.

"Wait here for just a few seconds," he instructed Arman, who really didn't feel like standing there for even half a second. He watched, mouth gaping, as Atrin ran about ten feet back into the bullet-riddled hallway, grabbed a bag hanging on the door of an empty cell, and sped back to safety. After turning the corner he rummaged through the bag, eventually pulling out a wallet. His breathing was labored, but not too heavy, when he said his final words to Arman.

"This is yours. Now run!"

Arman grabbed the wallet quizzically, then leaped onto the stairs, climbing close to two floors, even though it was pitch black, when he realized Atrin wasn't behind him. *What happened to him?* His instinct told him to just keep running, but he found that he couldn't take another step. He had to see if he was okay. He fell back down the stairs and burst the door open, fully expecting to find Atrin wounded and needing help. But he saw… nothing. He heard nothing as well. The fighting had stopped! *Is this good or bad?* Considering the thought only briefly, he came to a conclusion. *That depends on who won.* Arman felt his way to the corner and risked a glimpse down the long corridor.

Atrin walked slowly and calmly, hands in the air, toward men pointing flashlights in his face. His silhouette floated down the hallway, a lamb to the slaughter.

"Stop where you are! This is the police!"

"I'm the one you're looking for." Atrin's voice was calm and purposeful.

Arman's mouth ran dry, his feet like metal posts in the floor. He knew he should run, but he just stood there, mesmerized. *What is he doing? Should I help him?* Variations of these two questions spun him in circles until he heard something crack. It was a sickening noise, one he'd heard before. He looked up and saw Atrin slump to the floor as a policeman raised the butt of his rifle for another blow. Arman knew he couldn't do anything to help, but he continued to stand there, paralyzed. Finally, he remembered Atrin's words, the ones that gave him such inexplicable peace less than an hour earlier.

"I want to set you free."

It made him nauseous to think about leaving without Atrin, but he ran back into the stairwell and climbed faster than he thought possible. He felt his way upward by holding onto the rails, continually turning right as it led him higher. He guessed he had climbed the equivalent of five floors when the stairs suddenly ended and he crashed into a wall. He hit it head first and careened to the ground. *What now?* He began feeling the walls for a door when he heard footsteps in the stairwell below. Frantically, he continued searching until he knew there couldn't possibly be a way through the walls around him. He was at a dead end.

Footsteps crept ever closer as he waited in silence. He saw flashlights now and realized there would be no opportunity for him to jump on anyone in the dark. There was nothing to do but wait for the inevitable. It was odd, he finally realized, that the footsteps weren't coming toward him with any haste. They were dutiful and deliberate, not hurried in the slightest. As a flashlight pointed up the center of the stairwell, Arman saw something above him sparkle for an ever-brief moment. He reached up and, to his incredible relief, felt a steel ladder. As quietly as possible, he pulled his body upward a few rungs until his feet were solidly on the bottom rung, then darted up and away from the unwanted visitor. As he climbed into further darkness, he kept waiting for the flashlight to shine directly on him. And perhaps to hear gunfire. To his great surprise, this never happened. Eventually he realized that there was no noise below him at all. *Is he even trying to follow me?*

2 8

THE NEWS

In a dream last night I saw an ancient one in the
    garden of love, beckoning with his hand, saying,
    "Come here."
On this path, Love is the emerald,
the beautiful green that wards off dragons.
— *Rumi*

His head smacked the top of the tunnel but he was unfazed, raising his hands and pushing it open all in one smooth motion. He jumped to his feet and fought the temptation to bask in the unusually cool breeze, not to mention the fact that, even though it was the middle of the night, he could actually see the shapes of objects and light in the distance. It was now almost a full day from when he'd last been above ground with Habib, searching for the entrance into the Hell he'd just escaped. He knew he was still in the Forest Eco Park because of the trees, the foliage, and the enormous KL Tower still pointing in one clear direction toward the sky, but he had no idea how to get out the way he came in. Finally, he realized he was holding his shirt and a wallet. He threw the shirt on, unaware in the low lighting whether or not it was on straight or backward, and held up the wallet to the best available light and realized it was actually his own. *Why did Atrin risk getting his wallet for him? And why did he give himself up?*

He didn't want to draw any attention to himself, but there was no choice except to find the common tourist entrance. The back entrance, which had been used to smuggle him in, was under the control of Habib's friends. He followed a couple of lamps until he reached a dimly lit path, fluorescent light bouncing off large banana leaves, and walked up a steep hill until he saw stairs that looked like they led to a walkway out of the park. So far he hadn't seen anyone, so he sprinted up the circular steps to the top, saw two more walkways that looked like they were situated in the top branches of nearby trees, and chose the one that led to KL Tower.

He made two miscalculations before hitting the walkway. The first one was not seeing the Malay couple, obviously wanting to be alone, kissing on the side of the path, partially hidden by a tree branch. The other was forgetting that a concave, wooden walkway usually meant it was a swaying bridge. His first two footsteps hit hard and solid, propelling the young lovers into the air, grasping at the branches for stability. His third step missed completely, sending him crashing to the ground under their feet. They screamed in unison with no discernible cadence to differentiate the boys from the girl. The couple grabbed the rail and were able to gain their balance, but that meant, unfortunately, landing on various parts of Arman. He scrambled out from underneath them, jumped to his feet, and apologized in a panic. He expected to be hit or yelled at, but all he received were breathless gasps and bulging eyes. Realizing he wasn't the only one in this scenario preoccupied with not getting caught, Arman sped into the city.

He ran down the steep roadway leading to KL Tower, onto Jalan Puncak, took a right on Jalan P. Ramlee, and continued like a convict through the darkest roads he could find. He knew very quickly he was lost, but at first he didn't care. He just needed to know he'd escaped from the police in the dungeon. Now that it was apparent he was free from immediate danger, he wanted to figure out where he was in the city. He remembered how Farzin had taught him to look at the Petronas Towers as kind of a North Star, an immovable fixture revealing their general location in the city. He looked up reflexively to see what they would reveal about his location, but they were invisible to him.

Because he hadn't seen a single police car on the streets, he stood in the shadow of a palm tree next to an empty road and pondered what had just transpired. He thought about Atrin telling the police, "I'm the one you're looking for," but blew it off as inconsequential. After all, he thought, they'll clearly see that he's not the same person in the security camera videos. *But why would he even try that?* While he found the thought of no one chasing him incredibly appealing, so was the idea that the government in Iran would change. He would not let himself hope for either. Meanwhile, he was starving and began hunting for a nasi kandar. He took out his wallet and found he had no cash. His ID and credit cards were still there, but that obviously didn't help him. If he wanted to eat, he'd have to steal.

Eventually he reached a shop lot and recognized it as the neighborhood where he lived - Bandar Raja! While this felt comforting, he knew he had to be careful not to be seen by anyone he knew. He crept toward the nasi kandar he'd become so familiar with until he reached the edge of the open air entrance. The smell of roti canai hung so thick in the air it made him feel like he'd gained three pounds already. Chicken curry and rice appeared to be easily accessible, but he didn't know where the workers were yet. He decided to walk casually past the store and glance around. As he did so, he saw two young Indian men behind the counter, dark collared shirts and mustaches, each laying with a chair to the back of a wall and their legs propped up on another chair in front of them, dead asleep.

Arman tiptoed into the restaurant, ears attuned to any noise outside of the flat panel TVs hanging on the bare walls, and past a long row of white tables with metal chairs lining each side. One of the televisions showed a soccer game between Manchester United and Everton. Another was playing a Bollywood film in the middle of a dance scene. It was the third screen, however, that froze him in his tracks. Arman was reaching for a plate when a woman's voice, interrupting several seconds of on-air silence, abruptly inquired, "Arman Javadi, is that you?" The hair on his arms stood on end and his limbs stiffened. It was all he could do to avoid knocking the stack of plates over. He jerked his head around to see who was behind him, but only saw a woman on a blue screen instead. At the top left of the TV, there was a picture of a young man in a green shirt with a similar beard as Arman, but his face wasn't perfectly visible. She continued. "This is what authorities are asking now that a man named Atrin Shirazi confessed both that he was with the Petronas Tower bombers and that he was the coward who let go of the stroller on the crosswalk." Arman tried to take in these words, but it was too disorienting in the moment. He walked closer to the TV and stood on the opposite side of a pillar from the restaurant workers so they couldn't see him. And to steady himself.

The camera shifted from the newscaster to a policeman who was being questioned live outside of a police station in downtown KL. He had his right hand on his head in a look of bewilderment. "We raided an underground bunker where the terrorist network was hiding," he said. "There was a shootout lah! Most of them are dead, but we took Atrin Shirazi into custody. He fits the description of the young man in the white t-shirt on the security cameras." He stopped to take in a few labored breaths. "And he was wearing the same shirt when we caught him! It didn't take long for him to confess to the whole thing lah." They showed a picture of Atrin taken a few months earlier, standing on a boulder in Cameron Highlands, burnt orange sunset in the background, arms spread wide.

He looks a lot like me. Arman put a hand to his mouth and began to tear up. *He's confessed to doing something he didn't do? And how is he wearing the same shirt I was wearing?* Arman stood there astounded, the implications beginning to sink in even through the confusion.

"Previously we thought the accomplice was Arman Javadi, the cousin of one of the bombers. But now we're convinced Arman is actually the young man in the green shirt, the one who saved the child in the security camera footage on the crosswalk." The reporter, an older Chinese gentleman with slicked back hair, pulled the microphone away from the policeman. "Then why do you think Mr. Javadi ran away?" The policeman explained, "We're not sure lah, but perhaps it's because they look a bit alike. It makes sense that seeing a picture of a wanted man who looked like him, and being a cousin of the bomber, made him believe he'd be blamed. Remember, it was only later that footage of the hero in the green shirt showed up." The policeman stopped looking at the reporter and peered into the camera. "Arman, no need to hide lah! We see what you did and we want to thank you. Terima kasih, Arman Javadi!"

Unable to see the TV clearly, Arman reached for his shirt to wipe his face. It was at this moment that he made the most humbling and overwhelming discovering of his relatively short life. Ever since he'd left the underground bunker and threw his shirt on, he'd been running in the middle of the night through the darkest alleyways he could find. He'd also been too extremely preoccupied to notice. But now, in the bright neon light of the Bandar Raja nasi kandar, he was looking down at the piece of cloth in his right hand, dumbfounded. His shirt was green. The beautiful color of freedom.

The screech of a metal chair clamored behind him. Arman looked back to see one of the young Indian workers transfixed, staring at the screen with a quizzical smile. Arman looked back at the TV to see that it was a picture of him with a caption underneath. He didn't catch all of what it said, but it included the phrase, "local hero." He looked back at the young Indian man, who was now pointing at him. It was understandable that Arman's instinct was to think that someone extending a finger in his direct was bad news. He froze, waiting for what would happen next. The restaurant worker bobbed his head back and forth slightly, his expression changing to one of wonder. "You're the hero lah!"

Arman managed a slight smile, but that was all he could take of the awkward moment. It was too overwhelming and seemed too good to be true, so he did the one thing he knew how to do. He ran.

~

He sped down the Lebuhraya Bandar Raja sidewalk, avoiding the light from the lampposts as much as possible. The long rows of palm trees were a comfort to him, as was anything else that temporarily blocked the light from revealing his identity. He instinctively looked at the street corners ahead for the reflection of blue and red lights, but there was nothing. He saw the large field in front of Bandar Raja Secondary School to his left and swung open the gate to let himself inside, thirsting for solitude. He just needed time to think. The darkest place in the field was next to the wide, bowl-shaped rain trees, so he jogged in their direction and collapsed on his back in the dark. Just thirty minutes ago, darkness was captivity. Now it was solace. He laid on his back in the dry grass and peered into the starless sky.

Did I really just see that on TV? His fists clenched nervously and his eyes shut tightly, as if he could gain clarity by the sheer effort. There were so many details to sort out. He'd have to take them one at a time. *It's just a mistake. There's no way he'd get beat up for me and take the blame like that. Nobody does that. Especially for someone who isn't family or a close friend! But the switched shirts… Yeah, that was just a mixup as well. It was so dark, how would he know? And just because he said, 'I'm the one you're looking for…'"* Remembering Atrin's last words stumped him and made his previous arguments feel shaky at best. He rose to his feet and paced and forth in the field next to the grove of trees, taking care to remain in their dark shadows.

Atrin was on the crosswalk with us! Why didn't he tell me? Why did he sit there and listen to all my problems without even mentioning what he did? He replayed the events in his head. The only image he had of Atrin on the bridge was what he'd just seen on TV. It occurred to him that he'd blocked these events out of his mind because he couldn't bear to picture Farzin and Banu reaching for explosives. Regardless, he forced himself back to the place of terror, then he remembered. *Someone reached down to help me off the bridge before it fell… He was wearing a green shirt! Wait… it was the same guy who returned my wallet!* Arman grabbed a handful of his new shirt.

Atrin's shirt. The one that identified him as a hero instead of a suspected terrorist. He thought about Atrin throwing his wallet back to him in the underground bunker. *A weird coincidence to have done that twice*, he thought, before moving on to the greater issues at hand.

Eventually all of his arguments that Atrin hadn't really tried to save him fell short. The extreme act of compassion left him undone. Not only was it clear that he switched places with him on purpose, it was also becoming evident that, against all logic available to Arman, Atrin had known he would save him even before he entered the Petronas Towers.

I was so angry when he wouldn't give me an answer for Mahnaz's death. There were so many questions I would've demanded an answer even if he'd answered the first one. But now, after seeing what he's done for me… what could I possibly demand of him? As he pondered Atrin's actions, he realized another layer of pain his new friend endured. *His father! Atrin lit up the dark when he spoke of him. What would he think? How would it affect their relationship? And… how will his father handle the shame of people thinking his son is a terrorist?!* Arman rehashed the same arguments that Atrin couldn't have done this on purpose, but came to the same conclusion as before. It was planned.

He laid back down, hands covering his face, intently trying to remember everything Atrin said to him. While they were together, some things resonated and others he dismissed. But now, lying in stunned wonder at what just happened in his own personal Green Revolution, every word Atrin said in that horrid place seemed like soft and precious gold. He gathered up his teachings like a mother cradling an infant child, immediately uncovering layers of truth made clearer in light of his sacrifice. He was shocked, wonderstruck, transformed, and profoundly humbled. This was not how he thought it would happen, but for the first time, he felt…

Free.

Not just free from punishment. But he was also free from being shunned by family and friends. While Arman had been running from the authorities, he only imagined a slight hope that he could physically escape. But Atrin gave him the possibility of once again having meaningful and joyful relationships, which was suddenly understood as a gift equal to an entire kingdom.

He lay there for thirty of the most peaceful minutes he'd ever known, occasionally sitting up and looking around just to remember where he was and where he'd been. He eventually decided it was time to leave. While considering his next step, however, another voice interrupted the sanctity of the moment. *So I'm really just supposed to accept what he's done and act like it's true for the rest of my life?* The question didn't come out of a concern for truth. It came from pride. *Surely I can figure something out and explain it so we can both go free. After all, it's one thing for me to be declared innocent. But a hero?! While he suffers? It's not fair. There has to be a better way. A way that will keep him from being punished any further. A way that will clear his name and remove his shame. And when it's all over, I won't owe him so much. In fact, I could practically make things even!* Having a plan that allowed him to make things better on his own terms gave him a certain amount of satisfaction. He didn't want to live the rest of his life owing so much to one person. He marched toward the gate with more purpose than he experienced while lying down just a few moments ago, although the moment carried a little less joy and a lot less wonder. But he now felt as though he were in charge, and he clung to this emotion as a drunkard grasps the bottle.

"You're an imbecile!" The voice came from the blackness of the grove. He suddenly recognized the trees. He certainly recognized the voice, for it was the only sound in his world that made him long to listen to Habib. The three voices of Dahag exploded in his head. The high-pitched voice, like someone drilling into a steel door, the chanting of an old sage, and the frenzied voice of a woman being attacked. He stopped dead in his tracks, peered underneath the canopy of branches, and slowly backed away. The leaves shook and the three heads of Dahag emerged into the dim light, all six eyes emanating a piercing red glow as they fixated on Arman. His three mouths worked in perfect sync and unbearable dissonance at the same time.

"You think someone would do that for you?! Pathetic! Atrin's just like you, Arman. He may try to convince you he has some kind of self-sacrificial love, but deep down he just wants to be liked. As soon as he realizes his plan isn't working, he'll sell you out in a second!" Every syllable pierced through Arman's left ear, tunneled through his head, and slithered out the other side, causing both emotional and literal pain. As much as Arman despised Dahag, however, the monster was only confirming what he already felt was true.

"You're right about one thing," the three-headed snake dragon hissed. "You're going to need another story! And you'd better make it a good one because he's about to turn on you any second now!" Dahag leaped out of the tree, spreading his enormous wings and gliding through the air toward Arman. He landed five feet in front of him, slammed into the earth with such force it shook like an earthquake, knocking Arman to the ground.

An intense reddish glow rose behind Arman, showering Dahag in a light unfamiliar to the frightened young Persian. The dragon's teeth glittered as he lifted all three heads, towering above his prey. His scales shone in hues of red, orange, and yellow, some of them bright enough to almost blind Arman. He lifted his hands to shield himself from the reflective light and looked the other way, causing him to see its strange and horrifying source. It was at this point where the city seemed to fade into alternate reality.

Behind Dahag was a fire, beginning about a hundred feet away, as long and as wide as the Caspian Sea. Billows of smoke spewed out of random pockets like geysers in a valley. A wave of heat emanated from the flames with such violence it would've blown Arman into Dahag's fangs if he'd been standing up. The roar from the inferno intensified until he couldn't even hear the jaded screams of Dahag behind him. He was beyond terrified.

Dahag lifted himself up with his wings, head still raised high above his body. Then, in a swift and sudden movement, he raised up his steel-tipped tail above him, positioning himself for the dive that would be Arman's end. He twisted his three necks around each other like a coiled rope, wrapped his wings tightly around his body, and spiraled downward like a jet fighter for dramatic, and even whimsical, effect. But he never touched his intended victim.

Arman's hands covered his face and his eyes were half closed, just open enough to see a shadow pass over him. Out of the corner of his eye, he saw an enormous serpent, green and sleek, uncoiling into the side of Dahag, grabbing him with its fangs and then, with a twist of his body, slung him away from Arman. Dahag shrieked, stunned into silence by the unexpected enemy, then unfurled his wings to again try an attack from above. But the snake, shaped like an enormous pit viper, was too fast. It bounded upward and met Dahag on his own terms, in the air, impossibly wrapping its body around the dragon until his wings were useless. They tumbled to the ground and the viper, completely in control, rolled him in the direction of the flames. In one swift and final motion, it uncoiled and hurled Dahag deep into the sea of fire, never to be seen again.

It was in this moment, at long last, Arman became aware that he was in a dream. He also realized he'd been dreaming for a long time.

This awareness, however, only lasted for a few minutes. He would later declare, while shaking his head in wonder, that the rest of the dream felt more real than anything that ever happened to him. It was as if all of his previous life on earth had been a mere shadow and the dream, instead, was the ultimate reality. As if all nightmares in the world had somehow been undone and the only thing he doubted were all the unpleasant memories which previously haunted him.

2 9

———

THROUGH THE FIRE

Arman wasn't sure what to make of the viper, but several things took place very quickly. First, the voices stopped. The accusations, half-truths, and outright lies… They just went away. It was as if someone removed a tumor from his lungs and he was truly breathing for the first time. Second, the sea of fire began to change. Its howling came to an abrupt stop and the flames died down until they smoothed out into an endless body of water, clear as glass. He found himself standing on sand instead of grass and, somehow, knew that he was looking at the Caspian Sea on a beach in Shomal, Iran.

The Malaysian humidity was gone, replaced by a cool breeze mercifully washing through his shirt and sweat-filled beard. Stars emerged in the clear night sky like the eyes of owls in a black forest. The fire didn't completely disappear, however. As it dissipated over the sea, remnants of its flames gathered together, climbed onto the shore, and organized themselves into small patches like campfires, cozy and inviting. Then, as Arman's eyes adjusted to the dark, the green snake curled toward a pier a few hundred feet away. It surprised him to know that he felt no fear whatsoever. Instead, he calmly followed the huge serpent as it crawled with purpose down

255

the beach. Its diamond-shaped scales collected the available light and reflected it back to Arman like emerald mirrors. He only saw a few lampposts in the distance and the stars above, but the snake seemed to both absorb and multiply the light until it became its own unique source of illumination. The viper reached the pier and slithered onto a supporting pole, close to where the water met the shoreline. It scattered a green warmth across the beach, underneath the pier, and onto the water like a strobe light as he circled its way up the pole. Arman assumed it was taking a shortcut to the pier, so he turned to find his way to the entrance designed for two-legged creatures like himself. He only took one step when something stopped him.

"Just look."

This wasn't the first time he'd heard a voice inside his head, but Dahag's was a taste of Hell. This was the aroma of Heaven. He was completely lost to any other reality except what lay before him, including the preposterous idea that this could just be a dream. He stared, transfixed on the serpent. The longer he looked, the more he saw personality in its eyes. In direct contrast to everything he would've expected, he didn't see the usual emptiness that one sees in the pupils of a reptile. He saw love. He also saw wisdom.

"Accept it, Arman."

He stood there with his hands in his pockets, unsure if it was okay to speak but just as confused about what the serpent meant. Eventually, he managed a response.

"Accept what?" He watched the snake's mouth to see if it would move, but the voice remained inside his head only.

"Accept what Atrin did for you. Accept the great sacrifice and the extravagance of his love. Let him accept your guilt and your shame. He can take it. His father can take it. Trust in what Atrin has done and let yourself be transformed."

The serpent paused to let Arman absorb its words. The only sound came from waves gently breaking on the shore. The breeze became sweeter and his lungs continued to increase their capacity to breathe. He remembered the way he felt after he first grasped the implications of the news. His newfound freedom. Gratefulness.

Humility. Wonder. Then he thought about what happened as soon as he decided to take things back into his own hands. Pride. Stress. Futility.

"Just look." The glistening viper repeated its first words. Arman was beginning to understand the rest of what he said, but not this. He hesitated to question the serpent, but he needed to know.

"What do you mean by 'just look?'"

The snake somehow had a countenance that communicated both intensity and joy. It wasn't a smile, but somehow Arman knew it was happy to give him this final message.

"You need to talk with Yusuf."

Yusuf? Isn't he dead? Everything seemed so surreal in the moment, it somehow seemed easy to just assume he was still alive. Still, he loved and respected Yusuf, but he'd only known him for over a month.

And he hated the idea of having to wait until sometime in the future to get an answer. As he pondered this disappointment, the serpent crawled down from the pole and slithered into a dark shadow under the pier. Arman wanted to follow, but somehow he knew he wasn't supposed to. Green light scattered onto the bottom of the tall wooden structure, but he could no longer see its source.

It was when the snake was no longer visible that the light began to intensify. Instead of glittering, it became stable and consistent. This was calming at first, but it continued to strengthen until, in a flash, it developed a sudden energy and weight to it that knocked Arman to the ground. The soundless explosion stunned him, leaving him in the sand with his hands covering his face to protect his eyes as if he were lying next to the sun itself.

Even with his face covered he noticed the light was changing from green to white. His pulse raced with fear, but his curiosity increased as well. Every few seconds he would risk cracking one eye open to see if he could catch a glimpse of what was happening. After several unsuccessful attempts, his eyes finally adjusted to the brightness. Or was he being adjusted? He peered through a slit between his fingers to see, not a serpent, but a man. At least, he could tell it was the outline of a man, but it was impossible to look directly at him. His clothes blazed like fire, radiating with a force Arman could actually feel, pressing him down and calming him at the same time. His heart rate unexpectedly slowed and, as it continued to do so, the light slowly dimmed and the pressure also disappeared. He risked more frequent glimpses of the man if for no other reason than to make sure he wasn't coming any closer.

"Stand up, Arman. You have no reason to fear."

Arman wasn't exactly convinced of this, but he stood at attention nonetheless. The light dimmed until he could discern some details of the man's features.

"Who are you?"

The man chuckled, like someone laughing at a friend. "I'm fiery," he said with a slightly discernible smirk. "And full of energy."

"Atrin!" Arman's hands flew to his mouth and he stood still, unsure if he should hug him or fear him. *Did he really take the blame on purpose or will he be angry with me?* It was all still too absurd for Arman to completely believe. Finally, he stammered, "How… how did you get out?"

Atrin smiled, took the three steps necessary to reach Arman, and began to raise his hands. Arman flinched, only to find himself enveloped in Atrin's arms. He was still confused, but the fear had melted away completely. He placed his hands lightly on Atrin's back, hesitant to return the embrace with equal strength. Atrin placed his hands on Arman's shoulders and looked him in the eyes.

"Everything you know is about to change, Arman."

He put his right arm around Arman's shoulders and faced the pier. Now that both the green and white light had faded, the only sources of illumination were interspersed patches of fire, each about five feet in diameter, and the soft glow coming from Atrin himself. Arman saw the silhouette of a woman, hunched over, lurching forward with halted and labored motions. She moved inch by inch with great effort, but she wasn't walking toward them.

Instead, she seemed to be walking toward a fire only a few feet from where the water ended its course, drifting back into the sea. Her face more visible now, Arman saw the creases marking her life's journey. Lines fell from the corner of her eyes down the side of her pale cheeks. Locks of long hair, gray and tangled, fell out of her dark head covering. Now only a couple of feet from the campfire, and not slowing down, Arman started to rush over to stop the frail woman from falling in, but Atrin held him by the shoulder.

"She's going to burn herself." Arman trusted him, but he was confused. Atrin returned his question with an enthusiastic smile. His voice was calm.

"Watch, Arman."

She looked down with an intelligence in her eyes, but also a weariness communicating she was almost out of hope. One of the logs collapsed into the middle of the pile, the ensuing sparks causing the fire to spike in both height and intensity. Flames of orange and yellow, occasionally carrying a hint of green, seemed to lean toward the woman as if inviting her to enjoy their warmth. She began speaking, but was still looking at the fire. Arman thought she was just mumbling something to herself since he couldn't hear the words, but as her volume gently increased, he realized she was chanting, repeating the same lines again and again as if to convince herself of some ancient truth concealed inside a simple poem. He was still unable to audibly discern what she was saying, but as soon as she took a few steps, still staring at the fire, he knew.

Give me your healthy glow. Take my sickly pallor.

"You can't let her jump!" Arman looked at Atrin in bewilderment, but his expression was unchanged. Arman felt Atrin's strong hand clutching his shoulder, keeping him in place. The weary woman no longer just quoted the poem. She lifted her head back, inhaled deeply, and sang it with all of her might.

Give me your healthy glow! Take my sickly pallor!

"I realize your last jump didn't go well, Arman, but I promise you this won't be her fate."

Give me your healthy glow!

Take my sickly pallor!

Her voice became stronger and strangely beautiful to Arman. It occasionally cracked and some of the words were strained, but it was an alluring melody, both haunting and hopeful. He was so familiar with the words, however, that he really didn't think about their meaning at all. To Arman it was just a tradition. Sure, he knew Iranians repeated it as they expressed hope for the new year, but mostly it was just about the fun of jumping over a fire. Since it now reminded him of pain and shame, the meaning of this moment was only more obscured. When the woman looked up at Atrin with a playful smile, joyful and full of faith, Arman finally realized what was happening. She hadn't been singing. She was praying.

She staggered forward with three long steps and leaped into the air, Atrin still holding Arman in place. There was no way, he thought, that she could make it over, especially with only three steps. Her loose dark clothing created a ghostly silhouette as she ascended over the fire, her hair swirling freely in the breeze. In the first moment after jumping, Arman could tell that something, or someone, seemed to help her climb, but something else was happening as well. The stars in the background grew brighter and stronger. As the brave woman reached her apex above the fire, there was yet another exposition of light, this one more like a camera flash, temporarily blinding Arman and preventing him from seeing the rest of her journey over the abyss.

Realizing Atrin had let go over his shoulder, he ran to the woman to see if she was okay. His instinct was to bend down on the other side of the fire to help the lady to her feet, but no one was there. He looked inside the fire, on the side where she began the jump, and then around the other sides, but saw nothing. He rubbed his eyes as the scene came back into focus, but he heard the woman before he saw her. She was laughing. Not at Arman, though. It was the kind of laughter you might hear from a young woman experiencing snow for the first time. He turned around to see that she was about five feet behind him. *How could she have jumped that far?!* Whatever the explanation, it had surely happened. As a matter of fact, she was still jumping. Her smile was like the innocent serenity of a child. The lines were gone. Her hunched posture gave way to a confident stance, though she didn't seem focused on herself in the slightest. She was looking at Atrin. She ran, jumped, spun in circles, and crashed into his arms. He embraced her with the same acceptance Arman had encountered only moments ago. Beautiful tears, both quiet and joyful, gently flowed from the corners of their eyes. They stood still as the woman expressed her gratefulness in hushed tones meant only for him. They turned and looked at Arman.

"This is Farah, a dear sister for you, Arman." Arman blushed, confused by what Atrin meant by "for you."

"It's a pleasure to meet you, Farah."

Farah took a few steps toward Arman. Now that he could see her face clearly, he was in wonder over what could only be described as a complete transformation. He couldn't tell her age for sure, but she was no longer the older woman he saw approach the fire. Her cheeks were flush with color, smooth as the sea lying only a few feet away. The greatest changes, however, could only be described in terms of countenance. Strength and humility. Passion and sobriety. Bursting with energy and yet calm and serene.

"It's your turn, Arman." Her smile reminded him of Mahnaz. He put his hands in his pockets and looked at the fire. The breeze from the Caspian Sea fanned the flames as if on cue. He wasn't sure what had happened with Farah, but he knew he was supposed to follow her lead. The longer he stared at the flames, however, the more he was filled with shame. In his mind, his last Charharshanbeh Suri had marked him forever.

"Arman!" Atrin diverted his attention from the fire to himself. "There's nothing you can do about it. You can't take away your shame. You'll never be able to restore your own honor." His words were ominous, but his tone was hopeful, eyes flooded with sincerity as he pleaded with Arman. "Trust me."

He walked toward the blaze and stopped about ten feet away, just enough distance to reach full speed. His heart beat slowly, but erratic and pounding. And for the first time since standing on the beach, his scars burned like hot wax. He clutched his chest, instinctively gasping for air. At the same time, the fire grew longer and wider. He'd been fairly sure that he could clear the flames before, but now the fire was at least ten feet in diameter. He looked to Atrin, eyes pleading for either an explanation or a reprieve.

"Why is it longer for me?"

"It only needs to be a little longer than you believe you can jump."

Still holding his chest, Arman was frustrated. "Well… how is that fair?"

"Oh, it's not fair at all," Atrin said flatly. "Fair is the last thing you want. But if you trust me, I promise you'll reach the other side and what you'll receive is beyond anything you've ever deserved."

Arman walked a few feet closer, knowing this was no longer about his ability. As he let go of the idea that he needed to prepare, concentrate, and execute. An unexpected peace came over him. It wasn't logical, of course, since this fire was significantly longer than any fire he'd ever cleared by himself, but somehow he knew he was dealing with a differently reality now. He looked at Atrin again to find him both resolute and encouraging.

"So you're going to help me?"

"Yes," Atrin replied. "Do you believe?"

Arman hesitated, searching his heart and considering everything that had happened in the last couple of days.

"I do believe," he managed. "But…" "But what?"

Arman was worried if he said what he was thinking, Atrin would call the whole thing off. Finally, he found the courage to be honest.

"There's a part of me that's struggling to believe."

Atrin smiled, unfazed. "I can help you with that."

Closing his eyes, Arman took the first two large steps toward the flames. As he looked back on this later, he wouldn't remember the next steps at all, not even the jump. Before he knew it, his arms were flailing and his legs were moving as if he were running, but he was mid-air. Not only was he mid-air, but it was as if he was floating. And time slowed down into an impossible crawl.

Looking into the flames, he saw something in the wood that sent him into a panic. Red glowing embers on top of two cross-shaped logs scattered and moved around until they formed images. The first one was his father. As soon as he was able to discern who it was, it changed into moving pictures as clear as a computer screen. Jalal was alone in their living room, his face soured in anger and disappointment. Still hovering over the fire, Arman's heart dropped. The scene dissipated until he was confronted with an outline of embers in the image of his mother. Zia was alone in her bedroom while Jalal was brooding on the other side of the house. She clutched a picture of Arman in her arms, tears dripping onto the the frame. Arman was almost halfway over the fire now, but he felt as if he may as well be inside it. Finally, the last image was of himself in the back of the video game store wearing the virtual reality headgear. Then he understood. Atrin knew everything. Surely he was about to face the eternal punishment he'd always been warned about. The one he'd simultaneously feared and convinced himself would never happen.

A flame shot out of the fire like orange lightning. It entered into the scar on Arman's ankle, shot up his left leg, through his torso, and into the wound on his chest, which was now emanating a dark yellowish glow. It flew out of his chest and slammed into his face, knocking his head backward.

Every day for almost a year he'd dealt with the pain of trying to clean his wounds in the shower. It felt both horrible and hopeless. Not just because the scars always seemed to get worse even while trying to do whatever he could to heal them, but also because it was a reminder of his failures. The surge running through his body at the moment, however, was entirely different. There was no question that it hurt much worse, and not just on the surface.

It coursed through his flesh and bones with an immobilizing force, drawing the very air out of his lungs. And yet, he began to understand that this was not a hopeless pain. It was more like a doctor wrenching a dislocated shoulder into place.

He landed on both feet, steady and unharmed, and immediately knew he'd been changed. The first thing he saw was the smiling face of Atrin. The first thing he heard, however, was Farah, cheering and singing Atrin's praises. She twirled and danced in circles, kicking up sand all around them.

Atrin put his right hand on Arman's left shoulder and looked deeply into his eyes. "Show me your scars." Arman met his gaze and, for a brief moment, saw something that stopped him in his tracks. Something mysterious and ancient, burning like the forges of the firmament. It was a power to be feared for sure, but he discerned, even in the span of a few seconds, that this was a constructive force.

The command, however, seemed quite cruel. Why should he have to expose the ugliest and most shameful part of himself? Arman pointed to the top of his beard on his left cheek, to his ankle, and then pulled up his shirt to reveal the mark he'd never shown to anyone but his mother.

"I don't see anything, Arman. Are you sure you're pointing to the right place?" He revealed a mischievous grin and waited. Arman lifted his right hand to his face and felt for the old familiar scabs. Nothing. He hastily bent down and reached underneath his jeans to feel his ankle. Smooth as a newborn baby. He slowed down, now staring at Atrin, and slid a trembling hand underneath his shirt to feel for any evidence of Dahag. There was none. He was healed! Finally, after nearly a year of pain and embarrassment, an excruciating cycle of thinking he was healing only for new cracks to form and old cracks to re-emerge, his skin was finally restored. And not only the skin, even his thick chest hair had regrown, blanketing his former wound.

"How did you…?" He didn't know how to finish the sentence and, instead, just stared in awe.

"Let me show you," Atrin replied. He reached for the bottom of his brilliant white shirt and slowly lifted it up.

CASPIAN TREE

Arman's breath halted. He collapsed to his knees in tears, undone by what he saw.

This can't be real. No one would do this for someone else. Especially for someone they barely know. And definitely not for me.

He reached under his own shirt and placed his hand over his newly healed chest while staring at Atrin's.

"It's real, Arman. And I know you better than you realize." There was acute joy in Atrin's eyes, yet his smile carried a hint of sobriety. "You can feel my wounds if you need to."

His wounds… All Arman could do was stare at the scar. He knew every crack, scab, and puss-filled bump. He'd tended this monstrosity daily for what seemed like a lifetime. Every day he watched to see if there was some sign of healing. There had been many times he was convinced it was improving only to slowly realize this was just wishful thinking. And now his scars belonged to Atrin.

Who would do this? Why did he have to take it on himself? Couldn't it have just been healed? A thousand questions whirled, but he wasn't allowed much time to dwell on them. Apparently, it was time to celebrate.

Farah jerked him to his feet by his left arm, startling Arman and making Atrin laugh.

"It's time to watch our people set free!"

Arman looked up to see a steady stream of men and women emerge from the shadows of the pier. Withered and limping, they walked zombie-like toward the various pockets of fire scattered across the beach. An older woman in a black hijab, oblivious to Arman's presence, lurched past Arman and was just close enough to the light emanating from Atrin to see the contours of her face. Her forehead was wrinkled, worrisome lines crawling from the corners of her eyebrows to her jaws. A tuft of grey hair inadvertently fell out of her head covering and fluttered over her eyes, but she paid no attention. Like others around her, she quickened her pace toward an open fire. Without hesitation, she leaped over the flames, a flash of light temporarily blinding those around her. Arman looked up to see her on the other side, or was that a different woman? The stressed lines on her face were gone, replaced by a ruby gleam and a bright smile that radiated with new life. Her head covering had fallen off during the jump, revealing shiny black locks which had fallen to her shoulders, framing her glowing countenance. Arman watched in awe as the scene was repeated hundreds of times in front of him. Young men in jeans and t-shirts, older men in suits or traditional Iranian clothing, women in chadors, young women in tank tops… all moving forward in faith and re-emerging as new creations.

The bursts of light, much slower for those being transformed, appeared to Arman like a lightning storm ravaging the shores of Shamol. All along the beach, as far as his eyes could see, his fellow Iranians were being re-made, their numbers like the sand underneath them. He swelled with the joy of a man discovering a treasure he'd never known to seek.

Spontaneous celebrations erupted all over the banks of the Caspian Sea, some dancing, some singing, others doing backflips into the water and swimming into the modest waves. A few of these waves suddenly jumped, as if to join the party, lifting several of the women fifteen feet into the air before dropping them safely near the shore. They sprang up and pulled their hair out of their eyes, laughing in wonder. Some of those on the beach saw what happened by the flashes of light still emanating from above the fires. Hundreds of wonder-filled Persians suddenly rushed into the water, shouting praises and howling with laughter at the same time. They threw themselves with abandon into the harmless waves, knowing any second they would be flung into the air like a father playing with his children in a pool. Arman didn't know what would be more fun, continuing to just watch everything unfold or jumping into the sea himself. He stood in amazement as his greatest hopes for his people were fulfilled before his very eyes.

They were free.

Farah grabbed Arman's hand and pulled him up the beach toward the top of the pier, giggling and skipping in anticipation. "I was told you like piers on the Caspian Sea," she said. He hadn't thought of it since arriving, but now he remembered.

"It feels like home," Arman replied. "And a little bit like Heaven." As he said this, he took in his first real glimpse of the top of the pier. There was soft yellow lighting on both sides from lamps resting on top of thin brown lampposts, leaves circling around them from top to bottom. Arman assumed it was ivy around the posts, but he didn't have a theory about how it could be growing on a pier above the sand. Reflecting on Farah's comments about feeling at home, he realized that, although this pier was clearly different than any he'd ever seen, it somehow felt more like home than the others.

Feeding off of Farah's energy, Arman started to run onto the pier when she suddenly stopped him.

"You wait here first."

Arman was curious, but not irritated. At this point he assumed there was yet another marvel to be discovered. He'd just met Farah and yet she acted as if they were old friends. Normally he would've considered this behavior as flirtatious, but there was something different about this place. Or was there something different about him?

Atrin joined them and helped Farah lift something from behind a bench. It was ten feet long, cylinder-shaped, and more than six feet in diameter. Not only was it large, but Arman thought it looked incredibly unwieldy and offered to help.

"Stay where you are!" There was a playful tone in Farah's voice and a twisted grin on her face. Incredibly, she and Atrin seemed to have no problem carrying the large object and quickly laid it in place. She beamed at Atrin, satisfaction in her eyes, and they bent down in unison, placing open palms on the object. They paused briefly, Atrin making sure he caught Arman's gaze, then lunged upward and flung their arms forward.

A rug, both ancient and pristine, unrolled toward Arman. Every few feet unveiled cross-stitched patterns woven primarily in deep red, with yellow borders and highlights. The outer border, filled with hunter green fig trees, framed a stunningly beautiful Persian carpet. An enormous crimson cross, the cross of St. Thomas, almost reached all sides of the rug.

"It's time to welcome the prince," Atrin said to Farah before turning to Arman.

A sound like the creaking of wood and rustling of leaves materialized from both sides, briefly disorienting Arman. He looked up to see the lampposts bending down toward the center of the pier, covering the area above the rug. Like ancient warriors standing in a row with swords held high, they formed a saber-arch, inviting him to walk underneath. Incredibly, he realized that the "lampposts" weren't really lampposts at all. They were branches. And the entire area below him wasn't made with pieces of cut and varnished wood. They were large and ornate roots. The entire pier was a living tree!

As wondrous as this discovery was, however, the most surreal aspect of the moment was the undeserved attention. And did he hear Atrin use the word "prince?" This was ridiculous, of course, so he remained in place, uncomfortable with walking forward and yet also feeling uneasy about refusing the invitation. Seeing that he needed some encouragement, Farah chirped, "Oh, just do it!"

Atrin smiled as others around them, fresh from the fire, cheered him on. "Prince Arman! Prince Arman!" While loud and joyous, their ovation fell well short of worship. It was more like siblings encouraging their little brother to kick a soccer ball. Their deepest reverence was reserved for another. Although Arman knew he wasn't deserving of this particular honor, it was ultimately his gratefulness for Atrin that gave him the final push.

Stepping forward, he noticed different scenes woven into the spaces formed by the four corners surrounding the cross. On the bottom right, a stone tablet in various shades of yellow, Hebrew characters etched in the middle, was enveloped by a deep red fire tinged with orange. To the left was a simple crown with 12 thin spires, elegant but cracked in the center. At first he perceived this as the traditional Persian flaw, but upon further inspection realized that it was intentionally and perfectly woven into the fabric. Arman trudged over the center of the cross, looking up in wonder at the bowed branches, stopping to touch one of the lamps. Peering inside, he saw dancing flames of yellow with a green tint, but he could discern neither a candle nor any evidence of gas lighting. Just flames. Continuing across the ancient rug, at the top right he saw the golden image of a shepherd wielding a thick staff as a weapon while sheep behind him safely entered a narrow gate. A few of the flock, however, wandered in the opposite direction. The scene on the top left of the rug stood out from the others, both for of its multicolored imagery and the large number of etchings. Still walking toward Atrin, Arman didn't have time to investigate, but a short viewing revealed people from every ethnic and cultural background imaginable, and across the ages by the appearance of their clothing, gathered around a bright golden throne. A burning white emanated from its center, causing Arman to avert his gaze until his eyes adjusted.

By the time he reached the end of the rug, Arman was in tears. As he closed his eyes and wiped his face, the shouts from the crowd were deafening. He looked over to the people, still on the sand, to see what had excited them, when he felt something on his head. Atrin's hand on his shoulder, he reached up to find he was wearing a crown. Atrin turned him around and placed both hands on his shoulders. The cheering stopped abruptly, providing space for the sacred moment.

"In this place, you are a prince. Not because of what you've done, but because you're a son of the king."

Atrin's words entered into the deepest parts of Arman's soul. Years of inadequacy disappeared like ice in a desert as he took the crown into his hands. It was similar to the crown on the rug in its simplicity, yet different in that it had a lone jewel in the center. A glowing emerald illuminated Arman's forehead as he shook his head in astonishment. *A son of the king.* The bewildering honor sealed up deep crevices of shame he'd carried for as long as he could remember, allowing Arman to hold his head up and see the world differently. Not in arrogance, as an earthly prince may be enthralled with the idea of common people seeing his greatness. Just the opposite. He was now free, as if for the first time, to truly see his surroundings, including those around him, without reference to himself at all. Clear-eyed, he beheld Atrin with joy and deep reverence, finally comprehending his true nobility. With sudden haste, he fell to his knees, gently placing the crown at Atrin's feet.

The crowd erupted and rushed to the front of the pier, one by one receiving their own honor as sons and daughters of the king. They glided under the arched branches like brides, eagerly awaiting to be embraced by the arms of royalty. As men and women joined Arman on the other side, they continued to watch each individual with the same awe and anticipation as the first, until everyone had crossed the sacred rug and received their crown. When the last person was through, a spontaneous shout jolted the night sky, shaking the pier underneath them. Arman turned around to see the celebration morph into the most beautiful - and most Iranian - response he could imagine.

Dancing.

As far down the pier as he could see (he now realized it was much longer than he thought), they were jumping and whirling in sheer delight of the moment. As he looked back on this later, he couldn't remember what music they were dancing to or what people were wearing. It wasn't about style and it certainly wasn't about sensuality. The focus wasn't on themselves at all. It was about the presence of a king and the honor of being with his people.

After what seemed like hours of celebrating, the dancing waned and everyone again looked back to Atrin standing at the end of the rug. It was time for more additions to the royal family. This time, however, the people were black, brown, white, yellow… from every ethnicity and culture Arman had ever known and more, they poured onto the pier to join their new brothers and sisters. More dancing.

After what seemed like an immeasurable amount of time spent jumping, spinning, and hugging people he'd just met, Arman slowed down and decided to walk to the end of the pier. After all, the closest he'd ever felt to home, before today, was when his legs were dangling next to his sister's over his beloved sea. Soon after he started in this direction, however, he again was in awe over how much longer it was than he previously thought. Although there were still lanterns along its sides, the light wasn't overwhelming and no one at the front of the pier could really see clearly to the end of it. It was so long, in fact, that the longer he walked, the more he began to wonder if it was, in fact, a bridge.

Arman looked up to see the stars, astonishingly bright and clear, and peered into the Milky Way. Suddenly he felt a touch of vertigo, as if the wood was spinning. But the movement wasn't coming from underneath him. It was the stars! Or, at least some of them. At first, the motion seemed haphazard, but soon he discerned a pattern. They circled around each other in perfect symmetry, each individually moving in the shape of the number eight, except sideways, the symbol of infinity. As this repeated action continued, these "stars" slowly drifted downward, becoming discernibly larger. It was at this point that he knew these weren't stars at all, though he was far from certain what they were. Floating lamps? Large bulbs? Whatever they were, he was transfixed and couldn't have averted his dumbstruck eyes even if he'd wanted to. Between the stars, the mysterious lights, and their collective reflections off of the glassy sea, there was just enough glow that anyone within a hundred feet would've seen his astonished grin.

The lights changed their fixed pattern, suddenly darting in all directions and drawing nearer together at the same time. Then they slowed down, lining up like stringed Christmas lights, and began to form a word. Still hovering, Arman couldn't quite read it until, finally, they became still, revealing the word "MESSIAH" splashed across the heavens. No sooner than he was able to read it, they shimmied and sparkled until, amazingly, they exploded above the pier like fireworks, briefly torching the sky like the midday sun.

"Well, I've never seen that before." Farah's voice was playful, the curls of her dark hair glistening in the starlight.

"I didn't know you were there," Arman replied.

"I guess that's understandable. We're all pretty overwhelmed." Arman looked back to see there were many people heading in the same direction, drawn out of the same curiosity.

"Do you see that?" Farah pointed toward the end of the pier. Narrowing his eyes, Arman recognized something in the distance. On the horizon, where the stars met their reflection, he saw the tiny silhouette of a tree.

"Do you think that's the end of the pier?"

Farah smiled broadly. "Let's go find out!" They turned and rushed across the beautifully grooved roots, hand in hand, suddenly feeling a greater capacity to run than in their previous life. They looked at each other, slightly shaking their heads in disbelief as they sprinted down the wooden trail with ease, lungs functioning as if on a morning stroll. The silhouette, which Arman had expected to grow larger by now, remained fairly small. *How long is this thing?* As he pondered, a rumble approached from behind, footsteps from the happy throng of worshipers. They skipped, spun, occasionally stopped to dance again, and continued the journey further into the Caspian Sea. As the tree finally appeared larger, a green tint emanated from the leaves. They were glowing! It wasn't bright, just a soft and inviting gleam. Little by little, Arman grew more amazed at its enormous size. As he finally reached the nearest low-lying branches, it felt more like approaching the base of a mountain. *How tall is this thing?*

The leaves were thick and verdant and its branches rested low to the ground, covering the width of the pier, which was now a few hundred feet. It briefly reminded him of the branches of the rain trees in Bandar Raja, but there was no fear in this moment, regardless of what lay unseen. Farah and Arman watched as eager men, women, and children threw aside glowing leaves and branches to see what they revealed. Farah, still holding Arman's hand, grinned at him and led the way inside.

He pulled away the branches and leaves, shaped like maples, and climbed over a few roots until they entered a clearing. A much larger clearing than he expected. An area approximately fifty feet wide, with branches overhead forming a vaulted ceiling about twenty feet high, framed a stunning space inside the tree that looked like a ballroom. Crystal chandeliers hung from the lowest branches, gathering and scattering the soft green light. The floor, presumably part of the same tree as the pier, was flat and shiny with no spaces in between planks, adding its own glowing reflection. Arman was so taken by the atmosphere, he hadn't noticed the people. "I need to make some introductions," beamed Farah. Arman looked around to find that he was in a room full of women. Some short, others tall. Some dark-haired, others light brown or blonde. All of them the most beautiful women he'd laid eyes on.

There were too many introductions, conversations, and shared laughs to write about here. The most amazing aspect of it all, something that only occurred to him later, is that he was never the least bit uncomfortable nor did he ever feel the slightest temptation toward thoughts of objectification. Yes, he saw that they were gorgeous and, of course, noticed they were very much shaped like attractive women. Yet he freely watched them dancing, sometimes joining them, and never once did he feel the old familiar inability to honor them with his eyes. Although he enjoyed their beauty, he talked and laughed with them for the sake of enjoying the laugh only. He asked them questions simply for the pleasure of enjoying their intellect. There were no thoughts of trying to make a good impression in order to win them, for complete acceptance was already a mutual reality. In the hours he spent in the chandelier-laden tree room, he felt new relationships deepen in a way he never thought possible. It was a gift so fantastic that he'd never known to seek it. Because of their inward change, these new creations loved each other perfectly and equally. Arman had no fear, nervousness, or corrupt thoughts to ruin the moment. He was free. And he now realized what Atrin meant when he said that Farah was "for you." She, like these other daughters of the king, were his sisters.

The sound of a horn shook the tree and the pier underneath, exciting the guests and drawing them toward the source of the noise. Arman followed the women through a maze of glowing leaves, sometimes having to crawl over large roots and at other times walking through narrow and neat corridors. The trumpet blared again, letting them know they were close, apparently underneath the gathering place. Looking to the left, he and Farah finally saw the trunk of the tree and gasped. They weren't even sure how wide it was since the other low lying branches on either side hindered a full view, but what they were able to see was much more like the side of a building than a tree. The bark reminded Arman of an ancient walnut tree in the Alborz Mountains that his family would occasionally visit on the way to Shomal. A thick vine wound around the side of the trunk and, upon further inspection, formed a perfect walkway. Farah and Arman laughed in amazement, then flung themselves upward onto a stunning winding staircase. Half covered with moss, it nevertheless provided solid footing as they occasionally ducked under or climbed over thick limbs protruding from this life-giving wood. Finally they came to another opening, much larger than the ballroom. The base of this one was only about seventy-five feet wide, but the branches were arranged with rows and terraces, much like stadium seating. Other sections, like balconies, surrounded the room and rose as high as Arman could see. In the middle of the floor sat a wide and long table, apparently made of wood protruding from the living tree itself, containing every food and drink imaginable. At the head of the table stood Atrin, noble and serene, love overflowing toward everyone present. He raised his hand and the room hushed in anticipation. "It's time for a feast!" Cheers erupted from every direction and the tree again shook beneath and above.

The dinner was unmatched, but fellowship was the source of satisfaction on this evening. He made new friends among his new brothers and sisters and again felt them deepen even within a relatively short time. The main difference between this world and what he'd always known was the level of trust they implicitly had for each other. In his previous life, it sometimes felt like a risk even to trust family and friends. But here, there was no need to hide information out of fear of the Basij. No insecurity about what others may think about him. No oppressive government to enforce opinions no one agreed with. And the only competition consisted of each one trying to outdo the other in showing honor.

They talked, laughed, and occasionally played games throughout the night until Arman thought he saw a sliver of golden light peeking between the outer branches. He climbed up and walked without fear toward the thinner section on the outside of the tree. To his left, there was a platform inside a clearing under a few large branches and a bench, the latter attracting his immediate attention. Facing perfectly East, it was obviously designed to provide a view of the sunrise. Looking down at the seat, he stroked its soft padding, smiling upon realizing it was made of heather. He heard the footsteps of someone else entering the platform, so he turned to offer a greeting and invitation to join him to watch the sunrise. Instead, he stared blankly, unable to move.

A familiar woman with bright eyes, dark eyebrows, and black hair stood between Arman and the budding sunrise. Angelic and graceful, he knew her immediately, yet she seemed different. She held herself with more confidence and more humility at the same time. She wasn't wearing much make-up, if any, yet her face was more full of color than ever. Her demeanor was marked by peace, and the morning sunlight shone through the edges of her hair. Tears flooded Arman's eyes as his greatest nightmare was coming untrue.

"Mahnaz?! Is it really you?"

HONOR THY FATHER

Banu was silhouetted by a harsh fluorescent light as Arman slowly regained consciousness in his hospital room. A blue haze from a television on the wall further clouded his vision, delaying his ability to process the scene.

"Farzin! He's waking up!"

Arman's eyes opened a little wider as he tried to focus on the girl in front of him. "Mahnaz? Is that you?" Banu turned to Farzin and froze, unsure how to respond. Unable to focus in one place for long, Arman's eyes drifted to a corner of the ceiling where he saw an arrow with the word "kiblat" in the middle, a courtesy to guests wanting to pray in the direction of Mecca. Eyes a little wider now, he looked back in front of him to see both Banu and Farzin. Banu was deadpan, but Farzin's eyes were wide with excitement. He leaned over the bed and put his hands on Arman's shoulders, his face only inches from his cousin.

"Arman! Are you okay?! Man, we've been so worried!"

Arman, now fully conscious, beheld the terrorist before him with disdain. "What are you doing here?!" He shook Farzin's hands off of his shoulder and pushed him away. His first instinct was to run, but when he tried to raise his body up from the bed he became dizzy and slouched back into a resting position, holding his hands over his eyes.

Farzin was both undeterred and entertained. He looked at Banu, who was a bit shaken, and laughed. "Arman, it's me. Farzin. Your cousin. This is Banu."

The door flung open as Barbara came in shouting, hands held high. "Woo hoooo! Let me get my hands on that boy!" Yusuf followed Barbara, wide smile on his face and Starbucks coffee in both hands. Arman watched in disbelief as friends and family came back from the dead, circling around him in the hospital room. Barbara was the first to hug him, of course.

"We've been praying for forty-eight hours straight!" she exclaimed, every word succumbing to at least four syllables.

"Tom?" The large Texan was the only person he could see over the shoulders of Barbara, who was squeezing him so hard he thought he'd pass out. Mercifully, she drew back and Arman was able to scan the others, his eyes settling on Yusuf, whom he'd last seen falling from the Petronas Towers. Slowly realizing he didn't know where he was or how he got there, he knew there were some major gaps to fill. "Where am I?"

Farzin leaned down and grinned, his teeth bright against his brown skin. "You're in Damansara Specialist Hospital. You fell in the back of the IT store in the KLCC mall and hit your head. They said you had a severe concussion and thought there was bleeding in your brain, but everything seems to have cleared up now."

Arman covered his beard with his palms, looking down at his bedsheet in disbelief.

Everyone quieted down to give him time to process this new information.

Farzin and Banu didn't bomb the towers. Tom and Yusuf are still alive!

He moved his hands slightly upward to cover his eyes. As he did, the skin under his beard on his right cheek was noticeably smoother than before. He felt for his scar.

Nothing.

He looked down at his skin just above the sock on his left ankle and saw no burn. Slowly and deliberately, he reached under his shirt and ran his fingers across his chest. Nothing but skin and a natural Persian rug of chest hair. Then he passed out.

Arman stared at the mirror with a razor in his right hand and shaving cream in his left. It was three days after he woke up in the hospital, and his parents, who arrived the day before, wanted him to stay with them at One World Hotel. The bathroom was still foggy from spending roughly thirty minutes under a rainfall shower head, the first time Arman had experienced this particular sign of human progress. He'd been standing in his current position for about ten minutes listening to the opposing arguments for and against shaving the beard. Miniature angels and demons shuffled around on his shoulders, punching back and forth while Arman tried to decide who was who in the midst of the melee. On the one hand, he'd wanted to shave for a very long time. The only reason he grew the stupid thing was to hide his scar. In his mind, thick beards and Persians were too often connected with religious radicals, and he'd looked forward to cutting it off every day for almost a year. But now, staring in a clouded mirror in a beautiful new hotel, he saw things a little differently. He put down the shaving cream and set the razor on the bathroom counter as well. *Why not keep it? After all,* he thought, *God did create us to be a pretty hairy people.*

He threw on a pair of grey shorts and blue t-shirt, slipped his feet into razor thin flip flops, and gingerly walked out of the hotel room. It was 10 a.m., but Jalal and Zia, still jet lagged and exhausted from both the trip and the angst of their firstborn lying unconscious in a foreign hospital, slept like babies in their king-sized bed. After Farzin called to tell them Arman was in the hospital, they jumped on the first flight possible. Unfortunately for them, the earliest flight they could find was still a few days after hearing about the incident. By the time they settled on the plane, Arman had awakened and was getting ready to leave the hospital. At one point Jalal proposed that perhaps they didn't need to go to Malaysia since their son was feeling better. Zia flashed a singular glare in his direction and the "conversation" was over.

Arman walked through the hotel lobby into the enormous corridors of the adjacent megamall, 1Utama. Most of the shops were just opening, yawning young men and women pulling up metal security gates one by one like dominos as he passed. Chinese New Year's decorations still filled the open spaces and walkways as he wandered down three floors of escalators to the ground floor. He stopped for a quick breakfast at Burger King, then took his intentional aimlessness into the surrounding neighborhoods outside. He wandered through the city like ancient magi through an unknown land, only partially knowing what he sought. He followed the sidewalk down Jalan Leong Yew Koh, inspecting yet another section of Kuala Lumpur he'd never seen, winding around a few more roads until he happened upon Taman Tun Park. A lake crowned by a beautiful fountain was in the center, which had benches and a clean walking path winding into the woods. Arman had left the hotel to find somewhere to think, and he quickly decided this was the perfect spot.

Every night since waking up from his concussion he had the same dream, or at least parts of it, as the one he had while in the hospital. He didn't entirely know what to make of it, but neither could he stop thinking about it. He was obviously getting nowhere, but he was hesitant to talk to Yusuf. Why should he listen to the voice of a talking snake in a dream?

But even though he didn't understand it entirely, he knew two things: First of all, it was ultimately about Jesus. But was it *from* Jesus? That was another question entirely. Second, a profound change was happening within. He couldn't completely explain it, but he felt that he was becoming both different and more himself than he'd ever been.

The dream replayed itself even as he sat on a bench next to a wide and full waterfall. White crests flowed generously over golden brown stones, the fruit of four straight days of afternoon thunderstorms. *I guess I must've heard thunder in my sleep*, Arman reasoned, recalling his memory of The Dark Cave. As the scene of lying on the pathway looking up through the opening of the cave appeared in his mind, clear as day, he caught a glimpse of something moving on his left. A troop of monkeys scurried onto a couple of benches under a red canopy, helping themselves to the contents of a plastic bag. *That's one picnic someone will want to forget.* A Malay couple with several small children ran from a swing set to chase the macaques away from their food.

The dream conjured thoughts and feelings ranging from terror to pure elation. On the one hand, there was the horrible angst of running from an inevitable judgment. Sure, he wasn't guilty of taking down the towers, but that didn't exactly make him innocent. It wasn't lost on Arman that the entire episode occurred because he was in the back room of a shady IT store indulging his lusts. On the other hand, his encounter with Atrin seemed so real. So beautiful and pure. Love. Forgiveness. Honor. Fellowship with his sons and daughters. It wasn't just better than he imagined life could be. It was beyond anything he could've imagined.

He thought about being in a room under the tree alone with the most beautiful women he'd ever seen, contrasting it with his virtual reality experience. The latter was based on a perverted promise of "Heaven on Earth," the former based on something that was, in reality, other-worldly. Arman had grown up with a vision of Paradise consisting of seventy-two perpetual virgins assigned to fulfill his every fantasy for all eternity. He had no idea whether or not the Qu'ran actually taught this, but he recalled nodding along as Habib and other friends would laugh and roll their eyes as they hoped beyond hope they would make their way to this glorious place. Now, however, while listening to the cascade of a waterfall in a Kuala Lumpur park, it seemed a veil had been lifted, and he knew he'd been sold a cheap imitation. *And by the way, who were these seventy-two virgins? Where did they come from? Was that really going to be their Paradise? Could I really not find it in myself, for all of eternity, to care about what they wanted? How they felt? What kind of relationship was that?* Having tasted the purity of acceptance, honesty, joy, transparency, fearlessness, and genuine laughter, he realized his appetite for pleasure hadn't been too great, as he'd always imagined. It was embarrassingly modest. It was sex without intimacy. Self-indulgence without joy. Servitude in place of love. Shackles disguised as liberty.

~

"Dad, can I ask you something?" Palpitations making his upper body tremble, Arman finally found the courage to talk to his father. He didn't know when they would be alone in the hotel room again, so he knew it was now or never.

Just one day ago Farzin had introduced Zia and Jalal to Banu, the mirror image of their deceased daughter, and Arman was there to observe the fallout. It started with a collective gasp and quickly devolved into tears. Zia reacted as if Mahnaz had just reappeared from the dead. After the initial shock, however, she threw her arms around a disconcerted Banu and hugged her tightly. Jalal, looking more like he'd seen a ghost, remained on the couch and stared at the floor, trying desperately to steady himself. Eventually everyone calmed down, opening the way for more proper introductions. Zia and Banu bonded more quickly than Arman thought possible. Jalal, however, remained sullen, staying put and giving the impression he didn't want to talk. In fact, not much had changed in his mannerisms since yesterday. So while Arman sat on the hotel bed with his arms nervously crossed over his stomach, Zia and Banu were enjoying an afternoon of shopping in 1Utama.

Jalal startled, as if wakened from a daydream, and focused on his son. "Of course, Arman."

Not only had their relationship suffered from the events of the last year, but they never really talked about anything too personal before that either. After the accident, however, it appeared to Arman that his father felt a new tenderness toward him. He sat up on the side of the bed and turned toward his father, sitting on the couch.

"Dad…" Only one word in and Arman choked on it. Then Jalal did the last thing Arman expected. He rose to his feet, sat down next to his son and placed his right hand on his back, looking at him intently through his wire-rim glasses. Arman looked up in astonishment and uttered the only two words he could conjure in this moment. "I'm sorry." He wept as the words left his mouth and his father surprised him again. Wrapping both arms around him, Jalal said the words he'd never uttered to either of his children.

"I'm sorry, too."

They remained in the same position for what seemed like hours, though it was only a couple of minutes. For the first time in years, Arman felt accepted by his father.

Emboldened by the embrace, he stood up, walked toward the sliding glass door, then turned around and faced Jalal. He knew it was a risk, but he had to do it.

"Dad, while I was in the hospital…" His voice trailed off and he took a few seconds to swallow and clear his throat. Jalal's eyebrows widened just a little, but his expression was one of assurance. Arman looked back up until their eyes met. "I had a dream."

"Was it a good dream or a bad dream?" Jalal grinned, attempting to lighten the mood. Age and anxiety had produced more than a few lines on his face, but his perfect smile remained intact.

"Both."

For the next two hours, Arman poured out his heart, and every detail of the time he spent both unconscious and yet more alive than ever. Jalal listened intently, stone-faced throughout most of it, and occasionally asked questions for clarity. His sympathy for Arman was palpable while he described running from the authorities and the shame he felt for choosing his own safety over the child in the stroller. There was laughter as well. The shark scene felt so over the top ridiculous that it left Jalal holding his side. When Arman started talking about Atrin, however, Jalal's countenance changed altogether. The shirt exchange. Taking the blame. Overcoming Dahag. Charharshanbeh Suri on the shores of Shomal. The crown and Persian rug. His eyes glistened with what looked like both longing and hope at the same time. But when Arman described the love he felt for his sisters underneath the great tree, Jalal was wrecked. Arman stopped, deciding to spare him the part about Mahnaz.

They took a break, each spending a generous amount of time in the bathroom before coming back into the open. Arman had one more thing he needed to address.

"Dad, I know how much Mahnaz's choices hurt you and Mom. I swore I would never do that to you."

"Talk to Yusuf." His response was immediate, almost interrupting the end of Arman's sentence. Jalal sat on the couch and looked down, his face in his hands. "Talk to him, Arman." He looked back up and met his son's gaze. "And tell me what he says."

"Last month, you asked me what I was longing for. Do you remember that?"

Yusuf stifled a grin as he finished shoving the rest of his roti canai in his mouth. He raised his head slowly and looked relieved to see the smirk on Arman's face.

"Yes, I remember. Sorry if it was too intrusive."

"No, it was okay."

"I believe you said you were longing for seconds, right?"

Arman laughed as he dove into his banana leaf plate at the local nasi kandar in Bandar Raja. Indian waiters carrying silver trays circled around them during the lunchtime rush. Fans spinning with the force of a helicopter helped to ease the heat and humidity of the open air restaurant, but Arman could still feel sweat dripping through his beard. No amount of heat, however, would keep him from enjoying his teh tarik. He washed his rice and curry down with a satisfied grin and continued the conversation.

"Yes, I said seconds. The food was very good."

"Yes, it was," Yusuf concurred. "So what is the real answer?"

"Freedom," Arman replied in a matter-of-fact tone. "But…" He hesitated, deciding it was a good time to finish off his drink. "If I'm honest, I'm no longer sure exactly what that means."

For the second time in two days, Arman spent a couple of hours nervously telling the grand story of his hospital dream. Yusuf followed along with great interest, eyes occasionally widening in apparent recognition of the significance of an event or quote from Atrin. Wrinkles on his forehead revealed the sincerity of his interest. When they got to the part where Yusuf was mentioned by name, he nearly spit out his drink. By the time Arman was finished, they had plowed through two roti canais, two garlic cheese naans, their respective banana leaf meals, and four refills of teh tarik. It was now mid-afternoon and the crowd was sparse, not that either of them noticed.

"Yusuf, does this dream fit with what you believe about Jesus and the Bible?"

"Yes." There was no equivocation in his voice.

"Okay, then can you explain the part about the large room full of women?" Arman hesitated before asking the next question, then blushed slightly. "I'm not sure how to ask this, really." His mind searched to find the most delicate way to put it. "They were beautiful, but my relationship with them wasn't at all about sexual attraction." Yusuf nodded, but wasn't sure where Arman was going with it. "So if that's Heaven, then does that mean we're supposed to avoid sex here as well?"

"Oh." Yusuf let out a breath. "That's a good question. Most people ask 'How can it be Heaven if there's no sex?'" They both laughed and Arman suddenly realized how odd it was that this wasn't, in fact, his burning question. "The answer is that God created sex as a beautiful gift to be enjoyed between a man and a woman in marriage, but Jesus taught that there would be no marriage in Heaven except for the marriage between himself and his bride, the church. For now, we are charged to be faithful to our wives, cherish the gift of marriage, and treat all other women as sisters and mothers. Unfortunately, even the most holy among us will still experience brokenness in this fallen world." This brought up more questions for Arman, but he decided to stay on task.

"I don't believe that was the main point of the dream, but I guess I could've started with weirder questions than that."

"Like what?"

"Oh, I don't know. Like 'What in the world is going on with a talking snake on a pole?'"

Yusuf's dark eyes lit up. "Believe it or not, that's the easiest question you could have asked lah!"

Arman's expression was somewhere in between stunned and amused. His mouth remained open as Yusuf reached into his backpack to pull out a Bible. He turned the pages for a few seconds before landing on what he was looking for. He closed his eyes in prayer, then looked up at Arman, shaking his head in wonder.

"Now it's my turn to tell a story."

W hat a terrible way to end a story, right? I mean, some of you have some serious questions about now. Others, however, already know that Yusuf is about to talk about Jesus, Nicodemus, Moses, and a bronze snake on a pole. If you're in the latter category, you may leave now. But wait! Before you go, I'll assume that you also knew that "Yusuf" is another word for "Joseph." You know, the Joseph in the Old Testament? The interpreter of dreams? Okay, you can go now.

But if the biblical references above are either unknown to you or not as fresh as you'd like to admit, I would be honored if you'd stick around for a story much more important and reliable than the one you've just finished. It's from John 3 and Numbers 21.

One of the most famous stories in the Bible began when a man named Nicodemus came to Jesus at night to talk to him privately (John 3, CSB). He was a Pharisee (religious leader) so he most likely wanted to talk to him privately to avoid being seen by others. The first thing Nicodemus said to Jesus was, *"Rabbi, we know that You have come from God as a teacher, for no one could perform these signs You do unless God were with him."*

After giving Jesus a compliment, he was probably surprised at Jesus' blunt response: *"I assure you," Jesus said, "unless someone is born again he cannot see the Kingdom of God."* Since Nicodemus had never heard the phrase "born again," it wasn't surprising that he was confused. He replied, *"How can anyone be born who is old? Can he enter his mother's womb a second time and be born?"*

"Jesus answered, "I assure you: Unless someone is born of water and the Spirit, he cannot enter the kingdom of God. Whatever is born of the flesh is flesh, and whatever is born of the Spirit is spirit. Do not be amazed that I told you that you must be born again."

If you don't understand what Jesus is talking about here, don't feel bad. Nicodemus' response was, *"How can these things be?"* Again, Jesus was very direct in his answer. *"You're Israel's teacher and you don't understand these things?"* Perhaps Jesus knew that Nicodemus's greatest obstacle to understanding the truth of salvation was that he would no longer be able to trust the things he thought he knew. In order to come to Jesus, it required faith, a life of simple trust in him, and nothing else. All of the laws that Nicodemus followed (and sometimes failed to follow) could not save him. He needed to be "born again" spiritually.

In order to explain how Nicodemus would need to place his faith in Him, Jesus pointed to a story about Moses. He said, *"Just as Moses lifted up the serpent in the wilderness, so the Son of Man must be lifted up, so that everyone who believes in Him will have eternal life."*

Since Nicodemus was a scholar of the Old Testament, he already knew this story about Moses – the prophet God used to rescue the Israelites from slavery in Egypt. When God delivered them, he performed incredible miracles that displayed both his power and his faithfulness to his chosen people. Because Pharoah would not let the Israelites (his slaves) leave, God sent ten different disasters on them until Pharoah finally let them go. After the Israelites left Egypt, Pharoah changed his mind and went after them with his army. Just when it looked like the Israelites were trapped in between the Red Sea and the Egyptian army, God split the waters apart and let the Israelites cross on dry ground. When the Egyptian army tried to go after them, God let the waters close back up so that the entire army drowned.

Even after these amazing events, there were many times that God's people worshiped idols instead of the God who rescued them and even complained about how he wasn't taking care of them. During one of their journeys, *"they spoke against God and against Moses, and said, 'Why have you brought us up out of Egypt to die in the desert? There is no bread! There is no water! And we detest this miserable food!'"* (Numbers 21) Even after all God had done to show his love and care for them, they accused him of leading them to the desert to die.

So what was God's response? He sent poisonous snakes. All of a sudden, there was an infestation of dangerous serpents all around them. Many people were bitten and died. Can you imagine how paranoid they must have been? Everywhere they stepped, every time they laid down to sleep, and every time they sat down to rest, they were on the lookout for the snakes. Finally, they came to their senses and confessed their sinful attitude to Moses and begged him to ask God to take the snakes away.

God listened to Moses' prayer, but he didn't take the snakes away. Instead, he chose to come up with His own solution, as he often does. His directions were confusing, yet simple. God told Moses to tell the people to make a snake out of bronze and put it on a pole. Then, if anyone is bitten, they can simply look at the bronze snake and they would not die. It could not be more counter-intuitive. God took the very thing that threatened to kill them and turned it into a source of life.

We can guess that the Israelites would have preferred that God just get rid of the snakes. Wouldn't you? After all, there were still poisonous snakes all around them! They could still be bitten and they were most likely still very scared of them. They probably would have also preferred that God would give them a logical way to rid themselves of the poison – something that would have made sense medically and didn't seem so arbitrary. What God left them with, however, was something that would not help them in the slightest unless they actually believed that he would do what he said he would do. If they believed God, then they could have a measure of peace even though poisonous snakes were among them. If they didn't believe him, then they would be hopeless.

When we disobey the laws and ways of God (sin), we dishonor him and bring shame on his name in the same way a rebellious son brings shame on the name of his parents. We are all guilty of sin and we all deserve punishment. When Jesus said that he would be "lifted up" like the bronze snake, he was talking about the cross on which he would die. When he was crucified, he took the deserved punishment for the sins of the world on himself. He wrapped himself in our shame, defeated it by conquering death by rising again, and restored us to a place of honor in a relationship with himself as sons and daughters of an eternal kingdom.

It's only when we know the story about Moses and the bronze snake that we can truly understand the most famous words in the Bible. In John 3:16, Jesus said, *"For God so loved the world that he gave His one and only Son so that whoever believes in Him will not perish, but have eternal life."* **In this verse, Jesus is the snake on the pole to whom we look for salvation**.

Our response to what Jesus did, however, is very important. If you believe that you are basically a good person who doesn't have many sins to be forgiven, you probably won't look to him for forgiveness. Instead, you will be like an Israelite who, after being injected with poison, refuses to believe that there is anything genuinely wrong. If you believe that you do, in fact, have some sin but you're convinced that your good works will earn forgiveness, then you will trust in your obedience to a religion or other moral rules to save you.

However, if you realize that we have *"all sinned and fallen short of the glory of God"* (Romans 3:23) and have been injected with a poison called "sin" and that there is nothing you can do to heal yourself, then you may react as the Israelites who were bitten and had faith in God. Trusting his words, they just looked to the bronze snake and lived. In a similar way, we can look to Jesus on the cross, trusting him with our lives, and avoid the spiritual death of eternal punishment.

Your life on earth will change as well as you experience what Jesus called being "born again." Honored sons and daughters of the King of Kings. For those who place their faith in Jesus as both their Savior and Lord, they have the peace of God's presence and the assurance that death is not final. In the same way that the Israelites no longer had to fear the snakes, we have the assurance that death will only lead us to Heaven. In that place we will know no shame and will love each other without a thought of hiding in fear. In the meantime, we also have the joy of knowing that our lives have purpose and that doing God's will and loving others gives us meaning in life.

If I needed to explain the way of faith in Jesus versus the natural way of thinking about God in two short sentences, I would quote an Iranian who I've known both before and after becoming a Christian. "Before, I tried to do good things to be saved. Now I do good things because I am saved."

Missiological Issues and Resources

Most Christian readers of Arman's Freedom will understand the main theological themes presented. They may not, however, be familiar with the missiological themes that the story engages. Below is a brief overview of the topics embedded into this novel that one would routinely encounter in a missions class, followed with a couple of suggested resources for further study.

Dreams and visions: The main storyline of the book is a dream which led Arman to want to ask a Christian about Jesus. While the dream in Arman's Freedom is a rather fantastical tale (I mean, if you're going to write fiction, why go halfway?), the basic components of a dream that includes Jesus followed by a conversation with a Christian are more common than many would think. I'm not exactly what you would call "charismatic," so when I first came across these stories while in seminary studying missions, I was skeptical. I lost that skepticism long ago, based both on study and personal experience with Iranians. I should quickly add that it's always a danger to let experience be the foundation of a church or movement instead of the clear Word of God. It should be no surprise to us that this happens since we already know there are Christians around the world (including America!) who have a tendency to elevate experience over doctrine. But just because there are some who have overemphasized dreams doesn't mean that we should be any less encouraged that God has used them to lead non-Christians to seek more about Jesus.

Shame/Honor Gospel: Much of Western theology does a good job of explaining how Jesus saves us from our guilt, but we're not as clear on how he saves us from our shame. For some this isn't a big problem, but when you're from a culture that revolves around an honor/shame understanding of life, presentations of the gospel that only deal with guilt and innocence often fall short. In Arman's Freedom, Atrin doesn't just take the punishment for Arman. He takes on Arman's shame and grants him an honor beyond what he could have imagined. *The 3D Gospel*, by Jayson Georges, is a very accessible and clear explanation of the Scriptural narrative of the gospel of honor.

Worldviews and World Religions: You may have seen that Arman's dream was also a journey of encounters with various belief systems. Pantheism, polytheism, monotheism (both Christianity and Islam), modernism, and postmodernism are all competing for Arman's allegiance. You may have also noted that it was important that Yusuf made the effort to be Arman's friend. Yes, God did the main work through the giving of a dream, but this doesn't eliminate our need to be able to engage Islam or other beliefs. For a foundational understanding of worldviews, I highly recommend Paul Hiebert's *Transforming Worldviews*. Hiebert is a deep dive. If it looks too intimidating, start with the chapters that describe individual worldviews. Beware. The chapter on modernism may reveal an idol or two. You will also get more of a sense of why I'm encouraging Iranian Christians not to place their entire hopes in a different system of government. I used *Transforming Worldviews* and Winfried Corduan's *Neighboring Faiths* recently for a class on worldviews and world religions.

No doubt there will be some who read the scenes about

Thaipusam and will instinctively feel that I am being unfair and exaggerating the intensity of the religious festival. Feel free to go to YouTube and search "Batu Caves," "Thaipusam," and "possession" to decide for yourself. I would add that it's not celebrated by all Hindus. It's mainly among Tamil-speaking Hindus in India and the diaspora in places like Singapore and Malaysia.

Persecuted Believers: The story of Mahnaz is an echo of real life martyrs such as Bishop Haik Hovsepian, who disappeared in 1994 after speaking up for persecuted Christians in Iran. One resource for understanding the persecuted church is Nik Ripken's *The Insanity of God*. It is a difficult but hopeful account of how the gospel continues to grow throughout the world despite severe persecution. A great online source of information for the persecuted church is www.opendoors.org.

ABOUT THE AUTHOR

David Parks is from Birmingham, Alabama and is the Director of the Global Center and Contextual Learning for Beeson Divinity School on the campus of Samford University. He is married to Jenn Parks and has four children, three of whom were born in Southeast Asia. He enjoys hanging out with the family, hiking, tennis, and teaching.

9 798887 580029